THE DRAGON BREATH CHRONICLES

David Turnbull

THE DRAGON BREATH CHRONICLES

DRAGON CLAW BOOKS

TABLE OF CONTENTS

Part One
The Stolen Boy

1. The Birthday Surprise

"Euan Redcap," snapped my mother. "You haven't heard a word I've been saying, have you?"

She was right. I hadn't.

I'd been daydreaming about a story my grandfather once told me about how a blood red dragon had made its nest amongst the craggy rocks up in the high hills. It hadn't been such a big dragon, not much bigger than a small pony. But it proved troublesome and problematic for all the hill folk.

It had stolen sheep away in its powerful talons and burned the crops in the low fields with its fiery breath. According to my grandfather it had skimmed over the church and knocked a big chunk of masonry from the steeple. And it had landed on someone's barn roof, splitting the wooden support beams from the pressure of its weight.

It had made a terrible nuisance of itself. Folk were afraid to come out of their cottages in case it fell upon them from the sky. Folk couldn't get to sleep at night for its nocturnal screeching and keening. Folk would look out of their windows in the morning and find piles of fresh dragon dung steaming on their lawns. Eventually when they couldn't take it any longer some men were hired to take their hunting dogs up to the craggy rocks and . . .

"Euan?" repeated my mother. "Are you listening? I asked if you'd finished your porridge."

I looked down my empty bowl and gave her a nod of my head, blushing slightly.

That morning my father had caught a rabbit in one of the snares he'd set out along by the fence that surrounded my mother's vegetable patch. It was a hefty catch with plenty of meat on the bone, which meant we were going to have a big pot of rabbit stew for my sister Isla's birthday supper.

My mother was holding it up by its long ears. Her forearm strained against its dead weight. She jabbed her finger at its underbelly, then turned to Isla, who had just finished her last spoonful of porridge. "I need you to go down into the glen and pick some wild mushrooms to put in the stew."

"You're sending me on a chore on my birthday?" complained Isla.

"Mushrooms won't pick themselves," said my mother.

She gave my father a sly wink.

I held up my hand to cover the grin that was spreading on my face. I knew that sending Isla to pick mushrooms was just a ruse so that my mother could get on and bake the birthday cake she had been secretly hording ingredients for.

"And you're to take your brother with you," she added.

The grin fell rapidly away. What was she talking about? She didn't need to hide the cake from me. I already knew all about it. The last thing I

8

needed was the humiliation of having to trail along at my big sister's heels.

"Him?" complained Isla. "He'll only slow me down."

My mother rolled up her the sleeves of her blouse, hefted the rabbit up by the scruff of its neck, and laid it down by the sink. "This has to be skinned and gutted," she said. "I don't want your brother getting under my feet all morning."

"I could help *you* instead," I suggested.

My mother shook her head. "You'd be more of a hindrance than a help."

Now she was at it! Why didn't either of them have any faith in me? Maybe I did have a tendency to be easily distracted. Maybe my attention did wander sometimes. And maybe that could be the cause of the occasional mishap or accident. But I wasn't half as bad as they always seemed to make out.

"He'll be a hindrance to me as well," Isla moaned.

"All he'll need to do is hold the basket while you pick the mushrooms," said my mother. She began sharpening her gutting knife against the whetstone.

I drummed my fingers impatiently on the top of the table. It was always like this with my mother and my sister - they seemed to feel free to make all sorts of plans for me, without ever actually including me in the conversation. But I had solemnly promised my parents that this year I would be on my best behaviour for Isla's big day, so

I fought down the strong urge I had to give them both a piece of my mind.

When it became clear that my mother wasn't going to back down Isla let out an exaggerated sigh. She folded her arms tightly across her chest and pursed her lips. I could see the freckles standing out against the bridge of her nose, the way they always did when she was annoyed.

"Why can't you send him up the hillside to help tend the sheep with Pa?"

By then Pa had already picked up his shepherd's crook and left through the back door. I could hear his dogs yipping and yapping as they followed him up the path to the hillside. He was a fast walker. I would have to run if I was going to catch up with him.

My mother lifted the rabbit and slapped it down onto the chopping board that sat on the kitchen table. Her braids went swaying from side to side like twin pendulums on a big grandfather clock. "He's too young. If the mist comes down from the high hills your father will need all his wits about him to make sure none of the sheep wander off. It won't help if he has to keep a watch on Euan as well."

That was nonsense. If the mist came down Pa wouldn't need to keep a watch on me at all. I would be a huge help to him. I could listen out for the bleating of the sheep. I could point him in the right direction to go and fetch them. I could help him shepherd them down the hill.

Isla sighed again. "I'm going to need my wits about me as well. I'll need to look for good sized

10

mushrooms. Euan will only go and do something stupid like fall in the stream."

"No I won't!" I yelled, finally deciding that I couldn't just stand there and hold my tongue.

"You will," insisted Isla. "You're always doing stupid things! Especially on my birthday."

Not this again. Was I never going to hear the end of it?

"No, I'm not," I huffed.

"Yes, you are," said Isla. "Last year you went and got yourself stuck in the ditch. Up your armpits in stinking mud, as I recall. And the year before you fell off the dyke and knocked out the last of your baby teeth."

"We'll nothing has happened to me this year." I said, defensively.

"Not yet," Isla shot back.

"Quiet! Both of you!" snapped my mother. She wiped her hands on her apron. "Isla, you'll do as you're told and take your brother with you down the glen. Euan, you're to behave yourself. You're to hold the basket for your sister to put the mushrooms in. And you're not to go anywhere near the stream. You hear?"

Realising that there was absolutely no point in arguing, I nodded my head moodily.

"Come on then, if you're coming," snapped Isla.

Grabbing the basket, she turned to my mother.

"I bet something stupid happens to him. You wait. I guarantee it!"

2. Down in the Glen

We zigzagged across the wide meadow, tramping a winding trail through the white and yellow carpet of daisies and dandelions. Bumblebees with fat black stripes went buzzing past my ears. Blue and red butterflies fluttered lazily around us. At the far end of the meadow I caught a glimpse of a fox dashing swiftly for cover.

I picked up a piece of old tree branch that had snapped in half when I stepped on it. I pretended it was a sword, swiping down blades of grass before me like imaginary opponents. "Stop messing around," complained Isla.

"How come you're always think you've got the right to tell me off?" I called after her.

"How come you're always messing around?" she called back.

Turn it back on me, I thought. *That's just typical. That's all she ever does. Euan's messing around. Euan's getting in the way. Euan's gone and done something stupid again. What would she do if I just disappeared in a puff of smoke? She'd be sorry then. Wouldn't she?*

I tossed the branch as far across the meadow as I could.

"Watch out!" cried Isla, as it sailed over her head. "That could have hit me!"

I growled back at her. "It was miles away from you."

"Stop messing around!" she snapped again.

That did it!

12

She had no right to boss me about!

I began to deliberately drag my heels, slowing my pace till the gap between Isla and myself grew considerably wider. With a bit of luck I'd be able to sneak off and claim that I lost her somewhere down in the glen. Then without warning she came to a sudden halt. I stopped too. Did she have eyes in the back of her head, or what?

Isla swung around on her heels and marched furiously towards me. Her face was as red as her freckles. Her hand was so tightly wrapped around the handle of the basket that her knuckles were turning white. With her other hand she grabbed me by the wrist and yanked me forward. "Ma told me to keep an eye on you! So you better stop messing around!"

It never did any good to get on the wrong side of Isla once she got herself into one of her tempers. I put aside my indignation and allowed her to haul me down the tree-lined slope that descended into the shaded glen. It was cool down there. The ground was soft under foot. When I breathed in, the air was full of the perfume of pine needles and scent of wild flowers.

After five minutes or so of searching we found a big cluster of mushrooms near the foot of a contorted old rowan tree. The soil they were growing in was black and spongy. Their caps were wide and creamy and their stems long and fat.

"You stay here out of the way," said Isla. "And hold on tightly to the basket. I don't want you clomping around with your big feet and squashing everything."

She removed her shoes and socks and went tiptoeing amongst the beige-coloured mushrooms. Crouching gently down she began snatching the base of their stems and plucking them out of the soil. When she'd collected six or seven mushrooms she came over to me and tipped them into the basket.

Down in the belly of the glen I could hear the gurgling of the stream as it gushed over the smooth, flat pebbles. Despite the shade of the trees the hot sun was sending darts of light down through their branches, making my back feel sticky. I glanced dreamily towards the sound of the water. I longed to go down and paddle there in my bare feet. I would build a dam with some big stones from the bank. Then would use one of my socks as a net to catch sticklebacks that drifted into the pool it created.

Isla noticed the wistful look in my eyes. "Don't you dare move from there," she cautioned me. "And don't you dare tip the basket. I'm not going to spend the rest of the afternoon trying to pick mushrooms caps out of the nettles."

"I'm not that stupid," I said.

Isla's eyebrows went up.

"Oh, yes you are."

She wove her way back through cluster of mushrooms.

It was then that I heard a low droning noise coming from somewhere high above us. I looked up through the leafy interwoven latticework of branches toward the white clouds that were billowing in the pale blue sky. The sharp shaft of sunlight that came streaming through the spidery

14

bows of the rowan tree made me squint and narrow my eyes.

"Pay attention to what you're doing!" barked Isla. "If you drop those mushrooms I'll knock your head into next Tuesday."

The droning grew louder. I could feel it vibrating in the ground beneath my feet. Isla came back and tipped another handful of mushrooms into the basket. "Can you hear that?" I asked her.

"It's an airship," she said.

"An airship?"

Once I had seen a pencil sketch of an airship in the big encyclopaedia that was usually kept under lock and key in the library at the village school. I remembered a boat-like structure, apparently called a gondola, suspended on wires beneath a fat balloon. I started to feel excitement build up inside me. I had never actually been lucky enough to see one in real life.

Isla let out one of her pronounced sighs. "From Tennanbrau City. They rarely come this way. But sometimes there are thunderstorms that send them off route."

"I know where airships come from," I told her.

"Dragon hunters I expect," said Isla.

My mouth dropped wide. Dragon hunters? In the Low Counties? I closed my eyes and conjured up images of brave men, kitted out in protective armour, risking life and limb to bring down monstrous fire breathing beasts and draw the wonderful breath from their lungs. Dragon Breath, the very name sent a shiver down my spine. It was the power source upon which all of Tennanbrau City was driven.

What a glorious and valiant profession drawing Dragon Breath must be.

"Just pay attention to what you're doing," snapped Isla. "It'll pass over soon enough."

The droning grew even louder. So loud now that the leaves on the rowan tree began to rustle and tremble. I couldn't help but look up again. I craned my neck and gasped in shock as the most enormous thing that I had ever seen in my life came descending down from the clouds. The glen was swallowed up in its shadow.

3. The Drunken Molly

The first thing that I was able to make out was the gondola, hanging below the balloon on silvery wires, just like the sketch I'd seen in the encyclopaedia. The tarred hull gleamed with condensation as its big iron anchor swayed from side to side.

Then came the balloon itself came into view, starkly crimson in colour and as long and round as a fat marrow. I could feel the churning of the turbines that drove the airship's engines trembling through me. I could see the dizzying spin of the propellers that jutted out from wide housings at its tail end.

A column of steam came shushing out of the pistons. A huge glob of sump oil came oozing blackly down, landing with a wet smack in the undergrowth nearby. Lower and lower came the airship. It was so low now that I could read the name that had been painted along its side in ornate golden letters.

The Drunken Molly, I thought. *What an odd name.*

I had always imaged that an airship would have an excitingly appropriate name, like *'Cloudburster'* or *'Skyslicer'* - *Drunken Molly* seemed somehow a bit of a let-down.

Nevertheless, she was an awesome sight.

I saw people leaning over the wrought iron railings that encompassed the deck of the gondola. They were pointing down at Isla and me. I couldn't actually hear their voices over the thrum and clank of the engine. But I could tell from the animated way that their faces moved that they were shouting eagerly to each other. One of them produced something that glinted in the sunlight and held it to his eye.

A telescope!

I waved my arm enthusiastically back at him and almost tipped over the basket of mushrooms with my enthusiasm.

"Isla!" I cried. "Look!"

But she was already looking, still as statue below, neck stretched skywards, mouth gaping wide. Following her gaze I looked up again. The airship had descended even lower. It was so low now that I could make out the outline of the wooden slats that criss-crossed the belly of the gondola. It was so low that it was actually bending the tallest shoots on the highest bows along the canopy the glen.

Through the shaking leaves, I could see that several of the crewmen were leaning over the railings with what appeared to be looped lengths of rope held in their hands. They began to swing these around and around above their heads.

"Run!" cried Isla and broke into a sudden, unexpected sprint.

I found myself frozen to the spot as she came dashing past me.

"Your shoes and socks," I called after her. "You left your shoes and socks!"

She didn't look back. "Run, Euan!"

Isla was already halfway up the slope that led from the glen to the meadow.

"What about the mushrooms?" I cried.

Isla glanced back over her shoulder.

"Just drop the basket and run, you idiot!"

There came a loud crack as if something was falling rapidly down through the branches. This was immediately followed by a dull thump from somewhere behind me. When I looked back one of the rope loops had been thrown down from the gondola and had landed amongst the clump of mushrooms. A second later it was swaying in the air above my head as it was hauled back up to the airship.

Isla was at the top of the slope now. "Run, Euan!" she screamed down at me.

I had no idea what was going on. But the look of sheer terror on her face was more than enough to spur me on. I threw the basket to one side. The mushrooms scattered, spinning and somersaulting away. I ran for the slope. From behind me I could hear the crack-crack-crack of more branches snapping, followed a dull whump-whump-whump as rope loops were hurled down from the gondola to land in the glen.

I stumbled up the slope.

"Come on!" yelled Isla.

Her face was deathly pale.

I was three quarters of the way up the slope when she turned and broke into a sprint again. "Move it!" I heard her call back.

I crested the slope and ran after her.

"Wait!" I cried. "Not so fast!"

But the gap between us was growing wider with every frantic churn of her legs. I could feel the drone of the airship's engine humming in the ground below my feet. I could feel its ominous shadow creeping closer to my shoulders. It was like being chased by a huge, lumbering bear. The shadow seemed to drain all the warmth from the sun, shrouding me in a melancholy chill.

Whump-whump-whump went the tumbling rope loops behind me.

I tried desperately to make my legs go faster. My heart thumped against my chest. My lungs felt fit to burst. A sharp stitch stabbed at my side. Isla was way ahead of me now. Far across the meadow. Almost at the stone dyke. The drone of the airship's engine seemed to be burrowing right into my head. I started to cry. The tears blurred my vision. I wasn't even sure if I was still running in the right direction.

Then something caught hold of my left leg.

For the briefest moment, I thought that a thorny branch had hooked itself onto the bottom of my trousers. But it clearly wasn't a thorn. As I tried to yank myself free whatever had hold of me yanked forcefully back. I lost my balance and fell face first onto the sun-baked grass. I tasted dirt and straw in my mouth and spat it out.

"Isla!" I screamed. "Isla! Help me!"

Ahead of me Isla skidded to a halt and spun back around.

In an instant the world turned swiftly upside down.

Everything went into a whirl.

It took me a moment or two to realise that I was rising high above the ground. Something was contracting tighter and tighter around my ankle. The pain in my leg was excruciating. I realised with a horrible jolt that I had been caught by one of the rope loops and I was being hauled up toward the airship.

"Isla!" I screamed, kicking out with my free leg and waving my arms desperately. "Isla!"

I could see her running across the meadow. Her voice was carried up to me on the wind. I could hear it above the drone of the airship's engine.

"Euan! Euan!"

Higher and higher I was dragged. The wind whipped around me and set me into another wild spin. I saw my father on the hillside with his sheep. He was watching the airship and I could tell instantly that he saw me. He came hurtling toward the meadow, his dogs barking like crazy at his heels, his sheep scattering before him and galloping off in a dozen different directions.

The wind spun me again. Now I saw our cottage, with its thatched roof and the thin streamer of smoke trailing from its stubby chimney. My mother came out of the kitchen door with a wooden bucket under her arm. She began to toss bits of rabbit innards out into the yard for the black crows to feed on.

She looked up to the hill where my father was running as if his very life depended on it. She looked over to the meadow where Isla had fallen to her knees in a fit of tears. She looked up to where the airship ploughed through the summer sky, coughing steam and wheezing smoke. She saw me dangling there on the rope.

She dropped the bucket and let out a scream.

Isla was directly below me, tiny as a mouse now. She was getting further and further away. I knew that as well as the rope being hauled up the airship was ascending too. From that height, I could see all of them in one go - my father scrambling down the hill, his dogs yapping at his side, his crook outstretched as if he could somehow reach into the sky and snatch me back down; my mother wringing her hands by the kitchen door, the wooden bucket rocking from side to side where it had fallen by her feet; my sister on her knees amongst the white daisies and yellow dandelions, staring up at me.

"Isla!" I yelled. "Ma! Pa!"

I knew that they probably couldn't even hear me. And I knew too that even if they could there was nothing at all they could do to help me. Then, in the blink of an eye, I was sucked away into the misty swirl of the clouds and the comfortable world that I had known for all the twelve summers of my life was gone in an instant.

4. Mrs Zachariah

With little recollection of how I had arrived there, I found myself flat out on my back on the grimy deck of the airship's gondola. Mighty crimson balloon billowed above me. Splintery wooded deck hard against my back. A bow-legged crewman came waddling up to me. Brandishing a keen bladed knife in his filthy hand he cut the rope from around my ankle.

Kicking my heels, I shunted myself away from him. The skin around my ankle was raw and chafed from the friction burn of the rope. I started shivering from the cold air that gusted about the deck. I found myself surrounded by a dozen or more rough looking men, dressed in greasy clothing that was a jumble of patchwork and stitching.

Some held smouldering clay pipes clamped between brown stumps of worn-down teeth. Others chewed sloppily on dirty big wads of tobacco that dribbled ochre trails of tainted saliva over their unshaven chins. Their faces were pockmarked and battered. Their fingernails were stained black with oil. They reeked of sweat and stale rum. They were the opposite of what I had always imagined brave dragon hunters would look like.

They began to poke and prod me as if I was some curious item they'd dug up in the dirt. I was pinched and jabbed and jostled and nudged. A gnarled hand with splintered fingernails shot out and tugged at my red hair, while another pulled up my top lip and an ugly face loomed in to take a good long gander at my teeth. They all started chattering at once. So fast and noisily that I couldn't understand a word they were saying.

Terrified, I started to bawl. As my face became sticky with tears a chorus of mocking laughter assailed me. Unsightly jeering faces leered down at me. One of them blew pipe smoke into my face, making me cough and wheeze. Through my stinging eyes I noticed a boy not that much older than Isla amongst the jostling crewmen. His ginger hair was long and matted. His narrow face was pale and splattered with freckles. From his appearance he simply had to be a Low County boy like me.

I sat up and pleaded with him. "Help me."

The boy came forward with a mischievous grin on his face. He gave me a kick to my shoulder. I fell back onto the deck, hitting my head with a painful thump. His grin spread wider. He whispered something to the crewmen. As they howled with laughter, he crouched down beside me. "Don't whine," he said. "It's all a big joke. They'll lower you back down in a basket once they've had their fun."

"They will?" I rubbed my eyes with the heels of my hands.

The boy nodded. "But the more you cry the longer it will take for them to grow bored of you."

A voice barked out what sounded like an order. A female voice - deep and gruff and officious. The crewmen stepped swiftly away from me, and a small woman appeared in the clearing they left behind. Hands on hips she glared down at me. I swallowed hard and did my best to stop crying. If she was in charge, then she would surely put an end to this and order them to lower me back down so that I could run home.

She was dressed in men's clothing; knee length boots, leather britches and a thick overcoat with wide lapels. Her black hair snaked out from under her wide brimmed hat and hung in twisted braids like sodden rat tails around her shoulders. Her dark, sullen eyes appeared to be swirling in wildly their sockets and her face seemed to dance and jitter with a thousand nervous tics and twitches.

She looked as if she was teetering on the verge of total madness. It seemed that at any minute she might fall to the ground in some sort of juddering fit. I felt my hopes replaced by a deep sense of foreboding. The woman poked me with a grimy finger and whispered under her breath in an odd lilting tone that sent a cold tingle down my spine. "We could have had a boy like you. Me and my bonny Captain. We could have had ourselves a son had the accursed White Sow not taken him from me."

I had no idea what she was talking about. Her eyes seemed to glaze over. It felt as if she was staring straight through me. The way the crewmen stood with their heads hung in silence suggested that they were somewhat wary of her. She reached out and ruffled my hair. "He has fine head of red hair, just like you, Angus," she said, turning to the Low County boy, who was still crouched down by my side.

The boy nodded. "But if we don't lower him back down soon he'll be too far from home to find his way back before sunset."

The woman's face began to twitch again. Her dark eyes went juddering crazily from side to side. "Who said anything about lowering him back down?" Her voice became gruff and officious once more.

"I thought." said Angus and shrugged his shoulders helplessly.

The woman lashed out with her hand and smacked him with a loud crack on the side of the face. "I'm the one who does the thinking round here." She leaned in close to me and a bizarre lopsided grin spread across her face. She licked her lips like a wild cat that had just hauled a trout from the stream. I began to whimper and tried to back further away. She reached out and pinched some of the flesh on my arm between her thumb and her forefinger. "You're a skinny little thing, so you are," she said. "Can you fetch and carry?"

From behind her Angus gave a barely perceptible wink of his eye. I took it that he meant to suggest to me that I played along with her I nodded my head. "I do plenty of chores for my Ma and Pa."

She turned to the crew.

"You know what I'm thinking, don't you lads?" she asked. Some of the men looked up, but she didn't wait for any of them to answer. "I'm thinking that this boy here would us make an excellent fetcher."

A wave of shock seemed to ripple through the men. One of them pulled his pipe away from his lips and coughed out a cloud of smoke. He stroked the bushy moustache that drooped over his upper lip. "I don't think that would be a good idea, *ma'am*," he said, somewhat nervously. "I mean a bit of fun is one thing - but kidnapping?"

The woman stiffened. She bit down on her lip. I tiny bubble of blood appeared where her tooth pierced the flesh. She turned on the man. "Why, Mister Grisling?" she asked. "Why do you always feel you have a right to question my decisions? I know you're the coxswain. I know you served for years under my husband. But is this not my husband's vessel? Bless his beautiful, departed soul. And I am not your captain now that he has been so cruelly taken from us?"

The coxswain bowed his head and stuck his pipe back into his mouth, as if plugging it up so that he wouldn't be tempted to speak out again. This didn't seem to appease the woman. She began to rant and rave at the crew. "Did every man Jack of you not pledge your allegiance to me? Did you not vow to avenge my Nathaniel's death? Are we not bound together by that vow? To take the breath of the White Sow, or die in the trying?"

The men shuffled their feet and, with a nod of their heads, let out a subdued "Aye."

The woman eyed them one by one. "So, if I say we employ the boy as a fetcher that's exactly what we will do!"

The coxswain removed his pipe and held it hovering by his lip. He cleared his throat. "But it would still be kidnapping, *ma'am*."

The woman flew into another rant. As her head snapped from side to side her rat-tail hair went slapping against her shoulders. "This vessel belonged to my husband, Captain Zachariah! You were his crew! Now the vessel is mine and you are my crew. Must I get down on my hands and knees and beg you to avenge my darling husband's death? We agreed. We swore an oath. Any of you who wants to go back on his word is welcome to jump over the side."

Again, the men bowed their head and shuffled their feet. Seemingly satisfied that she had re-asserted authority her attention returned to me. Again Angus flashed me a warning look. "You'd like to do some fetching for us, wouldn't you, lad?" she asked. Angus nodded his head at me in an animated manner. I had no idea what 'fetching' involved. I replied that on any other day I would love to. "But I can't. Not today."

She leaned closer. Her eyes danced a wanton jig in their sockets. "What's that? What's that?" she asked. "Speak up boy. I can hardly hear you. I thought you said that you can't?"

"It's my sister's birthday today," I told her. "And my Ma has baked a cake. And she's making a rabbit stew. And every year I do something stupid to spoil Isla's birthday. Not on purpose though. But this year I promised."

Mrs Zachariah shook her head and the black braids flapped around her shoulders. "Nonsense!"

she chuckled and pinched me hard on the cheek. "You wouldn't be spoiling your sister's birthday. You would be making it. What sister wouldn't be proud to have brother who is off soaring through the clouds in search of dragon breath? Why it's the best birthday present a girl could ever wish for!"

"But my Ma and Pa will be waiting for me," I insisted.

"And how do you think they would feel if you accidentally fell from the gondola?" she asked, a spiteful tone creeping into her voice. "How do you think they'd feel if a dead body came home to them instead of a heroic young man who had been off on the adventure of a lifetime?"

I could see several of the crew members stiffening and clenching their fists in obvious discomfort. But not even the coxswain seemed willing now to come to my aid. "Now what say you?" she asked, leaning in so close to me that the black braids of her hair trailed across my face like spider legs. "How do you fancy fetching for me and my lads?"

I saw Angus nodding his head urgently at me.

"I suppose I could," I replied, fighting back the urge to start bawling again.

Mrs Zachariah jumped to her feet. "You hear that lads?" she asked. "He's coming along of his own free will. You're all witnesses to what he said. We can't be accused if kidnap if he comes along of his own accord."

5. Fetcher

I discovered very quickly that the job of a *fetcher* was to do exactly that – run and fetch stuff for the captain and crew. Run here. Run There. Run everywhere. The first thing that I fetched for them was an urn of tea, which was prepared by the ship's cook. A lanky looking fellow called Smudger, who laced the brew with rum, and warned me on pain of my life not to spill any.

No sooner had I fetched the tea than I was called upon to fetch the tin cups to pour it into. Then I had to fetch the empty tin cups back to the galley to be washed. No sooner had I completed this task than Smudger ordered me to fetch him a sack of potatoes from his cramped little pantry. No sooner had I done this than Grisling, the coxswain, now back at the airship's navigation wheel, called on me to fetch him some fresh tobacco for his pipe.

And so it went on all day long.

"Fetcher! Fetch me a mop and bucket!"

"Fetcher! Fetch me a knife to cut this rope!"

"Fetcher! Fetch me my map and compass!"

I must have run up and down the length of the gondola a hundred times or more, trying to figure out where next to go to fetch whatever item I had been urged to fetch. My legs began to feel like lead weights. Despite the chill in the air, I was sweating profusely from the exertion. Perhaps it was a blessing in disguise. I didn't have a spare second to dwell upon my plight. No time to consider how badly I had spoiled Isla's birthday this time.

The sun was setting, turning the open sky a gloomy shade of pink, when Smudger came to me. "Captain says you can knock off for the day." He held up a threadbare woollen blanket that had been folded under his skinny arm and indicated with his head that I should follow him.

"I'll show you where you can bed down for the night," he said. I was led to a rusty looking cage, little more than chicken wire stretched across a rickety wooden frame, dirty looking straw spread out across its floor.

"In there?" I cried.

Smudger nodded. "We usually bring some hens on a long journey," he told me. "Only the ones we had this time round wouldn't lay no eggs. So we ate them."

"You want me to sleep in a chicken coop?" I asked.

Smudger gave a shrug of his shoulders.

"Best we can offer," he said. "All the bunks are already taken."

I didn't argue. I was so tired. It honestly didn't matter, so long as I could lay down and close my eyes and dream of home. I took the blanket from him and crawled in through the narrow gate of the coop.

"Sweet dreams," said Smudger.

I pulled the blanket around me and curled myself into a tight ball. I could hear the drone of the airship's engine and the creaking of her decking as she picked up speed and stole me ever further away from my loved ones. I could feel the gondola swaying on the silver wires that hung down from the crimson balloon. The motion seemed to emphasise how high up we were and how very far away from the Low Counties we must have already travelled. The whole thing started me crying again. Frightening noises came tumbling out of my mouth as I howled and yowled in my misery.

"Shut up!" hissed a voice.

When I looked Angus was standing in the front of the chicken coop.

"Help me," I blubbered.

"Shut up!" he repeated, handing me another threadbare woollen blanket through the gate. "You'll need an extra one to keep warm. We're headed far to the north. The winds up there are like driven ice."

I wrapped the extra blanket around my shoulders, trying desperately to control my crying. "You're h-hill f-folk like m-me?" I sobbed.

The nod of his head was barely perceptible. "My name is Angus Stonedyke," he said. "My father was as a weaver in a woollen mill. I was supposed to follow in his footsteps. But couldn't see myself working the looms all my life. First chance I got I ran away from home. Made my way to Tennanbrau City. Took up with the dragon hunters."

"You have to help me escape," I said.

"Can't do that." He shook his head solemnly. "More than my life is worth."

I started to cry again. "What's wrong with your captain? She's like a mad woman."

"Her husband was our true captain," he said, leaning closer to the chicken wire. "Nathaniel Zachariah. This vessel belonged to him. He named

32

her *The Drunken Molly* after an inebriate old aunt he had a soft spot for. Captain Zachariah was the greatest dragon breath gatherer to sail the skies. Everybody in Tennanbrau City loved him. And Mrs Zachariah loved him more than anyone. Worshipped the ground he walked on, so she did."

"What happened?" I asked. "Where is he now?"

Angus leaned in even closer to the coop. So close that his face was now pressing against the chicken wire. He whispered almost conspiratorially. "On our last voyage with him he took us out beyond the vast wilderness of the Far Tundra and into the canyons of the Serrated Mountains. To hunt the White Sow."

"White Sow?"

"A she-dragon," he explained. "He-dragons are called boars. She-dragons are called sows."

"Like pigs?"

Angus nodded.

"The White Sow has eluded dragon hunters for years. She's an albino. Scales as white as freshly fallen snow. Eyes as red as ripe cherries. She's grown to be the biggest she-dragon in the world." He took a quick glance over his shoulder. "Bigger even than this ship. Huge wings." He spread his arms wide to demonstrate. "When the sunlight reflects from her scales it is so bright it almost blinds you. Her teeth are like daggers. Her claws are like spears."

"Did he get her?" I asked, wide eyed. "Did Captain Zachariah get the White Sow?"

Angus shook his head.

33

"She got him.

Yanked him overboard. Lasso and all. Then she disappeared into the clouds. Too fast for us to keep up. It was the last we ever saw of him. Mrs Zachariah was expecting his child. She lost the baby shortly after we brought her the terrible news. She's been crazy with grief ever since. She's vowed to avenge him and their poor, dead son. Or die herself in the attempt."

I looked into his eyes. I could see in them more than a trace of the simmering madness I'd observed in Mrs Zachariah's eyes. "And we have all vowed an allegiance to her cause." His voice trembled disturbingly as he spoke. "Sworn a blood oath. A pact to avenge the death of our captain. To bring down the Sow. No matter the cost."

Now the madness rose fully to the surface of his eyes. They seemed to redden as his face took on a maniacal continence. "The hide of the Sow will fetch us a fortune from the Tannery merchants," he jabbered. "The finest restaurants in Tennanbrau will scramble to outbid each other for her tender flesh. The traders from Scavenger's Market will squabble over her teeth and her bones and her claws. Her wings will be hung on the wall above the Imperial throne. Old Emperor Julian himself will sing our praises."

He looked at me with wide eyes. "But it's her breath, Euan. When we capture the precious breath of the White Sow, we will be kings amongst men. And Mrs Zachariah will be Queen of all the dragon hunters!"

He let out chilling little chuckle. And with that he turned and walked away.

"Wait!" I called after him. "What has any of this got to do with me? I didn't take any blood oath."

"You're with us now, hill boy," he called back over his shoulder. "You're our fetcher. And when we catch the White Sow, you'll get to share in the glory!"

6. A Drove of Dragons

Darkness fell quickly up there above the clouds. I wrapped the blankets tightly around me as the temperature plummeted. The persistent hum of the airship's engine and the melancholy whistling of the wind blowing through the silvery wires that hung down from the crimson balloon gnawed at my ears.

I pulled the blankets tighter and curled myself once more into a ball. I tried to shut it all out of my head; the cramped chicken coop with the straw floor that was to be my makeshift bed, the terrible noises all around me, the stinging rope burn that still smarted around my ankle. I felt that if I could somehow force myself to sleep, I would wake up in the morning and find that it had all been some dreadful nightmare.

My thoughts turned to my family and the green hills of the Low Counties. I tried to pretend I was lying safely in my own bed. For once Isla's birthday had gone off without a hitch - we had eaten big, steaming bowls of rabbit stew and blown out the candles on her cake - the fire was burning down in the hearth and the last trail of smoke was whispering up through our stubby little chimney - my world was just as it always had been.

***

"You!" rasped a harsh voice. "Wake up!"

My eyelids flickered open. There was straw stuck to my cheek where my tears had dried to a sticky mess. I could feel bits of it woven into my

36

hair and poking into my scalp. I had no idea how long I had been asleep, squashed up inside that awful, cramped place. I could tell for sure that it was not yet daytime. But it was a little lighter than it had been when I'd lain down.

"Stop dithering," insisted the voice. "Get up and shake a leg!"

In the dingy half-light of the pre-dawn, I sat up and saw Angus Stonedyke standing once more in front of the coop. He opened the gate and slid a hunk of dried bread and a mug of goat's milk towards me. "Best I can do for you," he said.

"Not hungry," I pouted moodily. "I just want to go home."

Angus shrugged his shoulders.

"Too late for that," he said. "We've come too far now to turn back. You're with us for the whole voyage - to the Far Tundra and back to Tennanbrau City. Like I said, you'll share the glory when we take the Sow. Then you can make your way back to the Low Counties as a hero."

"What all of you have done is against the law." I curled my fingers into the chicken wire and rattled it noisily. "You kidnapped me and you're all going to be in big trouble."

"Ever seen a dragon?" he asked, seemingly oblivious to my threats.

I shook my head.

"My Grandpa used to tell a story about a dragon that once made its nest in the high hills back home. And I've seen sketches in the school encyclopaedia. But I've never seen a live dragon."

"Stand up," he said. "Stand up and take a look."

He pointed over the railings of the gondola and way off into the distance.

I crawled out of the coop, grabbing the mug of milk in one hand and hunk of bread in the other.

I rose to my feet and stood on tiptoes, craning my neck. Some distance away, where the sky was tinted pale red from the slow rising of the morning sun, strange serpentine objects, turquoise and emerald in colour, were swooping gliding through the wisps of clouds on raggedly unfurled wings.

"Dragons," breathed Angus.

The word sounded almost mystical as it floated out of his mouth.

I squinted my eyes to get a better look.

"A drove of Common Greens," said Angus. "Not the one we seek. Not the White Sow. But we're going to hunt them, nonetheless. Mrs Zachariah says the opportunity is too good to pass up. We'll take their breath and sell it for a profit when we return to Tennanbrau."

"What is this breath you keep talking about?" I asked.

"Don't you know anything?" he replied. "Dragon breath is the most powerful element known to man."

He leaned in close to my ear, as if he was about to share some great secret.

"There is a form of gas that occurs naturally deep within the lungs of dragons. It's the ignition of this gas in the back of their throats that causes them to breathe fire. If you can steal a dragon's breath the raw gas has countless uses. It drives the factories in Tennanbrau. It's the basic ingredient in the mortar bombs of the Imperial Army."

He pointed up at the fat crimson balloon above our heads. "Dragon breath!" he cried. "It's lighter than air. It's what helps dragons to fly and it's what keeps huge airships like this aloft."

"But how do you take it?" I asked.

"Sup your milk," he said. "You'll see soon enough!"

Then he was gone in the blink of eye. I heard the hum of the engine distinctly change tone as the airship set course for the direction of drove of dragons. The churning noise of the turbines seemed to intensify. Some of the milk slopped over the side of the mug as the gondola tipped slightly leftward. Around me the deck burst into hectic activity as crewmen ran this way and that. As watched, I took a reluctant gulp of the vinegary tasting milk and nibbled at the bread crust.

Mrs Zachariah came slinking up to me - mad eyes rolling in their dark sockets. Rat tailed hair whipping around her shoulders. She gave me a creepy smile that made me shiver. "We could have had a boy like you." Her upper lip quivered. "Me and my bonny captain. He would have been dark and handsome like his father. And I would have absolutely loved him to pieces. And he would have been such a comfort to me in my grief."

She reached out and stroked my hair. "What a fine boy he would have been," she said. "He would have grown up to be as strong and handsome as his father. He would have loved his mother as much as his mother loved him."

"My mother loves me," I said. "She'll be crying for me now. Wondering what has happened to me. Praying that I'll come home safely."

Mrs Zachariah blinked as if she was seeing me for the first time. Her mouth went slack. She cocked her head to one side and narrowed her eyes, scrutinizing me from head to toe. "All mothers love their sons," she said. "And all wives love their husbands. Wives should not have to mourn for their husbands without sons to comfort them. But first I lost my bonny captain and then I lost my bonny boy."

Now it seemed as if she could no longer see me at all. He eyes stared straight ahead. She swayed slightly against the rocking motion of the gondola. "The damned White Sow took him from me," she sighed. "She took my bonny captain. And I lost my bonny boy. It was left me to mourn my husband without a son to comfort me."

"And you've taken me from my mother," I told her. "Stolen me from her."

Again, her eyes blinked. Again, it seemed as if she was seeing me for the first time.

"Stolen you?" She seemed genuinely taken aback. "A boy like you? Some poor mother's son? Who would do such a thing? Tell me their name and I'll have them strung and up lashed to within an inch of their lives!"

"You did!" I yelled back at her, the rest of the milk spilling from the mug. "You ordered your crew not to let me go. You said I was to be your fetcher. You tricked me into agreeing."

Mrs. Zachariah stumbled clumsily back along the deck. Her hand went up to her mouth. The tics on her face stopped fidgeting. The dancing strands of her hair settled as the wind momentarily fell calm. "I did?" she cried. "What was I thinking? How could I contemplate such a terrible thing?"

Then a shout went up from farther along the deck. "Dragons ho!"

Mrs Zachariah froze. Her eyes began snapping left to right. Tics and twitches began to break out once more all over her face. The wind came howling around her, causing her overcoat to flap against the sides of her boots and the locks of her hair to rise and gyrate.

A crewman came running along the deck. "We're almost upon the drove, *ma'am*."

Mrs Zachariah snapped to attention. "Man the rope cannons!" I heard her yell.

Then she turned back almost instantaneously to me.

"Fetcher!" she roared. "No time for nibbling on that bread. Fetch me my telescope this instant!"

7. The Dragon Hunt

From that point on everything seemed to unfold around me at a fantastical speed. The airship banked and swung a hard left into the midst of the gyrating flock of green dragons. No sooner had I fetched Mrs Zachariah's telescope than she climbed up onto a raised gantry to the rear of the gondola and began to bark out orders, her arms flailing wildly, as the snaky tails of her black hair danced in the wind.

Several of the men began attaching metal hooks to lengths of ropes. "Fetcher!" they called to me. "Fetch the bait!" I had no idea what they were talking about. Arms spread wide in hopelessness I cast my eyes frantically from left to right. Angus ran past me, a leather helmet on his head, strap pulled tightly under his chin, goggles balanced on the brim.

"The bait!" he yelled. "It's in the hold."

Hurriedly I climbed down the uneven rungs of the wooden ladder that led into the stuffy depths of The Drunken Molly's hold. In the gloom I could see the bleached dragon bone beams that made up the airship's frame and, gathered here and there in nooks and corners, four or five crewmen, busily uncorking fat looking clay vessels. One of them handed me a basket filled with rough-cut chunks of salted meat. "Bait!" he said over his tobacco-stained teeth.

With the basket strap over my left shoulder, I hauled it up to the deck of the gondola and dragged it to where the men were waiting with their hooked ropes. They made a wild scramble for the salted meat and, having pierced these with the pointed ends of the hooks, tossed the ropes over the sides. One of them winked at me "Just like fishing, laddie. Cast your line. Catch a dragon."

Mrs Zachariah was screaming out orders upon her gantry, her hair squirming wildly like a nest of eels. Now I saw canvas covers being stripped from what I assumed must be the rope cannons. Six in all, they were a mixture of darkly stained wood and grey metal cladding. Each one stationed at a regular interval all around the circumference of the gondola's deck.

Angus jumped up into the little cockpit seat behind one of the emplacements as another crew member loaded the barrel with a long length of rope, looped and knotted at one end. As soon this was in place Angus swung the mouth of his cannon around so that it was facing out into the open sky.

The dragons were far smaller than I had imagined they might be. Most of them were no longer than four or five feet from nose to tail. They looked a lot like overgrown lizards, ridged backbones and swishing tails. But they were beautiful. Not in any way ferocious or intimidating. Their hides, armoured in overlapping scales, ran through every imaginable shade of green. Their underbellies were all of a similar pale, yellow hue. Their wings, at full span, were twice as long as their bodies and when they swooped close to the airship the gust of wing beat whipped frostily against my face.

I could tell that they were panicked by the intrusion of the noisy, smoke belching airship into their midst. But rather than flying away they were circling around the vicinity of airship's crimson balloon. I had no doubt that they were held there by the temptation of the enticing meaty rewards that dangled from the gondola like baubles on a solstice tree.

There came a sudden jerk and the airship lurched slightly forward. A cheer went up from the crew and seconds later an emerald hued dragon rose swiftly upward, wings beating, a hunk of salted meat clamped between its razor-sharp teeth. One of the rope gunners swung the barrel of his cannon around and let his lasso fly. The loop sailed over the dragon's serpentine head and yanked tight around its neck. It let out a high-pitched squeal, spitting fiery blue sparks. The red meat fell limply from its mouth and tumbled downwards.

Another cannon sent its rope flying and this one took hold of one of the dragon's hind legs. Now the crewmen grabbed both ropes and began to haul the dragon in. It thrashed and pulled against them; the men drawing in the rope pulled harder so that the lasso around its neck tightened and prevented it from throwing flames from its mouth.

The poor thing reeled and lashed out with its claws. Starved of air, however, it was soon overwhelmed. Its wings folded back close to its ridged back and it began to drop. The men strained against the ropes as a wide net was thrown over the edge of the gondola to catch it. In no time at all it was yanked over the side and tipped onto the deck.

Two crewmen pinned its thrashing legs down. Two more wrestled its flailing wings and held them tight. Yet another straddled its scaly neck and forced its head into an upright position. I could see the fear etched in the poor creature's eyes as erratic puffs of smoke stuttered out of its flared nostrils.

"Don't just stand there, fetcher!" yelled the crewman as the dragon tensed its rippling neck muscles and tried to buck him off. "Go and fetch the fire extractor!"

Again, I had no idea what he was talking about. I stood there gaping at him as the dragon kicked out and sent one of the crewmen tumbling across the deck.

"Fetcher!" called out a voice from behind me. "Over here!"

I turned to see Smudger holding out a piece of odd-looking apparatus. It had a leather muzzle at one end and a long length of rubber tubing trailing from the other. "Give this to the wrangler," he yelled. Snatching it from him I rushed back and passed it to the crewman straddling the dragon's neck. In truth I had no idea who the wrangler was, but I thought it was safe to assume he was it.

The muzzle was yanked over the dragon's snout. The straps were pulled tight and the buckles fastened behind its scaly head. Another crew member came lurching along the deck bearing one of the clay vessels I'd seen earlier in the hold. He placed the vessel in front of the dragon and stuffed the rubber tube running from the end of the muzzle into its narrow neck.

"Ready!" he yelled.

The wrangler began to loosen the noose of the lasso around the dragon's green neck. There came an odd clicking noise from inside the creature's throat. The wrangler reached down and pressed two fingers against the scales just beneath its jaw line. The clicking ceased. The wrangler nodded to his crewmates.

"Ready?"

"Aye," came the response.

The wrangler relaxed his fingers. As soon as the pressure was released from her neck the clicking commenced again in earnest. The dragon let out a furious roar. The muzzle sparked blue as its fire was forced through the insulated tubing and into the clay vessel. After no more than a few seconds the crewman pulled the tube away and re-corked the neck of the vessel. It sat there hissing and steaming till someone else, wearing thick heatproof gantlets, appeared to haul it back to the hold.

Meanwhile the wrangler had once more pulled the lasso tightly around the dragon's neck. "She'll be good for two more!" he cried, as another clay vessel was brought up from the hold. When I looked along the length of the gondola, I could see that three more of the green dragons had been lassoed, netted, held down and muzzled. Up on her gantry Mrs Zachariah danced and laughed like a mad woman as their fiery and potent breath was brutally drawn from their lungs. The last of my illusions about dragon hunting were well and truly shattered. As far as I could see there was no bravery or glory whatsoever about was happening.

All in all the hunt could have lasted for no more than an hour. As soon as two or three roars of breath had been taken from the dragons they would be unceremoniously tossed over the side of the gondola. I watched them as they beat weakly on their wings, seeming to drop ever lower in the sky as they flew feebly away from the airship. When it was finally over, I was dispatched to fetch a rum barrel so that the crew could celebrate. While the accordion player started warming up his instrument and I found Angus amongst the raucous crowd.

"What did you think of that?" he asked me.

What I had seen made me feel sick. But I didn't think he'd want to hear that.

"Amazing," I lied. I could feel my stomach churn with disgust. I had grown up on a farm, so I wasn't exactly squeamish, but what I had witnessed seemed wholly cruel and unnecessary.

"Did you hear how they clicked?" asked Angus.

I nodded.

"You know what it was?"

I shook my head.

Angus pointed at his neck. "All dragons have two little organs at the back of their throats. They click together like flint stones and when they spark that's what ignites their breath."

"What happens to the dragons after you take their breath?" I asked.

Angus grinned. "The lucky ones will make it back to their lairs in the canyons of the Serrated Mountains."

"And the unlucky ones?"

"They'll fall foul to the crossbow bolts fired by the crews below us in the scavenger ships."

"Scavenger ships?" I felt my brow crease.

"Smaller airships," said Angus. "They travel in the wake of dragon hunting vessels, at a slightly lower elevation. They're crewed up with skinners and boners and butchers."

"How come I didn't see them when the *Drunken Molly* flew over the glen and the meadow?"

"They were at a higher altitude than us at that point," explained Angus. "Waiting above the cloudbank. They fell in behind us as we ascended."

I didn't like the sound of skinners and boners and butchers.

"And if a dragon drops down into the path of a scavenger ship and gets hit by a bolt?" I asked.

Angus grinned maliciously and ran a finger across his throat in a slicing motion.

Along the deck the accordion player stuck up a song.

"Now I was born in Tennanbrau," he sang in a deep baritone.

"Haul away above the clouds," joined the rest of the crew.

"And grew as tall as I am now."

"The Dragon Hunter's Sky Shanty," said Angus, and pitched in with rejoinder.

"Haul away above the clouds."

The song continued back and forth.

"I signed on with my captain bold."

"Haul away above the clouds."

"We travelled north to where it's cold."

48

"Haul away above the clouds."

"And there I swore on pain of death."

"Haul away above the clouds."

"To take the precious dragon breath."

"Haul away, haul away - haul away above the clouds."

It was the first time I'd ever heard the song, but I would hear it sung many more times before we reached the Far Tundra.

8. Across The Far Tundra

A week dragged by. *The Drunken Molly* coursed ever northward. The hum of her engine became like the ticking of a familiar clock – so constantly present I no longer noticed it. The often-repeated call and refrain of the Dragon Hunter's Sky Shanty echoed endlessly inside my head. I soon knew the words by heart and would catch myself singing it under my breath as I ran here and there, fetching this and that. It grew colder. Far colder than I'd ever experienced in my life, even in the snow bound depths of winter back in the Low Counties. My teeth chattered constantly. My cheeks blushed purple. My nose seemed always to be running and dripping.

I did what I could to keep warm, improvising and scrounging unwanted items from members of the crew. I tore a hole for my head into one of the blankets and hung it around me like a sort of cape, bunching it up around my waist with a frayed piece of rope to stop it flapping around as I dashed here and there, fetching stuff for Mrs Zachariah and hefting ingredients for Smudger's stodgy stews and broths.

I padded out the insides of my shoes with old straw from the floor of the chicken coop. I retrieved a pair of gloves with a missing thumb that one of the crew had thrown in the bin. Angus gave me a slightly dented rope gunner's helmet with a faulty strap that had to be tied together with string.

I no longer felt anything like the boy who had been kidnapped only seven days earlier. I missed my family. I longed to be back home with them in the Low Counties. But I had stopped crying myself to sleep. I had become totally focused on my tasks as the ship's fetcher. A mental map of The Drunken Molly had constructed itself inside my head. I came to know automatically where one thing might be kept and where another thing had to be returned. I was forever devising route plans across the deck or down into the hold. The quickest way to fetch an item and a quicker way to fetch it back. Many of the objects that I was called on to fetch were unbelievably heavy and I could feel an ache in my arms as my muscles hardened. The throbbing in my legs from the constant running around was almost as bad.

Over the days Angus appeared increasingly keen to fill me with all sorts of facts about how an airship was constructed and how the dragon trade worked. He was passionate in what seemed to be a highly personal mission to try and convert me to the cause of the dragon hunters and make me into a fully-fledged crewmember. "See the balloon," he'd say, pointing up enthusiastically to the billowing crimson giant above our heads. "It's made from the membrane of dragon wings, stretched across a frame constructed from dozens of dragon ribs. The membrane is so tough that keeps the dragon breath inside. Nothing can leak out. Cold air can't leak in."

"Tennanbrau is built on the dragon trade," he'd say. "The airship docks, the warehouses, the huge factories. All of it centres on the dragon trade."

Once he brought me a strip of cured dragon meat to taste. "Dragon meat jerky," he said. "Better than the gristly old mutton they used to give you back home in the Low Counties."

I found it bitter to the taste and far too salty. Chewing on it I remembered the terrible scenes I had witnessed when the flock of green dragons been wrestled to the deck and muzzled. I recalled the rows of clay vessels in the hold, filled with the breath stolen from their lungs, and wondered how many of the weakened creatures had fallen into the paths of the unseen scavenger ships still apparently trailing below us.

"What exactly would have happened to the Common Greens who were caught by the scavengers?" I asked once.

Angus responded in a matter-of-fact manner. "The meat goes for canned food in the processing plants. The hide and the scales are used for schoolbags and purses and shoes and such. The teeth and the claws for cheap jewellery. There's a tradition in Tennanbrau when a new baby is born. The parents give it a pendant. A tooth for a girl and a talon for a boy."

I thought of Mrs Zachariah's dead baby and a talon pendant never given.

"The wings that are not big enough to use for airship balloons go for lady's umbrellas," he went on. "The bones of Greens and some other species are too small for use as scaffolding in the construction industry, so they'll be ground down to use in fertilizers for the farms around the townships. None of it will sell for near as much as a good batch of pure dragon breath, but all added up the scavengers will still turn tidy little profit."

Occasionally Angus would show up in an extremely apologetic mood. "Sorry, sorry, sorry," he'd say over and over, pushing his straggly red hair behind his ears. "We're both Hill Folk. You could be my little brother. I wish I'd known exactly what Mrs Zachariah was planning. If I did, I'd never have let them catch you in that rope."

"I think in her heart Mrs Zachariah regrets it too," I'd say. "In fact, I even think she was ready to set me free. Maybe of you were to talk to her?"

"I couldn't do that," he'd reply. "I swore an oath to be loyal to her. I couldn't challenge an order. Besides, we can't turn back now."

"Even if the order is wrong?" I'd ask him.

He would shrug his shoulders. "I might be able to have word with the coxswain," he'd say. "Mister Grisling sailed the skies with Captain Zachariah for years. She trusts him. She might listen. If he picked the right time."

But the time never seemed to be right.

"Did you speak to the Grisling?" I'd ask.

"Not yet," he'd reply.

"When then?" I'd whine at him.

And his mood would change in an instant. He'd become cold and belligerent. "You should be grateful, little hill boy," he'd yell at me. "You're going to help us catch the White Sow and avenge the name of the famous Captain, Nathaniel Zachariah. It's an honour and a privilege."

His eyes would take on that crazed look and he would gabble on and on about the White Sow and how she would be taken.

"I'll be the one. It'll be my lasso that hauls her in. You'll see. Mrs Zachariah will give me a handsome bonus for my bravery. I'll be far richer that the rest of the crew. I'll be famous. When I walk down any street in Tennanbrau people will turn their heads. 'That's him,' they'll say. 'That's Angus who brought down the White Sow.'"

Once we saw another flock of dragons on the horizon. They looked far bigger than the Common Greens that the crew had hunted with such glee. The sunlight seemed to bounce in sparkling yellow darts from their hides, making them glisten and glimmer like stars in the night sky. They were flying in a formation, dozens of them, great wings outstretched as they glided down through the thermals.

"Horned Goldbacks," said Angus. "Almost as rare as the White Sow herself. If we had waited instead of hunting the Greens, their breath would have brought us a pretty penny. But it's the Sow we're after now."

His eyes went wide in their sockets.

That morning *The Drunken Molly* began passing slowly over wide, seemingly endless miles of flat and monotonous frozen tundra. In between fetching this or that I would lean over the railings and look down the bleak landscape. A cold shiver would run through me at such a stark contrast with the green rolling hills of the Low Counties. There was nothing to be seen but moss and lichen and straggly, grey looking shrubs. I was so far from home that I despaired of ever returning.

***

Late in the afternoon that same day, as I was fetching some onions from the hold for Smudger, I saw Angus and most of the other crewmen gathered by the railings. As the skies around us grew more and more overcast they had been singing the Dragon Hunter's Sky Shanty to lighten the mood. Now a stony silence had fallen over the entire gondola. With a small sack of onions under my arm I pushed the battered helmet back over my forehead and peered down to where they were pointing.

A group of thirty or so figures was trudging in single file across the tundra in a meandering procession. From that high up it was difficult to make out exact details. But on squinting my eyes and forcing myself to focus on the exact spot where they were I could make out that that some of them were carrying what appeared to be wooden staffs, while others were drawing sleds that were laden with animal furs and various pots and pans.

Even from that height I could tell that there was something odd about their lumbering, broad shouldered frames. The hue of their flesh seemed as grey as rock or slate and the tufts of hair on their heads was an odd shade of mossy green. I noticed that some of them carried wooden shields as well as staffs. Some of them even wore leather breastplates over their fur garments.

"Who are they?" I asked Angus.

"Ghibelline nomads," he replied.

55

"Foul creatures with nothing better to do than wander back and forth across the tundra all day long," added one of the crewmen.

"No friends of dragon hunters," said another.

"We'll never forget our comrades from *The Freedom Moon*," said his companion.

"Aye," agreed several of the crew.

"*The Freedom Moon*?" I asked.

"An airship that went down in a thunderstorm," replied Angus. "When a search party found the wreck all that was left of the crew was their bones."

"Eaten alive," said the first crewman.

"Gnawed down to the marrow," said the second.

I looked down again at the slow procession weaving its way across the tundra.

"By the Ghibelline?" I asked in a tremulous voice.

"The very same," said Angus, running his dirty fingers through his increasingly greasy ginger hair. "Their appetite for human flesh is insatiable!"

9. The White Sow

I was roused at the crack of dawn the next morning by the keening sound of Mrs Zachariah's voice. "Shake a leg, fetcher!" she screeched and rattled noisily at the wires of the coop. "Go fetch my telescope. I've seen something on the far horizon that warrants a closer look." I pushed my head through my blanket cape, pulled it down over my shoulders and tied the rope around my waist. As I was scrambling through the cage door, I realised that tiny flakes of white snow were floating down on the dawn breeze. I grabbed my helmet and tied the strap under my chin as I ran to fetch Mrs Zachariah's telescope from the little nook on the deck where it was housed, skidding slightly on the slush that was accumulating on the deck.

Through the snow flurries I could see that overnight *The Drunken Molly* had almost traversed the entire width of the tundra. Ahead of us loomed a huge and foreboding mountain range, its craggy fissures zigzagging downwards from grey piercing peaks that were caked in a thick icing of snow. Mrs Zachariah snatched the telescope from me and scrambled up onto the scaffold of her raised gantry. Snow began to dot the snaked braids of her hair and gather on the shoulders of her man-sized coat. "Come on, come on," she muttered under her breath as she scanned the peaks. "I swear that I saw you."

Standing on my tiptoes I peered in the direction that Mrs Zachariah was scanning. All I could see in the distance was the snow-capped zenith of a tall mountain, poking its jagged peak up into the cloudbank. I looked down to where the tundra was turning white as sheet as the snow began to lay on its frozen surface. Mercifully I could see no longer see any sign at all of the raggedy band of apparently man-eating Ghibelline we had passed over the previous day. Then, as I turned my attention back to the mountain range, something huge and vibrantly white seemed to glide over the summit. At first, I thought that an immense shelf of snow had shifted and avalanched over the edge. Then I saw a pair of mighty wings spread magnificently wide as an enormous pale hued dragon circled the range.

"It's her!" whooped Mrs Zachariah. "It's the White Sow!"

I watched the colossal white monster as she beat her gigantic wings and rose towards the cloudbank. A tremble shuddered through me at her awesome sight. For a moment the Sow was lost amongst the billowing bulge of the swollen snow clouds. Then she broke through once more and came swooping down at such a terrifying speed that I felt sure that *The Drunken Molly* would be batted out of the sky by her powerful wing beat. But just as it seemed as if she was flying straight toward us she banked away and flew towards the east.

"Coxswain!" screamed Mrs Zachariah. "Hard astern! Follow her! Follow the brute who took my bonny captain!"

Grisling had been half asleep on his wooden stool, with his boots resting lazily against the airship's navigation wheel. At the sound of Mrs Zachariah's voice, he leapt to his feet and shook his head vigorously, as if trying to jerk himself fully awake.

"The Sow, man!" she railed at him. "The Sow is in our sights. Give chase before we lose her!"

With one quick look to where Mrs Zachariah was pointing Grisling smoothed down his moustache, then grabbed the wheel and swung it full circle. The crimson balloon strained against its silvery wires. I was nearly thrown from my feet as the airship went into a wild swerve. Mrs Zachariah stumbled and almost toppled from the gantry.

"Smudger!" she cried, righting herself once more. "Rouse the crew! Rouse the crew!"

The drone of the turbines grew louder. Smudger came gangling lankily out of the galley and set about banging the gong he normally used to call the crew to meals. I could feel the cold wind blowing snow back into my face as the airship's speed picked up. Rudely roused from their bunks and hammocks, half dressed and tousle haired, the men formed a somewhat confused congregation on the deck.

"The Sow, lads," Mrs Zachariah told them, pointing in an eastwardly direction. "Luck is with us this day. We're on the trail of the White Sow. Vengeance is ours for the taking. Glory is in our grasp. Man the lasso guns. Get the nets ready. We'll draw her breath this day, so help me. And when were done we'll have the rest of her. Not a single scale of her hoary hide will we leave for the scavengers!"

Just as it had when she'd ordered the hunt of the Common Greens the deck erupted into a noisy and chaotic hive of activity. I stood there peering into the distance, watching the far white image of the Sow beating her mighty wings through the snow-laden skies. Mrs Zachariah looked down saw me there. "Fetcher!" she snapped at me. "No time for daydreaming. Get down into the hold and fetch the bait this instant."

10. The Hunting of the Sow

When I climbed back onto the deck, hefting a sack of dried meat for the bait, Mrs Zachariah was yelling out orders from her perch up on the gantry. The black braids of her hair whipped and writhed once more in the wind thrown up by the tail end of the gathering blizzard. I glanced into the distance and saw that the gap between the Sow and *The Drunken Molly* was steadily being reduced. Now we were outrunning the gusting snow flurries and were heading into a clear blue sky. The engine and the turbines droned unremittingly as the speed was notched to full throttle. Steam hissed from the pistons. A trail of black smoke fanned out behind us. The steel wires hanging down from the crimson dragon wing balloon complained and groaned. I opened the sack and emptied the dried meat onto the deck. Immediately chunks of it were pierced by hooks attached to ropes and were tossed over the side.

Angus came rushing past me pulling on his lasso gunner's helmet. "What did I tell you!" he cried. "She's as big as an airship!"

Perhaps even bigger, I thought, eyes fixed again on the image of the Sow pounding her gigantic white wings as we drew ever closer. Her legs were curled up under her belly and I could clearly make out the scimitar curve of her talons, starkly lacquered black against the contrasting snowy whiteness of her hide.

"If you catch her, how are you going to get her on board?" I called after him. "She's far too big!"

"We'll drag her behind us and descend to the tundra," he called back. "We'll take her breath and then finish her once and for all."

I looked towards the Sow again. How could they even think of destroying a thing of such majestic beauty? As I watched her, she turned her head looked back over her shoulder directly at us. Her wings stopped beating. She held them outstretched at full span and came gliding around in a wide arc. She raised her muzzle as if she was sniffing at the air and let out a single piercing shriek.

A deathly silence fell over *The Drunken Molly*. Up on the gantry Mrs Zachariah stood as still as a statue. Even the wind seemed to have blown itself out. The braids of her hair hung limply down the side of her face, straight and unmoving. Every member of the crew seemed to be holding his breath. I realised that I was holding mine too. Only the thrum of the airship's engine broke the silence.

With a single beat of her wings the Sow came straight for us.

The spell was broken.

"Cut the engines!" cried Mrs Zachariah. "She has the scent of the meat."

The engines came to a slow, clanking, hissing halt.

"Mister Grisling, hold fast. Let her come to us."

Grisling steadied the navigation wheel, digging his boot heels against the deck of the gondola.

The huge form of the White Sow loomed closer.

"Lasso gunners make ready!" came the order from Mrs Zachariah.

Angus and his fellow gunners adjusted their cannon turrets and lined up their eyes against the sights. The Sow was so close now that the next beat of her gigantic wings sent a gust of wind that tipped the crimson balloon and the set the gondola rocking. The Sow bared her teeth. Her red eyes sparkled like rubies in the cold sunlight. She tossed back her slender neck and, letting out a hungry roar, swooped down below the gondola to take her prize.

Immediately Mrs Zachariah snapped into action, screaming garbled orders at the lasso gunners, arms flailing wildly around. It was highly unlikely that they understood a word of what was being yelled at them. Nevertheless, they swung their cannons around and pointed the barrels downwards. The gondola suddenly juddered forward, signifying that the bait had been taken. My stomach did a dizzying somersault as the entire airship dropped by at least ten feet. The Sow was dragging the airship with her as she tried to fly off with her catch. Several of the crew cried out in fear. Mrs Zachariah had to grip the side rails to stop from tumbling from her gantry. Grisling cranked up the engine to try and pull *The Molly* back.

There came a horrendous splintering noise. When I looked down into the hold, I saw that a gaping hole had appeared. The gondola veered and seesawed wildly on its wires. Two of the men who had been passing dragon breath vessels up the ladder from the hold to the deck were knocked from the rungs. They became awkwardly tangled up with each other and in their panic slid across the floor and fell straight through the ragged hole.

Their screams faded on the wind as they plummeted towards the foothills below.

The Sow rose ominously to the left side of the gondola. Her teeth were clamped tightly shut. There was no sign of the meat. But the frayed remains of the rope trailed back from her mouth, with a jagged section of decking attached to the end. It was then that everyone saw what had been concealed from us on the Sow's approach. Lashed to her side by a tangled length of lasso was a hideous sight. It appeared to be a hand, sheathed in a leather gauntlet, fingers curled around the rope.

"Captain Zachariah!" gasped Grisling still holding the navigation wheel in place. "Is that all that is left of you?"

Up in the gantry Mrs Zachariah let out an anguished howl of grief. "Nathaniel!" she cried. "My precious husband! My bonny captain!"

The Sow beat her massive wings and the gondola rocked crazily again. Clinging to the gantry railings Mrs Zachariah screamed at the lasso gunners. "Fire at will! Bring the vile creature down. Avenge your captain! Avenge my husband!"

Three lasso gunners fired in unison. Their ropes went hopelessly wide as the Sow circled the airship. I saw Angus and the two other gunners in their cockpits on the other side of the deck tracing her progress. But by the time they had fired the Sow had already beat down on her wings and was easily

64

far out of range. The rope loops spun through the air to their maximum range before dropping slackly down. As the tethers were hauled back up Mrs Zachariah began screaming at the top of her voice.

"Re-load! Re-load! She's coming back for a second bite."

The sure enough the Sow had changed direction and was racing for the airship. She plunged low and dipped beneath the gondola once more. As she went the ghostly, gloved hand of Captain Zachariah seemed to wave ghoulishly at us. Again, the whole of *The Drunken Molly* juddered as the airship was pulled forcefully into a plunging descent. Again, Grisling tried to get the engine to pull back. Again, there came a sudden jerk, followed by the horrible sound of splintering wood. This time the Sow did not rise. When several of the crew ran to the iron railings, I ran with them. The Sow had gone into a sharp dive, white wings tightly pressed against her side. I found myself hoping that she would escape.

But Mrs Zachariah had other ideas. "Release some dragon breath from the balloon!" she yelled. "Take us down. She'll not outwit me. I'll have my revenge. I will have my revenge!" One of the crewmen began to shimmy his way up one of the silver wires attached the crimson balloon "Be ready," Mrs Zachariah warned the lasso gunners. "A curse on any one of you that misses his mark."

Then her eyes fell upon me.

"Fetcher! Get down the hold and fetch some fresh bait."

I lurched across the deck, my stomach churning as the crewman on the wire twisted open a valve that allowed the crimson balloon to deflate sufficiently that *The Drunken Molly* began to noticeably loose altitude. I fell to my hands and knees and looked down into the hold. Another huge hole had been torn in the belly of decking.

Only one man remained down there. He was desperately clinging to one of the curved dragon bone beams, the wind tearing his clothes to shreds around him. Through the twin holes I could see the clear blue sky and the distinctive outline of the White Sow heading back in the direction the Serrated Mountains. I called out to the terrified crewman. "We need more bait!"

"Gone," he called back over the roar of the wind. "All gone. The bait and all our supplies. The jars with the dragon breath we took from the Common Greens. Out through the holes. Just like our poor brothers."

I turned and yelled to Mrs Zachariah up on her gantry.

"Bait's gone. Hold full of holes. Everything gone."

"What?" she screamed. "This can't be happening. I'm so close. So close to avenging my bonny captain."

"We need to turn back, *ma'am*," warned Grisling. "With no bait to draw the Sow it's pointless. And if the hold is as badly damaged as the boy says we're going to have to put down to make repairs before the whole gondola breaks up."

66

"And the leave the scavengers to take the Sow?" screeched Mrs Zachariah. "Never!"

"The scavengers are miles behind us," said Grisling. "They're no match for *The Molly* at full tilt."

For a moment Mrs Zachariah seemed somewhat hesitant, unsure of what to do or say. Then her eyes sparked as if an idea had just taken hold. "That boy!" she cried and pointed straight at me. She took on that odd look, as if she was just noticing me for the first time. Her brow furrowed as the black braids of her hair whipped around her face. "That boy," she said again, climbing hurriedly down from the gantry. "We can use that boy as bait."

I heard several of the crewmen let out gasps of shock.

"Fetch the fetcher," said Mrs Zachariah, heading straight for me. "Tell him to fetch me a rope."

"The boy is the fetcher!" said Coxswain Grisling.

"Is he?" Mrs. Zachariah blinked as if she wasn't really aware of where she was. She began prowling around me, sniffing at my hair like some beast of prey, eyes narrowing, and her teeth chewing on her lower lip. After a moment she turned on the group of crewmen who were hovering cautiously behind her. They jumped back a little. "Don't just stand there," she bawled. "One of you fetch me a rope."

11. Dragon Bait

Mrs Zachariah attended to me herself, making the preparations her own personal responsibility. Gently, almost tenderly, she tied the rope under my arms and pulled the knot tight. For a moment I caught the tiniest hint of the kind-hearted woman she might once have been before the White Sow took her husband and robbed her of her sanity.

She had calmed the protests led by Grisling by assuring everyone that I was only to be dangled as bait until I had drawn the attraction of the Sow. She promised faithfully that at the last minute I was to be hauled back to safety. I could see the looks of doubt that were etched the men's faces. Grisling had his pipe clamped between his teeth again. He looked like he was forcefully holding his temper. Smudger was twisting his hands into his apron and avoiding looking directly at me. Angus Stonedyke had turned a ghostly shade of pale.

But not one of them said a single word to challenge her.

She started talking to me in an odd and eerily affectionate voice. She brushed my hair out of my eyes and stroked my chin. "Good boy," she crooned. "Don't be afraid. Soonest done. Soonest over."

"If I'm eaten by the Sow my mother will never forgive you," I told her.

"Mother?"

A look of utter surprise flashed in her eyes - the way it had that day when she had spoken to me in the chicken coop that first day. Her features softened a little. "I could have been a mother," she muttered, swallowing hard. Her upper lip trembled as she stroked my chin again. A tear rolled down her cheek. Then the madness took hold - her eyes grew dark and began to fidget and twitch, her lip curled into a ferocious grin.

She tore open the neck of my shirt and produced a pointed stiletto knife from the scabbard that hung from the wide leather belt around her waist. Her hand moved in a rapid blur as she slashed a shallow cut across my chest. I heard the crew gasp in shock at what they were witnessing.

I bit down hard on my lip, determined not let her see me cry. She dipped her finger into the blood that oozed from the wound and held it up to her nose. Her nostrils flared as she sniffed loudly. She let out an inane chuckle "Your blood is sweet, little fetcher. The Sow will come quickly to you."

Just then the wind picked up and sent the black braids of her hair into a wild dance. Her face took on a demonic countenance. She looked over my shoulder to where the crew had gathered, heads bowed as if they were ashamed of what she was doing. When she barked out a series of commands Angus ran swiftly past me and glanced guiltily over his shoulder as he climbed back into the cockpit behind his lasso cannon.

A pair of strong hands lifted me from behind and one of the dragon wranglers carried me over the mouth of the hold. Hand over hand the rope was lowered down through the larger of the two holes ripped in the gondola's belly. Dangling in the open sky the wind tore at me, howling in my ears and spinning me around as the knot pulled tighter and tighter around my chest. The terrible cold made me so numb I was no longer able to feel the throbbing pain that emanated from the oozing wet scar on my chest.

The last time I had hung on a rope like this I had been dangling precariously upside down as I watched my family, and the green hills of the Low Counties, disappear before my eyes. This time, although I was the right way up, the experience was no less terrifying. I glanced down to see how far below the ground was. All I could see was the vast columns of billowing grey cloud that had rapidly smothered the blue sky. Blustery squalls of sleet began to stab at my eyes. Was this to be my end? I had seen how fast the Sow could travel once she beat down on her wings. It didn't seem at all possible that the crew could haul me back up to the gondola before her teeth snapped shut around me.

Beneath the raggedy remnants of my blanket cape, I could see the blood from my chest wound slowly causing a bigger and bigger red stain on my shirt. I thought of how my mother had sewn that shirt with her own hands. How the thread she had used had been spun from wool that my father had sheared from one of his best sheep. How Isla had griped and moaned when she had been given the task of fixing the buttons in place. I wondered what my family were doing at that very minute. Were they waiting by the window of our little cottage, fire roaring in the hearth, hoping that I'd find my way back home to them?

70

I knew in my heart that they would never give up hope.

And I knew then that I owed to my parents and my sister not to give up until every possible thing that I might feasibly try failed. I decided in that instant that I had to find a way to defend myself against the White Sow. It would be like a new-born lamb, weak and separated from its mother, trying to confront a hungry wolf. But if it were my fate to die thousands of feet up there in the cold, cold sky then I would do it fighting for my life.

I felt my chin jut forward in defiance.

From above me I heard a loud cheer go up from the deck. When I looked to the horizon I saw the outline of the White Sow wheeling around in the distance and beating her blanched wings as she prepared to advance through the clouds. She had the scent of my blood now and nothing was going to stop her. I pulled on the rope. It went into a slight swinging motion. Kicking out my legs I set it swinging in the opposite direction. I had learnt this with the rope swing that hung from the branch of the old oak tree at the back of our cottage. I pulled on the rope again. Soon I had built up a considerable back and forth momentum.

I watched White Sow heading towards me at breakneck speed, snow coloured head dipped low, claws tucked up into her pale, creamy belly. Above me I saw the barrels of the lasso guns swinging outwards. Over the howl of the wind, I heard Mrs Zachariah, cackling like a crazy woman. The Sow went into a dive, wings set back tight against the frosty scales of her flank.

It was clear that no one was making any effort at all to pull me back up to the gondola, so I yanked on the rope and went swinging rapidly backwards. The Sow came gliding menacingly towards me. Her teeth were like serrated tombstones. Her tongue lashed hungrily around the sides of her mouth like some ravenous purple pulsing serpent. She roared and in the heat of her breath I felt the terrifying hint of the terrible fire that brewed in her lungs. She moved in for the kill, jaws gaping wide. As she did so I kicked out with my legs and swung the rope towards her.

My father had always taught me that if I was ever charged by an angry ram, I should slap it as hard as I could on the snout, and it would be so shocked that it would turn tail and run. I intended to treat the Sow as if she were a charging ram - but if my plan didn't work it would surely be the end of me.

12. The Molly's Downfall

"Yah!" I cried as the rope swung me directly into the Sow's path. The wind pulled at my hair. The sleet went beating relentlessly against me. I raised my hand and aimed for the rapidly approaching crest of her slimy pink snout.

SMACK!

The sound echoed in the sky.

The Sow threw her head back and let out a dreadful ear-piercing scream, wings spread wide. I was showered in froth and spittle. The pale membrane of her wings rippling the Sow reached up with her front leg and clawed at her injured muzzle, her head jerking from side to side. I thought that at any minute she would turn and snap me up in her jaws. I tried to kick out and set the rope swinging again. But I just didn't have the strength left in me.

The Sow began to howl as if she was in great pain. She beat her massive white wings and went into a deep dive. She went so fast that it was as if she'd blinked out of existence beneath the grey density of the clouds. I could feel the rope beginning to spin from the powerful back draft left in her wake. Above me I heard Mrs Zachariah screaming out in frustration. The hull of *The Drunken Molly* let out a long groan as she was manoeuvred into a sharp dip, following the Sow's descent.

I imagined a crewmember clinging to one of the silver wires, loosening the balloon's valve, as the airship's engines drove her down through the clouds. I could feel the rope around my chest pulling even tighter as it slipped painfully up under my armpits. I could feel the knot grinding into the wound where Mrs Zachariah had cut me with her knife. It was becoming more and more difficult to breathe. The turbulence within the churning chaos of the clouds knocked me sideways and back again as I was dragged and buffeted wildly behind the airship.

Engulfed in the gritty black smoke from *The Drunken Molly's* turbines I could taste the rank odour of her fuel tanks in my mouth. I was terrified that a sudden gust of wind would whip me upwards into the blades of the rapidly rotating propellers. In the heat of the hunt Mrs. Zachariah and the crew had either forgotten all about me, or, in their obsession with bringing down the Sow, they simply no longer cared.

Then suddenly we were through the clouds and back out into the crisp blue skies. The foothills of the Serrated Mountains were behind us and below me I could see the rolling tundra, dusted in a light covering of snow, stretching like some vast undulating carpet towards the horizon. The plummeting body of the Sow came into view, pure and white, as beautiful as some angel falling from heaven, wheeling awkwardly in a huge circumference as her head went jerking left and right.

I looked up in time to see the barrels of the lasso cannons begin pointing downwards as Angus and the other gunners trained their cannon upon their quarry. I hoped that they would miss. That the

74

wind would send the ropes skewing wide and the White Sow would muster the strength to fly off and outrun them. Why should the crazy Captain's wife and her covetous crew get their way? Why should a magnificent creature such as the Sow have the breath from her lungs stolen, only to be brutally butchered and skinned so that they could profit from her downfall?

"Fly!" I screamed into the wind. "Fly, White Sow! Fly away!"

But the first volley lassos had already been released, slicing down through the sky with a sickening hiss. Three ropes whizzed past her head, missing by mere inches. But those that followed hit their mark. Two seized her left wing - one at the bony joint close to her ridged spine, and the other at the wingtip. As her head swung round in panic a third caught her by the hind leg. Desperately clawing at the ropes tightening around her wing she went into an erratic spiral. She roared and tried to beat her wings. Only one wing rose. The other had been rendered useless from the constricting ropes.

A cheer went up from the airship.

But the crew were being over optimistic. There was no rope around the Sow's neck to restrict the flow of the fiery gases that boiled deep within her. I heard the organs in her throat go click-click-click. I watched in terror as her jaw yawed wide and, with a mighty roar, out belched a column of raging blue fire. Flame scorched the hull of *The Drunken Molly*, singeing my hair where it hung down below the brim of my helmet and causing the skin on my forehead to bubble into blisters. The ropes that bound her wing and her hind leg burst into flame and severed within seconds.

Momentarily out of control from the fire that was rapidly eating into the hold *The Drunken Molly* was pitched this way and that. She tipped precariously to the right and had it not been for the balancing effect of her crimson balloon she would have capsized completely. Several of the crew were thrown overboard by the motion. I watched them tumble through the sky. As the ship rocked itself upright again nets were thrown over the side. The crew were clearly not ready to give up yet. But Sow batted them easily away with her hind legs. Her long tail cracked upwards like a whip and smashed into *The Drunken Molly's* damaged hull, leaving yet another jagged hole.

Still the crew persevered. More lasso ropes were launched from the cannon emplacements. With a snap of her head the Sow caught one in her teeth and pulled back. When she let go the airship went hurling into another rocking roll. This time in the opposite direction. I could see that the Sow's left wing had been terribly weakened by the rope nooses still attached to it. Unable to fly properly she began to drop like a stone from the sky. As she fell, she gave a final flick of her snowy white tail. The barbed tip skimmed the length of the crimson balloon cutting a huge, gaping slash as it went.

I watched the Sow tumbling down below me, while above me the dragon breath gas from ship's balloon gushed incessantly outwards. With nothing to keep it afloat the nose of the gondola dipped into a dive. She nose-dived, dragging me behind her.

The tundra was still miles below us, but it was drawing closer with frightening speed. It was then that a spark from the flames still licking the underbelly of the airship's hull hit the rope tied around my chest and took hold. Things blown clear from the deck went tumbling past my head, cages and rum barrels, mops and buckets. Even my chicken coop bunk.

As the rope burned I could see several small emergency balloons being rapidly inflated along the deck of *The Drunken Molly*. Great gushes of steam were being evacuated from the pistons into the hold an effort to douse the flames before they ignited the dragon breath still hissing out of the main balloon. It seemed that those still on board were in with a chance of survival. But it was clearly too late for me. The fire gnawed the rope till all that was left was single precarious thread.

Just as the emergency balloons began to slow down the descent of the airship the last thread of the rope snapped. *The Drunken Molly* rose in an upward direction as I fell away. I screamed and squeezed my eyes shut, preparing for my bones to be shattered against the frozen tundra.

13. The Lair of the White Sow

With a sudden, painful thud that knocked the wind out of my lungs I came to a halt a lot quicker than I had expected. I lay flat on my belly wheezing and gasping for breath, wondering why my ribs were not horribly broken and by what miracle I came to be still alive. A chill wind was whipping about my head. The ground beneath me seemed to be pulsating in an odd, rhythmic fashion. Afraid to open my eyes I began patting all around me with my hands. Instead of frosted ground and spiky blades of snow dusted grass, as I had expected, what I felt like a polished leathery surface.

Slowly I opened my eyes and found that I was still in the air, high above the tundra. By some fluke I had landed on the back of the White Sow. What I had been feeling with my hands was her white, overlapping scales. The pulsating sensation was that of her heartbeat and breathing. She seemed to have regained some of the strength in her left wing, but her wing beat had become stilted and irregular. She progressed across the sky in juddering fits, sometimes gaining altitude, only to drop lower once more when her wing gave out and fell limp by her side.

For fear of slipping and falling again I clung tightly to the hoary folds of white flesh around her neck. It was like clinging to the overgrown trunk of an outsized tree. I wondered if she could feel me there and trembled at the thought that she might turn and blow me into oblivion with her fiery breath. I listened intently for any sign of the organs in her throat beginning to click. From the corner of my eye, I could see Captain Zachariah's gauntlet still lashed to the Sow's side. It seemed pretty clear from that close angle that his severed hand was not still encased there. Nevertheless, the way it seemed to wave spookily at me sent shivers down my spine.

As we lunged across the vastness of the sky I could feel the wind whistling past my ears, almost yanking the battered old helmet from my head. Surrounded by swirling wisps of cloud vapour I looked back at the fallow land that stretched out mile after mile behind us. Far below I could see the craggy foothills that rose steadily in height till they merged with the vast grey range of the Serrated Mountains. My stomach turned at the thought of how high we were.

Clutching the Sow's scaly skin, I scanned the skyline to see if I could spot *The Drunken Molly*. For as far back as I could see the sky was empty. I wondered if the emergency balloons I had witnessed being inflated would hold enough dragon breath for the airship to be able to make it back to Tennanbrau City. Or would they have to put down on the tundra and risk being eaten alive by the Ghibelline? Despite what they had done to me, and their obvious lack of concern as to whether the Sow would devour me, I felt that my best hope still lay in trying to find my way back to them. I wondered whether, if the Sow were to fly low and close enough to the ground, I might be able to jump off safely.

If could somehow do that, what then?

I looked back at the barren wilderness of the open tundra and then at the foothills, which seemed far steeper and much more treacherous that the gently sloping hills back home. The distances involved seemed incomprehensible. Searching for an airship that had set down on the tundra would be like looking for a needle in a haystack. Thinking again of the tribe of flesh-eating Ghibelline and the gruesome fate of the crew of *The Freedom Moon* the idea of somehow jumping down began to seem a far less attractive option. Clinging tighter to the Sow's furrowed neck I watched with fatalistic acceptance as the grey mountains grew nearer and larger.

Minutes later the Sow went gliding through the middle of a gigantic canyon. Huge, ribbed walls of rock to either side of her, dropping endlessly, endlessly down into darkness, hardly enough room on either side to accommodate the spread of her wingspan. I clung for dear life as she rose over a pointed column of rock, her talons almost clipping the summit. We passed above a series of snow-crested mountaintops, each one higher than the next.

I could make out movement on the ridges and in the jagged gullies. When I looked down, I saw that the mountainsides were teeming with dragons of all colours. Green and gold and red. Some speckled with assorted shades. A few which were as glossy and black as the burnt syrup my mother used in her treacle scones. I saw dozens and dozens of nests, constructed on ledges or in wide fissures in the rock. Some bore clutches of mottled eggs, while others housed tiny baby dragons, bawling to be fed.

We came upon the highest peak of all. So high that its apex penetrated the fat bank of snow clouds that hung lazily in the sky. Just when I thought that Sow would rise and fly into the clouds she dipped into another canyon. This one led directly to cavernous entrance on the mountainside. Deep into the belly of the mountain she flew. At first the light penetrating inwards from the entrance was enough for me see the enormous chamber we were traversing. Magnificent pillars of solid rock, sparkling with minerals, supported a vast stone ceiling from which jagged stalactite fingers pointed down to a rocky floor.

As the Sow went deeper and deeper the light gradually faded until we were engulfed in total darkness. Without warning there came a chaotic shrieking and wild fluttering of wings directly above my head as the passing of the Sow disturbed a huge colony of bats. I had to press my head flat against her scaly hide as I was buffeted this way and that by their panicking wings. Moments later the air fell still. The Sow went gliding slowly down into the belly of the cavern. She came to land, keening in pain out as the rope nooses around her left wing restricted her ability to fold and tuck it back in a comfortable manner. I lay as still as I could as she curled her massive tail around herself and rested her muzzle on her front legs.

I had no idea of how deep inside the mountain we had come, but it was clear that I was in the lair of the White Sow. I knew vaguely from which direction we had entered the cavern and the first thing I planned to do was to try and find my way back to the chasm in the mountainside. I made a promise to myself that I would not even think of what to do after that until I got there. One step at a time - that was the way I had to do things - if I thought too much of the challenges that lay ahead the whole situation might overwhelm me.

For now, I had to focus on escaping from the Sow's lair without being eaten or burned alive. I was pretty sure now that she had no idea that I was on her back. From the way her wing kept twitching I could tell that she was pre-occupied with the obvious pain it was causing her. A low whining was emitting from the back of her throat and echoing around the walls of the cave. I lay there, not moving a muscle. Finally, when the Sow's breathing had slowed and fallen into a steady pattern that suggested she had drifted into sleep, I plucked up the courage to slowly slide my way down from her shoulders.

The rocky floor of the cavern was icy cold. I bit down hard on my lip to stop my teeth from chattering as I felt my way blindly into the darkness. I kept an attentive ear out for the any small change in the Sow's breathing. When I dared a glance back over my shoulder, I could make out the huge bulk of her shape traced in the slightly luminous glow that emanated from her pure white scales. I had cautiously edged a good six feet away from her when I tripped over a scattered pile of discarded of animal bones and fell down hard, skinning my knees. The sudden shock of it made me cry out in surprise and pain. The Sow awoke and let out an irritable roar that was ominously amplified by the hollow cavern.

I heard her rise to her feet and sniff the air, turning in a laborious circuit as she tried to catch my scent, her claws clattering disconcertingly on the cavern floor. I may have been able to make out the incandescent image of her lumbering form, but she clearly could not find something as small as me in the darkness. This didn't stop her from lashing out wildly with her tail. I heard it whipping through air and immediately pressed myself flat against the ground. The tail flew over me, slicing above the back of my head with no more than an inch to spare. Then I heard a sound that chilled me to the bone – click-click-click. The Sow roared again and spat a great raging ball of fire from her jaws. The cave lit up as bright as a summer's day. The intense heat from the flames that licked the tall ceiling of the rocky chamber sent prickles up and down my flesh. I glanced up and was astounded to see a hooded figure step out from behind a rock. As the light from the Sow's fire faded the figure reached down and yanked me to my feet.

"Run, lad," rasped a raw voice. "Run for your life!"

14. The Mysterious Hooded Stranger

I ran faster than I would have ever imagined possible, stumbling over rocks, arms outstretched in case something unexpected loomed up ahead of me in the pitch dark. The mysterious hooded stranger chased close behind me, barking out directions in his strained and abrasive voice.

"Left!"

"Duck down!"

"Sharp right!"

Blind in the darkness I did as he bade me. I had no to time to consider whether he was driving me towards the entrance of the huge network of caverns or deeper into the labyrinth of its dark belly. The sound of the White Sow bellowing and roaring in her lair echoed all around us and spurred me on whenever I began to flag. We ran like this for almost fifteen minutes, weaving rapidly through the rocky outcroppings, clattering down dipping slopes and scrambling up steep inclines, my shoulders often barging painfully against the narrow walls of the tunnels. Then without a word of warning his hand grabbed my shoulder and pulled me to a halt.

"Slow down, lad," he wheezed. "I'm not nearly as young as I was. There's enough distance between us now."

Over the sounds of our laboured breathing, I could hear that the Sow's agitation had settled into anxious bleating, somewhat like that of a sheep lost somewhere on a hillside.

"She'll be asleep soon enough," said the hooded stranger.

He squeezed past me and began walking along the remainder of the passageway through which we had been running. "Come," he called back over his shoulder. "My chamber is nearby. There's a fire to warm yourself by and some hot broth for your belly."

"Your chamber?" I called out. "You live down here?"

***

I sat across from my peculiar rescuer, watching him through the flickering flames of his campfire as he ladled portions steaming broth into a pair of clay bowls, his facial features still tantalisingly hidden beneath the shadowy hood of his cape. The heat from the fire was a mixed blessing. While it warmed my shivering body I had to keep moving back when it caused my blistered forehead and singed scalp to prickle and sting.

"Eat," said the hooded man, passing me a bowl and a wooden spoon.

I looked at the greasy, grey liquid.

"Toadstool and bat meat," said my companion.

My thoughts immediately turned to the delicious rabbit stew my mother had been about to prepare and the mushrooms that Isla and I had gone to collect. A lump came to my throat. I let out a loud, involuntary sob.

"Bad manners to baulk at another man's hospitality," came the sharp reprimand from the opposite side of the fire.

"Sorry," I said, and hesitantly lifted a spoonful of the broth to my trembling lip. It tasted far better than it looked and the warmth of it felt wonderful as it slid down into my belly. In no time at all I had cleaned the bowl.

"Now," said the hooded man, "suppose you tell me how you came to find yourself in the lair of the White Sow?"

"I didn't find myself there," I replied. "I was carried there on her back."

He raised his head. Although I could not see his eyes under the shadowy gloom of the hood, I could tell that they were thoroughly scrutinising me. More than a little uncomfortable I bowed my own head to avoid his gaze. "Tell me," he said.

So, I cleared my throat and told him my tale, starting with my mother sending Isla and myself to fetch mushrooms and ending with the flight of the White Sow deep into the cavernous mountains.

"And you are sure it was the crew of *The Drunken Molly* who kidnapped you?" he asked when I had finished.

I gave a solemn nod of my head.

"And the wife of their dead captain has taken over the run of the ship?"

"Mrs Zachariah," I nodded again.

"She lost her child?"

"I think the grief of losing both her husband and her baby has driven her a bit crazy," I said. "She blames the White Sow. All she thinks about is

86

revenge. Sometimes she doesn't even know where she is – or what she's done."

"This is my fault," said the hooded man, rising to his feet. "I've been too wrapped up in guilt and self-pity to think of anyone but myself."

With that he pulled back the hood and let it drop to his shoulders. What I saw before me was a terrible sight. A face that was burnt and warped beyond anything that might be remotely recognisable as human - hideous raw scars, barely healed; pitiful tufts of hair poking out from a scorched scalp that was otherwise completely barren. Lopsided lips beneath the shrivelled nub of what once was a nose and sad blue eyes that peered out from under eyelids so scalded, they could hardly blink.

He gave me a little bow.

"Captain Nathaniel Zachariah, at your service. Or all that is left of him."

15. Nathaniel Zachariah

Edging cautiously away from the embers of the fire I scanned the chamber. At least four tunnel entrances were illuminated by the flickering glow. The closest to me was to my left. If I was quick, I could reach it before he made it to my side of the fire. But could I outrun him? I recalled how he'd kept close on my heels as we fled the Sow's liar. And how he called out directions as if he knew every dip and turn like the back of his hand. It was no use. I couldn't escape him. I was at his mercy.

"What are you going to do to me?" I asked.

"Do to you?" he asked, a quizzical crease forming on his misshapen brow. "I may look monstrous. But I assure you, I am not a monster."

"It's not what you are," I told him. "But who you are."

"The name of Captain Zachariah strikes such fear into your heart?"

His voice sounded confused and hurt.

"After what happened to me, I have good reason to be wary of dragon hunters," I said. "And I've been told that you were the most famous dragon hunter of all."

He pulled the hood back up over his head. "You have no reason at all to be wary of me, lad," he sighed. "My dragon hunting days are well and truly over. The White Sow saw to that." He tossed a piece of wood onto the fire. "The day I tried to capture her she fled back here to her lair, dragging me with her. My hand was trapped beneath one of the lasso ropes lashed to her side."

I remembered the eerily waving glove.

"But I did not have your luck, lad," continued the captain. "As I made my escape, she caught me with the full force of her fiery breath. My chest and my upper arms are burned as badly as my face. Had it not been for the Ghibelline I would surely have perished."

"The Ghibelline!" The pace of my heart quickened at the very mention of their name.

"They found me unconscious in one of the stone corridors leading away from the Sow's lair. I must have dragged myself there. They nursed me back to a semblance of health with their herbal remedies."

I gulped loudly. "They didn't try to eat you?"

Captain Zachariah threw back his head and let out roar of rasping laughter. "You've been listening to too many exaggerated tales about the crew of *The Hunter's Moon*, lad. The Ghibelline are gentle folk. It was pack wolves that did for the survivors of that wreck. By the time the Ghibelline reached them they were too late to save them."

Kneeling down he rifled around amongst some scattered belongings laid out on a flat rock two or three feet away from the fire. When he had found what he was looking for he stepped over to me and forced it into my hand. I looked down at a crumpled photograph depicting a beautiful pale skinned woman with lush dark ringlets hanging down to her shoulders and pearl necklace around her neck.

"The woman who captained *The Drunken Molly*," he said. "The one who claimed to be my wife? Is this her?"

At first, I was going to say no. The delicate looking lady in the picture could not possibly be one and the same with the mad woman with the rat tail braids and nervous tics that danced on her hardened features. Then I looked more closely at the eyes and recalled the occasions when Mrs Zachariah's own jittering eyes has stilled and softened. And I knew.

"It's her," I said.

Captain Zachariah snatched back the photograph and pressed it to his chest. "And she said that our child died?" he asked.

"Yes," I whispered.

"Again my stupidity has had disastrous consequences," he barked.

"It's not your fault," I said.

"But it is," he insisted. "My arrogance led me to believe that I had some pre-ordained right to take the breath of the White Sow. I suffered the consequences of that. Once I was back on my feet, I could easily have made my way back to Tennanbrau. The Ghibelline could have seen me safely across the tundra. I could have boarded a scavenger ship that had set down for repairs at Forgsnur's Footprint."

I wondered where Forgsnur's Footprint might be and whether that was the place I would have to get to in order to make my own journey home.

"I could have saved my wife from the terrible grief that brought about the death of our child," said the captain. "But my pride got the better of me and I

90

chose to hide myself away down here in these caves."

"You didn't want people to see how you looked?" I asked.

"There's that," he replied. "But there are also the truths that I have learned from the Ghibelline. Truths that have made it extremely hard for me to come to terms with the consequences of all the things I have done as a dragon hunter."

"What things?"

Captain Zachariah sighed and shook his head. It seemed to me that he was done with talking. His shoulders slumped. I thought it must be terrible to be him. Mrs Zachariah had called him her 'bonny' captain - but he certainly wasn't 'bonny' any longer. All I had was some blisters and a bit of singed hair, a faded rope burn on my ankle, and scar that was already caking dry on my chest. They were nothing compared to what he must have endured.

Wearily he pointed at a scattered pile of bearskins in a far corner of the chamber. "You must be exhausted. Go and take a nap. I need contemplate on what I might yet do to right my wrongs."

16. Illagnor and the Ghibelline

I awoke to the sound of hushed voices whispering in the gloom of Captain Zachariah's chamber. I'd enjoyed the deepest sleep since I'd last had the luxury of my own bed back home in the Low Counties. It wasn't just exhaustion that brought this about. There was no comparison between the soft warmth of the bearskins and the hard straw covered floor of the empty chicken coop aboard *The Drunken Molly*. It was also relatively quiet down there in the caverns. No crew singing drunken sky shanties to keep me awake. No thrumming of an airship engine or the howling of the wind to disturb my sleep. The only sounds were the occasional crack of cinders in the fire and the steady drip-drip-drip of water seeping into one of the stone corridors.

But now, I could hear voices. Many voices. Talking in muted tones, as if not wanting to be heard. They seemed to be coming from all around, echoing through the corridors leading to the chamber. My eyes flickered open. Without raising my head, I glanced across to the fire.

The flames had died down, but in the pulsing glow of the red embers I could make out that Captain Zachariah was still pretty much seated where I had last seen him. His hood was pulled down over his disfigured head. He was leaning forward, elbows resting on his knees, suggesting that he too had fallen asleep.

I began looking around the chamber, my eyes tracing the outline of rocks and peering into the murky entrances to the corridors. I was beginning to think that maybe I was misinterpreting the sounds that the wind might make as it hushed through the corridors when I saw something moving a few feet behind Captain Zachariah's stooped form. An upright figure was slowly creeping up on him. Pausing whenever the captain twitched or let out a snore. I could tell that it was not entirely human. The shoulders were too broad. The head too big and wide. I drew in a breath and held it, my heart pounding in my chest.

Ghibelline!

The sinister thing drew slowly closer to Captain Zachariah. When it was almost upon him, muscular arms outstretched, ready to grab his shoulders, I leapt from the bearskin, snatching up my battered old helmet in case I needed to defend myself.

"Watch out!" I yelled.

Captain Zachariah swung round instantaneously to face his would-be assailant. The two grappled with each other onto the cavern floor. I heard the thing with the broad shoulders and oversized head grunting in an odd hog-like voice. "I would have had you this time, hermit. If your young visitor not cried out."

"I had already heard you coming you clumsy buffoon," came Captain Zachariah's rasping reply.

"You won't best me," said the creature. "I wrestled big old bears with more to them than you."

From the size of the thing, I could well imagine that to be true. I watched as the two of them rolled around the floor, each seeming in turn to get the better of the other. Then there was laughter as the wrestling transformed into an affectionate hug. Processions of shambling figures poured into the chamber from each of the tunnel entrances. The air filled with more loud, gruff laughter. Captain Zachariah and his opponent rose to their feet, politely dusting each other off. The other figures gathered around them, some reaching out to vigorously shake the captain's hand.

In the midst of all of this he called out to me. "Over here, lad. Let me introduce you to my good friends, the Ghibelline."

With more than a little trepidation I made my way to the fire. There must have been thirty or forty Ghibelline crowded into the chamber. Men, women, and children. As I drew closer, I could make out their features in the glow from the embers. Their skin was a pale shade of grey, almost as craggy and pitted as the rocks around us. Their noses hooked and their chins narrow and curved. All of them had the distinctive broad shoulders and wide head that I had noticed on the one who had crept up on the captain. High up on the side of their heads sat small, pointed ears and on their scalps - spiky crops of mossy green hair. The small black pellets of their eyes followed me intensely as I approached.

Captain Zachariah placed his hand on my shoulder. "Ladies and Gentlemen," he announced. "May I present, Master Euan Redcap, formerly of the Low Counties." The Ghibelline crowded in on me. They seemed fascinated by my red hair. It was ruffled, stroked, and tugged, sniffed at, scrutinised, and cooed over. I felt dwarfed and somewhat intimated by their enormous, imposing forms. Even the children seemed huge in proportion to my small, skinny frame.

Finally, Captain Zachariah came to my aid. "Give the lad some air!"

The Ghibelline dispersed and settled themselves amongst the rocks. Only one remained standing; the one who had crept up on the captain as he dozed by the fire. Close up I could see that his grey flesh was criss-crossed with innumerate scars. A chunk was missing from his left ear and his hooked nose was warped on the bridge, as if it had been broken and badly set. Clearly, he had been through many battles. I wondered how many big old bears he had wrestled with.

"Euan," said Captain Zachariah. "This is Illagnor, Chieftain of the fifth tribe of the Ghibelline. I owe him my life and much more."

Illagnor stepped forward and ruffled my red head of hair, his pinprick black eyes seeming to spark with marvel at its colour. "So, a companion has come to live with you, hermit?" he said.

"Not of his volition," sighed Captain Zachariah. He turned to me. "Euan," he said. "I want you to tell Illagnor and the others what happened to you. And when you are finished, I will say what I believe must be done."

***

Once more I recounted my tale.

95

The Ghibelline listened intently, sometimes demanding that I speak up when my voice trailed off and could not be heard by those seated towards the back of the chamber. Whenever I mentioned the White Sow, I noticed that they seemed to bow their heads in a sort of reverential gesture. When I had finished Illagnor stood and addressed his people.

"For generations now the White Sow has been a symbol of hope for the Ghibelline. Whenever we see her cross the sky it is taken as a good omen. Her form guides us home when we are lost on the tundra.

Now she needs us.

From what the Redcap child says the dragon hunters have wounded her far more seriously than our friend hermit did in his misguided former life. We must sooth the Sow with the sleeping smoke of the crabwort root so that we can release the ropes that bind her wing and tend to her wounds."

The assembled Ghibelline clapped their calloused hands and stamped their huge flat feet in approval. Amid this Captain Zachariah appeared beside Illagnor, his hood concealing the terrible burns on his face. "I too applaud you," he said. "But again, it is me who is at fault here. Once more it was my crew and my ship that were responsible for the pain inflicted on the Sow. It was my wife who drove them on. Had I gone back to Tennanbrau City, as I should have, she would not have lost her mind and none of this would have happened."

"Hermit," said Illagnor. "You are not responsible for the actions of your people."

96

"But I am responsible for my own," replied the captain. "From what the lad said *The Drunken Molly* was so badly damaged they would have had no choice but to steer a course for Forgsnur's Footprint to make repairs."

That name again.

Illagnor nodded. "This is true."

"Then I will need to beg the services of the Ghibelline to guide the lad and myself across the tundra to where my wife and my men will be."

"For what purpose?" asked Illagnor.

"I must finally return to Tennanbrau," came the reply. "I must convince Emperor Julian of the dire consequences if the taking of dragon breath is allowed to continue unabated. And, just as importantly, this boy must be returned to his parents."

17. Of Crabwort Root and Other Things

On Illagnor's instruction a party of the Ghibelline departed to gather crabwort. From what I could gather this was a sturdy little plant, which grew in only in the damp and gloomy conditions that prevailed on the shores of a subterranean lake, deep with the bowels of the mountains. When burned its leaves let off a heavily scented smoke, which, if inhaled by any person or creature, would act as a sedative, and send them into a deep sleep. My head was racing with questions and, while we awaited the return of the gatherers, I fired them in rapid succession at Captain Zachariah.

"What is Forgsnur's Footprint?"

"It's a natural crater towards the edge of the tundra. It takes its name from a mighty giant in an old Ghibelline folktale. Forgsnur was said to have stamped his foot in a temper and left his huge imprint on the floor of the tundra.

For a long time, it was used by dragon hunters as a dumping area for damaged and unwanted parts of airships. Then an enterprising fellow by the name of Rusty Reeves saw that there was a business opportunity to be had out there."

"What type of business?"

"He set up an airship repair shop on the rim of the crater. He reconditions and adapts all the discarded items and uses them as spare parts."

I understood immediately why the captain was so sure that *The Drunken Molly* would head there. But I still had other questions.

"Why will there be dire consequences if the taking of dragon breath continues unabated?"

"Because there are no longer enough dragons left alive. It's a cold and sober fact, Euan. If the practice continues dragons will surely become extinct."

"Angus Stonedyke told me that the whole of Tennanbrau is built around the trade in dragon breath. It's the power that runs the factories and all sorts."

Captain Zachariah nodded under his hood. "Those are the dire consequences, lad. Tennanbrau relies too heavily on regular supplies of dragon breath. If those supplies run low, or cease completely, everything will collapse."

I felt him looking at me from the shadows beneath his hood, studying the puzzled look on my face. "I know it may be hard to understand for one who grew up in the Low Counties," he said. "You have a far simpler way of life. But believe me terrible things would happen in Tennanbrau if there was no longer a continuous supply of dragon breath. There would be riots. Perhaps even civil war."

"But how can there be too few dragons?" I asked. "When I flew through the mountain range on the White Sow's back, I saw nests. Nests filled with eggs – and dozens of baby dragons."

"There are far fewer than there used to be, lad. Fewer and fewer each year. Just think about the number of dragons taken by the scavenger ships.

That alone would have a huge effect.

But we always believed that the strongest of the dragons flew back to their nests and, over time, regained the fire in their lungs. What I have learned from the Ghibelline is that we were wrong in that assumption. More than half of them simply die down here in the caverns. Some of the nests you saw would have been abandoned. The eggs will never hatch."

"So, what is it you plan to do?" I asked him.

"I was the most famous of dragon hunters," he replied. "I will return to Tennanbrau, and I will use my fame. I will petition those with power and influence in the Imperial Court. I will seek an audience with Emperor Julian himself. I will make them see, as I have come to see, the error of our ways."

"You want to put an end to dragon hunting? But won't that have the exact same effect. There will be no dragon breath for the airship balloons and the factories."

"Not all at once," said Captain Zachariah. "There are other types of gas; other types of materials that could be used to construct balloons. The trade in dragon breath has made people too lazy and indifferent to invest the time and money to make these viable. But if there was a phased approach things could be different."

"Do you think you can really convince people?" I asked.

"I can but try, lad," he replied. Then he bowed his head and said in a sad whisper. "But first I will return to my wife and my men."

"Are you really going to take me back home?" I asked. Captain Zachariah raised his head once more. "You do want to go home, don't you, lad? You want to return to your family in the Low Counties?"

He didn't need to ask me twice.

I nodded enthusiastically.

"When I am once more captain of *The Drunken Molly,* I promise that she will carry you back there. Just as she carried you away."

***

It was mid-afternoon the following day when we set off for the tundra.

Since Captain Zachariah had confirmed his intention to take me back home, I had been filled with elation. So much so that I barely noticed the foul-smelling reek that emitted from the herbal balm that one of the Ghibelline mothers had applied to my blistered forehead and the half-healed scar on my chest.

I was going home. Back to the green hills and the meadows and the glens. To my little stone cottage. To my mother and father. To my sister, whom I promised myself I'd never argue with again. I knew it would be a long and arduous journey. We had to traverse the barren tundra to Forgsnur's Footprint, before even setting out across the vast miles of the open sky. Nevertheless, I was going home.

But when the party of gatherers returned from their expedition to the underground lake, I suddenly found myself conflicted. I wanted to go with them first to the White Sow's lair. From what I understood their plan was to set fire to clumps of the crabwort root and toss them into the lair. They were confident the potent smoke would quickly render the Sow unconscious, allowing them to remove the lassos and tend to her sprains and rope burns with a similar herbal concoction to that which had been applied to my own wounds.

Despite the excitement I felt at the thought of returning to the Low Counties I desperately wanted to help in easing the Sow's pain and discomfort. What had been done to her was terrible and what the crew of *The Drunken Molly* had planned for her was ten times worse. I had no direct hand in any of it, other than that loud smack on her snout, but I still felt a nagging sense of guilt. Besides a part of me ached to see her again - to wonder at the sheer size of her and feel that sense of astonishment at the magnificence of her wingspan. To marvel at the snow-white purity of her scales and the contrasting black sheen of her lacquered talons.

But Captain Zachariah would have none of it.

"There's no time, lad," he insisted. "They will already have set about repairing the damage to the gondola and the balloon. Before we even start our journey across the tundra, we have to descend deep down into the very lowest caverns to be able to come out in the foothills. We simply have no time to spare."

We parted company. A small band of half a dozen Ghibelline, hefting a sack of crabwort root and baskets of herbs, heading to the lair of the White Sow, and a far bigger group, led by Illagnor, working our way ever downwards through the honeycombed labyrinth of hollow caverns and narrow, rock walled passages. A third group, consisting of children and some of the elderly tribe members were left behind in the captain's stony chamber.

18. Forgsnur's Footprint

It took us an entire day to emerge into the crisp sunlight of the foothills and a further two days after that to traverse the endless bleak and desolate miles of the tundra. We ploughed through wind and sleet and fat flurries of snow, across a land that was endlessly, endlessly flat and hardened by frost. Often the only sign of plant-life lay in the erratic patches of pitiful scrub we trudged across. We rested and dozed fitfully for only an hour or so at a time under animal hide bivouacs hastily assembled by the Ghibelline's expert hands.

Sometimes when fierce blue bolts of lightning illuminated the overcast skies, I would catch fleeting glimpses of dragon droves dancing amongst the thunderclouds, twisting streaks of intense green and vivid red amongst the dreary drabness of grey. I would find myself wondering if airships were prowling above the clouds ready to launch their lassos, with hungry scavenger ships stalking their wake. I would listen intently for the tell-tale hum of engines and turbines and breathe easily when there seemed to be none.

The Ghibelline maintained a relentless pace, to which even Captain Zachariah appeared to have difficulty matching. My legs ached. I felt that I was in a constant state of weariness. The bearskin that one of the Ghibelline had given me kept me warm, but also weighed me down. Sometimes I became so exhausted that I would stumble and lurch as I struggled to keep upright.

When it clearly became too much for me Illagnor lifted me into one of the sleds that were being dragged behind us, bearing provisions. I lay there, head resting against my battered helmet, keeping my spirits up by imagining the joyful reunion with my family when I finally arrived back home.

**

We reached Forgsnur's Footprint at first light on the third day.

The jagged crater was around a mile in circumference. A ramshackle compound of rickety huts was situated behind a listing fence, in a huddled area facing towards the expanse of the tundra. Smoke was billowing up from a large campfire and we could make out group of men congregating around a long trellis table, where the clatter breakfast dishes came echoing to us on the wind.

Beyond the compound a dozen airships, about a quarter of the size of *The Drunken Molly*, were at anchor around a large platform quay raised a good twenty feet from the ground. The multi-coloured array of dragon skin balloons swayed against their steel support wires as the wind from the tundra whipped around them.

Scavenger ships.

I thought of all the dragon carcasses that might be stored in their holds and a cold shiver ran down my spine. Captain Zachariah came alongside me, his hood pulled over the disfigurement of his face. "Look, lad," he said. "Your transportation back home is almost ready."

I looked to where he was pointing.

To the left of the compound the huge gondola of *The Drunken Molly* had been raised up on a wooden platform and surrounded by a latticework of dragon bone scaffolding. I could see different shades of colour on her hull where all sorts of mismatched planks of wood were being used to repair the holes torn away by the White Sow. Immediately next the scaffolding stood a wide frame, across which *The Drunken Molly's* scarlet balloon had been stretched and was in the process of being patched and sewn.

"She'll ready to fly in a day or so," said Captain Zachariah.

My heart fluttered.

I might be back home in just over a week.

***

We approached the compound, Captain Zachariah in the lead, me close behind, fixing the string bound strap on my helmet. Illagnor and the Ghibelline seemed uncharacteristically cautious, trailing a good twenty paces back. The entrance to the compound was a tall wind-bleached arch, constructed from the dragon bone frame of an old airship hull. From it hung a chain bearing a scrawled handwritten sign.

Rusty Reeves

Reclamation and Repair

Beneath this sign two sentries stood guard. One was armed with a battered looking rifle. The other with a crossbow. From his lean frame and his greasy looking shoulder length red hair I recognised the one carrying the rifle straight away. So did

106

Captain Zachariah. "Angus Stonedyke," he whispered to me. "We're in luck, lad. The other fellow is from a scavenger ship. He'll be a crack shot with that crossbow. That's how they down dragons once their breath has been drawn. But good old Angus will vouch for us."

As we drew nearer *good old* Angus raised his rifle and aimed it at us. His crossbow-wielding companion did likewise. "Don't come any closer, stranger," he called to Captain Zachariah.

Apparently not wishing to take any risks Captain Zachariah signalled with his hand and came to a halt. Glancing back over my shoulder I saw Illagnor bid the Ghibelline to do likewise. "You found our ship's fetcher, did you?" asked Angus. "We thought he was goner, for sure."

"As if you cared!" I spat back at him.

Captain Zachariah squeezed my shoulder and whispered in my ear. "Let me do the talking."

"I would like to speak to your captain," he told Angus. "I believe her name is Mrs Zachariah."

"Who are you under that hood?" demanded Angus, jabbing his rifle barrel at the captain. "A monk or a missionary or something?"

With a disdainful sneer he nodded towards Illagnor and the Ghibelline. "You're mad if you think you can consort with those filthy creatures. They'll have you in the cooking pot as soon as look at you."

"I have something important to say to Mrs Zachariah," said the captain calmly. "I think she would be more than a little peeved if she were to find out that I had left without you having called her here."

Angus relaxed his grip slightly and lowered the rifle.

He narrowed his eyes and chewed his lip.

"Fine then," he said, after a while. "I'll send for Mrs Zachariah. But what you have to say better be important."

"Believe me," said Captain Zachariah. "She will want to hear it."

Angus dispatched his companion to fetch Mrs. Zachariah.

Five tense minutes passed. Angus watched Captain Zachariah intently, nervously glancing beyond him to the Ghibelline, who stood as still as statues, staring back at him with their beady black eyes. He only spoke once. "Come into the compound, Euan. Go warm yourself by the fire."

I shook my head and stepped closer to Captain Zachariah.

A few minutes later a screeching commotion announced the arrival of Mrs Zachariah. Behind her came a gaggle of *The Drunken Molly's* surviving crew, including Coxswain Grisling and Smudger the cook. Accompanying them a squat bald-headed man with filthy oil streaks smeared across his face. I guessed that this must be the famous Rusty Reeves.

"This better be important, Angus," ranted Mrs. Zachariah, the black braids of her hair snaking about her shoulders. "There's work to be done. The White Sow is still flying free."

"This stranger says he has something to tell you," said Angus, pointing at Captain Zachariah with the barrel of his rifle. "He brought back Euan Redcap. But they're in the company of the Ghibelline."

"Euan Redcap?" Her fidgeting eyes fell upon me. "Fetcher!" she cried. Then, as so often before confusion crept across her face. "You're so young. So small. How ever did a boy like you sign up for service aboard my airship?"

"The lad didn't sign up, my Isabella," growled Captain Zachariah. "And well you know it."

Mrs Zachariah turned her head to face him. "Isabella?" she gasped. "How would you know to call me that? Only one man ever called me *his* Isabella."

"And that man stands before you right now," came the reply.

Mrs Zachariah let out another short gasp.

"Nathaniel? My bonny captain?"

"The very same," replied Captain Zachariah. "Only not so bonny these days."

With that he pulled back his hood and revealed the horrible molten scars on his disfigured face. Mrs Zachariah let out an anguished howl. She staggered backwards and would have collapsed into a faint had Grisling not stepped forward and held her upright.

"Am I so repulsive?" asked Captain Zachariah.

"She did this?" cried Mrs. Zachariah. "The White Sow?"

Captain Zachariah nodded his head.

"But you've come back to me," said his wife. "Together we will have our revenge for all the pain the Sow has caused in our lives."

"No," said the captain.

"What are you talking about?" asked Mrs Zachariah. "You are Nathaniel Zachariah, the greatest dragon hunter ever to fly an airship out of Tennanbrau City."

"I am not that person any longer," said the captain.

"He's gone mad," said Grisling. "All that time out there on the tundra, it's addled his brain."

"I'm not mad," insisted Captain Zachariah. "I've simply come to my senses. Hunting dragons to steal their breath is wrong. I see that now."

The crew descended into a commotion of shouts of protest and waved fists.

"Hear me out," pleaded the captain. "The least you can do is to hear me out."

110

19. The Captain's Plea

Captain Zachariah climbed up onto a rock. He cleared his throat and pulled the hood back over his head. "You men know me," he began. He looked at Mrs Zachariah. Pale and trembling, she was still being propped up by Grisling's grimy hand on her elbow. "Isabella, you know me better than anyone. I swear to you that what I am about to say is the absolute truth."

As he spoke, I noticed that more men were arriving from the compound. It was obvious to me that they were crewmen from the scavenger ships. They carried a frightening array of weapons. Rifles and pistols, crossbows, daggers, and wooden clubs. Illagnor noticed their arrival too. When he and the Ghibelline moved closer to Captain Zachariah and myself, and formed a protective arc behind us, the scavengers tightened their grips on their weapons.

I felt my pulse quicken.

Captain Zachariah pushed on with what he had to say, at times having to shout to be heard over the relentless assault of heckling jeers. As he spoke Mrs Zachariah's face seemed to flit from one emotionally charged expression to another. One moment tremulous and tearful, the next teeth grindingly furious, the moment after than glazed and vacant.

"How would we make a living if we no longer took dragon breath?" demanded Angus Stonedyke.

"There are other uses for an airship," replied Captain Zachariah. "Trade and transportation for example."

"Become merchant men?" spat one of the scavengers. "Where's the adventure in that?"

Grisling eased his hand away from Mrs Zachariah's elbow and reached up to stroke his moustache. "If we stop taking dragon breath, how do you propose we inflate our balloons?"

"I accept that the taking could not stop over-night," said the captain. "But you know as well as I do that there are learned men in Tennanbrau who have designed alternative airship balloons that rely on natural gases for buoyancy. If Emperor Julian were to endorse their development, we would not be so reliant on dragon breath. Eventually we could leave the dragons in peace."

"Then we needn't worry," countered Grisling. "We can carry on hunting dragon and taking their breath till none are left and there will always be this other type of gas to fall back on."

A loud cheer went up from the dragon hunters and the scavengers.

"You would really hunt them into extinction?" demanded Captain Zachariah.

"Aye!" came the rapturous reply.

Now Rusty Reeves stepped forward.

"Captain," he said. "No one here would ever disparage your reputation." He nodded his head towards the Ghibelline and spat on the ground. "But these flesh-eating monsters have clearly taken advantage and filled your head with all sorts of superstitious nonsense."

112

"The Ghibelline are not monsters," Captain Zachariah yelled back. "The suggestion that they eat human flesh is the superstitious nonsense. You know that full well, Rusty Reeves. You trade with them often enough."

Rusty Reeves' face blushed deep red. He bowed his head to avoid the outraged glares that were being directed towards him. "I also know which s-side my bread is b-buttered on," he stammered. "If there is no trade in dragon breath and no scavengers taking dragons for their flesh there will be no airships traversing this far north and I will go out of business."

"Like thousands of others like him," agreed someone in the crowd.

"It doesn't have to be like that," pleaded Captain Zachariah. "If things are gradual and properly planned out."

Now catcalls and insults started flying at the captain from all quarters.

"Rubbish!"

"Idiot!"

"Get down off that rock and stop talking garbage!"

"Enough!" Mrs Zachariah's high-pitched intervention soared above the din.

"Enough of this!" she cried. "Let me speak to the impostor who claims to be my husband."

Everyone fell silent at once.

Captain Zachariah stood as still as the rock on which he was balanced.

His wife looked up at him.

"You never asked about our child," she said in a quiet voice. "We had a son. A bonny baby boy. I held him in my arms, and he died. My husband should have been there to comfort me. If you were truly my husband our child would have been the first thing you asked about."

"I . . ." began Captain Zachariah, and then seemed lost for words.

"You apparently care more about the wellbeing of White Sow and the fate of the dragons than you do for your family."

"I . . ." said Captain Zachariah and was unable again to finish his sentence.

"We believed Nathaniel Zachariah was dead," said Mrs Zachariah. "We wept for him. We mourned for him. We swore to avenge his death."

"I should have made my way back to Tennanbrau," agreed the captain.

"No, you should not!" screeched Mrs Zachariah. "Not as you are. You are nothing but an impostor."

Captain Zachariah bowed his head. "I know that I look repulsive."

"It is not how you've come to look," Mrs Zachariah told him. "It is the nonsense you speak. The nonsense that has wormed its way into your head. If you were truly my husband, you would be preparing this very minute to take revenge on the White Sow."

She turned to face the crewmen and scavengers.

"Nathaniel Zachariah is dead!" she announced. "You hear me? Captain Zachariah, the greatest dragon hunter ever to fly an airship out of Tennanbrau City is dead. It is down to all of us avenge his passing. We will show no mercy. And if every single dragon must die before we get to the White Sow, then so be it!"

A cheer went up from the crewmen and scavengers.

Mrs Zachariah pointed at the captain. "This pitiful impostor will not stand in our way. And neither will his Ghibelline cohorts."

"I am not dead," protested the captain. "I stand here, living and breathing."

Mrs. Zachariah looked him up and down, an expression of contempt etched on her face. "Nathaniel Zachariah is dead. Dead as my poor, lost son." Then she turned to me. "*The Drunken Molly* still needs a fetcher if you are of that mind, Master Redcap."

I shook my head.

"Then go," she said. "Both of you. Just get out of my sight. Scurry back to the tundra with your Ghibelline friends."

***

We retreated a mile or so back into the tundra and set up a camp. I could feel a deep, hollow ache in my stomach. My hopes of returning home to the Low Counties were dashed. Dejectedly I watched as Captain Zachariah paced around the campfire, his hood billowing about his shoulders.

"I should have been more assertive," he muttered. "More forceful."

"No matter what you said they would not have listened," said Illagnor.

115

"I'll walk all the way to Tennanbrau if I have to," said the captain. "There are people there who will hear me out."

My heart sank even lower. Based on my experience of crossing the tundra I would have no chance of keeping up if he set out to walk all the way. I was never going to get back home.

"Could you fly a scavenger ship single handed?" asked Illagnor.

"If I could get my hands on one," replied the captain.

"Then the Ghibelline will help you to acquire one," said Illagnor.

"I'd never steal another captain's ship," said Captain Zachariah.

He thought for a moment and then turned to Illagnor.

"But I would borrow one and allow the rightful owner to reclaim her once I had steered her safely back to Tennanbrau."

Then he shook his head, seeming doubtful once more.

"It would be too risky. You saw how heavily armed the scavengers are. I will not have the deaths of any of your kin on my hands."

An idea came to me. "It's a pity we don't have some of that crabwort stuff with us," I said. "We could use it to put everyone in the compound to sleep."

"But we have," said Illagnor, his craggy grey features breaking into a smile. "We always carry crabwort with us on a long journey. In case anyone has an accident and needs to be sedated."

116

"Euan Redcap, you're a genius!" cried Captain Zachariah, slapping me heartily on the back. "If this comes off, I'll make good on my promise to deliver you safely back to the Low Counties before I head for Tennanbrau."

20. Capturing the Compound

Things moved swiftly once I had made my suggestion. Illagnor split the Ghibelline into small groups of twos and threes and despatched them to surround the compound. On his signal they ignited clumps of crabwort root and used slingshots to hurl the flaming missiles over the perimeter fence of Rusty Reeves' yard.

When Illagnor gave a second signal we all rapidly retreated in the opposite direction to which the cold tundra wind was blowing. We crouched down low on the frozen ground so that any stray wafts of the crabwort root smoke passed safely over our heads. After ten minutes or so, when Illagnor judged that the potent smoke would surely have done its work, we snuck cautiously towards the compound. Angus Stonedyke and his fellow sentry were slumped by the gate, heads lolling to the side, jaws slack and drooling.

Without a sound we crept past them.

Inside the compound the bodies of crewmen and scavengers lay strewn around the fireside, snoring and muttering sleepily to themselves. Some curled up like babies, some sprawled out like drunkards. Around the long trellis table those who had been seated there lay collapsed amongst a mess of crockery, cutlery, and overturned mugs. On the porch of a gaudily painted shack that must have been his personal living quarters Rusty Reeves was fast asleep in a battered old rocking chair. In front of him, on the uneven steps that led up to the porch,

118

sat Coxswain Grisling, head resting slackly on his chest, pipe still smoking in his mouth. By the coxswain's feet, face down in the dirt, lay Mrs Zachariah. Her hat, blown by the wind, was tumbling around the compound.

Captain Zachariah ran to her and had me help him turn her gently over onto her back. Her face looked calm and peaceful. It was almost possible to see in her the beautiful woman with the dark ringlets from the crumpled photo the captain had shown me. Pulling back his hood the captain leaned down and brushed a stray braid of hair from her eyes, before kissing her tenderly on the lips.

"I may be dead to you, Isabella," he whispered. "But my love for you will never die."

Then he rose, pulling his hood back over his face.

I thought that he might be crying.

"We need to hurry," warned Illagnor. "The effect will only last a short time."

"My friend," said Captain Zachariah. "I will never forget all that you have done for me and all that your people have taught me."

"And the Ghibelline will never forget *our* good friend, the hermit, who lived deep within the Serrated Mountains," said Illagnor.

The captain and the grey skinned Ghibelline chieftain hugged each other. Then, one by one, Captain Zachariah went to each of the Ghibelline tribesmen and women and took them in a warm embrace. Then it was my turn. My red hair was tugged and patted and ruffled. Some of the women planted big wet kisses on my cheeks. Finally, Illagnor himself held out his huge, calloused hand.

"Safe journey Euan Redcap," he said. "May you soon be home in the bosom of your family."

Looking up at his craggy face I asked the question I had been burning to ask since we left Captain Zachariah's chamber. "Do you think the White Sow will fully recover?"

Illagnor smiled.

"The Ghibelline I sent to tend to her are expert healers. She is in good hands."

"Come on, Euan," urged the captain. "We have to be away."

I followed Captain Zachariah up a rope ladder that hung down from the raised scaffold of the airship quay. Once on the platform he moved rapidly along the row of moored scavenger ships, trying to select the one that would be easiest for him to handle alone. He settled on a narrow gondola with a deep hull, which had the name *The Hawk's Cry* painted onto her bow. Above the gondola a balloon of bright yellow dragon skin bobbed and swayed against the buffeting tundra winds.

"This will do for me," he said and set about untying the mooring ropes.

It was then that I saw Angus Stonedyke staggering into the compound. His straggly red hair hung limply over his eyes. He seemed to be having difficulty placing one foot before the other, but clearly the crabwort smoke had not totally overwhelmed him and he'd managed to rouse himself. My mouth went dry when I realised that he was carrying a scavenger crossbow. Swaying

120

unsteadily, he flicked his hair away from his face and raised the hairpin sight to his eye.

The crossbow was pointed up at the platform. I could see the bolt glinting in the sunlight as his finger curled around the trigger. He seemed to be tracing our movements in the same way he would trace a dragon through the sights of his rope cannon.

"Look out!" I cried and I dived flat onto my belly.

Whether his intended target was myself, Captain Zachariah, or the balloon of *The Hawk's Cry* I'll never know because Illagnor ran at him and engulfed him in a big, restraining bear hug. Angus kicked and struggled. The bolt shot from the crossbow, hissed through the air, and embedded itself in one of the wooden support legs of the scaffold. "Get going!" cried Illagnor, as Angus slumped in his arms and fell unconscious once more.

Captain Zachariah pulled me up from the platform and swung me over the side of the gondola. He finished untying her mooring ropes and tossed these onto the deck. Released from her restraints the *The Hawk's Cry* began to rock from side to side as she floated slowly upwards.

"Farewell, my friends!" the captain called back to Illagnor and the Ghibelline.

With that he vaulted onto the deck and ran to the ship's wheel.

21. Homeward Bound

We began to ascend high above the jagged crater of Forgsnur's Footprint. Below us the Ghibelline dashed here and there amongst the sleeping bodies, gathering up weapons and sabotaging the balloons on the remaining scavenger ships.

I looked to where *The Drunken Molly's* own crimson balloon was being removed from the tall repair frame that it had been stretched across. It was to be loaded onto one of the Ghibelline sleds, hauled back across the tundra and hidden in one of the deep caverns. No chances were being taken that Mrs Zachariah would commence her crazed threat to slaughter as many dragons as she felt necessary.

Beyond Forgsnur's Footprint I could see the vast expanse of the tundra and beyond that the foothills that rose to jagged peaks of the grey Serrated Mountains. Although I had only been there for a few eventful days I felt oddly sad to be leaving. It felt strangely as if it had become a second home to me, with Illagnor and the Ghibelline an adopted family.

My thoughts, however, turned quickly to my own home and my real family.

"How long do you think it will be before we reach the Low Counties?" I called out.

Captain Zachariah stood at *The Hawk's Cry's* wheel with his hood pulled over his head.

"The engine on a scavenger ship like this is nowhere near as powerful as those on a full-blown airship like *The Drunken Molly*," he replied. "And she won't gain half as much altitude. But I'd estimate just under a fortnight."

A fortnight?

It seemed like a lifetime. But the important thing was that I was going home. Back to the rolling hills of the Low Counties, my little stone cottage, and my family. I looked down and saw that we had already risen high enough that the crater of Forgsnur's Footprint looked like nothing more than a tiny, ragged puddle in the ground with the Ghibelline appearing as little grey gnats scuttling around its edge.

"When we get to the Low Counties will you stay with us for a few days?" I asked. "You'll need to rest before you carry on to Tennanbrau. Our cottage is only small, but my parents wouldn't mind. You could sleep in my bed. The mattress is soft, and I have a real feather pillow. It would be no problem at all for me to sleep on the bench in the kitchen. I spent enough nights squashed up in a chicken coop on *The Drunken Molly* and I had to sleep on a Ghibelline sled when we were crossing the tundra. A bench would be luxury compared to that."

Captain Zachariah held his hand up.

"No need to go on, Euan," he chuckled. "I get the picture. But I really couldn't impose on your family like that. They'll want to celebrate your homecoming. I'd just get in the way." He drew his hood tighter around his face. "I would not be the most handsome of houseguests."

"Couldn't you at least share one meal with us?" I asked. "My mother always says it's not what a person looks like that counts - it's what's inside them that's important. And she is sure to have some mutton broth on go. If we're lucky there might even be a rabbit stew. With wild mushrooms, fresh from the glen."

"Rabbit stew?" asked the captain. "Wild mushrooms?"

I nodded vigorously.

"And a big open fire to sit before while we eat it."

"Perhaps I could share one meal with your family," said the captain. "And a good night's sleep would set me in good stead for the task that lies before me in Tennanbrau."

"I'm sure they'd like to thank you for bringing me safely back home," I told him.

"And I'd like the opportunity to apologise for my wife's actions and to tell them what an excellent job they've done in raising you," he said.

"You think?" I gasped.

"You're smart and quick witted, Euan Redcap," he said. "Brave with it."

I blinked in surprise. No one had ever said anything like that about me before. "You don't think I mess stuff up and get in the way all the time?"

"Absolutely not," said Captain Zachariah. "Your parents should be proud. I would have been more than proud had my own son grown up to be just like you." His voice seemed to trail off a little at the mention of his son.

"And you'd tell that to my big sister?" I asked.

Captain Zachariah nodded his head and chuckled from within the folds of his hood. "I'd tell it to the world without a moment's hesitation." He turned the wheel and the scavenger ship swung sharply to the right. "Will you agree to do something for me, Euan?" he asked.

"Anything. Just say the word."

"When we are finished with the meal, I want you to tell your tale to your family. Just the way you told it to me. Starting from when my wayward old crewmates caught you up in that lasso as you tried to escape across the meadow with your sister."

"Sure," I said. "But why?"

"I want to hear it just once more," he replied. "I want to get it down right in my head. I want to be able to re-tell it to the folk that count when I get back to Tennanbrau City. Word for word. The tale of Euan Redcap is going to help me change things for the better."

"The tale of Euan Redcap?"

"The tale of how the lust for dragon breath can drive good men and women do unthinkable and unspeakable things. Of how innocent boys can be stolen away from their homes and end up being used as dragon bait."

His hoarse voice seemed to crack with emotion. I couldn't imagine important people in faraway Tennanbrau City being at all interested in the misfortunes of a poor Low County boy. "Do you think anyone will listen?" I asked him.

"There is a movement opposed to dragon hunting," he replied. "They will be more than a little surprised when I offer them my services. But your story will surely help them in their cause. There are plenty of people in Tennanbrau City who are blinded by greed, Euan. But my belief is that there are just as many who have consciences just waiting to be pricked."

I could feel the chilled air growing decidedly colder as we climbed towards the cloudbank. Soon Forgsnur's Footprint and the wide tundra beyond would disappear entirely from view. As I turned to take one last look at the jagged outlines of the Serrated Mountains something came gliding over the crest of one of the highest ranges. I felt my heart leap with joy as the sunlight was reflected back from the pounding motion of huge white wings.

"Look!" I cried.

Hurriedly Captain Zachariah retrieved the scavenger ship's telescope from its housing on the deck rail. "It's her, lad," he said. "The White Sow. She's healed fast with the help of the Ghibelline. Good old Illagnor was true to his word."

He handed me the telescope and I watched as the Sow soared magnificently above the tundra, scales as pure as the driven snow, black talons curled back, and dazzling white wings hypnotically rising and falling. How could anyone in his or her right mind ever wish harm upon such a beautiful creature?

"It's a good sign," I told Captain Zachariah. "Illagnor said so. Whenever the Ghibelline see the White Sow crossing the sky, they take it as a good omen. Do you think it means we'll get to the Low Counties safely?"

"Aye," said Captain Zachariah. "We have the luck of the Sow and a helping wind at our backs."

We rose up into the churning mist of the clouds and although I finally lost sight of the White Sow, I knew that the wonderful image of her in full flight was so vividly fixed in my mind that it would never be erased for as long as I lived. The wind began to pick up, singing eerily through the silver wires that hung down from *The Hawk's Cry's* yellow dragon wing balloon.

I watched as Captain Zachariah reached down and notched the scavenger ship's droning engine up a gear. "To the Low Counties," he cried. "The promise of a soft mattress and a feather pillow - and perhaps a bowl of rabbit stew!"

Part Two
A Trial in Tennanbrau City

1. Homeward Bound?

"Euan, fetch me the telescope!"

Captain Zachariah's raw voice interrupted the hurried preparations I was making for our lunch. Blinking against the sunlight I stepped from the cramped galley onto the narrow deck of *The Hawk's Cry's* gondola and watched the captain as he gently spun the navigation wheel to bank the scavenger ship leftwards. His hood was down around his shoulders, revealing the terrible disfiguring scalds and scars that had been inflicted upon his face by the fiery breath of the White Sow. He no longer felt it necessary to conceal himself in my presence and I hardly gave him a second glance. His scorched facial features were all I had ever known.

My own burns and blisters were almost completely healed now. A few pink blotches were all that remained, my singed eyebrows had grown back, as thick, and red as ever, and the scar on my chest had scabbed over, the rapid closing of the wound assisted greatly by the herbal healing balm applied there by the Ghibelline.

The captain looked at me, warped eyelids drooping over his blue eyes. "The telescope?"

"Aye, Captain!" I said and dashed along the deck.

There was something about the tone of Captain Zachariah's voice that suggested he was worried. Perhaps a storm was brewing in the distance? The possibility put me on edge. We were less than half a day's journey from the little stone cottage that was my home. I couldn't bear to think of a storm throwing us off course. *The Hawk's Cry's* hull was already skimming only a few dozen above the dark emerald canopy of conifers and pines in the forest that marked the northern approach to the Low Counties. When I squinted my eyes, I could make out the undulating outline of familiar green hills in the near distance.

In my head I had constructed an image of what would happen when Ma and Pa saw *The Hawk's Cry's* yellow balloon slowing to a halt in blue sky above the stubby smoking chimney of our cottage and how they would react when my slightly bedraggled form climbed down the rope ladder that hung down into the yard - my red hair uncut, unwashed, and uncombed for longer than I cared to remember. I felt sure that Pa's sheep dogs would be the first to recognise me and would come dashing as I dismounted the ladder, yipping and yapping, front paws pressing against my chest as they affectionately licked my face. Then Ma would cry out when she realised who it was. Pa would wrap me a huge hug. All the while Isla, my sister, would be ogling in open-mouthed surprise at all the muscles I had grown.

First though I had a telescope to fetch.

During our journey back from the bleak expanse the Far Tundra I had gradually assumed the role of ship's fetcher, a position I had previously been forced into during my abduction aboard *The Drunken Molly*. Being only a quarter of the size of a dragon hunter's airship it had been much easier to memorise *The Hawk's Cry's* more compact layout. I'd quickly assembled a mental tally of exactly where everything was kept, the quickest way to locate a thing, and the swiftest route return it to its rightful place.

By far the worst thing about *The Hawk's Cry* was the regular need to retrieve items from her dank and morbid hold. I hated going down the ladder into that awful place. It was crammed with the cruel accoutrements of the scavenger's trade - wing clamps, scaling knives, chopping blocks and bone saws. The wooden floor planks were stained blood red and scored with deeply furrowed claw marks from the terrified struggles of countless captured dragons that had been fatally weakened by ruthless attentions of dragon breath extractor equipment used on airships like *The Drunken Molly*. On a crooked shelf in the hold sat two glass jars. One filled with extracted dragon teeth. The other with dozens of severed black and red talons. I remembered how Angus Stonedyke had told me these were given as good luck charms to new-born babies in Tennanbrau City. A tooth for a boy. A claw for a girl.

Despite the downside of regularly descending into the hold I felt that fetching for Captain Zachariah was very least I could do. After all, he was taking on all the roles aboard scavenger ship that would usually be performed by a full crew and had hardly slept a wink since we waved goodbye to Illagnor and his Ghibelline kinfolk at the crater of Forgsnur's Footprint.

I would prepare simple food for him in the galley and fetch it to him so he could eat standing at the navigation wheel. Sometimes he was buffeted by strong winds. Sometimes he was lashed by pounding rain. But never did I see him so much as flinch or falter. Occasionally though, when we passed through calm skies on a steady course, he would let me take the wheel for a short while. Even then he stubbornly refused to rest. Instead, he would use the time to adjust any of the steel wires attached to the ship's gondola that required tightening, before checking the pressure on the valve feeding the bottled dragon breath into *The Hawk's Cry's* yellow balloon.

"Euan?" he called again from the wheel. "Where's that telescope? Have you gone all the way back to the tundra to fetch it?"

I retrieved the telescope from its housing on the decking rail and turned to run back along the deck. I had come to know Captain Zachariah a lot better during the long days and nights of our journey together. He spoke to me as he worked, telling me all about his childhood in a suburb of Tennanbrau, under the guardianship of his wealthy but befuddled and increasingly intoxicated aunt (the famous drunken Molly after whom his airship had been named).

He told me too of his life as young crewman aboard another airship owned by a grisly old dragon hunter named Gulliver Quat. "In those days, Euan,"

131

he said. "No more than half a dozen airships were engaged in the taking of dragon breath. The dragon population was so huge that it wasn't uncommon to encounter flocks as far south as the fringes of the Low Counties."

I recalled the story my grandfather used to tell of how a small dragon had made its den in the high hills and caused a proper nuisance of itself amongst the Low County folk. I thought of the miles and miles of open sky between the Far Tundra and the Low Counties and tried to imagine how many dragons there might once have been. A cold shiver ran down my spine when the stark reality of how many thousands of them must have been killed to fuel Tennanbrau's appetite for their breath hit home.

Captain Zachariah had been second in command on Gulliver Quat's airship, *The Cerulean Beauty*. During the disastrous encounter with the White Sow Quat had lost his left foot when it became hopelessly tangled in a wayward lasso. His airship had been left fit for nothing but the reclamation yard and a surgeon had removed the rest of his leg below the knee, ending his days as an airship captain. It had been this encounter that had set a tiny cinder smouldering in the Nathaniel Zachariah's mind. A cinder that erupted into the unquenchable flame that had finally driven him to attempt to hunt down the Sow himself.

"What an arrogant fool I was," he'd sighed after recounting this to me. "I wanted the glory of being the dragon hunter to finally bring down the White Sow. Not once did I give a thought to the consequences of my actions."

Often, he'd speak in a much quieter voice about Mrs Zachariah. The woman he described was entirely different to the half-crazed person upon whose orders I had been kidnapped. He told me that had fallen in love with her from the first moment he had cast eyes upon her beautiful dark hair at the Annual Dragon Hunter's Ball. Once they married it had been the happiest day of his life when she announced that she was pregnant with his child. The child she had subsequently lost in the grief-stricken aftermath of his supposed death.

In my haste to fetch the telescope to the wheel, and wrapped up in my thoughts, I tripped over my own feet and went sprawling across the deck. The telescope rolled out of my grip. I scrambled to retrieve it. "What's wrong with you today, lad?" the captain called to me. Blushing I picked up the telescope and handed it to him. He immediately raised it to his lopsided eye. Placing my hand over my brow I peered in the same direction as he was looking. A dozen or so hooded crows were wheeling darkly in the skies above the approaching hills. Not an unusual sight in the Low Counties and clearly not what the captain was looking at. Narrowing my eyes I scanned the horizon and a caught a glimpse of a group of tiny figures flying in a 'V' shaped formation and seemingly heading in our direction.

"What would an ISC patrol being doing this far north?" muttered the captain under his breath.

"ISC?" I asked.

"Imperial Sky Constabulary," he replied, and handed me the telescope so that I could look for myself.

I could make out five of them - one in the lead and two on either side, forming the wings of the 'V' pattern. I could see that they wore goggles on their faces and round helmets on their heads. They were seated upright, upon strange looking single manned crafts that looked a bit like bicycles without wheels; attached to these were narrow cucumber shaped balloons.

"The pedals act like a crank shaft to fire up their engines and rotate their propellers," explained Captain Zachariah. "They use the handlebars to manoeuvre the rudder left or right."

I lowered the telescope and looked up at him.

"Where do you think they're going?"

"They're not going anywhere," he replied. "They're coming to meet us."

Again, I could tell from the tone of his voice that he was worried. "They're like the police, right?"

Captain Zachariah gave a terse nod and pulled his hood up over his head, hiding his burns and afflictions amongst its shadowy folds once more.

"Can't we just rise up and hide in the cloud bank until they pass?" I asked.

The captain shook his head.

"They've seen us now."

He took the telescope back from me.

"Their craft are lightweight and swift, Euan," he said. "The pilots are handpicked for the job. Three quarters of them are women. The ISC are the

134

only division of Emperor Julian's police force that insist on diminutive height and stature as an entry requirement. But don't let that fool you. They're tough and determined - and they always get their man."

I swallowed down the hard lump that was rising in my throat.

"What should we do?"

"Slow down," he replied. "Wait and see what they want."

I watched the ominous 'V' shape as it drew ever closer.

Down below I could also see the steady approach of the green hills. Dotted here and there amongst them were little cottages with smoking chimneys, identical to the one I had grown up in. On the gentle slope of one of the nearest hillsides I could make out a flock of black-faced sheep, like those Pa tended, grazing on the lush expanse of grass. I breathed in and caught the unmistakable scent of fresh, blooming heather. Only a few more miles and I could be back home at last, but I had this terrible feeling that all my hopes and dreams were about to be shattered.

2. Under Arrest

It took little more than ten minutes for the lead ISC rider to pull up alongside the hull of *The Hawk's Cry*. I watched her gauntlet-encased hands apply the breaking mechanism on her craft's handlebars as her knee length boots clicked the foot pedals into a fixed position. The drone of her engine fell to a soft put-put-put. She hovered to our left, suspended by the blue, pencil thin balloon that held her craft aloft on its slender wires.

Like a miniature airship, I thought.

As well as her helmet and thick goggles she wore a padded dragon leather jerkin, with a thick woollen collar. The letters ISC were embroidered in gold lettering above the left breast pocket, while the pocket itself bore an insignia depicting a red dragon entwined around a flagpole bearing the Imperial pendant of Emperor Julian. The right arm of the jerkin boasted three stripes, which I thought must signify some sort of important rank.

Within moments of her arrival her four companions came to a halt at a slightly higher altitude, bringing them level with *The Hawk's Cry's* yellow balloon. They stationed themselves two abreast to the front and rear of the scavenger ship, effectively blocking any remote chance Captain Zachariah may have had to make a break for it.

"Captain Nathanial Zachariah?" called the lead rider.

"Aye," he replied from under his hood.

"Sergeant Cecilia Caulder of the Imperial Sky Constabulary. I have a warrant for your arrest."

I felt Captain Zachariah stiffen at my side. "Arrest?" he cried. "On what charges?"

"There are several," replied Sergeant Caulder.

She pushed her goggles up over the front of her leather helmet and reached inside her jerkin to pull out a sheet of parchment. Deftly unfolding it with her right hand she steadied the handlebars of her craft with her left. Then, clearing her throat, she began to read. "Charge one - Assault by poisoning and rendering unconscious, with a substance unknown, of several Imperial Citizens, including Mrs Isabella Zachariah, legitimate registered owner of the airship known as *The Drunken Molly*, Mr Hubert Maurice Grisling, coxswain of the airship known as *The Drunken Molly* and Mr Reginald 'Rusty' Reeves, proprietor of *Reeves Reclamation Yard*.

Charge two - Theft of property, namely the scavenger ship known as *The Hawk's Cry*, belonging to Mr Eulugio Barnard, legitimate registered owner of said scavenger ship, along with fixtures, fittings and items of personal value contained therein.

Charge three - Theft of property, namely one scarlet dragon skin airship balloon belonging to Mrs Isabella Zachariah, legitimate registered owner of the airship known as *The Drunken Molly*.

Charge four - Wilful unlawful damage and wanton vandalism toward the balloons of the following scavenger ships - *The Owl's Eye, The*

Kestrel's Wing, The Eagle's Talon, The Buzzard's Beak, The Vulture's Tail and *The Kite's Swoop.*

Charge five - Collusion in the aforementioned felonies with potential enemies of the Empire, namely a renegade band of unidentified Ghibelline tribal folk of the Far Tundra."

"How does she know all this?" I whispered nervously.

"My wife obviously managed to get a message back to Tennanbrau ahead of us," Captain Zachariah replied.

Sergeant Caulder looked up from the charge sheet and called over to *The Hawk's Cry.* "My orders are to bring you back to Tennanbrau City to face fair trial at the Imperial Court of Justice."

"I will not resist arrest," Captain Zachariah called back. "But I have a passenger onboard. I would request your indulgence in order that I set him down at his home. I would estimate fifteen minutes or so would suffice."

Fifteen minutes, I thought. I'm almost home.

Sergeant Caulder turned and peered towards me across the gap between her craft and The Hawk's Cry. "Euan Redcap?" she asked. "Master Euan Redcap, formerly of the Low Counties?"

A gave a nervous nod of my head.

"I also have a warrant for your arrest."

"Don't be ridiculous!" blurted Captain Zachariah. "What offence can the boy possibly be accused of?"

Sergeant Caulder referred to her charge sheet. "Aiding and abetting Captain Nathanial Zachariah

138

and his alleged confederates in the execution of the aforementioned felonies," she called out.

"That's preposterous!" protested Captain Zachariah. "The lad is only twelve. You can't seriously be intending to arrest him."

"I'm here to carry out my orders, not to debate them," came the terse reply.

Captain Zachariah turned his hooded head surreptitiously towards the wheel of the scavenger ship.

"Don't try anything stupid, sir," warned the sergeant. "I have the power at my sole discretion to bring this craft down if I in any way suspect that you intend to resist arrest." She pointed upwards. Captain Zachariah and I craned our necks to see the other four ISC riders aiming crossbows at *The Hawk's Cry's* balloon. "One word from me," warned the sergeant.

"You win," conceded Captain Zachariah. "We'll come quietly. Although I wish you to make an official note of my objections in terms of the boy's arrest."

"Duly noted," said sergeant Caulder. "Now, on my signal, steer a course away from the Low Counties and head due south for Tennanbrau City."

For a moment I couldn't quite get to grips with what was happening. I tugged at Captain Zachariah's sleeve. "Does this mean I'm not going home?" He wrapped his arm around my shoulder. I couldn't see the expression on his face amongst the shadows of his hood, but his voice was calm and reassuring. "Not yet, lad," he said. "But I swear to you I'll keep my promise. One way or another I'll get you back home."

3. Tennanbrau City

Day turned into night and back into day once more.

The Hawk's Cry sliced her way through the misty vapour that swirled beneath the cloudbank. Already the Low Counties were miles behind us. Unable to hold back the tears that flooded out at the realisation that I had been robbed of my long-anticipated reunion with family I had cried myself to sleep in one of the scavenger ship's crew bunks. All night long my dreams were plagued by terrible visions of the consequences of being under arrest.

When I awoke my eyes were swollen and red, but if Captain Zachariah noticed he said nothing. His attention remained doggedly fixed on the sky ahead. Sergeant Caulder was still riding in front of *The Hawk's Cry*, every now and then peddling furiously to crank up the growling engine housed beneath the seat of her odd-looking craft. Above us, the four members of her patrol maintained their steadfast guard on either side of the yellow balloon.

Captain Zachariah told me that they had taken it in turns to come onboard to rest, lashing their craft to the side of the scavenger ship and each taking two hours to sleep in one of the bunks close to where I had slept. "Sergeant Caulder didn't rest though," the captain said. "Just kept on peddling through the night. Made of tough stuff that one."

As the morning sun climbed higher in the sky the tiny farms and hamlets we passed over gave way to larger and larger villages, which, in turn, became increasingly crowded and sprawling townships. I had never seen so many buildings and people in one place at one time. Further south, towards midday, these townships became interlinked by a latticework of railway lines, criss-crossing the countryside, along which steam engines, pulling jiggling lines of carriages, seemed to endlessly huff and puff.

It struck me that compared to the sloping meadows and shaded glens of the Low Counties this densely populated terrain was as strange and alien as the vast tundra had seemed when I first observed it from the deck of *The Drunken Molly*. I was as far from home as I had been on that day - only now I was heading in entirely the opposite direction.

The skies around us began to fill up. Commercial air vessels the size of *The Hawk's Cry*, with patchwork balloons of multi-coloured dragon wing membrane, crammed with passengers who apparently preferred the gentle rocking motion of aerial travel to the bump and jostle of the steam train. And hulking great dirigibles with long, cigar shaped balloons twice the size of that of *The Drunken Molly*. "Merchant airships," said Captain Zachariah. "Bringing in goods from all corners of the Empire."

"That would be how Isabella got word back to Tennanbrau so quickly," he added. "They would have made hurried repairs to one of the scavenger ship balloons and she would have been sent up to rendezvous with the nearest merchant airship. *The*

142

Hawk's Cry's engines are no match for the speed of one of those giants."

"Are their balloons filled with dragon breath?" I asked.

"Aye, lad," said the captain. "And they're hungry beasts, so they are."

As I watched the huge merchant ships my thoughts returned to our plight. "What's going to happen to us?"

"I have faith in the Imperial justice system," he replied. "In the end this will all be straightened out."

"But we're guilty!" I had been thinking hard about this since Sergeant Caulder read out the charges. "We did everything on that charge sheet. We stole *The Hawk's Cry*. We encouraged Illagnor and the Ghibelline to steal *The Drunken Molly's* balloon and damage the balloons of the other scavenger ships. It was my idea to use the crabwort root to knock everyone out."

"Don't take on so, lad," said Captain Zachariah. "There are three possible pleas we are entitled to submit in an Imperial court."

"Three?"

"Guilty," he explained. "Not Guilty. Or Guilty, with mitigating circumstances."

I screwed up my brow.

"What does Guilty, with mitigating circumstances mean?"

"It means that while you freely admit to doing everything you are accused of, there are certain circumstances the court has to take fully into account."

"And that's what we're going to plead?"

Inside his hood the captain gave a nod of his head. "Once you tell your tale on oath the judge will see that were good motives behind our actions and that everything we did was fully justified."

I wasn't all that convinced.

"Believe me, Euan, I've seen men on far worse charges than these walk free on a plea of Guilty, with mitigating circumstances."

Although he was trying to offer me reassurance a kind of mental barrier went up inside me. My hopes of returning home had already been dashed and I didn't know if I could cope with another bitter disappointment. I decided that the best policy was to expect the absolute worst. In that way anything even slightly better might come as a bonus.

"Could you fetch the telescope?" he asked, interrupting my glum thoughts.

"You want to look at something?"

"I want you to look at something."

Captain Zachariah pointed to a huge, jagged silhouette that had just become visible in the far distance. It looked like dozens upon dozens of long fingers pointing skywards. "Your first glimpse of Tennanbrau City," he said. I fetched the telescope and brought it up to my eye, peering past Sergeant Caulder and her peddle powered craft towards the jagged outline. The finger shaped objects turned out to be a wild assortment of soaring buildings and structures. They were of varying widths and heights; even the shortest was far taller than any man-made structure I had ever seen in my life.

They were all crammed in and around each other, giant factory chimneys, belching columns of

144

black smoke, side by side with endless arrays of turrets and spires, which Captain Zachariah explained belonged to Imperial palaces and institutions. Around these stood rows of pencil straight, soot blackened columns, peppered with row upon row of impossibly narrow windows. Tenement towers, the captain told me, each apparently housing hundreds of families, all squashed into tiny dwelling spaces called apartments.

"Since the advent of the airship Tennanbrau has had an unchecked tendency to grow upward as well as outward," said the captain.

I thought of my parents' cottage and tried to imagine what it would be like to live with your neighbours' cottages all crammed up alongside and piled up on top of each other. It would be terrible. No back yard to play in - no meadow to run across - no glen with sturdy boughs on which to construct a rope swing - no stream to build a dam and catch sticklebacks in your sock.

The ache that I had to set foot once more on the grassy slopes of the Low Counties intensified the closer we came to the city. Through the telescope I could make out more detail and the more I saw the more outlandish the place appeared. In stark comparison to its own legend the 'so called' magnificent city of Tennanbrau seemed to me to be bewilderingly dirty and unwelcoming.

Wooden bridges and chain-linked walkways connected many of the structures to each other. Here and there zigzag ladders climbed from one level to the next. Spiral staircases wove around and around and around some of the spires and turrets. Some buildings bore tiered layers of verandas seemingly made from the same type of wrought iron that was used for the railings along the decks of airship gondolas. They rose one above the other, like giant stairwells. Others sported wide crescent shaped balconies with dragon motifs carved into their stonework.

Between some of the taller buildings ran cables bearing small box shaped carriages that transported folk crosswise and diagonally from one part of the city to another. Elsewhere pulleys, hoists and winches conveyed baskets and creels, crammed with merchandise and commodities, back and forth, and up and down, and across and around. The whole place appeared to be in a tumult of endless motion and upheaval. I could feel in my bones that I was going to absolutely hate the place.

4. The Imperial Palace of Law and Judiciary

We passed over the sprawling suburbs and into sky above Tennanbrau City, descending lower and lower as we progressed. As Sergeant Caulder expertly guided *The Hawk's Cry* between rows of tenement towers, we glided so close to the building walls that I feared a hole would be ripped into the side of the gondola's hull at any minute. But Captain Zachariah was a skilled pilot. I marvelled at how the minutest movement of his hands on the wheel could adjust the delicate course of the scavenger ship's progress, giving that all important inch or so between wall and hull where I was convinced there was none at all.

Nevertheless, there were occasions when he had me use what was called the *long pole* to prevent an impending collision. As the name suggested this was a long wooden pole. Its purpose was to nudge *The Hawk's Cry* away from the side of a building whenever she drifted too close. I found the pole was heavy and unwieldy. But focusing intently on how to use it distracted my thoughts momentarily from my consternation at being under arrest.

I could tell that we were heading in the direction of a raised mooring port that sat to the front of an imposing brown stone edifice. The building sported a dozen or more spires and a set of tall stained-glass windows depicting what looked like the scales of justice. Captain Zachariah told me that this was The Imperial Palace of Law and Judiciary, where the Imperial Courts of Justice were located. My hands began to tremble around the long pole as I mentally recounted the list of charges that Sergeant Caulder had read out.

The closest I had ever come to being in serious trouble was once, when running through the village to avoid being late for school, Isla and myself had been severely scolded by the Borough Constable for accidentally knocking over a basket of apples outside the greengrocer's shop. Clearly the punishment for the crimes we had been charged with was going to be far more than a dressing down and I couldn't help thinking that it wasn't going to be half as simple as Captain Zachariah was making out.

Turning my attention back to the tenement towers I saw that some of the narrow windows had knotted washing lines hanging vertically down the outside wall. These bore items of clothing that flapped in the turbulence caused by the scavenger ship's passing. I could see people moving on the other side of the grimy glass in the windows. They were going about their household chores. Cooking, making beds, dusting furniture, barely giving *The Hawk's Cry* a second glance, as if the sight of an airship passing by a window thirty-five storeys high was an everyday occurrence.

Sooner than I would have liked the great edifice of The Imperial Palace of Law and Judiciary loomed directly before us. With Sergeant Caulder calling out directions Captain Zachariah manoeuvred *The Hawk's Cry* into the mooring bay.

The bay was constructed from a mixture of timber and bleached white dragon bone and it seemed to be set on a jutting shelf, housed about halfway up the side of the palace. Glancing down I saw that as much of the grand building stretched down below the shelf as did above it.

The mooring point boasted a huge iron bollard, around which a rope could be tied to secure an airship into place, and a cleft housing that seemed designed to fit an anchor. Beyond this was a walkway leading to a wide set of steps, which in turn led up to a tall iron gateway. The walkway itself was crammed with a jostling crowd of Tennanbrau citizens, jeering and baying as *The Hawk's Cry* came to a juddering halt.

I didn't like the look of the crowd at all. They seemed angry and irate. They were shouting things that I couldn't quite make out. Some of them were shaking their fists. Others were carrying placards with the words *'Zachariah the Traitor!'* painted onto them. Without warning a hail of missiles came raining down onto the deck of the scavenger ship. Squashed tomatoes, rotten eggs and rancid potatoes splattered all around us.

"Looks like the dragon hunting fraternity have been busy getting everyone riled up," said the captain, ducking low and trying to shield me from another sudden barrage of inedible projectiles.

Having docked their own crafts Sergeant Caulder and the other ISC riders hurriedly formed small protective arc between *The Hawk's Cry* and the walkway. No sooner had they done this than two dozen, truncheon wielding men in blue capes and matching blue berets came charging down the stairs and began to push back the crowds to clear an open space.

"Imperial Foot Constabulary," Captain Zachariah explained.

A burly looking man with tattooed arms stepped up to the docking point. Captain Zachariah slowly lowered *The Hawk's Cry's* anchor and the man's muscles strained as he slotted this into the cleft housing. Then the captain threw him a rope and he secured this to the iron bollard with a deft twist and a clearly practiced knot. Having completed his task, he stepped back and watched as Captain Zachariah lowered *The Hawk's Cry's* gangplank.

"Hold on to me, Euan," said the captain. "And don't be afraid." I took hold of his hand and gripped it as tightly as I could. As soon as we both stepped on the gangplank the crowd surged forward. The foot constables linked arms and tried to hold them back. The jeering rose to a crescendo. "Traitor!" they cried. "Turncoat!"

Below this came a low, monotonous hooting, almost like the lowing of cattle. It took me a moment to realise that we were being booed. "Boo!" they cried. "Boo! Boo!" For someone who had not so long ago been hailed as the greatest dragon hunter ever to sail the skies this was not the sort of reception I could imagine Captain Zachariah ever having experienced before. Another hail of eggs and tomatoes came hurtling through the air, splattering against the gangplank and spraying our leg with red slop and yolky gunk. Afraid that I

150

might become separated from him I gripped tighter to the captain's hand as we stepped from the gangplank onto the walkway.

The ISC patrol formed a defensive cordon around us, using the same formation as they had used when guarding the scavenger ship - sergeant Caulder to the front and two each to either side of us. Now that the sergeant was standing upright rather than sitting astride her craft, I could see how short she was. Much shorter in height than the rest of her patrol members, I thought, and probably even a good inch shorter than me.

However, her diminutive height seemed to be no handicap as she marched ahead of us, confidently brushing aside placards and grasping arms that shot erratically out of the crowd. Her self-assured, unflinching air seemed to bolster the metal of the other ISC pilots. They began to march brusquely towards the stairs, shielding Captain Zachariah and myself as they went.

Now the baying crowd heaved and surged against the line of foot constables.

"Boo!"

"Traitor!"

"Turncoat!"

"Boo!"

A toothless old woman managed to jut her crooked walking stick through a space in the cordon. Its tip made painful contact with my shoulder. "Low County hick!" she hissed at me in a mean and spiteful voice. Then without warning another hand shot swiftly out of the crowd and pulled back Captain Zachariah's hood. The terrible disfigurements of his scalded face were exposed for all to see. An audible gasp of shock rippled through the crowd. Everyone fell silent. I saw sergeant Caulder glance backwards, eyes wide with shock. For a long drawn-out moment, the chaos around us seemed eerily still.

Then a tremulous voice spoke out from the crowd. "Monster . . ."

Then the same word screamed at the top of someone else's lungs. "Monster!"

The crowd took up the call, pitching forward, more infuriated than ever.

"Monster!"

"Fiend!"

"Ogre!"

"Run!" yelled Sergeant Caulder, making a desperate dash for the steps.

Captain Zachariah followed, dragging me behind him.

5. To Courtroom 708

We ran through the iron gateway and into a marble floored courtyard that sprawled out beneath a high, glass-roofed atrium. As soon as we were safely through two of the ISC patrol members slammed the gates shut and locked them. Outside, at the head of the steps, the harried officers of the Foot Constabulary formed a barrier as the enraged crowd bayed and remonstrated to be allowed access. With no more than a fleeting glance backwards Sergeant Caulder hurried us across the courtyard. Here and there, seated on benches, or huddled around the lush verdant flora of overgrown pot plants, members of the legal profession, in their white wigs and black gowns, were mulling over case files.

As we hurried past many of them looked up and exchanged whispers behind concealing hands. Some scowled and shook their heads, others openly clicked their tongues in studied disproval. It seemed that Captain Zachariah and I were as unpopular amongst Tennanbrau's lawyers and barristers as we were amongst her citizens. I found my doubts Captain Zachariah's assurances deepening. If we were both so despised, then I couldn't see how the tale of my kidnap was going to make any difference. What could I possible say to appease these people who seemed so very angry? And what good was a plea of guilty, with mitigating circumstances going to be when everyone already appeared to have tried and condemned us?

I still had hold of the captain's hand and I was almost running to keep up with his determined stride. Somehow in the confusion of the melee he had managed to pull his hood back over his head - so while the looks we were getting were most unwelcoming I didn't suppose they were half as bad as they might have been if the hood had still been down. We entered a doorway at the far end of the courtyard and were immediately confronted by a bespectacled official seated behind an imposing desk.

"Names of prisoners?" he asked, without looking up from his paperwork.

Sergeant Caulder stepped up to the desk. "Captain Nathanial Zachariah and Master Euan Redcap," she announced.

The clerk entered our names into his papers. "Charges?" he asked.

Sergeant Caulder unfolded her parchment and recited the list of dreadful charges.

As the clerk began filling out the details, she removed her helmet and her goggles. A wiry thicket of auburn curls seemed to spring to life on her head and I noticed for the first time the faint dusting of pink freckles that speckled the bridge of her nose. She turned and winked at me, appearing a lot less stern and foreboding than she had done up to that point. "My mother was a Low County lass," she told me with another wink.

"Preliminary hearing," interrupted the clerk. "Courtroom 708, on level fourteen."

He handed the paperwork to Sergeant Caulder and without another word she marched off again, beckoning to us to follow. She led us up a narrow stairwell and along a winding corridor, our footsteps echoing noisily against the smooth grey walls. At the end of the corridor, we passed through another set of doors and into a much wider corridor. As we strode along this corridor I noticed that doors to either side had descending numbered designations above them. Courtroom 931. Courtroom 930. Courtroom 929. Outside some of these lawyers were seated on narrow benches, consulting with worried looking individuals that I assumed were their clients. Some of these 'clients' were in handcuffs and shackles. Quite a few seemed to me to be decidedly unsavoury characters.

At the end of this corridor, we passed through yet another set of doors and found ourselves on a huge descending stairwell. "Level Fourteen is two floors down," said sergeant Caulder, her auburn curls bouncing as she took the stairs. On the next landing a young lawyer, almost swallowed up in a flowing cape that seemed several sizes too large for him, stepped up to Captain Zachariah and introduced himself. "Danby Caruthers. I'm your designated defence lawyer." With that he hurriedly reached up to stop his unstable wig from slipping down over his eyes.

"How many cases have you defended?" asked Captain Zachariah.

"This is my first since graduating from the Imperial Law Academy."

"That figures," said the captain. "They wouldn't want to risk providing me with an experienced lawyer."

"What plea do you intend to enter?" asked Caruthers, almost tripping over the billowing hem of his cape, and tumbling down the stairs.

"Guilty, with mitigating circumstances," replied the captain from under his hood.

"And you . . ." He glanced frantically at his file. "Master Redcap?"

"The same," Captain Zachariah replied for me.

We followed sergeant Caulder down another flight of stairs and then another. Then through one more set of doors and into another corridor. The place was a veritable warren and almost as much of a labyrinth as the caves and tunnels where the captain had once made his home beneath the Serrated Mountains. The numbers above courtroom doors on either side of this corridor climbed in ascending order. Courtroom 700. Courtroom 701. Courtroom 702. I felt sick to the stomach. Any minutes now we would arrive at Courtroom 708. Just as we were passing the courtroom with the number 705 above its door a fidgety looking clerk stepped out into the corridor.

"Professor Thaddeus Mayhew," he sang out. "Calling, Professor Thaddeus Mayhew."

An elderly man with shoulder length grey hair bustled past us. He was swinging a walking cane and mumbling distractedly to himself. Behind him came a young woman in her early twenties. She was dressed in a brown leather waistcoat, worn over a white blouse - and baggy trousers that were tucked into a pair of knee length boots. Her long blonde hair was braided and tied back in a ponytail. As she hurried past, she leaned in and whispered into my

156

ear. "Don't worry. We're on your case. We won't let you end up in the Institute."

The Institute?

What was that?

Before I had time to consider what any of this might mean, we arrived at the door to Courtroom 708. A female clerk seemed to materialise as if from thin air on our approach. Sergeant Caulder handed her the paperwork the desk clerk had completed then turned to me.

"My duty is done." She shook my hand. "Good luck to you, Master Redcap." Then with a curt nod to Captain Zachariah she beckoned to the members of her patrol and was gone.

The clerk ushered us into the Courtroom.

6. His Infallible Worship

We entered the courtroom chamber, my eyes scanning the tall ornate ceiling - the carved wooden furnishings - the deep blue pile of the carpet, trying to take it all in at once. I had never been inside a room that felt so daunting and intimidating. I felt the pace of my heart quickening. Sharp nervous pains began to shoot through my stomach. I found that I could hardly catch my breath. The clerk escorted the two of us to a boxed area she referred to as the dock and bade us both to be seated. I slumped down into the hard wooden chair, knees trembling as my pulse pounded loudly in my ears. Danby Caruthers sat down immediately in front of the dock. To his left a fierce looking woman with intense blue eyes gave him a polite nod accompanied by a sharp scowl.

"The prosecuting lawyer," Captain Zachariah whispered.

I looked beyond the two lawyers to a huge commanding desk that sat on a platform raised two or three feet above the chamber. On the desk sat a quill pen and gold bell with a wooden handle. Behind the desk was a high-backed chair upholstered in blue velvet. I guessed that this was where the judge would sit. On the wall to the back of this chair was a raised wood carving, depicting the same image of the scales of justice that I'd seen on the stained-glass window as we'd approached the palace. Immediately above this image was spread a huge set of dragon wings pulled to full span. They

158

were of the same crimson hue that had been sported by *The Drunken Molly's* balloon. I could make out the jagged blue veins that traced crooked trails beneath the outstretched red membrane. I thought of the dragon that had once soared upon these wings and the cruel suffering it must have endured at the hands of the scavengers who had cut them away.

Now the sound of voices and the shuffling of chairs from above my head made me look up. People were filing into the public gallery. They looked as angry and as agitated as the crowd at the mooring point had been. I half expected them to start showering us with rotten vegetables. Instead, they just sat in silence gazing scornfully down on us. One man in particular caught my attention. He came hobbling in with a crutch under one arm and placed himself by the railings. A huge salt and pepper beard engulfed the lower half of his face. Wedging the crutch beneath his armpit he gripped the railings with both hands and stared with what seemed to be frighteningly intensity at Captain Zachariah. The captain bowed his head, clearly trying to avoid the man's unremitting glare.

"It's Gulliver Quat," he whispered in a faltering voice. "My old airship captain."

I looked up again at the bearded man. His eyes remained fixed and unblinking on Captain Zachariah's hooded form. Beneath the thatch of his beard his jaw seemed to be rotating as if he was grinding his teeth. It looked to me as if he was taking everything the captain was accused of as an extremely personal insult.

Suddenly the clerk stood up.

"All rise for His Infallible Worship, Barnabus Greyling!"

Everyone rose from their seats.

Beside me Captain Zachariah stood up and tugged my sleeve, indicating for me to do likewise. From a doorway to the side of the grand desk a frail looking man in a red, ermine trimmed cape shuffled slowly to the desk and took his seat. With trembling hands, he placed his white wig on his head. Then with some considerable effort he lifted the hand bell on the desk and clanged it twice. "I declare these proceedings duly open," he said in a high-pitched, decidedly boyish voice. "Be seated."

As everyone settled back into their seats I looked up to the gallery. Gulliver Quat was still standing with his hands gripping the railings and his crutch under his armpit, staring at Captain Zachariah.

"You there," said the judge suddenly. "The man in the dock. Is that a hood you're wearing on you head?"

When I looked over to the bench Judge Greyling was squinting through narrowed eyes towards Captain Zachariah. After a moment he reached inside his ermine trimmed cape and brought out a large magnifying glass. Holding this up to his right eye he peered again in the direction of Captain Zachariah. "It is!" he cried. "You're wearing a hood. You'll remove that hood at once, sir. I will not have such insolence in my courtroom."

"I would plead you indulgence, Your Infallible Worship," said Captain Zachariah, the rawness in his voice becoming noticeably apparent to me for the first time in ages. "I have good reason not to wish this courtroom to be exposed to my facial features."

"Nonsense," snapped Judge Greyling. "You will remove that hood, or I will have a constable come in here and remove it for you!"

With a resigned sigh the captain pulled back his hood.

Cries of shock and gasps of horror echoed across the gallery.

The judge clanged his bell somewhat clumsily.

"Order!" he cried. "Order in this courtroom!"

The judge brought his magnifying glass up to his eye again and peered across at Captain Zachariah's horribly addled face. "Good grief, man!" he exclaimed. "What happened to you?"

"It was my own doing," replied the captain. "Greed and blindness drove me towards an unfortunate encounter with a ferocious albino dragon known as the White Sow!"

"I knew it!" Gulliver Quat called out from the gallery. "She took your handsome looks the way she took my foot. You should have finished her when you had the chance, lad."

Captain Zachariah looked up at him, his mottled flesh stretching and distorting as he raised his neck. "It's not the way, Gul," he said. "I know now it's not the way."

"Damn you, Nathaniel," the bearded man cursed. "What's become of you? You were like a son to me."

His outburst was loudly interrupted by another clang of the judge's hand bell.

161

"Silence," barked Judge Greyling. "How dare the two of you engage in a private conversation in the middle of legal proceedings? Just where do you think you are? You up there, any more of this and I will have you forcefully evicted!"

"I've heard enough anyway!" spat Gul Quat and hobbled angrily out of the gallery.

Judge Greyling turned to the clerk.

"Read out the charges if you please."

The clerk cleared her throat.

"Be it known," she commenced in a loud and officious tone. "That in Courtroom 708 of the Tennanbrau Imperial Palace of Law and Judiciary the following charges are laid this day against the defendants in the dock. Captain Nathanial Zachariah, airship captain and former resident of Tennanbrau City…" She then ran through the list of charges. Somehow, they sounded ten times worse than they had when sergeant Caulder first recited them. When she was finished, she moved swiftly to me.

"Master Euan Redcap, airship fetcher and former resident of the Low Counties…" The list was recited again, only each charge against me was preceded with the prefix, aiding and abetting Captain Nathanial Zachariah and a renegade band of as yet unidentified Ghibelline of the Northern Tundra.

Judge Greyling addressed Danby Caruthers.

"Which pleas do your clients wish to enter?"

Caruthers rose somewhat shakily to his feet.

"Guilty, with mitigating circumstances, Your Infallible Worship," he replied. "Both of them. To all the charges laid."

"Tish," said the judge. "Why is it that every felon who enters my courtroom seems to think they can wrangle out of accepting the consequences of their criminal activities by coming up with some sort of cock and bull story?"

He turned to the prosecuting lawyer.

"What do you have to say about this, Miss Belmarsh?"

The fierce looking woman rose to her feet.

She placed her hands on her hips and turned slightly, so that it almost appeared as if she was addressing the members of the public up the gallery, while somehow maintaining a respectful amount of eye contact with Judge Greyling. "Your Infallible Worship," she intoned. "The Imperial Department of Prosecutions fully recognises the right of the defendants to enter whichever plea they deem fit to. However, our assertion at this preliminary hearing today is that an order for the custodial remand of both defendants, pending the full trial, is of the utmost necessity. In order to ensure they do not both abscond."

I didn't fully understand what she was saying, but I didn't like the sound of it at all. The pace of my heart began to quicken once more.

"Quite," nodded the judge. "What do you wish to say in response, Mr Caruthers?"

"Captain Zachariah . . . is . . . a man of property," came the hesitant response. "He has apartments here in Tennanbrau City in which both he and Master Redcap can reside until the trial takes place. I can assure His Infallible Worship that neither of these gentlemen has any intention of absconding."

"If I may, Your Infallible Worship?" the prosecuting lawyer interrupted.

Judge Greyling gave her a nod of his head.

"Captain Nathanial Zachariah was declared officially dead over a year ago," she said. "All of his property, including his apartments, passed lawfully to his wife, Isabella Zachariah. The Imperial Department of Prosecutions fully acknowledges that, under the circumstances, Captain Zachariah has the right to mount a legal challenge in order to have his property re-assigned. But that will take some time to resolve."

"Quite," nodded the judge. "I am of the mind in the circumstances to issue an order for custodial detention in the Imperial Penal Complex."

"If I may, Your Infallible Worship?" asked Caruthers.

Judge Greyling gave him a nod.

"Master Redcap is only …" He shuffled hurriedly through his papers. "Twelve years old. I hardly think the Imperial Penal Complex is appropriate."

"If I may, Your Infallible Worship," said the prosecuting lawyer.

Now Judge Greyling nodded to her.

"As a precaution the Imperial Department of Prosecutions has taken the liberty of establishing that there is sufficient bunk space within one of the dormitories of the Pym Street Institute for Wayward

Boys and Girls. The Institute Comptroller would be more than happy to accept Master Redcap into his custody."

"Ah," said the judge. "Now that seems to me a perfectly sound proposition."

Suddenly Captain Zachariah was on his feet beside me. "You can't send the boy into that serpent's nest," he railed. "You know that the Pym Street Institute is full to the brim with petty crooks and junior cutthroats!"

The judge clanged his bell loudly. "Keep your client in order, Mr Caruthers," he warned. "I will not have such outbursts in my courtroom."

Captain Zachariah reached over and squeezed my arm. "Sorry, Euan," he whispered to me. "I don't want to cause you any alarm. But if you do get sent to Pym Street keep yourself to yourself and remember it'll only be for a short period."

"Captain Zachariah!" barked Judge Greyling, scrutinising us both through his magnifying glass. "Do I have to warn you again about having private conversations in my courtroom?"

"Sorry, Your Infallible Worship," said the captain, dropping down into his chair and bowing his head.

Judge Greyling rang his bell again.

"Enter into the records that I have set the trial for three weeks from today," he said to the clerk. "And that until that time the defendant Captain Nathanial Zachariah will be held in precautionary detention in the Imperial Penal Complex, while the custody of his co-defendant, Master Euan Redcap, will be entrusted to the Comptroller of the Pym Street Institute for Wayward Boys and Girls."

He rang the bell once more.

"Session closed."

With that he rose and shuffled back towards the doorway.

7. Slug Martin

Given no time at all to say goodbye to each other Captain Zachariah and I were escorted from the dock by burly officers of the Imperial Foot Constabulary. I was taken one direction and the captain the other. Captain Zachariah was my only friend in this strange city of incredibly unfriendly and hostile people. Now I was on my own and it terrified me.

As I was being bustled past courtroom 705 the door opened and the elderly man that I had seen going in earlier came out. His walking cane tapped loudly against the floor tiles and his shoulder length grey hair swayed from side to side as he engaged in a deep and apparently irritable conversation with a lawyer in a white wig and black cape. Behind the two of them came the young woman with the braided blonde hair. She flashed a reassuring smile at me. "We got the order."

I still had no idea what she was talking about.

"Who are you?" I called back over my shoulder.

"The name's Hari," she called back. "Don't you worry the paperwork will be ready in two or three minutes."

But already the two officers who formed my guard were barging through a set of double doors and nudging me with rough prods to my shoulders down the winding stairwell. "Where are you taking me?" I asked, having to raise my voice against the clattering echo of our footfall. Stone faced neither of them answered.

Several floors down we barged back through another set of double doors, and I was hauled up in front of a wide desk. Behind it sat a bespectacled clerk who looked so similar in dress and appearance to the clerk who had checked our paperwork on our arrival that he may well have been his twin. He observed the officers over the rims of his glasses then looked me up and down with an expression of officious distain. "Come on, man, hurry along," he said to one of the officers. "Prisoner's name and destination?"

"Master Euan Redcap," grunted the one to my left. "Transportation to the Pym Street Institute for Wayward Boys and Girls."

He handed over my paperwork. The desk clerk pushed his glasses back along the bridge of his nose and gestured to a surly looking youth with spiky black hair who was slouched down on a nearby bench chewing absently at his dirty fingernails. "You there. You were sent to fetch this lad to Pym Street, were you not?"

The youth spat a crescent of bitten off fingernail onto the floor. "I suppose," he shrugged.

"Don't be so insolent," snapped the clerk. "Have you come from Pym Street to fetch this lad? Yes or no?"

The youth folded his arms over his chest and glared sulkily back at the clerk. "I suppose," he said again.

"Well get up on your feet and get over here," said the clerk. "Or do you want me to get one of

168

these officers to give you a good clip round the ear?"

Looking as if he would be only too happy to oblige, one of the officers turned to face youth. With an exaggerated sigh the youth ran his hand over his spiky hair and lurched up onto his feet. He was dressed in a threadbare woollen jacket with patches on its sleeve. Beneath this a moth eaten and badly creased shirt was stuffed into a pair of baggy trousers a good two sizes too big for him. He approached the desk with a swagger that was almost comical in its contrived arrogance.

"Can you write?" the clerk asked him.

"What's it to you?" came the defensive response.

The clerk slid a document across the desk. "I need you to sign this to say the prisoner was delivered safely into your possession."

The youth sighed again and scrawled a chicken scratch signature onto the document.

One of the officers took me by the elbow and guided me toward the youth.

"They give you a leash?" he asked.

The youth nodded, a sly grin breaking out on his surly face. From the pocket of the woollen coat, he produced a length of leather with narrow loops at either end. One of these he placed over his wrist. The other he slipped over mine.

"Wait a minute," I cried. "I think there's more paperwork to come?" The clerk peered at me over the rims of his glasses. He turned to the officers who shrugged their shoulders. "What paperwork, boy?" asked the clerk. "There was this person," I said, floundering to explain better. "I think her name was Hari. She said more paperwork would be ready in two or three minutes."

The officers shrugged their shoulders again.

"The hand-over documentation has been duly signed," said the clerk. "So, if any other paperwork is expected it's not my concern."

"All yours then," said the constable to the youth.

"And there's not a bruise on him," added the other. "You make sure that he arrives in Pym Street in the same condition, you hear?"

The youth arched his eyebrows. "Oh please," he huffed and walked swiftly away from the desk. After a few paces he yanked the leash, and I was forced to follow.

***

We emerged from the Imperial Palace of Law and Judiciary on one of the lower walkways, six or seven floors below the docking point. Looking up I could see the tarry hull of *The Hawk's Cry*, rocking in the breeze that whipped through the tenement towers. The paperwork the girl called Hari had been talking about was obviously taking longer than the two or three minutes to complete. If it had anything at all to do with me, it was clearly too late now.

"Put this on," the youth growled, handing me a seedy looking cloth cap that had been stuffed inside the waistband of his baggy trousers. I screwed up my nose and held it between two fingers, convinced that it was teaming with head lice. "Put it on," insisted the youth. "That red hair of your is a dead giveaway. It don't make no difference to me. But

I'm not about to be pelted with rotten eggs and tomatoes for the sake of a Low County hick like you."

Recalling the jeering crowd on the landing dock I pulled the cap over my head, wishing that I'd had the foresight to keep hold of the battered rope gunner's helmet that I had obtained when I was onboard *The Drunken Molly*. The youth yanked the leash again and set off at a rapid pace along a dirty, litter-strewn walkway.

"What's your name?" I called, running to keep up with him.

"What's it to you?" he called back.

"My name is..." I tried.

"I know your name," he said. "All of Tennanbrau City knows your name. Euan Redcap. Airship thief and vandal. Confederate of the traitor, Nathaniel Zachariah."

Suddenly I was full of pent-up rage and affront. Blood rushed to my cheeks. I yanked back on the leash with all my might. "Captain Zachariah is no traitor!" I yelled. "And I'm not a thief or a vandal!"

The spiky haired youth's arm was heaved backwards so roughly I thought it would come out of its socket. He stumbled and almost fell face first onto the walkway. Somehow, he managed to hold his balance. Face fuming, he turned on me.

The next thing I knew I was pinned up against the wall, his left fist twisted around my shirt collar. "The name's Slug Martin," he growled at me. "Short for Slugger. They call me that on account of my terrible right hook."

171

He held his right fist up to my chin, his knuckles so tight that I could see the white of the bone through his dirty skin. "Don't you mess me around, Low County boy," he warned. He unclenched his fist and held the open palm up in front of my face. On his flesh the letters 'PS' had been etched in dark blue ink. "Stands for Pym Street," he told me. "I've got a week to go till they release me and remove this mark. The last thing I need is for you to go provoking me into giving you a shiner. So don't you mess me around, you hear?"

I nodded my head slowly and the cloth cap slipped down my forehead. Slug let me go. Then we were off again. Slug striding away. Me running to keep up as the leash went taut. We ducked under a narrow passageway and down a set of winding spiral stairs that eventually brought us down to street level. Then away marched Slug again, dragging me through a grimy back alley and then out into a bustling thoroughfare, where more people than I had ever seen in my life jostled and jockeyed to get past each other. Above us I could see the walkways and bridges and zigzag stairwells I'd witnessed from the deck of *The Hawk's Cry*. A cable carriage passed overhead, traversing the space between one tall building and the next. I saw a baker placing loaves of fresh bread into a basket that was then drawn up on a rope to a window several feet above ground level.

"Stop dawdling," complained Slug, pulling at the leash. "Trust me to get lumbered with a Low County hick. You lot are nothing but trouble.

172

Especially that crewmate of yours, Angus Stonedyke."

I ran after Slug, the tension on the leash slackening as I reached his side.

"You know Angus Stonedyke?"

"Worst luck," replied Slug. "Me and my gang took him in when he first came to Tennanbrau. But he messed up a robbery we planned. He got clean away and we all ended up in Pym Street. I could have dobbed him in. But I kept my mouth shut. That don't mean that if I ever see him again."

I saw his fists balling up at his side.

I had mixed feelings about Angus. As a fellow native of the Low Counties, he had been a friend of sorts to me when I'd first been kidnapped and forced to be fetcher on *The Drunken Molly*, but any notion of friendship had gone out of the window when he'd fired a crossbow bolt in a bungled attempt to prevent myself and Captain Zachariah leaving Forgsnur's Footprint in *The Hawk's Cry*. I wondered what kind of robbery it been and how Angus had messed it up. But before I had time to ask another question Slug pulled at the leash.

"This way," he barked. "Shortcut."

We were passing under a stone archway and above it hung a wooden sign. It read:

"Scavenger's Market"

8. Scavenger's Market

Any curiosity I had to know more about what had happened between Angus and Slug was instantly washed away when we emerged at the other side of the stone arch and entered Scavenger's Market. The place teemed with people, heckling and bartering for all sorts of dragon related products that were laid out on wooden barrows. The barrows were covered by gaudily coloured patchwork awnings made from sewn together remnants of dragon wing membrane, probably left over from the construction of airship balloons. As Slug weaved determinedly through the crowds, dragging me behind him, my ears were assailed by the noisy commotion of market traders calling out their wares.

"Cutlery! Genuine dragon bone handle cutlery! Eighteen pieces for the price of twelve! Not just the forks and the knives, but the spoons thrown in for good measure!"

"Umbrellas! Dragon wing umbrellas! Good for sun and rain alike!"

"Pendants! Get your new-born pendants here! Perfect gift for the new arrival! A tooth for a boy. A talon for a girl!"

"Lucky dragon ear broaches! Pin them on your lapel! When you touch them, good luck rubs off!"

I dragged my heels remembering the dank hold of *The Hawk's Cry*. The claw marks on the bloody floorboards and the terrible accoutrements of the scavenger's trade.

"Keep up," warned Angus. "And make sure that cap doesn't slip off your stupid head. This is the last place in the world you would want to reveal your identity."

A podgy looking boy, not much older than Slug, came plodding along the crowded thoroughfare between the trader's barrows. Under one arm he held a bundle of what looked to be newspapers. In the other he held a single copy aloft. The front page bore a pencil sketch depiction of an airship captain with a menacing scowl on his face. Above the sketch in big block letter were the words - Nathanial Zachariah - Scourge of the Skies!

"See the whole sorry story in glorious pictures!" the podgy boy called. "How the turncoat dragon hunter and his Low County cohort poisoned innocent crewmen and went on a wild rampage of vandalism and theft!"

"The picture papers are how folk who don't read or write get their news," explained Slug.

"But that's not what happened at all." I snapped back at him.

Slug just grinned. "It's not me you have to convince."

A big crowd had gathered round the podgy boy and within the space of a minute they had bought every last copy of his picture papers. I watched them wandering off, engrossed in the pages, gasping in shock at what they saw, some of them shaking their heads in disgust. Clearly this exaggerated and sensationalised version of what had happened was having the opposite effect to what the captain had intended when he said he was going to tell my tale to the people of Tennanbrau City.

"Come on!" said Slug, jerking the leash and setting off again.

Another vendor loomed up before us on the busy thoroughfare - a red faced woman with a wide tray bearing neat rows of dark brown strips of meat. "Jerky! Jerky! Jerkee!" she cried in a high-pitched voice. "Get your dragon meat jerky! Jerky! Jerky! Jerkee!"

People were holding up coins and calling her over to them. Remembering the dry, salty meat that Angus Stonedyke had made me taste aboard *The Drunken Molly* I felt a gagging sensation in the back of my throat. Slug yanked the leash again and set off at a rapid pace. Soon we emerged on the other side of the market. A dreary grey building, with dark narrow windows and a set of huge black doors, stood before us.

"Pym Street," said Slug and gave me a ridiculously exaggerated bow. "Welcome to your new accommodation, young sir."

***

Behind the door was a cheerless hallway; its stone floor covered by a moth-eaten rug. Ahead of that a wide uncarpeted stairwell. On its banister a single candle, fixed in a pool its own melted wax, issued flickering ripples of insipid light against the mould-speckled walls. There was a horrible smell about the place, like a combination of boiled cabbage and blocked toilets.

From somewhere on the upper floors, I could hear the boisterous sound of children arguing and bickering amongst each other. More than one of them seemed to be crying. I heard a loud thump as if someone had fallen or had been thrown to the floor. I didn't like the sound of it at all.

"You're going to have to learn to toughen up if you're going to survive in here," spat Slug, patting his spiky hair.

"You are late, Mister Martin," hissed a sickly voice from deep within the gloom of the narrow corridor that ran parallel to the stairwell.

Slug began removing the loop of the leash from my wrist. "The Comptroller," he whispered to me.

A hunched man scuttled out of the shadows like some dreadful spider. The top part of his head was entirely bald, but below that his greasy black hair hung long and lank down his back and around his shoulders, a pair of pale perfectly rounded ears poked out through the curtains it made to the side of his head. He took out a watch on a chain from the pocket of his waistcoat and tapped the face with a long, bony finger.

"I said you are late, Mister Martin."

Slug removed the leash from his own wrist and handed it to the Comptroller. "I had to wait for ages," he said. "Then there was all sorts of paperwork to be signed. And to crown it all, this one insisted on cutting through Scavenger's Market on account of him never having set foot in Tennanbrau before."

I was about to protest, but before I could open my mouth the Comptroller fired another question at Slug. "How long before the trial?"

"Three weeks," replied Slug.

177

"Three weeks?" muttered the Comptroller. He held up his right hand and began tapping each of his long fingers with his equally long thumb, as if he was doing some sort of mathematical calculation. "Three weeks is almost a month. But I'd wager they won't pay anything more than food and accommodation for twenty-one nights."

"They'll send him back here once he's found guilty," said Slug.

He cupped his hand over the corner of his mouth and whispered to me. "All he's interested in is the court fee for putting you up."

The Comptroller looked me up and down before holding out his hand for me to shake. "Master Redcap," he said, flicking his tongue over his wet lips. "Allow me to introduce myself. Chadwell Glennis, Comptroller of the Pym Street Institute for Wayward Boys and Girls." The palms of his hands were disgustingly moist. His long fingers felt light as a feather. Not like Pa's rough and calloused hands. As soon as I could I pulled my own hand back and wiped it on my shirt.

"You'll get along fine in here," he said. "So long as you don't break any of the house rules."

"House rules," I asked, glancing around the mouldy walls.

Chadwell Glennis began to chuckle. His laugh was like the cluck of a broody hen. "I do believe he's looking for something in print, Mister Martin." His bony shoulders jerked up and down in time to his clucking. "We run a frugal house here, Master Redcap. Ink and paper cost money. The rules are the rules. You'll pick them up as you go along."

He turned to Slug. "Cook's gone home," he said. "But if you're quick there might be some bread crusts and a bit of broth left in the pot."

Then he turned back to me. "I'm afraid we can't provide anything in the way of refreshment for you till breakfast. Master Redcap. The court fees don't officially start accumulating till tomorrow morning."

I felt a shooting pain in my stomach. I hadn't eaten since the previous day. I did think however that I might at least be able to clean myself up. "I was kind of hoping I might be able to have a bath," I said.

Glennis began clucking again. "A bath he says? A bath? Anyone would think that hot water grows on trees!" He leaned in towards me, his eyes narrowing over the dark, saggy bags below them. "How old are you, Master Redcap?"

"Twelve," I answered. "Almost thirteen."

"You don't need bath then!" he cried. "Baths are for babies. If I had my way, I'd outlaw the use of bath water for anyone over the age of five."

He turned his attention to Slug. "Take him to the mess room. Share whatever you find with him, if you have the mind," he said, dismissing us both with a disdainful wave of his arachnid fingers. "Bath, he says? That'll be the day."

Slug turned to walk away, indicating with his head that I should follow.

Then there came a loud knocking on the door.

Chadwell Glennis looked at Slug and then at me.

His eyes narrowed.

179

"You two better not have engaged in any juvenile waywardness in the market," he warned. "Especially you, Mister Martin. What with you only having a week of your incarceration to go."

"We didn't do nothing," Slug told him, folding his arms in that surly manner of his.

The knocking on the door persisted.

"Answer it then, Mister Martin," said Glennis, slipping furtively back into the gloom of the hall.

9. Saved in the Nick of Time

Slug pulled the door slightly ajar. A thin wedge of light fell across the hallway floor.

A woman's voice said something to him. After a moment Slug looked back over his shoulder and called into the hallway. "It's for you, Mister Glennis."

Glennis scuttled back out of the shadows, a worried look on his face and a film of fresh sweat glistening on his bald scalp. "Who is it?" he asked.

Slug gave a shrug of his shoulders. "Some lady, with papers from the Palace of Law."

Glennis hesitated for a moment before brushing Slug to one side and pulling the door wide. The mysterious young woman from courtrooms stood on the institute's desolate doorstep. She flicked back her ponytail and waved at me over Glennis's hunched shoulder.

"How can I help you?" Glennis asked her.

With smile she handed him a folded sheaf of papers. "This is a new court order that supersedes the one issued by Judge Grayling."

"And what precisely does this new order state?" asked Glennis, holding the paperwork between his finger and thumb, as if it were something nasty he'd picked up from the floor.

"It states that Professor Thaddeus Mayhew has been declared temporary guardian of Master Redcap until the date of his trial. He's to come with me immediately."

Hurriedly Glennis unfolded the papers and began to scrutinise them. Meanwhile Slug sidled up beside and whispered in my ear. "Looks like you may have got lucky, Low County boy. But don't worry none, you'll be right back here after the trial."

Glennis had finished reading. "It seems as if these are in order," he conceded. "I hope that, in the circumstances the courts are going to compensate me for my financial losses. Food and board is what I was contracted for. This going to throw my budget to pot."

"That's something you'll need to take up with them," said Hari.

With a grunt Glennis turned to me. "Master Redcap," he said wetly. "You have a visitor."

I stepped forward, narrowly avoiding falling flat on my face as Slug maliciously stuck out his foot.

"Apparently," said Glennis, "you have been placed under the guardianship of Professor Thaddeus Mayhew until your trial comes up."

"What does that mean?" I asked, looking at Hari rather than Glennis.

"It means," said Hari, whipping her ponytail back over her shoulder once more, "that you'll be coming with me."

She nodded at the document that Glennis was still holding. With a grudged sigh he fished around in his trouser pocket and produced a tiny stub of pencil. Grunting in disapproval he licked the dull point of the pencil, then scribbled his signature.

"Go get your stuff," said Hari. "We're off."

My head was spinning. Things were moving so fast again that I couldn't think straight. "I d-don't have any s-stuff," I told her.

"Then, if Mister Glennis has no objections, we shall go right now."

Glennis nodded grudgingly and Hari held out her hand to me.

Apparently finding this quite amusing Slug began to snigger loudly. In an instant Glennis swung round and whacked him hard across the ear. Slug staggered backwards. "Ouch!" he cried.

"I saw that," said Hari. "You assaulted that boy." She stepped into the hallway. "If you want to make a complaint, I'll be your witness. And I'm sure Master Redcap will be too."

"Do you want to make a complaint Mister Martin?" asked Glennis. "What with you only having one week to go, and all?"

Slug bowed his head, still rubbing his ear. "I haven't got a clue what she's going on about," he mumbled. "I didn't see no assault on nobody."

Hari shook her head and snatched the paperwork back from Glennis. "Come on, Euan," she said. "The sooner I get you away from this dreadful place the better."

***

The late afternoon sun was still shining brightly when I followed Hari back out onto the streets of Tennanbrau. Even though I'd only endured the gloom of the Pym Street Institute for a little over ten minutes the sunlight still made my eyes sting. Squinting, I followed her as she strode across the road, her boots clomping loudly against

183

the cobblestones. She stopped in front of a ladder that led all the way up the side of a tall building.

"Can you climb, Euan?" she asked me.

"I used to climb trees in the glen back home," I replied.

"I take it you have a head for heights then?"

I nodded. Having spent weeks above the clouds on board both *The Drunken Molly* and *The Hawk's Cry,* as well as having rode on the back of the White Sow through the canyons of the Serrated Mountains, I was certainly no longer a stranger to heights.

"The quickest way to get anywhere in Tennanbrau is go up and across," she said, pulling herself onto the first rung of the ladder. "The Professor and the others are waiting for us."

"Wait a minute," I said, parking my feet firmly on the pavement. "Who exactly are you? Why do I have to go with you? And who is this Professor Mayhew?"

Hari jumped back down from the ladder. She smiled and flicked her ponytail back over her shoulder. "It's natural that you have questions," she said.

"And?" I wasn't planning on going anywhere till I got some answers.

"I work for an organisation called Friends of the Dragon," said Hari. "Professor Mayhew is the president of our organisation. We've been campaigning for a long time to bring about an end to the dragon hunting trade and the taking of Dragon Breath."

I recalled Captain Zachariah telling me about people in Tennanbrau who might help him.

"And as to why you have to come with me." Hari patted the folded document poking out of her waistcoat pocket. "There's a Court Order saying you have to. Besides, if I was you, and the choice I had was between having the Professor as my Guardian, and staying in that awful Institute, I wouldn't be hesitating."

"That still doesn't explain how this professor came to get the Court Order in the first place," I challenged. "The charges against me are serious."

"So is kidnap," she replied. "We successfully argued that, as you yourself are a victim of a crime, in tandem with being accused of a crime, you should not be incarcerated till this is all resolved."

That sounded quite complicated, but it also seemed that she knew a lot about me than I did about her. "No one is going to believe I was kidnapped," I said. "The way Mrs Zachariah planned it she made it look like I agreed to become ship's fetcher of my own accord. And all the crew of *The Drunken Molly* will swear that it's true."

"But we have the complaint filed by you father with the Low County Division of the Imperial Constabulary," said Hari. "And copies of the signed witness statements made by your mother and sister."

A lump came to my throat. "My father complained to the constabulary?"

"I don't know your family," said Hari. "But I'm sure you didn't expect them just to sit back and do nothing." She nodded across the road towards the Institute. "I think we'd better be on our way. We seem to have garnered quite an audience."

When I turned and looked, Chadwell Glennis was pacing the doorstep of the Institute, glowering across at us. Above him, their dirty noses pressed against the grimy windowpanes of the upper floor rooms, were the wayward boys and girls that I had heard arguing and bickering. They seemed to be of all ages, ranging from about five or six years old, right up to teenagers like Slug Martin. Glad now that I wasn't going to be staying there, I followed Hari as she began climbing up the rungs of the ladder.

"Nathaniel Zachariah sends you his regards, by the way," said Hari over her shoulder.

I stopped on the ladder, one hand gripping the rung above my head. "You've spoken to him?"

"Not directly," she replied. "But the solicitor who represented you both is an associate member of Friends of the Dragon. The message comes through him. It feels odd though. We would never have believed in a million years that we would find common ground with such a notorious dragon hunter as Captain Nathaniel Zachariah."

I found myself smiling for the first time in ages. "He more or less told me certain people would feel that way."

Hari was climbing up onto wooden platform. She held out her hand and, when I took it, she pulled me up the last few rungs. "We've gone up," she said. "Now we go across." She nodded in the direction a swing bridge, constructed from rope and wooden slats that spanned the wide gap between one building and the next. "Come on, Euan," she urged. "Follow what I do."

I watched her crossing the bridge, gripping the guide ropes on either side of her, first the left hand, then the right hand, then the left, then the right. I stepped onto the first section of wooden slats and mimicked her actions. The bridge swayed as I walked, but the hand over hand technique kept me balanced and helped me keep pace with her.

Ten, maybe fifteen, feet below us I could see the bustle of Scavenger's Market. The sound of the dragon meat vendor's high-pitched call came echoing up to the bridge. "Jerky! Jerky! Jerkee!"

Within a few minutes we reached the building at the other side - a tall, chimney shaped construct, with narrow slats for windows, and a spiral staircase snaking around its sooty walls. Hari began to climb - around and around - up and up. Increasingly breathless I followed her. We came to another swing bridge and crossed again to yet another building, then up another ladder and across a more substantial iron bridge.

The higher we climbed the more I could see of the crazy jumble of that made up the vast city of Tennanbrau. There appeared to be no plan whatsoever. It was as if people just attached ladders or bridges or stairs wherever they felt necessary to get them from one place to the other. How anyone could ever remember his or her way through this hotchpotch maze was beyond me.

Hari, however, seemed to know exactly where she was going.

Up above I could see the passing hulls of airship gondolas, their captains and coxswains expertly navigating the narrow gaps between the tall tenement towers, crewmen utilising long poles when necessary. To the west where the sun was now beginning to set, I saw a huge platform complex. People were disembarking onto this platform from airships far bigger than *The Drunken Molly*.

"The passenger terminus," Hari told me when I asked what it was.

I thought of all the Dragon Breath that was being used up in the balloons of all these airships. Captain Zachariah had been right when he'd told me that Tennanbrau depended on the dragon trade. In the circumstances I wondered how anyone could ever realistically hope to bring about its end.

We arrived at a long platform, where a line of people stood waiting in a queue.

"We're almost there," said Hari. She nodded to where four of the people in the queue were boarding a little boxed hut that hung down from a thick steel wire. "We're going to ride the cable carriage the rest of the way."

"Where exactly are you taking me?" I asked her.

"The Beehive." came her reply. "Headquarters of Friends of the Dragon."

I kept my eyes closed as the flimsy carriage climbed steadily along the steel cable to the next level of platforms. Despite my head for heights the notion of sitting inside a wooden box hanging precariously from a wire made my stomach turn cartwheels.

Thankfully the journey didn't last too long.

We emerged onto the higher platform and another group of passengers took our place for the ride back down. Hari paid our fare to a man who sat in cramped booth at the far end of the platform, and we were allowed the pass through a turnstile.

"Last leg now," said Hari, already climbing the rungs of the ladder that rose from the section of platform on the other side of the turnstile. I followed her up the side of yet another building. We were so high now that the wind that whipped around us was a strong as anything I'd experienced on the gondola of *The Drunken Molly*.

We came at last to a flat rooftop. For a moment I watched a group of three scavenger ships approaching Tennanbrau from the north, their coloured balloons of dragon wing membrane standing starkly out against the reddening sunset sky. I turned in time to see Hari crouching down and placing a key in the lock of a trapdoor set into the rooftop.

She lifted the trapdoor lid and beckoned me over. "Come on then. This is the way in."

10. The Beehive

Down a dimly lit flight of stairs we went, and along a narrow corridor that ended at a set of green double doors, adorned with ornate panelling. Doors and stairs and corridors, I thought. That's all this place ever seems to amount to. The ache in my heart for the green hills and open spaces of the Low Counties intensified.

Hari fumbled around in her pocket and produced another key. Before putting the key in the lock, she indicated with her head to some words painted above the doorframe in gold leaf. "That's the motto of Friends of the Dragon," she said. "Dare to Dream the Impossible!"

When I mouthed the words, something stirred inside me.

I had no time to think any further about this because as soon as Hari unlocked the doors, she bustled me through. Beehive was an extremely apt name for the crowded room that Hari led me to. There had to be at least a couple of dozen men and women crammed in the there. They seemed mostly around Hari's age, although some were slightly older. One group was pouring over books and documents spread out across a long table, others were pondering various charts and diagrams that hung from the wall. Here and there groups of twos and threes were deep in animated conversation.

Everyone seemed far too busy and distracted to even notice us.

At the far end of the table, I saw someone I immediately recognised. Daneby Caruthers, the nervous lawyer who had represented myself and Captain Zachariah at our preliminary trail. He was hunched over a huge pile of law books, shirt neck open and sleeves rolled up to his elbows. Looking up for a moment he gave me a cursory nod before returning his attention to his books.

I glanced around the room, trying to take it all in.

By the door where we were standing were three tall piles of paper. The sign above the first read pamphlets for distribution. The sign above the second read petitions for signing. The sign above the third read signed petitions. The entire wall behind where Daneby was seated was taken up by a huge bookcase, its shelves crammed with books of all shapes and sizes.

I began to look at the charts and diagrams hanging from the wall. One bore a schematic of what appeared to an airship with an oddly shaped and unusually long balloon above its gondola. The words *'The Hargmir - Rigid Balloon Dirigible (prototype)'* were scrawled above the schematic and handwritten just under the gondola someone had scribbled a mathematical equation that I couldn't even begin to understand.

The chart next to this bore the title 'Current Registered Expeditions by Dragon Hunting Vessels' and amongst the names listed was that of *The Drunken Molly*. Next to that was another chart, entitled 'Current Registered Expeditions by Scavenger Vessels'. The name of *The Hawk's Cry* was on that list. Next to it someone had pencilled an asterisk and words - returned to Tennanbrau in unusual circumstances.

The first chart on the opposite wall was entitled 'Estimated Dragon Population by Breed'. This chart bore three columns. One headed name of breed. The next headed estimated population. The final column was a pencil sketch of what that breed looked like.

I saw a couple of names that I remembered being mentioned during my time on *The Drunken Molly* - Common Green and Horned Goldback. But the rest of the names were new to me. Black Treacleshell, Speckled Shortwing, Lesser Wind Glider, Silvered Ridgeback, Crimsonjaw. The list went on. All in all, there must have been a good two-dozen or more different species. From the sketches I recognised some of the types of dragon I had seen in the nesting area in canyons of the Serrated Mountains.

The very last name on the list was Greater Albino and the figure in the column marked estimated population was a lonely number one, with a large question mark at its side. I looked at the pencil sketch beside this. It was a pretty good depiction of how I recalled the White Sow.

Had there once been an entire breed of dragons with the same snowy white scales and magnificent dazzling wings as her? Was the White Sow truly the last of her kind? Was this the fate that awaited all of the other breeds on the list? Having witnessed how much Dragon Breath the citizens of Tennanbrau were using, it wasn't difficult at all to imagine this happening.

It was then I noticed a tall, grey figure, with unmistakably craggy features and a tuft of moss green hair. Although she was dressed similarly to Hari, in a blouse and waistcoat, knee length boots tucked into baggy britches, there was no doubt that she was a Ghibelline tribeswoman. Her dark, beady eyes met mine. She smiled and waved at me with her big, rough-skinned hand.

"That's Fenisnoor," said Hari. "She used to be the Professor's assistant. She helped him found Friends of the Dragon."

I wondered if this friendly looking Ghibelline might be a member of Illagnor's tribe. I started to walk towards her, but Hari was tugging at my arm. "There's someone I want you to meet," she said, pulling me to where a rather dishevelled individual was seated before an artist's easel, sketching something with a pencil. Another pencil clamped between his teeth, and yet was another wedged behind his left ear. I counted two more poking out of his shirt pocket. Dark streaks of pencil lead were smeared on his cheeks and forehead.

"This is Jeremiah Jamieson, our resident artist," said Hari. "Show Euan what you're working on, JJ."

JJ nodded and swung his easel around to show me. There was a large sheet of paper divided into several boxes of differing sizes, some square and some oblong. One or two of these boxes had sketches drawn into them. The first box depicted a series of rolling hills and an upside-down red-haired boy being hauled up into an airship by a rope that

193

was tied around his ankle. Above this box the title of document of read *'The Tale of Euan Redcap'*.

My mouth fell wide.

"We're going to put this out to counter all of the nonsense in those dreadful picture papers," said Hari. "It was JJ's idea."

JJ removed the pencil from between his teeth. "It'll work a lot better that a pamphlet," he said. "I've based it on how Captain Zachariah recounted your tale to Daneby. But I want you to go through it when it's finished. In case I've gotten any of the details wrong."

"S-sure," I stammered. "A-anything."

I leaned in to take a closer look at the picture in the second box.

As I was doing so a loud voice boomed across the room. "Ah, you've arrived!"

"Thaddeus Mayhew," said the elderly grey-haired man I had previously seen outside Courtroom 706. He gripped my hand in a firm handshake. "I trust you won't find it too onerous having me as your legal Guardian for the next few weeks?"

I shook my head. "T-thank you for g-getting me out of Pym Street."

"Think nothing of it, lad," said the Professor. "I wouldn't wish that place on my worst enemy." He looked down at me and gave me a mischievous wink. "So, Euan, what do you think of what these reprobates have done to my apartments?"

"Your apartments? You live here?"

"I do," said the Professor. "And so will you. A room is being made up for you this very minute. Now, are you hungry? I don't suppose Harmony

194

here has asked you. She's so committed to our cause that she often forgets to herself."

I looked at Hari. Her face was flushing bright red.

"Don't call me that, it's too girlie," she said, placing her hands on her hips and jutting her chin forcefully forward.

My stomach rumbled embarrassingly loudly.

11. Friends

The days seemed to fly up there in Professor Mayhew's apartments. Although I was extremely well looked after, three meals a day, hot baths whenever I wanted, a bed that was twice the size of my bed back home, and twice as soft, I still pined to be back in the Low Counties and worried constantly about my impending trial.

I occupied my time coming and going between the Professor's private apartments and the area that was designated as the Beehive. No matter what time of day I wandered in there it always seemed to be busy. Groups of young people would be bringing back signed petitions calling upon Emperor Julian to outlaw the hunting of dragons and declare them a protected species. No sooner would they put these down than they would pick up fresh sheets, along with the accompanying flier.

Apparently, the city was becoming increasingly divided when it came to the question of dragon hunting. The affair involving Captain Zachariah and myself was causing all sorts of shifts in opinion. People who might previously have been won round to the cause of Friends of the Dragon were suddenly reluctant to put their name to the petition, while those who had been apathetic before were now being persuaded to add their signatures.

There seemed to be a lot of faith in my tale turning things more solidly around and I often found myself being asked to pour over JJ's drawings to make sure the unfolding story that was accurate, both in terms of the images and the short accompanying text in each box. It was one day while I was looking at his unfinished sketch of Captain Zachariah and myself rising high above the crater at Forgsnur's Footprint when I noticed that a meeting was convening around the long table.

Sometimes Daneby Caruthers would report back to these meetings on conversations he'd had with Captain Zachariah in his cell at the Imperial Penal Institute. I loved listening in on this and no one seemed to mind at all when I sat in. Seeing that Daneby was joining the meeting I made my way to the table. Hari was there, as was Fenisnoor, and several other faces that I was now becoming increasingly familiar with. In fact, I would go so far as to say many of them, particularly Hari and Fenisnoor, felt close enough to me that I thought of them as real friends.

Professor Mayhew took his seat at the head of the table and fanned his long grey hair about his shoulders. "What do you have to report, Daneby," he asked, dispensing with any formal opening of the meeting. "Would Nathaniel Zachariah be willing to be captain on our expedition?"

I knew about this expedition. I'd heard them discussing it on two or three occasions. They were planning to go to the Far Tundra to conduct an accurate census of the dragon population. This would replace the guesswork that the current tallies were based upon.

The airship that Professor Mayhew had designed, and whose plans hung on the wall of the Beehive, was to be their mode of transportation. Its balloon apparently relied for its buoyancy on gas known as helium that occurred naturally in huge pockets deep underground. This, I guessed, was the alternative gas that Captain Zachariah had spoken about.

The Professor's airship was called The Hargmir. Fenisnoor had told me that, in much the same as Forgsnur's Footprint took its name from an old Ghibelline folktale, The Hargmir was named after Hargmir, the ghost of fallen dragons, who according to Ghibelline legend endlessly roamed the far tundra. The utilisation of this name was symbolic and meant as a tribute to all the dragons that had lost their lives because of the trade in Dragon Breath.

From what I understood the airship was already under construction in a hangar at a secret location near Pennington Vale, one of Tennanbrau's many outlying townships. I had learned that the mathematical equations on the schematic on the wall represented the formula for refined version of helium that would be safe and suitable for use within balloons. The aim of the expedition was also to provide concrete proof that this gas was a viable alternative to Dragon Breath.

Despite all that I had discovered the suggestion that Captain Zachariah was to be invited to be airship captain for the expedition was complete news to me. It wasn't something I'd overheard them talking about previously. But I thought it was an excellent idea. Like the others I turned to Daneby and waited for his response.

"The captain said t-that it w-was always h-his intention to offer his s-services to F-Friends of the D-Dragon," he stammered. "If assisting on such an expedition would help further the cause he would gladly offer his services, present circumstances aside, that is."

"Excellent!" cried the Professor.

"Is it though?" asked one of the young activists.

"Pardon?" said the Professor.

"How can we trust him?" asked another. "His haul of Dragon Breath was consistently higher than any other captain since Gulliver Quat."

"If Illagnor and his tribe-folk trusted him then that's good enough for me," said Fenisnoor, casting a beady-eyed glance at the two of them.

"I believe he's a changed man," added Hari. "He was kind to Euan and tried to take him back home to his parents."

"I say that a leopard can't change his spots," said the activist who'd spoken first.

"And I say that it can," interjected the Professor, rising to his feet. "With my own history am I not living proof of that?"

***

"What did Professor Mayhew mean by his own history?" I asked Hari.

We were in the kitchen area near the Beehive with JJ. Having just checked though his drawings in the finished version of The Tale of Euan Redcap we were snacking on jam sandwiches, accompanied by tall glasses of milk. Hari wiped away a purple blob of jam that had dropped onto her chin and answered my question with one of her own. "When you were on The Drunken Molly did you get close enough to a Rope Cannon to see its patent mark?" she asked.

"Or the mark on a Dragon Breath Extractor?" added JJ, his inky fingers leaving black prints around his glass.

I shook my head. I had seen both contraptions in action. But I had never been close enough to either to see anything of that nature. Hari took another bite from her sandwich and chewed it down. "Mayhew's Patented Rope Cannon," she said. "And Mayhew's Patented Dragon Breath Extractor."

"You mean?"

Hari nodded. "My uncle invented them both. It was how he made his fortune."

"Those inventions were responsible for the rapid expansion in the dragon hunting trade," said JJ.

I took a big gulp of milk.

"You could say that Thaddeus Mayhew is more or less the father of dragon hunting as we know it today," said Hari.

I understood now. Rope Cannon and Breath Extractors were the key tools of the dragon hunters' armoury. Without them the efficient taking of Dragon Breath would be virtually impossible.

"He was also involved in some of the early attempts to refine Dragon Breath," Hari went on. "There used to be an experimental station near the crater Forgsnur's Footprint. That was where he first met Fenisnoor. She was part of a small group of Ghibelline hired to catch dragons to experiment upon."

"Fenisnoor was involved as well?"

I remembered how Illagnor had condemned dragon hunting and how Captain Zachariah had told me that it had been the influence of the Ghibelline that had changed his own views and made him come to realise the potentially disastrous impact his chosen trade was having on the dragon population. It didn't seem feasible to me that a Ghibelline tribeswoman would have been so closely involved.

"No one quite understood back then what it would all lead to," said Hari.

"Even the Ghibelline?"

"When the experiments first started it was simply about extracting Dragon Breath and seeing what its properties and applications might be," explained JJ.

"Even when the first airships started hunting dragons for their breath very few of them were actually dying," added Hari. "But then people started to find more and more uses for Dragon Breath and the demand increased."

"And someone else at the experimental station discovered that dragon wing membrane was a much more reliable material for airship balloons than the silk material previously used," said JJ. "The same person argued that dragon bone made a sturdier frame for balloons than wood or metal. And dragons started being hunted for more than just the extraction of their breath."

"And that's where the scavengers came in?" I asked.

They both nodded.

"Chefs at the Imperial Palace began creating dishes that featured dragon meat," said Hari, pulling a face. "Dining on dragon became all the rage for a while."

I remembered the vendor in Scavenger's Market – Jerky, Jerky, Jerkee!

"Soon people wanted dragon skin raincoats and dragon wing umbrellas," continued Hari. "And pendants made from a dragon tooth or a dragon talon."

"And more and more scavenger ships started trawling in the wake of the dragon hunter's airships," said JJ.

"By the time the Professor realised what was happening it was too late to stop any of it," said Hari.

"So, I sold the copyright to my inventions and used the money to found Friends of the Dragon."

We all turned around at the sound of the Professor's booming voice. None of us had noticed him entering the kitchen area. "Therefore, Master Redcap," he said, looking deathly serious. "I am indeed the leopard that changed its spots."

"And that's why you want everyone to trust Captain Zachariah?"

The Professor nodded and his grey hair rustled around his shoulders. "In a way he reminds me of myself."

I held up JJ's artwork. "It's ready to go to the printers," I said. "Do you really think it's going to help change people's opinions?"

"Every little thing helps in its own way," he replied. "Now if you're finished your snack there's a visitor waiting to see you in my study."

"A visitor?"

Who in all of Tennanbrau City could possibly want to visit me? A knot twisted in my stomach. This could only mean trouble. Was it another court order? Had Slug Martin or Chadwell Glennis come to fetch me back to the Pym Street Institute?

"I think you'll be pleasantly surprised," said Professor Mayhew, ushering me out of the kitchen. "He's from the Low Counties."

12. The Lanolin Merchant

As soon as we entered the room, I could tell that without a doubt the man who was waiting in Professor Mayhew's study was clearly from the Low Counties. Except for a few tufts of ginger hair poking up around his ears he was bald headed. The chunky freckles that were splattered across his shiny scalp gave the appearance of spots of red paint having dropped there from a great height. He had a cloth cap that he kept twisting and untwisting as he paced the floor.

"Euan," said the professor by way of introduction. "This is Mister Andrew Highbrae. He's a lanolin merchant by trade."

Lanolin?

As far back as I could remember lanolin merchants had been setting up their stalls in the village square back home. Low County folk used the oily ointment for all sorts of ailments, from insect bites and sunburn in the summer to chapped skin and cracked lips in the winter. It had always struck me as strange that a by-product of sheep wool should be produced so far away in Tennanbrau City, only to be transported back for sale in the sheep rearing communities of the Low Counties.

Highbrae stepped forward and held out his hand. "Pleased to meet you Master Redcap," he said. His hand felt damp and clammy. When I looked into his eyes, they seemed full of trepidation. Was my reputation as a notorious criminal so bad that even one of my own folk was afraid to meet me?

"Why don't you take a seat Mister Highbrae," said the Professor, nodding towards his sofa. "If you don't mind me saying you look as if you are about to faint at any minute."

Highbrae flashed him a nervous twitch of a smile.

"If it's all the same to you I'll stand, sir," he said. "Your seats are far too close to the windows for my liking. I fear that if I so much as glanced out of one my heart might give out." Swallowing hard he dabbed the sweat from his brow with his crumpled cap.

So that was it. Highbrae was afraid of heights. Given his name that struck me as quite funny. I bit down on my tongue to stop myself from laughing out loud with relief.

"I do apologise," said the Professor. "I can see how uncomfortable you are. But, unfortunately, the terms of Master Redcap's court order restrict him from leaving the confines of my apartments. A meeting at ground level was out of the question."

The professor turned to me. "Mister Highbrae has a proposal for you, Euan."

"A proposal?"

I looked at Highbrae.

"Once my wagon is loaded with stock I'll be travelling through your part of the Low Counties," he said. "I had this notion that if you wanted to write a letter to your parents, I could carry it for you and deliver it safely to their hands."

"A letter to my parents?" The offer took me by surprise. "Now? I don't have a pencil or paper. I don't know what to write."

Professor Mayhew smiled. "Don't worry, Euan. I'm sure Mister Highbrae isn't expecting you to just write something straight off. There's writing materials in my desk that you could use. And envelopes so your correspondence will remain private and confidential." He turned to Highbrae, long grey hair as ever swaying around his shoulders. "I'm sure tomorrow morning would be acceptable."

Highbrae nodded and twisted his cap into another knot.

"I'll be leaving Tennanbrau at ten sharp. If you could get it to me before then I'd be more than happy to ensure its safe delivery."

"How does that sound, Euan?" asked the professor.

For a moment I was slightly lost for words.

Then they all tumbled out in a jumble.

"That sounds... I mean it sounds... fantastic. A letter to my parents. So they can be sure that I'm safe? It sounds... great. I mean I'll get work on it straight away. And I'll keep my writing neat so they can read it. And I'll try not to smudge the paper. And... thank you so much, Mister Highbrae."

"Think nothing of it," said Highbrae, blushing slightly. "I know what it's like to arrive in this city for the first time, especially for someone from the Low Counties. Mind you the letter will have to be brought to me. I don't think I could face coming all the way up here again." He drew a sharp intake of breath and cast a worried glance at the windows.

"I'll have Hari or one of the others deliver the letter to you at the North Gate by nine thirty at the latest," said Professor Mayhew. "Now can I offer you a cup of tea, or perhaps something a little stronger?"

"Thank you, sir," replied Highbrae. "But if it's all the same I think I'd rather be off. The sooner I'm back down on solid ground the better."

He pulled his crumpled cap over his head and held his hand out to me once more. "Good luck to you, lad," he said.

"Thanks," I replied. "And thanks again for offering to take my letter."

***

I screwed up another sheet of paper and tossed it into the bin.

I just couldn't think what to write. It seemed so long since the day that I'd been hauled up onto the deck of *The Drunken Molly*. So much had happened that I hardly knew where to start. Despite my best efforts my handwriting seemed so bad that I wasn't at all sure that they would be able to read anything I wrote. Every sheet of paper I had tossed in the bin was full of smudges and crossed out words. I decided to go to the little kitchen next to the Beehive to get another glass of milk and see if a break would help clear my head.

I bumped straight into Hari and JJ who, along with a couple of others, were stacking boxes onto one of the tables by the door. "It's here," said Hari. "Back from the printers. Hot off the press, as they say." JJ tore open one of the boxes and handed one of the pamphlets to me.

I read the title on the cover - *The Tale of Euan Redcap* - beneath this JJ's depiction of me on board *The Drunken Molly* with the White Sow breaking through the clouds in the distance. I flicked through the pages. It was all there in pictures and descriptive text. Everything that had happened to me from beginning to end. Everything I somehow couldn't manage to put down in words in my letter home.

"Can I keep this one?" I asked.

Hari looked at JJ and tossed her ponytail back over her shoulder.

"Sure," said JJ.

With the picture paper clutched in my hand I dashed back to Professor Mayhew's study and grabbed a fresh sheet of paper. Taking time to go as slowly as I could so as not to make any smudges or spelling mistakes. I wrote a very simple letter to my family.

Dear Ma, Pa and Isla,

This is what happened to me. It's all true.

I am fine now. Good people are looking after me.

Hope to see you soon.

Love

Euan

I took the letter and folded it around the picture paper. Then I stuffed both into one of the larger sized envelopes and licked the seal. On the front I wrote *Mr and Mrs Redcap, The Low Counties*. After a moment's thought I added – *delivered by the kind assistance of Mister Andrew Highbrae*.

13. Running Away

It was pitch dark when I crept out of bed and hurriedly pulled on my clothes. Wincing when the door to my room creaked loudly, I tiptoed along the corridor to the professor's study. Feeling my way past his desk I pressed my ear to the door that joined the study to the Beehive and listened. When I was sure that no one was in there I pushed the door open and entered.

I had lain awake for hours, thinking about my letter and how it would soon be heading its way to my family in the Low Counties. What started off with me wistfully thinking that it would the best thing in the whole world if I could only go with it had slowly developed into a determined statement of intent.

"Why shouldn't I?" I'd muttered into my pillow. "Why shouldn't I just go back home myself?"

Soon I had managed to persuade myself that there was nothing at all to stop me. The more that I convinced myself that this was the case the more selfish I found myself becoming. I had only known Captain Zachariah for a short time, the Professor and Hari even less. I didn't really owe them anything, did I? Hadn't I been kidnapped and stolen away from my family? It was to them and them alone that I owed my loyalty. Wasn't it my duty then to find my way home by whatever means possible?

It came to me in a flash that Mister Highbrae could provide me with a way to get back home. He'd told the Professor that he would wait by Tennanbrau's North Gate in the morning. If I could wait there too, hidden from sight, I could stow away in the back of his wagon. Surely it wouldn't be too difficult to hide amongst the boxes of lanolin till he reached the Low Counties?

I was counting on no one realising I was gone until later in the day. During my first two or three days in the professor's apartments I had been so tired from all my adventures and misfortunes that I had slept till well past midday. As far as I was aware no one had come to check on me. If the same thing happened, I would be passing along the road that joined each of Tennanbrau's outlying townships to the next long before anyone discovered I was gone. My hope was that they would not realise where I had gone and would spend all their time searching the city for me instead.

My heart pounded as I snuck through the shadowy gloom of the Beehive and snatched the spare key that always hung on a hook near the back door. The key seemed to burn guiltily in my hand. I knew that once I slipped it into the lock there would be no turning back. If someone caught me now, I would simply say that I couldn't sleep from the excitement of knowing that my picture paper was going to be distributed in the morning and that I hadn't been able to resist having a look at another copy.

I saw a woolly hat that someone had left on top of one of the boxes of picture papers and remembered what Slug Martin had said when he'd given me the dirty looking cap before we entered Scavenger's Market.

"That red hair is a dead giveaway." Drawing a deep breath, I pulled the hat down over my ears and took one last look at the crowded chaos of the Beehive. Then I slid the key into the lock and turned it. Outside in the corridor I looked up at the words above the door that I had seen that first day when Hari brought me there. The motto of Friends of the Dragon. *"Dare to dream the impossible."*

"That's exactly what I am doing," I assured myself, passing along the corridor. "No matter how impossible it might seem I am daring to dream that I can get back home to my family."

***

It was cold and dark outside on the rooftop of the tall building that housed Professor Mayhew's apartments. Glad of the warmth from the woolly hat I shivered as I gazed down on the kaleidoscope of multi-coloured lights that illuminated the tenement towers, palaces, and layered levels of Tennanbrau. In my mind I was going back over the route that Hari had taken when she brought me there. The ladders, the stairwells, the bridges and the walkways.

I remembered that we had crossed from one rooftop to the flat roof of this building and before that we had climbed a ladder that led up from the platform on the other side of the turnstile that was the exit from the cable carriage station. Cautiously I retraced those steps, telling myself that if I did this a small section at a time, I would easily find myself back at ground level. There I could ask someone for directions to the North Gate.

I was halfway down the ladder when I realised that I had no money. How was I going to pay my fare to cross on the cable carriage? If only I'd had the sense to take some copies of The Tale of Euan Redcap. I could have sold these to people going in and out of the turnstile and raised my fare that way. I considered going back. But then decided that I didn't want to take the risk. However, when I stepped down from the ladder and turned to face the turnstile, I found that having no money was the least of my problems. The station was in total darkness. It was closed for the night. Not a soul was around.

What now?

I fought down the panic that fluttered in my chest.

There had to be another way down. All I had to do was keep calm. I followed the platform that I was standing on past the foot of the ladder to where it curved around the side of the building. At the other side there was a zigzagging stairway leading both up and down.

"Down," I told myself. "Down is the direction I need to go."

Slowly, trying to make as little noise as possible, I followed the stairway down, all the time convincing myself that so long as I ended up at street level it didn't matter. *In fact,* I thought. *It's better this way. If I retrace Hari's route back to where we started, I'll end right up across the road*

212

from the Pym Street Institute. And that's not somewhere I'd like to be.

I came to the foot of the zigzag stairway and found myself on a sloping walkway that was bolted onto the wall of one of the tenement towers. The railings that encompassed the walkway were caked in a crumbling layer of rust that was as red as my hair. It stained the palms of my hands, but the dip of its slope was so deep into parts that I simply had to hold on to keep my balance. The walkway passed beneath several windows with recently washed workmen's clothing hanging from their ledges on knotted ropes. The water dripping from them bounced from the railing and made it precariously slippery underfoot. If this was a regular occurrence it was no wonder the railings were so rusty.

The walkway came so close to the window of one of the tenement apartments that I was able to peep through the net curtain that hung there. In a cramped little room, lit by a gas lamp, there was a boy of around ten seated on a wooden stool. He was engrossed in the pages of a picture paper. On a sofa to his left a girl of twelve or thirteen was holding out her hands so her mother could unravel a ball of wool. In an armchair to the boy's right a stocky looking man, who was presumably the father, was smoking a clay pipe, apparently deep in thought. It could have been a scene from my own cottage back home playing out before my eyes. Me, Isla, Ma and Pa.

It convinced me even more that I was doing the right thing.

Getting back home was all that really mattered.

I hurried along the walkway. When I came to a chain link bridge, I crossed it in the manner Hari had shown me, pulling myself forward with one hand followed by the next. I could hear singing coming up from below. The familiar words of The Dragon Hunter's Sky Shanty were echoing drunkenly and boisterously skyward.

Now I was born in Tennanbrau
Haul away above the clouds

Looking down I saw that I was no more than a dozen feet above ground level, passing over the tiled rooftop of a slightly listing alehouse. My heart quickened. I was almost at street level. As soon as I was down, I would ask the first person I met for directions to the North Gate. Then I would find a place to hide and wait for the arrival in the morning of Andrew Highbrae and his wagon. In a few hours I would be on the first leg of my journey home.

A ladder on the opposite side of the bridge brought me down into a narrow alley just behind the alehouse. It was dark down there and it smelled of dustbins and rotting fruit. I caught another snatch of the sky shanty.

I travelled north to where it's cold
Haul away above the clouds

I knew that the alehouse would be packed with dragon hunters and scavengers back from voyages to the Far Tundra. There was no way I was going risk going in there and asking any of them for help. But I could see through the archway at the end of the alley that it led to a thoroughfare where people were still passing back and forth, even at that late hour.

I dashed under the arch and out onto the street. I was in such a rush that I didn't see the group of three youths who were loitering at the mouth of the alley. I ran right into one of them and knocked him off his feet. "Sorry!" I apologised. "I didn't mean to do that. It was an accident." I reached down to help him back up.

"Sorry," snarled a horribly familiar voice. "You knocked down my mate. Sorry just isn't good enough."

I looked up and the first thing I recognised was the distinctive spiky black hair.

"Slug Martin?" I cried.

"Who do you think you are, running into people like that?" he demanded, grabbing me by the shirt collar. "And how come you know my name?"

14. Slug's Gang

Doing my best to avoid making eye contact with Slug I tried to shrug myself free of his grip. "I'm sorry," I told him. "I was in a bit of a rush. I honestly didn't see your friends."

"Hang on a minute," said Slug, pulling me closer. "I recognise that Low County accent."

With that he pulled off my hat.

"I knew it!" He pressed his nose against mine and then pushed me back, still holding my collar so that my neck jerked painfully backwards. "Euan Redcap!"

"Euan who?" asked one of his friends, scratching at the flaky skin on his filthy neck.

"Redcap," replied Slug. "The one I told you about. The one who was arrested with Captain Zachariah. The one who was a crewmate to Angus Stonedyke."

The third member of Slug's gang came lurching up to my side – a girl - extremely large, with broad shoulders, muscular arms, and big, beefy hands. Despite her size I thought she might be only around fourteen years old. She had black, curly hair and a mean look on her face.

"Angus Stonedyke?" she asked. "Are you a friend of his?"

"Not exactly," I replied.

She pressed her right hand over her left and cracked her knuckles loudly. "I wouldn't advise you to get into a fight with me," she warned.

"I wasn't planning to," I said.

216

Slug finally eased his grip. "Let me introduce you to my good friends," he said. "This is Fidget." The boy that I'd knocked over smirked and gave me a little fake bow, all the time scratching at his armpit. "And this is Lullabeth." Lullabeth glared at me cracked her knuckles.

"I finally got out of the Pym Street Institute," said Slug, holding out the palm of his hand to show how the P and I inked there was already fading. "As soon as I hooked up with my old buddies, we started to discuss was how we could take our revenge on that dirty turncoat Angus Stonedyke."

Fidget spat on the ground at the mention of Angus' name.

"Dirty turncoat," repeated Lullabeth and gave her knuckles one more crack for luck.

"And I just was saying how I knew this other Low County boy who might be useful in helping us get reacquainted with Mister Stonedyke," continued Slug. "What was I just saying?"

Fidget scratched his ribs and reached awkwardly over shoulder to scratch his back. "You was just saying how it was a pity you didn't exactly know where this other Low County boy was."

"Exactly," agreed Slug. "And then, as if by magic, he appears out of the alley and knocks my old mate off his feet."

He leaned toward me. "What's it going to be, Low County boy?" he asked. "You ready to help us get to Mister Stonedyke?"

"I'm leaving Tennanbrau," I told him. "So even if I wanted to help you I couldn't. Besides, Angus

Stonedyke is still hundreds of miles away on the Far Tundra."

"He'll be back," Slug snapped. "Until then you can squat with us, in a little den we've set up not far from the Airship Terminus. We've got plenty of patience. We've waited long enough to get even."

"No thanks," I said. "I have to be on my way."

"Who said I was giving you a choice?" asked Slug.

"You can't force me to come with you," I said and tried to walk away.

Fidget stepped in front of me and blocked my path.

Slug made another grab for my collar, but this time I managed to dodge away from of him. I took a step back, wondering why the street suddenly seemed so deserted. As I did so Lullabeth's huge arms engulfed me in bone crushing bear hug. I kicked back at her with my heels, but she hardly seemed to notice.

"Want me to carry him all the way to the den?" asked Lullabeth. "I can. It would be dead easy. He's as light as a feather."

"You, there!" cried a woman's voice from across the street. "Unhand that boy at once."

Lifting me up Lullabeth turned around to face a young couple standing on the opposite side of the road. The bespectacled man was dressed in a long overcoat and in his right hand he was carrying a leather briefcase. The woman only stood as high as his chest, but it was the man who was cautiously hanging back as she confronted Slug and the others.

"I said unhand that boy," she repeated. "Put him down at once."

"What's it to you, lady?" demanded Slug, stepping out into the road.

"Yeah, what's it to you?" agreed Lullabeth. Her grip on me was so tight I was finding it difficult to draw breath. Fidget came sidling up behind Slug, scratching his bottom as he went.

"Are you going to do as I say?" asked the woman. "Or do I have to come over there and make sure you do?"

"I'd like to see you try," said Slug, strutting up and down the road.

"So would I," said Lullabeth, as Fidget followed Slug's footsteps, still vigorously scratching his bottom.

"Right," snapped the woman. "You've asked for it."

"I don't think you should do that," said her companion and made a feeble grab for her shoulder. She shrugged him off and came striding across the road. It was the determined stride and the confident manner in which she marched right up to Slug that made me realise exactly who she was.

Sergeant Caulder of the Imperial Sky Patrol.

"Good evening, Master Redcap," she said to me. "Are these hoodlums giving you some bother?"

"You know her?" Slug asked me.

Still clamped between Lullabeth's muscular arms I nodded.

"You sure know a lot of annoying people," Lullabeth growled in my ear.

219

"You do realise that this is the notorious criminal, Euan Redcap?" asked Slug. "We're only doing our duty as good citizens of Tennanbrau and apprehending him."

"Well, if that's the case, you're in luck," said Sergeant Caulder. "You can hand him over into my custody right now."

"Your custody?" cried Slug. "Why would we do that? There's probably a reward on his head."

"I'll tell you why you should do that," said the sergeant, producing a leather wallet that flipped open to reveal a silver warrant badge bearing the same dragon emblem I'd previously seen embroidered onto her jerkin. "I'm an officer of the ISC, that's why."

Fidget looked at the badge. "Looks like the real thing, Slug," he said and inserted a finger absently into his left nostril.

The colour drained from Slug's face. "Put him down, Lu," he said.

Lullabeth held stubbornly onto me. "Why should I?" she demanded.

"Because I just got out of the Pym Street Institute," said Slug. "And I've no intention of ever going back there."

Lullabeth dropped me to the pavement.

"I think you three had better be on your way," said Sergeant Caulder. "I'll take care of Master Redcap from this point on. And don't think that I don't know who you are."

Slug, Fidget and Lullabeth began backing away along the pavement. When they were a few yards away Slug called back to me. "Hey, Euan! Don't forget – when you see your mate Angus Stonedyke, tell him me and the old gang were asking after him."

He shook his fist at me.

Lullabeth cracked her knuckles,

Fidget scratched his neck and affected a grimace.

Then they all turned on their heels and ran.

"Am I in trouble?" I asked Sergeant Caulder, when they had disappeared from sight.

"What do you think?" she asked. "You are out at night, in clear breach of a court order that made you a ward of Professor Thaddeus Mayhew. You've been found in the company of a handful of known petty criminals. And, worst of all, I have a sneaking suspicion that you may have been attempting to abscond the city altogether."

Her companion crossed the road and joined us.

"Did you have to do that?" he demanded. "What if those ruffians had turned on you?"

"Well, I clearly wouldn't have received any assistance from you," snapped the sergeant.

"This is Ned Bendick," she said to me. "He works in accounts at ISC headquarters. He's been pestering me for a date for ages. But after tonight I don't think he'll be pestering me anymore."

The man blushed and bowed his head slightly.

"Are you going to arrest me?" I asked.

Sergeant Caulder regarded me with a green-eyed glare. "By rights I should. Do you know the trouble you could cause for Professor Mayhew by breaking the court order in this way?" she asked, as Ned Bendick hovered awkwardly behind her. "Had it not been for certain developments that have only come to light this evening I probably would have."

"Developments?" I asked. "Are they to do with Slug Martin and his friends?"

She shook her head. "Absolutely not," she replied. "But they do concern you. And they could make a considerable difference to the outcome of the case against both you and Captain Zachariah."

My heart began to pound. "In what way?"

"That's not for me to say," said the sergeant. "But I would suggest that if you were to make your way back to Professor Mayhew's apartments the news will most likely have arrived there by now."

"You're letting me go?" I couldn't quite believe my luck.

"So long as you give me to solemn promise that you'll make your way straight back to Professor Mayhew's apartments."

"I will," I said. "I promise."

I walked over to the alley, heading for the ladder.

"Euan!" she called after me.

I turned around to face her.

"Never forget that an ISC officer always gets her man," she warned. "So don't even think of leaving Tennanbrau before all of this is sorted out."

"I won't," I said and stepped onto the first rung of the ladder.

15. Certain Developments

It took me almost two hours to find my way back. I was distracted trying to figure out exactly what Sergeant Caulder meant by the term *certain developments*. I was also convinced that Slug and his gang might be hiding somewhere in the shadows, planning to ambush me. Every time I heard a slight noise up ahead of me on a bridge or a walkway I'd hang back, peering worriedly into the darkness. Sometimes I'd get so nervous that I'd retrace my steps and try to find another route and, in doing so, I would get myself even more lost.

Looking back I'm sure it was more by accident than design that I found myself at last in the corridor that led the doorway into Professor Mayhew's apartments. It took me by surprise when I pushed open the door and saw the Beehive swarming with people. It was well past midnight now, but they were all huddled into groups of two or three, excitedly chatting amongst themselves.

It seemed that nobody had noticed me slipping back in. Relieved at not having to face giving an explanation for where I had been I sneakily slipped the key back onto its hook. Seconds later my face blushed guiltily red when I felt a hand squeezing down on my shoulder. Convinced that I had been caught out I turned slowly around.

"Euan," said the professor, his grey flopping about his shoulder. "Did all this commotion wake you? Never mind, lad, this situation concerns you as

223

much as anyone. I'm going to convene the meeting in two minutes."

With that he rushed across the room to greet two more arrivals.

Heaving a sign of relief at my narrow escape I scanned the room. Hari was there, as was JJ. There were other familiar faces too. The people who updated the tallies on the dragon and airship charts on the wall. The young activists who handed out the fliers and gathered names on the petition. The only person who seemed to be missing was the lawyer, Daneby Carruthers. Nevertheless, the recent *certain developments* must have been pretty important for everyone to be summoned to at this late hour.

Then I saw Fenisnoor, standing alone in the corner. Her massive Ghibelline frame loomed over the rest of the people in the room. The craggy grey skin of her face was fixed into a scowl. Her black beady eyes were staring accusingly at me. From where she was standing it was obvious that she must have seen me as I crept in through the door. She knew and she clearly wanted me to know that she knew.

***

The meeting convened. Professor Mayhew was, as ever, seated at the head of the table. I watched where Fenisnoor sat chose to sit and made sure I sat three of four seats down from her at the same side of the table. That way she would not be able to either stare across at me.

I was sure that after the meeting she would tell Professor Mayhew what she had seen. I decided that I wasn't going to lie about what I had planned to do.

224

I only hoped that he would forgive me. It hadn't occurred to me till Sergeant Caulder pointed it out that he could get into serious trouble with the court if I ran away.

The Professor stood up and called the meeting to order. Everyone fell silent and turned their heads toward him. The beehive was so full that not everyone had a seat, but those who couldn't fit in around the table were sitting on desks and leaning against walls.

"I apologise for bringing you all here so early in the morning," said Professor Mayhew. "But there have been *certain developments* in the past few hours."

Those words again – *certain developments*.

"In order that this meeting is able to proceed on the principle that we all share the same information," continued the professor. "I am going call on Hari to give a brief outline."

The professor sat back down and Hari, who had been seated to his left, rose to her feet, flicking her ponytail back over her shoulder. "Three days ago, unbeknown to any of us," she told everyone, "Mister Grisling, the former coxswain of The Drunken Molly, arrived back in Tennanbrau, along with several other former crew members."

I sucked in a sharp inhalation of breath.

"If that's true," said someone toward the far end of the table, "it must surely bode well for Euan."

Hari nodded and carried on with her report. "Apparently Rusty Reeves helped Mrs Zachariah create a new balloon for *The Drunken Molly*. From a patchwork of old dragon wing membrane he had stored in one of sheds. But instead of immediately setting course back for Tennanbrau she has turned pirate."

Everyone began to mutter and exchange views on this revelation.

Professor Mayhew tapped the table for silence.

"She's recruited a crew made up of the few who remained loyal to her and any cutthroat or reprobate from the scavenger ships willing to join her," continued Hari. "Already they've carried out several raids on airships and stolen their cargo of Dragon Breath."

"But she can't possible hope to sell it on," said one of the young activists. "People would know that it was stolen. The Sky Corps would track her down."

"She doesn't plan to sell it, said Hari. "She plans to make bombs!"

"Bombs?"

"For what reasons?"

Again everyone started talking at once. Again the professor tapped the table for silence. After a moment everyone seemed to calm down enough for Hari to carry on.

"She plans to declare war on the Ghibelline tribes," she said. "She blames them for the way in which Captain Zachariah has changed."

"Outrageous," roared Fenisnoor, rising ferociously to her full height. "This cannot be allowed."

The Professor held up his hand. "I'm afraid there's more, my dear friend," he said and nodded to Hari to carry on.

"She also plans to bomb the nesting grounds of the dragons."

Remembering the nests full of eggs and young hatchling dragons that I had seen when I passed through the deep canyon in the Serrated Mountains on the back of the White Sow a tight knot twisted in my stomach. All around me the meeting had again descended into noisy chaos. It seemed that everyone was shouting at once.

"That's disgusting!"

"Is the woman mad?"

Hari looked at me. "I think we know the answer to that," she said. "Everyone now realises that Mrs Zachariah is quite unhinged. Even Emperor Julian has come to that conclusion. He has been in emergency session with his ministers all night."

Professor Mayhew rose to his feet again and called for order. "Thank you Hari," he said. "It is in fact a decision made within the past few hours by the Emperor and his ministers that caused me to call this emergency meeting. As a direct consequence of Mrs Zachariah's actions they have acknowledged finally that what we have been saying all along about the impact of dragons being hunted to extinction has some validity."

"Well maybe if he'd banned dragon hunting like we've been demanding he wouldn't have found himself in this situation in the first place," grumbled one of the young activists.

"An ISC patrol was dispatched patrol to intercept *The Drunken Molly*," the Professor continued.

"Told you," said the activists who had earlier mentioned the ISC.

"They were captured," said Hari. "Mrs Zachariah is holding them prisoner and threatening to kill them if anyone else tries to interfere with her plans."

"The Emperor, therefore, proposes to turn to Captain Zachariah for assistance," revealed Professor Mayhew. "He has offered a full pardon to both the captain and Euan if Nathaniel Zachariah can somehow persuade his wife to set her hostages free and surrender herself."

So this was the considerable difference to my case that Sergeant Caulder had referred to. Everyone seemed energized by the news. People started patting my back and ruffling my hair, as if it was somehow a foregone conclusion that the charges against me were about to be dropped.

But I wasn't so sure. I clearly remembered the last thing Mrs Zachariah had said to her crew following the captain's address to them outside of the compound at Forgsnur's Footprint. Words that made me doubt that the captain could hope to have any influence over her at all.

"Nathaniel Zachariah is dead!" she'd announced. "You hear me? Captain Zachariah, the greatest dragon hunter ever to fly an airship out of Tennanbrau, is dead."

"By now Daneby Carruthers will have collected Captain Zachariah from the Penal

Complex," Professor Mayhew was saying. "They should both be with us within the hour. I very much hope to persuade Captain Zachariah that his mission to rendezvous with his estranged wife should also be the maiden voyage The Hargmir."

***

Fenisnoor cornered me almost as soon as the meeting finished. My head was buzzing with all the news the Professor had relayed, but I was also burdened with guilt. Captain Zachariah was on his way to the Beehive. What was he going to say when he discovered that I had been planning to abandon him to face trial by himself? How would he react when he realised that after all that he had done for me was this how I had been intending to repay him?

Thoroughly ashamed of myself I wanted to go and hide in my room. I wove my way through the bustle of activists who were milling around, waiting for Daneby Caruthers and the captain to arrive. Then, just as I was reaching for the handle on the door that led into the Professor's private quarters, Fenisnoor loomed up in front of me and blocked my way with the bulk of her craggy grey form. "I think we have something we need to talk about, Euan," she said.

"Do we?" I asked, doing my utmost to avoid her beady-eyed stare.

"You know we do," she said, placing her huge hand on my shoulder and directing me to the kitchen area. I could tell how strong she was from the firmness of her grip. I knew that she meant me no actual harm. But I also knew she wouldn't let up till I told her everything. So I blurted it all out in one long, rambling sentence, hardly stopping to catch my breath. When I finished she looked down at me and the smile on her face was tinged with sadness. "I know what it's like to want to get back to your family," she said.

"Do you ever see your family?" I asked her.

She nodded and seemed to swallow back a sob.

"It is never the same though. They've changed in my time away. Things happen while I am gone that I have not been part of and therefore they have memories that I could never share. And I have changed much more than them. I've seen things and experienced things in my time away that are far beyond anything they can imagine."

"I'm sure I'll be able to settle in straight away when I get back home to the Low Counties," I assured her.

"Of course you will, Euan," she said. "But remember there are things that have happened with your family that you have been no part of. And there are places you have been, things you have seen and done, that are beyond their experience. You will not return to them as the same boy who left. Whether you like it or not, things will never entirely go back to the way they were."

I stood there in shocked silence. It struck how true this was. I had changed. Not only in what I had seen and done, but physically as well as in attitude. I knew that all the hard work as a fetcher had hardened the muscles on my arms and legs and I was positive I had grown an inch or two in height. I was also a lot more confident. I was no longer the

same Euan who was always getting in the
messing things up.

I was about ask Fenisnoor's advice on
way to handle all of this when the door ope
in walked Daneby Caruthers with
Zachariah at his side. The captain had his ho
but as soon as he entered he pulled it
revealing the scalds and burns that were so fa
to me.

Professor Mayhew stepped up to him
shook him warmly by the hand. But the others s
back, eying him with trepidation, as if he wer
wolf in the midst of a flock of sheep. In a sense
was just that. The most famous dragon hunter ev
to fly out of Tennanbrau City right there in tl
Headquarters of those who were formerly his mo
vocal opponents.

The captain saw me, dwarfed by Finisnoor's
mighty Ghibelline frame.

"Euan!" he called out. "Good to see you, lad.
Good to see you."

I ran to him and we hugged warmly.

"I'm glad Professor Mayhew managed to get
the court order before you had to spend a single
night at that awful institute," he said, his scalded
face creasing as his lips turned upwards to a warped
smile.

"Was it bad in the penal complex?" I asked
him.

He shrugged his shoulders in response.

"I'm out now," he said. "It looks as if the
charges against us may be dropped. That's all that
really matters."

"I suppose," I said. "Are you going to agree to what Emperor Julian asks?"

"I'm going to try," he replied. "But I'm not sure if I can exert any influence at all over Isabella's actions."

"Captain," interrupted Professor Mayhew. "I'd like you to take a look at the blueprints for my airship. It has a rigid balloon and does not rely in any way on Dragon Breath."

As the professor led Captain Zachariah across to the far wall I was about to follow them both when Hari caught me by the arm. "I think you need to catch up on some sleep, Euan," she told me. "You have to be in court first thing in the morning."

"In court?" I raised my eyebrows in surprise. "Captain Zachariah is going to agree to Emperor Julian's proposal. We're both going to be pardoned."

"There will still have to be a hearing," she replied. "The authorities at the Imperial Palace of Law and Judiciary are sticklers for due process. Even a pardon proposed by the Emperor himself requires their stamp of authority."

16. Back To Court

We entered the Imperial Palace along one of the raised walkways just after sunrise, Daneby Caruthers fidgeting nervously in the middle, Captain Zachariah to his left, myself to his right, Hari and Professor Mayhew bringing up the rear. There were huge, seething crowds of people to either side of the walkway being held back by lines of Imperial Foot Patrol officers, linked arm in arm.

To my surprise the citizens of Tennanbrau seemed to be cheering us rather than jeering us. The captain had his hood down but I could detect no negative reaction to his scalds and scars. I could hear people calling out my name. "Euan! Euan Redcap!" When I looked they were waving copies of JJ's picture paper. Hari leaned in and whispered in my ear.

"We've had the activists out distributing copies of The Tale of Euan Redcap since the early hours."

A woman who looked suspiciously like the woman who'd pulled down Captain Zachariah's hood the first time we'd entered the Palace caught my eye. "You poor child," she called out to me. "Taken from your Ma and Pa like that."

What a hypocrite, I thought.

Hassled through the main doors by a couple of officers we had to go through the same rigmarole of paper shuffling and signature signing before we were allowed to proceed once more. As we passed along the corridors and up and down the convoluted stairwells I realised that I wasn't afraid this time.

It was more than just the fact that the hearing had been described by both Hari and Daneby as a mere formality, it was that I really was no longer afraid. I had changed even more than Fenisnoor had suggested. Just as the boy who'd arrived in Tennanbrau aboard The Hawk's Cry was not the same boy that had been kidnapped from his home in the Low Counties the boy who now entered Courtroom 708 once more was no longer the naïve country boy, intimated and awed by these imposing surroundings.

As I took my seat next to Captain Zachariah I even managed to smile at Miss Belmarsh when the fierce prosecuting lawyer turned her head to scowl at us. Beside me the captain kept glancing up every time someone entered the gallery. It occurred to me that he might be looking for Gulliver Quat, in the hope this time that he may be able to mend some bridges.

Although the seats were filling up, members Friends of the Dragon side by side with citizens holding rolled up copies of The Tale of Euan Redcap, there was no sign of the one-legged captain. Just as I was about to say something to Captain Zachariah the clerk of the court appeared.

"All rise for His Infallible Worship, Barnabus Greyling!"

Everyone rose to their feet.

As before Judge Greyling entered from the doorway to the side of the grand desk, his ermine trimmed cape trailing behind him as he shuffled to his seat beneath the wood carved scales of justice and the unfurled set of crimson dragon wings. Once

234

he had installed his white wig on his head he took up the hand bell and clanged it twice, declaring in his boyish voice that the proceedings were duly open.

On his bidding we all sat back down.

Without further ceremony Judge Greyling turned his attention to the Prosecuting Lawyer. "I believe you are instructed to table a motion for amnesty against the two defendants, Miss Belmarsh."

Looking somewhat disappointed Miss Belmarsh nodded her head.

"Indeed, Your Infallible Worship. It is the will of the Emperor and the Grand Council of Ministers that all charges be dropped against Captain Nathaniel Zachariah and Master Euan Redcap."

The Judge squinted his eyes at her.

"You are sure that the petition to this court from the Emperor and his ministers is for all charges to charges."

Miss Belmarsh nodded grudgingly.

"All charges against both defendants to be dropped, Your Infallible Worship."

"And are there any conditions attached to this petition that are to be placed upon the defendants?"

"There are," replied Miss Belmarsh. "This amnesty is dependent on Captain Zachariah accepting a diplomatic mission to negotiate with his wife, Isabella Zachariah, the renegade airship captain, in order, not only to obtain the release of the members of an ISC patrol she currently holds hostage, but also to elicit the terms of Mrs Zachariah's own surrender."

Now Judge Greyling turned to Daneby Caruthers.

"Mr Carruthers? Is your client willing to accept this condition?"

"He most certainly is, Your Infallible Worship," replied Daneby, almost knocking off his own wig in his excitement.

Judge Greyling stroked his chin.

"And what of the boy?" he pondered, almost to himself.

"There are no conditions placed upon Master Redcap," replied Miss Belmarsh.

"I was rather thinking of his own wellbeing," said the Judge. "He hails from the Low Counties, does he not? His family are hill farmers, are they not? I would assume therefore that they are unlikely to have the wherewithal to charter an airship voyage to Tennanbrau. On that basis it could be a fortnight or more before anyone is able to come here to fetch him home. I think I would be failing in my duty if I simply dropped the charges against him without considering the potential impact of leaving a minor to his own devises in a strange city for such a length of time."

I saw a sly grin spread on Miss Belmarsh's narrow lips.

"If I may, Your Infallible Worship," she said, leaning slightly forward. "I feel sure that if you were of a mind to make an order for temporary custody our good friend Chadwell Gleniss would be able to provide suitable board and lodgings for Mr Redcap at the Pym Street Institute."

I couldn't believe it. Suddenly all my confidence seemed to drain away from me.

"No!" I wailed, almost bursting into tears. "You can't do that! I won't go!"

Judge Greyling picked up his bell and clanged it angrily.

"The defendant will be silent." His face flushed furiously red. "Silent, you hear? One more outburst and I shall hold you in contempt."

Fighting down my indignation I bowed my head and bit my lip. Then I saw Hari crouching low as she approached Daneby and began whispering animatedly into his ear. After a moment Daneby straightened his wig and addressed the Judge.

"I have an alternative proposal for you to consider, Your Infallible Worship," he said.

Judge Greyling placed the bell back down on his desktop.

"Proceed, Mr Caruthers."

"There's a merchant," said Daneby. "A lanoline merchant. He was due to depart Tennanbrau this morning and travel to the Low Counties by horse and cart. If you would be so gracious as to grant him temporary custody as an alternative he would gladly ensure that Master Redcap is delivered safely back to his parents."

"And this merchant is of good character?" asked the Judge.

Daneby nodded his head.

"He is, Your Infallible Worship."

"And his name? The name of this benevolent lanoline merchant?"

"Andrew Highbrae," replied Daneby.

"And is he here?" asked Judge Greyling. "Is Andrew Highbrae here to vouch for himself?"

The clerk leapt to her feet.

"Andrew Highbrae? If Mister Andrew Highbrae is in this Courtroom will he please rise to his feet and make himself known to His Infallible Worship, Judge Barnabus Greyling?"

Up in the gallery there came a shuffling of a chair as Highbrae clambered to his feet, twisting his cloth cap nervously between his hands. Judge Greyling squinted up at him. "Step closer to the railing so that I can see you properly," he called up. Andrew Highbrae stepped up to the railing and twisted his cap some more.

"You are the lanoline merchant, Andrew Highbrae."

"Yes, Your Infallible Worship."

Judge Greyling picked up his magnifying glass and scrutinised him.

"And you are about to embark on a journey to the Low Counties."

"To sell my wares, Your Infallible Worship."

"And you would willing take this lad with you and see to it he comes to no harm?"

"I would, Your Infallible Worship."

"And you would take good care of him until he was rightfully returned to his parents?"

"I most certainly would, Your Infallible Worship."

"And what sort of a fee would you ask for providing this service to the court?"

Andrew Highbrae seemed taken aback.

"Fee, Your Infallible Worship? I would not expect any fee. I would take the lad for nothing. Why would anyone expect a fee for doing a good deed?"

Judge Greyling turned back to Miss Belmarsh.

"Well that certainly settles matters for me," he said. "Chadwell Glennis earns quite a penny from the decisions passed in the courtrooms of the Imperial Palace. If this gentleman is prepared to the job for nothing and save some poor hill farmer the trouble of travelling all the way to Tennanbrau, then I think that is a sensible solution all round."

"If His Infallible Worship so wishes," conceded Miss Belmarsh, her face seething.

Judge Greyling rang his bell.

"Have it entered into the records that I have endorsed the recommendation of the Emperor and the Grand Council of Ministers that an amnesty be granted in this case. In exchange the defendant, Nathaniel Zachariah, will embark upon a diplomatic mission with the aim of intervening in the unlawful activities of his wife Isabella Zachariah. Meanwhile the defendant Euan Redcap will be handed over to the temporary custody of Mr Andrew Highbrae, who, in turn, will deliver the boy to his parents. On this basis all charges against the defendants are hereby dropped and I declare this case now officially closed."

A loud cheer echoed through the courtroom.

Daneby turned to shake our hands.

Hari rushed over and squashed me in a huge hug.

17. A Wagon Ride

I sat at the back of Andrew Highbrae's wagon, listening to the clink-clink-clink of the lanoline bottles rattling in their crates in time with the forward motion of the wheels. Although we had been travelling for more than half a day I could clearly still see the tenement towers and tall smoking chimneys of Tennanbrau away in the distance. I had specifically asked Mr Highbrae if I could ride at the back for this very purpose.

"Just till the city is out of site," I'd pleaded. "Then I'll come up front and ride with you."

"Suit yourself, lad," he'd said to me. "But I warn you, on a clear day you can see parts of Tennanbrau from as far away as the border to the Low Counties. That's a long time to sit at the back. It's far more comfortable up front. I've got cushions and everything."

"Just till sunset on the first day then," I'd suggested. "Then I promise I'll ride up front the rest of the way."

What I could see on the endlessly winding road that led north was such a contrast to what I had been able to see looking down from the gondola of The Hawk's Cry on my arrival. From The Hawk's Cry I had been able in one glance to observe the whole vista of townships and open countryside that surrounded Tennanbrau.

At road level the only evidence of the townships was the listing road-signs we passed every now and then on the grassy verge, bearing this or that name and pointing in the direction of narrow side roads. Often tall and unkempt hedgerows obscured the fields and woodlands that skirted the road and I could see nothing at all of my immediate surroundings, other than the receding wheels ruts the wagon had made in the mud.

Looking up though, what a sight there was to see. Up there airships of all shapes and sizes and designs were ploughing through the clouds - dragon hunters, scavenger ships, commercial vessels, each one either bound for or departing the Airship Terminus. The sky's the place to be and an airship is the way to travel, I found myself thinking. With the cold wind blowing against your face and everything as far as the horizon clear and visible.

Then I thought of all of the dragon breath stolen away to make airship travel possible and a shudder of guilt came over me. It was evident from the fact that we had hardly passed anyone else travelling in either direction on the road that many people now relied heavily on airships for their transportation needs, whether goods or passengers. As if to emphasise the point the wagon jerked heavily as its wheels hit a large pothole in the badly maintained road surface. Had this been a well-used route the holes would surely have been filled in and flattened down.

"You all right, lad?" Mr Highbrae called back. "You didn't fall off did you?"

"I'm fine," I called back – but I felt as if my bones had been well and truly rattled.

Then, just as I was settling myself, something came roaring past the tall row of bushes to the left of the road, hooting and screaming, causing the ground to tremble. For a moment I thought that a ferocious dragon had swooped down from the skies into one of the fields. Then I saw the trail of grey smoke that traced the canopy of the bushes and I remembered the train I had seen when looking down from The Hawk's Cry.

I wondered if trains might also rely in some part on Dragon Breath for their locomotion. It wouldn't have surprised me. As Captain Zachariah and indeed the members Friends of the Dragon had explained to me so much of what people took for granted relied on Dragon Breath that there would be a calamity if dragons ever became extinct.

That was why Professor Mayhew was so keen to offer the use of his dirigible to transport Captain Zachariah to the Far Tundra. He wanted to gather hard evidence of the declining numbers of dragons and confront Emperor Julian and his ministers with the real consequences of the dragon hunting trade being allowed to continue unabated. By now they would all be loading up The Hargmir with goods and supplies, ready for their planned departure.

A little lump caught in my throat.

Although I wasn't too sad to finally be leaving Tennanbrau, I was having difficulty in coming to grips with parting from all of my newfound friends. I was supposed to have spent the previous night sleeping in my room in Professor Mayhew's apartments, but I had crept on tiptoe to listen at the door to the Beehive as plans were made for the expedition to the Far Tundra.

It seemed that as well as Hari and several of the young activists Captain Zachariah had already struck up a deal to recruit Coxswain Grisling and the crewmen who had returned to Tennanbrau with him. "It takes more than just enthusiasm and commitment to crew an airship," I heard the captain tell the others. "We're going to need experienced hands. The Drunken Molly was one of the fastest and most agile airships ever to take to the skies – no-one can manoeuvre an airship better than Hubert Grisling."

JJ was going as well. Another deal had been struck with one of Tennanbrau's daily newspapers. Hari was going to send back regular descriptive accounts of everything that happened on the expedition, including, ultimately, a fly on the wall piece about the negotiations with Mrs Zachariah. JJ was going to provide illustrations for each piece. Both hoped to try and subtly put across the message about the disastrous long-term consequences of dragon hunting.

Fenisnoor, of course, would part of the team. She sounded excited, thumping heavily back and forth across the Beehive floor, gushing about how great it would be to feel the mossy floor of the tundra beneath her feet and how she was going to look up old relatives in the tunnels beneath the Serrated Mountains. Sometime grunting angrily about how outrageous it was for Mrs Zachariah to be planning to declare war on her kin.

Lastly there was mention in several of the conversations of sergeant Caulder and the members of her sky patrol. On Emperor Julian's instance they would be accompanying the professor's dirigible on its journey. Their orders were to take Mrs Zachariah and her outlaw crew into custody, voluntarily if Captain Zachariah succeeded in persuading her to surrender – by force if he didn't.

I had been so enthralled by it all that when I finally did creep back into bed I found it impossible to sleep. I kept imagining what it would be like to go with them on the expedition. I was sure they would need a fetcher onboard The Hargmir and surely there was no better fetcher than me. I understood that they all had my best interests at heart and that getting me back home was the most important consideration – but it kind of upset me that no one had even suggested, even as a joke, that I might come along.

The parting had been the worst. I had already been dressed when Hari had knocked on my door and told me it was time for her to take me to meet Mr Highbrae at the North Gate. One by one I shook their hands and said my goodbyes, some of the activists still working on projects in the Beehive, followed by JJ, Daneby Caruthers, Fenisnoor and Professor Mayhew. Last but not least, Captain Zachariah, his spoilt face contorting as he forced a smile and hugged me.

"One day, Euan," he said. "You'll look out of the window of your parents' cottage and you'll see the gondola The Drunken Molly descending through the clouds and it'll be me come to pay you that visit I promised."

"And I'll tell my Ma to get the rabbit stew on the boil," I promised him.

When Hari brought me to Mr Highbrae she cried when she kissed my cheek.

"I'm going to miss you," she sobbed. "Tell that big sister of yours that I took good care of you."

"I will," I called after her, stifling my own tears as she climbed up a ladder and dashed along a walkway on the side of a nearby building.

Just remembering almost had me crying again. I blinked my eyes rapidly and turned my thoughts to my homecoming. If Mr Highbrae's estimation was correct I was going to be home just in time for my thirteenth birthday. I had already decided that I was going to insist that it was a double celebration with Isla - to make up for what had happened on her own birthday.

I'd ask Ma to bake us a cake and Pa to catch a rabbit in one of his snares. Me and Isla would go down to the glen to pick mushrooms for the celebration stew and I'd take of my sock and shoes and help her to pick out the best caps. Ma, Pa and Isla would be surprised at how much I had changed in my time away.

I planned to start helping around the place and I knew I wouldn't get in the way and mess things up anymore. I would use my skills at a fetcher to figure out where everything in the cottage and the farm was kept and then when anyone needed anything they would just have to ask me and I would fetch it in the blink of an eye.

When the mist came down in the hills I would go with Pa to herd the sheep safely down and I wouldn't get lost and have him waste his time looking for me. I had found my way back to the

Beehive through all the convoluted bridges and stairways of Tennanbrau, had I not? Every morning when I woke up I promised myself that I would look out of my window to see if I could catch site of The Drunken Molly breaking through the clouds.

The wagon trundled past another listing sign at the side of the road. The name read Pennington Vale. At first I hardly paid it any attention. Then I realised with a start that I knew that name. It was the township where The Hargmir sat ready in its hangar.

"Stop!" I yelled. "Stop right now!"

I heard Mr Highbrae pulling his horse to a halt. As soon as the wagon stopped I jumped down onto the muddy road. Mr Highbrae came toddling round to the back, his cap for once still on his head.

"You had enough?" he asked. "You want to come up front now?"

"How far is to Pennington Vale," I asked him.

He removed his cap and scratched his head.

"About five miles, I would reckon," he said.

As far as I could remember it was nearly two miles from my cottage to the village school. Two miles there and two miles back. I used to walk almost four miles every day of my life. Five miles wasn't so far. I could easily get there before sunset.

"I can't go with you," I told him. "I can't go home yet. Not when Captain Zachariah still needs the services of a good fetcher."

"But I promised to see you home safely," he said. "What am I going to tell your parents?"

I reached inside my jacket and took out the letter and the copy of The Tale of Euan Redcap that

246

I had folded away in there. "Give them this," I told them. "Tell them that's what happened to me so far. Tell them my story isn't ended yet and I won't be back till it is."

Mr Highbrae looked down at the fat envelope containing the letter and the picture paper. "I don't suppose I can stop you if you're really that determined. If I grabbed you now and bundled you into the back of the wagon, you'd only run away the first chance you got."

I nodded my head and forced my face into a stern expression.

"I'm not happy about this," he said. "Not happy at all."

"I'll make sure everyone knows it wasn't your fault that I didn't come with you," I assured him and began walking along the track that led from the main road to Pennington Vale.

"I could take you there," Mr Highbrae suggested. "It wouldn't be that much of a detour."

"You've done enough," I called back to him. "Besides, I'm not afraid!"

Part Three
Return to the Far Tundra

1. The Stowaway

I pressed my eye to the hole in the hull where a metal rivet had fallen out and watched the green hills below as *The Hargmir* passed over the far reaches of the Low Counties. I could see the remnants of a morning mist clinging to the nearest hillside and mingling with the smoke billowing from the fat chimney of a hill farmer's stone cottage. Amongst the swirls of mist and smoke I could just make out the forms of black-faced sheep grazing on the dew-covered grass.

We were miles and miles away from my home and soon the Low Counties would be far behind us. I felt a little twinge of guilt at what I had done. Somewhere on a winding road Archibald Highbrae was geeing on his horse as it pulled along his wagon full of chinking bottle of lanoline.

I felt so guilty knowing that I was going to disappoint my parents by handing over a letter instead of delivering me back to them in person. My own headstrong actions that had robbed me of the homecoming I had so longed for. My confused feeling were made all the worse by the fact that things hadn't gone quite the way I had planned them.

After I left Mr Highbrae at the crossroads it wasn't too long before the doubts started to eat away at me. At first I had been in high spirits, looking forward to being reunited with all my old friends, and imagining the captain taking me in a huge, welcoming hug when I offered my services as his fetcher.

Then it started to occur to me that things might not turn out that way at all. Professor Mayhew had gone to a lot of trouble to make the arrangements with Mr Highbrae for my safe transportation back to the Low Counties and the last time I'd spoken to him Captain Zachariah had been very insistent that returning to my parents was the right thing to do.

As for sergeant Caulder, I knew she was a stickler for the law and I couldn't see her being happy at all at me trying to join an airship crew without my parents' consent. Fenisnoor, who was about to embark on her own journey back home, wasn't likely to be all that supportive of my decision. I looked back along the road and wondered how long it would take me to catch up with the plodding pace of Mr Highbrae's slow rolling wagon.

I stood there for a long time, hesitating, cursing myself for being the same old Euan, messing things up by jumping straight in without even bothering to think about the consequences of my actions. I was just about to turn back when I had another change of heart.

If I pushed on to Pennington Vale what could be the worst that could happen? It was going to be almost nightfall by the time I arrived. I was pretty sure they wouldn't send me back in the dark. And if they waited till the following day it would be too late for me to catch up with Mr Highbrae. They surely wouldn't let me set out on my own.

In my mind I began to form an account of what I thought would happen. They would obviously all agree that it was not right for me to join with them on their mission to the Far Tundra. So the Professor Mayhew would ask Captain Zachariah to take a small detour to the region of the Low Counties where my parents lived. The airship would hover high above our little cottage and I would ride down to the ground on the back of sergeant Caulder's peddle-driven craft. I would be home a lot quicker that if I had stayed with Mr Highbrae and in more stylish manner than in an old rickety wagon.

I hurried on along the road, somehow convinced now that this was exactly what would happen, while at the same time disappointed that my dream of accompanying them to the tundra and catching one more glimpse of the magnificent White Sow would not come true.

When I felt myself flagging and wanted to stop for a rest I would think about Illagnor and the Ghibelline and our long trek across the tundra from the Serrated Mountains to the crater at Forgsnur's Footprint. This would somehow give me the energy boost I needed to push on.

The sun was setting when I arrived at the outskirts of Pennington.

It wasn't hard to find out where the hangar in which Professor Mayhew's prototype airship was housed. The Hargmir with its odd design and its balloon that relied on natural gas, rather than Dragon Breath for its buoyancy was the talk of the town. Claiming to be the son of a crewmember I was directed to a nearby heath where the hanger was located.

On my approach the huge construct of the hanger was easily visible under the glow of the rising moon. I began to speculate on the size of The Hargmir. Maybe twice that of the Drunken Molly was my best guess. I felt a flutter of excitement in my belly. It was then that I changed my mind yet again. I felt suddenly sure that it wasn't yet time for me to go home.

Although I missed my family, in my heart I knew that somehow it was my destiny to return to the Far Tundra onboard The Hargmir. To be there to witness what happened when the captain confronted Mrs Zachariah and tried to negotiate her surrender. To be part of the mission by the Friends of the Dragon to somehow gather enough data to convince everyone in Tennanbrau that the taking of Dragon Breath could drive these wonderful creatures towards extinction.

So I decided in that instant that I would become a stowaway. That I would hide myself somewhere and not reveal myself to anyone until Professor Mayhew's airship was so far from the Low Counties that it would be impractical to turn back. I suppose I was being selfish, just thinking about what I wanted and not how my actions might possibly impact on their mission.

But to me, at that moment, it sounded like a wonderful plan.

I slept that night in an outhouse near the airship hangar and in the morning when some carts turned up with crates of supplies I took my chance to hide inside one of the crates and have myself smuggled onboard.

I lived like a mouse, hiding in the shadows whenever a member of the crew came down into the hold to collect supplies, sneaking out when it was dark to try and scavenge things to eat and drink. I slept with the hum of the airship's engines in my ears and the thrum of her turbines at my back. My face became dirty and my red hair tousled.

On my nocturnal forays I would try to commit the layout of the hold to memory, making a mental map of where everything was to be found and what the quickest route to get to it would be. I was preparing myself for the day that I would once more become Captain Zachariah's fetcher.

I could see that this was going to present the biggest challenge I had faced yet. Because I had been smuggled onboard and having only previously seen blueprints of *The Hargmir* on the wall of the Beehive back in Tennanbrau I was not at all familiar with the layout up on deck.

Wandering around down there at night the hull seemed far more complicated than the deep single compartment that made up the belly of the Drunken Molly or the far more compact area beneath the deck of the Hawk's Cry. The Hargmir's interior was divided into six inter-joining compartments and each seemed designed for a different purpose. Nevertheless I persevered and did my best to construct my mental map.

All the time I was counting down the days till I would be able to reveal myself. Regularly returning to area where I was now, pressing my eye against the rivet hole to look down and monitor our progress, rehearsing under my breath the little speech I intended to make when I finally revealed my presence to Captain Zachariah and the others.

**

Three more days passed by before I decided it was finally time to come out of hiding. By then the crew had started to notice that items of food were going missing. They thought that there was really a mouse in the hold. Hidden away I'd heard them arguing as they set traps. "There's no way a little mouse could carry away the amount of stuff that's gone missing," one of them had said. "I'll wager it's a rat. A big, fat hairy one at that."

I had almost laughed out loud, thinking about what a surprise he would get when he found out his big fat rat was nothing more than a red-haired boy from the Low Counties.

But when I snuck out that night I found that it was no laughing matter. Not only did I have to walk with extreme caution to avoid setting off the traps that were littered all over the floor but I founds that all the compartments where the crates foodstuffs were stored had been firmly locked and bolted.

So it was hunger that forced my hand.

I waited till darkness fell on the third day. I didn't want to risk coming out in daylight in case someone saw me and grabbed hold of me. I wanted to give myself up rather than face the embarrassment of being caught. Through the rivet hole I watched as the swirl of the clouds turned from sunset pink to gloomy grey. When I was sure that night had fallen I tiptoed past the traps and started making my way up the wooden stairway that led to the deck of the gondola. I was almost seen by crewmember checking and tightening the wires that attached the gondola. I ducked low on the ladder and waited till he had finished his rounds.

The first thing I noticed when I emerged through the hatch was that the deck area of The Hargmir was far narrower than that of either *The Drunken Molly* or *The Hawk's Cry*. But it was also much, much longer from one end to the other. I tried to imagine how tiring it would be to run that length back and forth all day as a fetcher.

When I looked up I could see that the balloon was also long and narrow, rather than the fat oval shape I had become accustomed to and the darkly glistening material from which the balloon was constructed was definitely not dragon wing membrane.

The next thing I became aware of was the smell of food. I have no idea what it was that the ship's cook had made that night. But in my hungry state it smelled to me like the most delicious meal ever concocted. I inhaled deeply through my nostrils and felt my empty belly rumble as my mouth began to drool.

I began to hear voices, the click of cutlery and the chink of crockery. Crouching low I eased my way along the deck. At the far end of the gondola I could see the silhouettes of everyone congregated around a huge table that was almost as big as the table they used to congregate around in the Beehive.

As they ate they were deep in discussion about something. Although I was still not close enough to make out anyone's face I found that I was able to recognise certain voices. I stood with my hand on the railings of the gondola, shivering slightly as cloud vapour blew back in my face, the thrum of the airship engine vibrating beneath my feet.

JJ was speaking.

"I've started work on some rough sketches of the White Sow based on descriptions that Nathaniel has given me."

"My words can never do her justice," said Captain Zachariah. "You need to see her in the flesh. Snow white scales and all."

"There are dragon paintings that my ancestors did on the walls of the caverns deep beneath the Serrated Mountains," said Fenisnoor. "I'll show you. I'm sure it will provide greater inspiration."

I had been in the caverns beneath the Serrated Mountains. I didn't recall seeing any dragon paintings. But then again the honeycomb of tunnels and caverns was so deep and extensive that I supposed that I had only ever seen a very small part.

"I will get my old friend Illagnor to try and help you get as close to the White Sow's lair as might be possible without placing you at risk," Captain Zachariah was saying.

"I don't want just to do sketches," said JJ. "I want to do oil paintings. I want them to be the best work I've ever done. I want people back in Tennanbrau to appreciate the true beauty of the dragon, especially that of the White Sow."

"We'll put on an exhibition of your paintings," interjected Professor Mayhew. "We will change a small entry fee to raise funds for our cause."

"We should launch the exhibition on the exact same night at the Annual Dragon Hunter's Ball," suggested Hari. "That would cause quite a stir."

Now sergeant Caulder chipped in.

"So long as it doesn't lead to any unrest. My colleagues in the ground Constabulary have quite enough on their hands.

"Well, well, well. If it isn't Euan Redcap in the flesh."

This voice came from behind me. It seemed vaguely familiar - but not immediately recognisable. I swung around, firmly believing I had been caught and the game was up.

I found myself momentarily confused by the scruffy looking boy who was standing before me. The last time I'd encountered him dark night on a street in Tennanbrau City. "What are you doing here?" I asked.

"I might ask you the same question," replied Fidget, scratching the flaky skin on his neck. "The last I heard you was headed back to the Low Counties."

I wondered if maybe Professor Mayhew had taken pity on him and offered him a job so he could make a fresh start. It would be just the sort of thing that the Professor might do. But what sort of job could he have offered to someone like Fidget who had no experience whatsoever of working on board an airship.

Then it hit me. There was only one possible position for someone who hadn't yet gained his air legs, the position of ship's Fetcher. I felt myself bristle. That was supposed to be my job.

Then I noticed the rope that was tied around his chest. My eyes traced the route of the rope up past The Hargmir's long balloon into the dark sky above. Fidget wasn't part of the crew at all. He had been lowered down onto the deck. This wasn't right. Something fishy was going on here. Captain Zachariah and the others were so engrossed in their conversation that there was no chance of them realising what was going on. I was just about to yell out a warning when I saw Fidget nodding his head as if signalling to someone else who had managed to creep up behind me.

Before I knew it there was a hand clamped over my mouth. Another hand swiftly drew something around my waist. I heard the sound of two metal clips clamping together. The thing around my waist was pulled so tight that the air was knocked out of me. The hand over my face squeezed tighter too. Its owner was digging sharp fingernails into my cheek so that I couldn't call for help.

I saw Fidget yank twice on his rope. In the blink of an eye he was lifted from the deck to ascend skyward. I tried to shake free from my captor's grip, but I felt him yank twice on his own rope. The next thing I knew we were rising up so rapidly that I hardly had time to look down at *The Hargmir* before it disappeared beneath the clouds.

2. Kidnapped Again

I couldn't believe that I was being kidnapped again.

But that, it seemed, was exactly what was happening.

I quickly realised that the worst thing I could do was to struggle. My captor had his hand clamped over my mouth. The other was wrapped around my chest and whatever he had strapped around my belly was still pulled tight. We were hundreds of feet above the ground. If I struggled and he let go of the strap I would go plummeting straight down.

I looked up and saw the bevelled wooden underbelly of a dragon hunter's airship. The trap door through which the bait would be dangled during a dragon hunt was open and immediately I had a terrible flashback to that dreadful day when Mrs Zachariah ordered her crew to lower me down on a rope from *The Drunken Molly* as bait to lure the White Sow.

Above me I saw Fidget hauled through the trapdoor and moments later we were likewise pulled into the hold of the airship. I found myself lying on top of him as he released his grip on my mouth. As soon as he unbuckled the strap I scrambled to my feet. Amongst the flickering glow of dozens of storm lamps I found myself surrounded by a filthy looking gaggle of dragon hunters, greasy faced and unshaven. Fidget stood amongst them, untying the rope around his chest, looking perfectly at home. Then I saw another face that I recognised.

Lullabeth, the second member of Slug Martin's gang.

When she saw me, she cracked her knuckles. "I know that one," she told the crew. "I could easily beat him in a fight."

Given that Fidget and Lullabeth were both there it didn't take a genius to work out who had grabbed me. I turned round and there he was, large as life, black hair as spiky as ever. Slug Martin.

"Euan," he said. "We really have to stop meeting like this."

"Euan?" asked one of the crew.

"I think we hit the jackpot, lads," said Slug. "This is none other than Euan Redcap, Nathaniel Zachariah's partner in crime."

"Get him up on deck," snarled another of the crew. "The captain is going to want to see this."

Slug grabbed me by one wrist, Lullabeth by the other. With Fidget at my back and the rest of the crew following behind I was pushed and manhandled onto the deck. More of the crew surrounded me, some of them holding lamps out before them to get a better look at my face.

It was like I was reliving the day I'd been hauled up onto the deck of *The Drunken Molly* all over again. I looked up, half expecting to see that the gondola was dangling from a crimson red balloon, and heaved a half-hearted sigh of relief when I saw that this balloon was actually emerald green.

Then I remembered that Illagnor and the Ghibelline had taken *The Drunken Molly's* deflated balloon with them when they fled back to the tundra. This was supposed to have been a precaution to prevent Mrs Zachariah and her crew following when Captain Zachariah and I made our escape. But it was one of the actions on the day that had consequently gotten us into all sorts of trouble with the authorities in Tennanbrau.

With the crew pushing and shoving all around me I began to wonder if I might be back onboard the *Molly,* held aloft by a dragon wing balloon of a completely different hue.

"Make way for the captain," came a voice to the back of the crowd.

The crewmembers began to part, leaving a sizeable gap. Slug stood next to me, hand wound tightly into the shoulder of my shirt, grinning smugly. Fidget scratched his neck. Lullabeth cracked her fat knuckles. I was curious as to how the three of them came to be part of a dragon hunting crew. Then, over the heads of the crew, I saw the bobbing approach of a captain's hat. I held my breath, expecting at any minute to come face to face once more with the twitching features and dancing braids of Mrs Zachariah.

But when the captain stepped into the clearing my heart almost leapt into my mouth. It was a man. He sported a huge bushy beard. His left leg was missing, replaced by a stump made from sun bleached dragon bone. I knew who he was immediately. I had last seen him in the public gallery of the Court Room at the Imperial Palace of Justice during the preliminary hearing on the changes laid against Captain Zachariah and myself.

It was none other than Gulliver Quat, the captain's former captain.

"Is this all you fetched for me?" he asked, hobbling towards Slug. "I wanted you to knobble someone who could tell me something of interest. Not some snotty fetcher."

The grin fell from Slug's face. He twisted his hand deeper into my shirt. "This isn't just some snotty kid," he said. "This is Euan Redcap."

Quat scratched his beard and narrowed his eyes as he leaned in to examine me.

"If anyone is going to have information it's going to be Euan Redcap," said Slug. "The notorious confederate of Nathaniel Zachariah."

Quat's bushy eyebrows arched upwards. I could see that he now realised exactly who I was. A wide grin spread beneath his beard. "Is that right, boy?" he asked. "Do you have information you'd like to pass on to Uncle Gul?"

"I've no idea what information you're looking for," I spat. "But even if I did, I wouldn't tell you."

"Well, that's just downright rude," said Quat.

He turned to his men. "What do you say, lads? We offer a poor Low County boy the hospitality of our ship and all we get back is rudeness."

"Shame," chorused some of the men, while others laughed.

Quat leaned back in and stared me in the eye. "All I want is a teeny bit of information, son," he said, holding his thumb and forefinger slightly apart. "I just want to know what my old friend Nathaniel knows about the current whereabouts of his wife, that's all."

"I don't know what you think you're planning," I said, as Slug held me tight. "But Captain Zachariah is going to negotiate her surrender and hand her over to the custody of the Imperial Sky Patrol."

Quat threw his head back and roared with laughter. "Surrender?" he bellowed. "There will be no surrender. Isabella Zachariah is going to join forces with me, my boy. And together we are going to bring an end to the damned White Sow."

"What is it about you dragon hunters?" I yelled back. "Why are you all so obsessed with killing the White Sow?"

"Because of what she's done," replied Quat, his red face deepening to an almost purple shade. "She destroyed my ship and took my leg. She burned Nathaniel beyond recognition and robbed him of his handsome looks. She's turned his head and caused him to join forces with those cowardly Friends of the Dragon. She's driven poor Isabella almost to the brink of insanity. She near destroyed *The Drunken Molly*. Need I say more? She's a monster, son, and monsters deserve to be hunted down."

He turned to his men again. "What do monsters deserve, lads?"

"To be hunted down," came the cacophonous reply.

Quat looked me in the eye once more. "So c'mon, boy," he said. "Tell me what I need to know. Tell me in what direction my coxswain needs to set my ship in order to find Isabella Zachariah."

"I've no idea," I said. "That's the absolute truth."

262

I recounted how I had stowed away onboard *The Hargmir* and how no one had known I was hiding in the hold. And how, as a consequence of my kidnap, I couldn't give Captain Quat even the slightest clue as to where they might be heading.

Quat started grinding his teeth. He turned to Slug. "Waste of time and effort," he grunted. "I should have known it was a mistake to give you three reprobates a chance."

He went into a rant, which largely answered my questions about how Slug and the others came to be onboard. "Pym Street wasn't punishment enough for what you tried to do. Attempting to rob the charity money from the Dragon Hunter's Ball was an absolute disgrace. So, I brought you onto my ship to let you make amends properly. I trusted you with a mission to bring me back information. And you've let me down. You'll be peeling spuds and slopping out the latrines for the rest of the voyage."

He began angrily barging his way back through the crowd of crewmen. Lullabeth clenched a fist and shook it menacingly me. Fidget traced his finger along the front of his neck in slashing movement. "Wait," said Slug, hurriedly unravelling his hand from my shirt. "He does know something, captain. Something really important just occurred to me."

Quat pivoted around on his dragon bone leg and hobbled right up to Slug. "This had better be good."

From inside his jacket Slug produced a rather tattered looking copy of *'The Tale of Euan Redcap'*.

"A child's picture paper?" snarled Quat. "Is this some sort of a joke?"

"It's no joke," insisted Slug, flicking through the pages till he came to JJ's illustration depicting myself riding on the back of the White Sow and passing through the high walled canyon where the dragons made their nests.

He held it up to show Quat. "See for yourself," he said.

Quat scratched his beard and furrowed his brow, seeming somewhat unsure as to what Slug was asking him to look at.

"He knows, captain," said Slug. "Euan Redcap knows exactly where to find the lair of the White Sow!"

3. No Trail Left Behind Me

Quat would simply not listen when I tried to insist that I'd never be able to remember where the canyon that led to the White Sow's lair was. He kept jabbing his finger forcefully against the illustration on the page. "This proves otherwise," he insisted.

"I've no idea!" I yelled at him. "I can't remember."

"You'll remember, lad," he said. "We'll take you all around the Serrated Mountains. Up and down and over and through and when you see that one particular canyon you'll know. And we'll lay bait at the cavern mouth to lure the Sow out. We'll lasso her with ropes from my canons and finish her once and for all. And Isabella Zachariah will be there to share in the glory that is rightfully hers."

With that he folded the picture paper into his pocket and hobbled off.

I slept the rest of that night near the area where Slug and his gang bunked down. In the morning I was set to work in the galley. It seemed that my previous experience as fetcher counted for nothing with Quat. His ship already boasted no less than three, somewhat lazy and, in my view wholly incompetent, fetchers.

Quat's old airship, *The Cerulean Beauty,* had been destroyed beyond repair in its fateful encounter with the White Sow. His new ship was called *Beauty's Daughter*. I estimated that she was of similar size and dimensions to those of *The*

Drunken Molly. I had no doubt that it would have only taken me a day at most to memorise her lay out and to make my mental map of where to find anything I might ever be asked to fetch.

I had no idea how long it had been since *Beauty's Daughter* left the airship terminus in Tennanbrau but it seemed to me that Slug and his two cohorts hadn't learned a thing in that time. If someone asked for something to be fetched, they would take ages to locate it and nine times out of ten one of them would come back with the wrong thing. Slug and Fidget seemed bicker endless between themselves. Lullabeth was surly, threatening to bash any of the crew who told her off for fetching the wrong thing.

I might have found the whole situation quite amusing had working in the galley not been such a dreadful and demoralising experience. On *The Drunken Molly* I had fetched stuff for Smudger, bags of onions and potatoes and such. I had witnessed how skilled he was at making something tasty out of the most basic and frugal of ingredients.

Bosworth, Quat's cook, was bad tempered and as inept as the ship's trio of fetchers. I never once saw him wash his hands. He regularly had a smoking pipe clamped between his teeth and would tap out the old embers on to the same grungy board he used for chopping meat and vegetables. He'd lick his big wooden spoon, slobbering all over it, before he dipped it back in to stir his stew pot. He seemed incapable of making anything without burning it and it was me who had to wash the sticky black mess from the bottom of his battered pots, elbow

266

deep in the greasy water that sat in the galley's rusted sink, Bosworth endlessly yelling in my ear to hurry up.

As I toiled in the galley, I did my best to keep an eye on what Captain Quat was up to. Most of the time he'd be stationed up on the airship captain's gantry. His telescope was always in his hand. Every now and then he would lean his weight on his dragon bone leg and press the lens to his eye. I guessed that he was tracking *The Hargmir*, hoping she, in turn, was steering a course in the direction of Mrs Zachariah and *The Drunken Molly*, all the time working out in his head how he was going to bring his plans to fruition. For my part I was engaged in the exact opposite. Every time I plunged my hands into the greasy water of the sink, I'd be trying to figure out some way that I might signal Captain Zachariah and make him steer away of the impending danger.

I thought that maybe I could sneak out of my bunk one night and use the one of the storm lamps or maybe I could use a piece of glass to reflect the sunlight. But what would that signal say to Captain Zachariah other than a random flash or a glint of light? The fact that *Beauty's Daughter* was heading in same northerly direction as *The Hargmir* wouldn't be any cause for alarm. Dragon hunter airships were traversing the skies back and forth to and from the Far Tundra all the time.

And how would he know the signal was from me?

He had no clue that I had ever been on board *The Hargmir*. I realised that no one knew I was missing. As far as Mr Highbrae was concerned, I was in the company of Captain Zachariah and the other members of *The Hargmir's* expedition and as far as Captain Zachariah knew I was headed back home in the company of Mr Highbrae. When my family received my letter and the message I'd asked Mister Highbrae to relay they too would think I was onboard *The Hargmir*. Unlike the first time I had been kidnapped, this time there was no trail behind me, no sequence of events that had been witnessed by others who could confirm what had happened. I was truly alone and wholly reliant on myself.

Rather than feeling discouraged this made me feel even more determined. Not only did the thwarting of Quat's plans require me to devise some sort of signal, my chances of escape relied on it. I decided on three flashes of a lamp or glints from a piece of glass. If I did that often enough and repeated the same sequence Captain Zachariah was bound to become curious and give the order for *The Hargmir* to investigate.

***

At first light on the day that I intended to put my plan into action I was awoken by a cry that chilled me to the bone. A cry that I had first heard when I was on board *The Drunken Molly*.

"Dragon's ho! Dragons ho!"

Around me the crew started rising from their bunks. I saw Slug and Fidget hurriedly dressing. Fidget shook Lullabeth by the shoulder. She grunted and slapped him away. I jumped down from my bunk and got dressed as well, taking the piece of glass that had been hidden under my pillow and concealing it in the pocket of my trousers.

Everyone began streaming out onto the deck. Lullabeth gave another grunt and pulled her blankets over her head. Slug tried to rouse her. She slapped him too. He barged past me, Fidget trailing at his heels. I followed behind. The night watchman was up on the gantry. The crew gathered around. Quat came hobbling along the deck, one side of his grey beard matted and flattened from where he had slept on it.

"Thunderstorm to the west," said the watchman. "Flock of Hammerclaws heading in its direction,"

Quat climbed awkwardly up onto the gantry. He took the telescope from the watchman and relieved him of his duty. Then he leaned his weight against his dragon bone leg and scanned the western sky through the lens of the telescope. Having done this, he turned and looked north. He scratched his beard, looking pensive.

The crew waited. I recognised the anticipation on the faces. I had seen that same look on the faces of the crew of *The Drunken Molly*. Quat turned the telescope again to the west and then again to the north. The gondola creaked as it swayed to the forward motion of the engines. The humming of the turbines and the gentle sigh of the wind sliced through the silence that pervaded the crew.

Quat lowered the telescope and address his men. "*The Hargmir* is headed north," he said. "We will easily pick up her trail again. The smoke she leaves in her wake is not at all like the smoke a dragon hunter or a scavenger leaves behind. Her balloon is so unusual we can't fail to notice it. What say you we ride into the mouth of the storm and do some dragon hunting?"

The crew needed no further encouragement. This was what they were waiting for.

"Aye!" they cried as one.

"Coxswain!" cried Quat. "Man the wheel. Full speed in a westerly direction. Rope gunners to the rope cannons. Netsmen and wranglers make ready."

In amongst melee Slug and Fidget just stood there slack jawed and totally perplexed. Lullabeth came wandering up onto the deck, scratching absently at her head. Despite her size and bulk, she was almost knocked from her feet by a diminutive, little rope gunner who was racing headlong to his station.

4. Hunting Hammerclaws

As *Beauty's Daughter* sliced into the darkly swirling churn of the storm clouds, blinding flashes of lightening illuminated deck, swiftly followed by deafening thunderclaps. Sheets of hail and furious gusts of wind assailed the gondola. Her green balloon was buffeted this way and that, causing the silver wires to screech and groan.

Up on the captain's gantry Quat leaned on his dragon bone leg, rainwater dripping from the matted strands of his beard, a look in his eye that was the equal of the crazed look I'd often seen in Mrs Zachariah's own fidgeting eyes. "Hard left," he barked, as the blurred form of a Hammerclaw shot past the gondola on outstretched wings.

Rain bouncing from my head and shoulders I retreated to the covered area of the galley. Having previously witnessed the cruelty of one dragon hunt I had no desire whatsoever to be caught up the middle of another. Shivering in my wet clothing I pressed myself back against the sink, wincing at the intensity of the thunderbolt that followed another blue fork of lightening.

This was crazy. If the balloon was struck by lightning, the dragon breath inside might ignite. I had seen how quickly *The Drunken Molly* had dropped when the White Sow ripped a hole in her crimson balloon. If the balloon of *Beauty's Daughter* were to explode, I doubted the crew would have enough time to properly inflate her emergency balloons before she went hurtling to the ground.

I wondered if this was my opportunity to send my signal to *The Hargmir*? It might turn out to be the entire crew that needed rescuing, not just me. Another sharp flash of lightening put paid to that idea. I was sure they would be able to see the storm from the deck of *The Hargmir*. How could I ever expect them to differentiate between a glint of sunlight and a flash of lightning? Besides we were so deep within the dark heart of the storm now that there wasn't a single ray of sunlight penetrating the thick, black walls of the clouds.

Quat barked out an order. "Lower the bait!"

Despite sluice gates situated below the airship's perimeter railings gallons of accumulated surface water was sloshing and swirling about the deck. I watched as three of the crew came slipping and sliding through the rolling waves caused by the keeling of the gondola. Down they ascended through the waterfall that was gushing into the hold. There they'd open the trap door and hang down hunks of salted meat on ropes to attract the dragons, just as I had been dangled beneath *The Drunken Molly* as bait for the White Sow.

"Rope loaders load the cannons," yelled Quat. "Rope gunners make ready."

I saw one of the rope gunners tighten the straps on his helmet as his loader stuffed the barrel of his cannon with a weighted lasso and hurriedly checked that the other end of the rope was firmly secured to the eyehook on the deck. Finger curled around the trigger mechanism the gunner swung the cannon skyward and wiped the steam from his goggles so that he could get a fix on his sight.

We were right in the midst of the Hammerclaw flock now, scaly charcoal-coloured hides and dark beating wings all around us. I watched the gunner trace the descent of a Hammerclaw sow as she caught the scent of the bait and dived low beneath the gondola hull of *Beauty's Daughter*. Almost instantly the sow rose, a fat chunk of meat firmly clamped in her powerful jaw. The gunner launched his lasso. It spun through the air, casting off spray from the incessant rain. Somehow its trajectory matched the exact moment the sow's left wing rose in an upward beat. The lasso tightened around the wing and the Hammerclaw roared as she was yanked to a violent mid-flight halt. The meat fell from her mouth.

The gunner operating the emplacement to the left of the first gunner released his lasso. It caught the Hammerclaw by the rear leg. The gunner to the right released his lasso. The loop fell over her thrashing head. Two of the rope loaders pulled back on the rope so that noose closed tightly around the sow's hoary neck, preventing the flint like organs in her throat clicking together to create a spark that would allow her to drench her assailants in fiery breath.

"Haul her in," yelled Quat. "Fetch the nets."

Lightening flashed and thunder roared. Fat hailstones bounced from the deck railings as men dragged nets through churning torrents of water. I saw Slug, Fidget and Lullabeth huddled together like a trio of drowned rats at the far end of the deck.

273

They looked as lost and confused as I had been the day that I had witnessed my first dragon hunt on *The Drunken Molly*.

The nets were cast over the side of the gondola. I saw the muscles on the arms of the crewmen tense as the pulled back on the ropes. The Hammerclaw was bundled onto the deck. She was rolled heavily out of the nets. Before she could rise back up her legs and wings were pinned down. She bucked and squirmed. The rope around her neck was pulled tighter to prevent her breathing fire.

One of the wranglers straddled the ridges on her back. I had seen this before on *The Drunken Molly*. He placed his hands around her hoary neck. The noose was loosened. Her head jutted left and right as it was removed. Over the hiss of the rain and the crash of the thunder an ominous click-click-click could be heard as the little organs in her throat began to strike together. The wrangler fingers expertly found their mark. He pressed them against the organs and prevented them from making further contact.

Now a leather muzzle with a long length of rubber tubing leading from it was hauled over her snout. I heard her keening in terror. To the left and right more of the rope cannons were being fired off as the rest of the Hammerclaw flock was drawn to the bait. It was so cruel. I wanted to look away. But my eyes were drawn back to the poor Hammerclaw sow, pinned mercilessly to the deck.

The straps on the muzzle were tightened. A crewman appeared, lugging the clay vessel that would be used to store the gaseous breath that was drawn from the dragon. The end of the rubber tubing was passed down through the neck of the vessel and the crewman nodded to the wrangler.

Just as the wrangler was about to release his grip on the sow's neck her tail, which the crew had somehow omitted to pin down, began to swish violently left to right. A crewman holding down one of her rear legs was sent flying across the water slick surface of the deck.

"You!" yelled Quat. "Sit on that tail! Hold it still."

Through the sheets of rain, I looked to where he was shouting.

"Me?" Slug Martin yelled back. "You want me to sit on that thing's tail."

"Yes, you!" roared Quat. "Now! Before it's too late."

Head down Slug ran forward. Two paces from the dragon he lost his footing and went into a comical skid just as the dragon's tail whipped round in his direction. It hit him full force on the back and sent him careening into the wrangler, who, in turn, was knocked from the dragons back.

As Slug and the wrangler fell into a twisted pile the Hammerclaw bucked and twisted. She swiped away the crewman holding down her right leg. Then she did the same with her left. Clawing at the muzzle on her snout she rose on all fours. The other crewmen rolled frantically away from her.

Seeming half dazed Slug staggered to his feet. The Hammerclaw finally tore the muzzle away. She smashed the gas vessel with her claws, shattering it into dozens of pieces. I heard the click-click-click of the organs in her neck.

"Out of there, boy!" yelled Quat. "Out of her way this instant!"

Slug looked back over his shoulder as the sow spread her jaws wide. He tried to run. His feet skidded on the rainwater. The Hammerclaw let out a roar that was as loud as the thunder. An intense shaft of blue fire shot from her mouth. Engulfed in vortex of raging flame Slug was knocked from his feet. He curled himself into a tight ball, screaming and covering his head. Flames licked the deck all around him, boiling and evaporating the surface water. For a moment it seemed as if there was nothing anyone could do to save him. Then the rain pounding down from the dark clouds doused the fire, leaving nothing behind but swirling fronds of grey smoke.

Slug lay still as a stone on the scorched deck. The Hammerclaw launched herself into the sky, the rope around her wing still attached by its noose and trailing behind like a streamer. No one moved to help Slug. Two more netted Hammerclaws had been dragged on deck. Wranglers were preparing them to have their breath drawn. Fidget and Lullabeth were still huddled together at the far end of the deck. They didn't seem remotely ready to come to their friend's aid.

I realised it was up to me. I ran from the galley, hail lashing against my face. When I reached Slug, I touched the charred shoulder of his shirt as gently as I could. He turned to look at me. His face was smeared in a sooty mess. His eyes were wide with terror.

"I was almost roasted alive, Euan," he said.

I helped him to sit up.

He began to sob. "I was almost roasted alive."

5. After The Hunt

After the dragon hunt the mood onboard *Beauty's Daughter* changed dramatically.

Some of the silver wires hanging down from the green balloon had been snapped during the thrashing about the airship had taken in midst of the storm. They were apparently beyond repair. The gondola listed to one side, making the deck slope precariously and causing the drone of the engine to sound somewhat off kilter. A huge section of the decking timber was scorched black from where the flaming breath of the Hammerclaw had momentarily evaporated the rainwater and taken hold. In the middle of this scorch mark was an untouched patch in the shape of Slug Martin.

Slug seemed totally defeated by what had befallen him. His singed spikes appeared to have had all the vigour washed out of them. His hair flopped listlessly around either side of his face like a pair of sad and neglected curtains. He moped endlessly around the deck, head bowed, shoulders slumped, face and hands covered in blisters, unresponsive whenever Fidget tried to engage him in conversation and oblivious to the scowls and knuckle cracking that Lullabeth sent in his direction whenever he sloped past her.

Slug's mood seemed slowly and surely to infect the crew. I heard some of them whispering that they thought he was jinxed. In response to this they become sullen and moody, snapping and cursing at one another, occasional fights breaking out when the insults became too personal. It wasn't just Slug's apparently unlucky presence that drove their moods, it also to do with the pitiful outcome of the dragon hunt. When the order had finally been given by Quat to steer out of the storm, they'd only managed a haul of five canisters of dragon breath. "Hardly enough to keep a balloon inflated for a single voyage," I'd heard one of them mutter. Afterwards they went through the motions of a lacklustre rendition of the Dragon Hunter's Sky Shanty. Their heart clearly wasn't in it, and it was nowhere near as boisterous as the version I'd heard aboard *The Drunken Molly*.

While they were singing mutedly and packing away the ropes and lassos Captain Quat had climbed back up onto his gantry and scanned the sky with his telescope, slowly east to west and then back again. "We've lost her, lads," he'd said. "We've lost sight of *The Hargmir*."

"I'll find her," the coxswain called back to him, muscles straining as he turned the wheel. "Just give the order and I'll find her."

"Three wires snapped beyond mending," interjected the crewman who had been tasked with assessing the damage from the storm. "Deck is tipping somewhat. We may have to inflate one of the emergency balloons to keep the gondola on an even keel."

"I can still find *The Hargmir*," the coxswain had insisted.

Quat reached into the inside of his jacket and pulled out the tattered picture paper bearing my story. I saw him flick through the pages. I knew exactly which drawing he was looking for. The one of me riding the back of the White Sow through the high walled canyon that led to her lair.

I saw him look at me and then back down at the picture. He leaned forward on his dragon bone leg and scratched his beard. "The reclamation yard at Forgsnur's Footprint," he barked out. "We'll head there for repairs. Perhaps our old friend Rusty Reeves will know the whereabouts of Isabella Zachariah. And, who knows, maybe if Master Redcap is reacquainted with Mr Reeves, it might also help refresh his memory too."

I felt a knot twist in my belly. The last place I wanted to go back to was Forgsnur's Footprint. That was where the supposed crimes Captain Zachariah and I had been put on trial for had been committed. The use of smoking clumps of crabwort root to put everyone who had been inside the compound into a deep sleep, the damaging of several scavenger ship balloons, and the stealing of the crimson balloon of *The Drunken Molly*. I had no idea how Rusty Reeves was going to react when he saw me, but I was pretty sure he wasn't going to welcome me with open arms.

Wishing that I'd stayed on Mr Highbrae's lanolin wagon I retreated to the galley and remained hidden away in there, avoiding everyone except Bosworth. The messy little place with its sticky floor and untidy worktops became a sanctuary of sorts. I found myself constantly hoping that Bosworth would burn another pot of stew so that I could occupy myself scraping and scrubbing the charred remains.

280

Elbow deep in greasy water my thoughts would turn to the dragon hunt that I had just witnessed. After my previous experience on *The Drunken Molly* a hunt wasn't something that I'd ever wanted to see again. But, with the lashing rain, and the flashes of lightening, and crashes of thunder, and the dreadful thing that had happened to Slug, this one seemed somehow ten times worse.

Sometimes my thoughts would turn to Captain Zachariah and all the dragon hunts he must have personally directed. I began to understand why he was so filled with remorse for the things that he'd done. And what about Professor Mayhew? According to what Hari had told me he was responsible for the invention of both the dragon breath extractor and the rope cannon. How guilty he must feel. No wonder he devoted so much of his time and personal wealth to the cause of Friends of the Dragon.

These thoughts raced around my head all day long. Even when it was time to sleep, I found that I desperately wanted to be alone to wrestle with them. So much so that I was often reluctant to leave cramped confines of the galley. I'd make myself a bed of teacloths beneath the worktop and sleep there. I had slept in worse places after all. A chicken coop on *The Drunken Molly*, the hard surface of the Far Tundra, the chilly hold of *The Hargmir*.

With the airship engines humming against the galley floor, I was so full of regrets for my foolhardy decisions that it would take me ages to drift into sleep. Even then I would awake gasping and drenched in sweat when I dreamed that the last of the wires attaching *Beauty's Daughter* to her green balloon had finally snapped and we were falling like a huge stone to shatter on the ground miles below.

6. Return to Forgsnur's Footprint

I awoke at first light one morning to find a strange fluttering sensation in my belly. I'd had enough experience of airship travel to know what this meant. *Beauty's Daughter* was passing down through the clouds in a slow and careful descent. We had reached our destination I swallowed down the lump that rose in my throat.

When I brushed away the pile of tea towels, I had wrapped around me I shivered at how cold the air had become. My breath hushed out in puffy clouds of condensation. Listening to the sound of the crew making their landing preparations I crawled out from under the galley table, yawning and stretching. For the first time in days, I ventured onto the deck of the gondola. Quat was up on his gantry, calling out directions to the coxswain. Some of the men were making the anchor ready, others were brandishing longpoles, ready to push the hull of the airship gently away if it drifted too close to any structure and risked being damaged.

Still shivering I crossed the gondola to the railings. The deck was slippery underfoot and still listing unevenly. I could see frost glistening on the remaining silver wires hanging down from the green balloon. Lullabeth stepped out from the side of one of the rope cannon emplacements and tried to deliberately trip me up. I managed to dodge her outstretched leg. From behind her I heard Fidget sniggering. Slug was nowhere to be seen.

Ignoring the two of them I stepped up to the railings and looked down. The last time I'd seen Forgur's Footprint was when I'd watched it getting smaller and smaller as *The Hawk's Cry* ascended. The ragged crater was exactly as I remembered. Wide at the front, like the sole of someone's foot, narrow at the back, like the heel. No wonder the Ghibelline thought it was the footprint of a giant.

I could clearly see the compound of Rusty Reeves' Reclamation yard on the lip of the wider part of the crater, tall perimeter fence facing the expanse of the tundra, dragon bone hull of an old airship forming the arch of the entrance. Here two sentries stood at guard, watching the tundra beyond.

Just beyond the compound interior, on scaffolds that rose twenty feet from the slope of the crater was the raised platform quay where quite few scavenger airships were at anchor, balloons billowing in the cold wind. On one of the wooden repair platforms that stood to the side of the quay a vessel as large as a dragon hunter' ship was covered in a vast patchwork sheeting of tarpaulin.

Down went *Beauty's Daughter* and the crater and the compound became larger. Men were emerging from the rickety huts that ran parallel to the perimeter fence. I saw some of them climbing the ladders that led up to the platform quay. One of them picked up a pair of red flags and began signalling up at us, giving directions down to an empty berthing dock. One of the crewmen relayed the directions being given back to the captain. "Straight down a few more feet. Then proceed in a rightward direction."

"Steady as she goes," Quat called to the coxswain.

I watched the coxswain as he expertly turned the wheel to manoeuvre the great bulk of the gondola into position. The longpole bearing crewmen assumed their positions by the railings. When I looked down at the compound, I could clearly see Rusty Reeves on the porch of his gaudily painted shack, his bald scalp glistening in the wintry sunlight as he observed our descent. My heart began pounding. What was he going to say when he saw that I had returned to the scene of my alleged crimes?

Now we were so close to the platform that I could hear the voice of the signalman as he called out directions to accompany those he was relaying with his flags. "Left, left, left. Right a little. Ease down slowly." The gondola drifted too close to one of the scavenger ships. The long poles were used to push it gently back.

"Cut the engines," called Quat.

The engines fell silent. The turbines spun slowly down to stillness. I heard the hull thump lightly against the quay. The anchor was dropped. Two of the yardmen secured it into the housing on the platform. Ropes were tossed over the side and lashed around raised bollards.

"Good job, lads," said Quat, and climbed down from the gantry.

* * *

I was one of the last to descend the ladder from the platform quay. I was dreading coming face to face with Rusty Reeves. Mending the damage that

Illagnor had ordered the Ghibelline to inflict on the balloons of the scavenger ships at anchor in the reclamation yard when Captain Zachariah and myself made our escape must have used up a lot of Mr Reeves' reclaimed materials. Whatever he might have to say to me, it wasn't going to be pleasant.

Quat himself came down from the platform after me. With his dragon bone leg, he couldn't quite manage the ladder, so some of Rusty Reeves' men lowered him down in a makeshift cradle that they'd cobbled together from a couple of lassos. Once he was on solid ground he began walking across the compound, dragon bone leg resolutely crunching against the gravel. Everyone fell in behind him. I hung back as much as possible, walking alongside Slug, who slouched several paces behind Fidget and Lullabeth.

More of Rusty Reeves' men were climbing up onto the platform to commence the repairs that needed to be conducted on the scavenger ships. I could see groups of sullen, unshaven crewmen milling around, smoking clay pipes and exchanging boisterous banter.

More men were seated at the long wooden table next the compound fire, eating bowls of what looked like an extremely thick and stodgy porridge. Some of the faces I could see looked unsettlingly familiar. I wondered if some of them might be from the same group of scavengers who had confronted Captain Zachariah, myself, and the Ghibelline at the compound entrance. My unease began to increase.

We were halfway across the compound when Rusty Reeves' mouth dropped wide, as if he'd finally recognised who it was that was approaching. As he placed his hands on his hips and shook his head in apparent disbelief, I bowed my own head and tried to make myself look as small and inconsequential as possible.

"Well, well, well," I heard Reeves say. "If it isn't Gulliver Quat. I thought you'd long since retired, old friend."

I looked up, heaving a sigh of relief. It wasn't me he had noticed after all.

"Circumstances have brought me out of retirement, Mr Reeves," said Quat. The two men embraced like long lost friends. "But my ship is in desperate want of repair. I need to source some fresh wires for my gondola and there's a scorch mark on my deck that could do with sanding down and varnishing."

"I'm sure I can give you a reasonable quote," said Reeves. His face was already streaked in oil. He wiped his brow with a dirty rag.

"There's something else I need from you," said Quat, leaning forward on his dragon bone leg.

Rusty Reeves narrowed his eyes, wiping his hands with his rag. "What might that be, Captain Quat?"

"I'm hoping that you might know the current whereabouts of Isabella Zachariah," replied Quat. "I have an important proposition that I wish to put to her."

"A proposition?" asked Reeves.

Quat gave a nod of his head.

"Well then," said Reeves, "I should think I would definitely be able to help you with that."

He turned to face his shack. "Isabella!" he called out. "There's someone out here who wishes to speak to you!"

Isabella?

My heart skipped another beat. I looked again at the men seated at the breakfast table and knew instantly why they seemed so familiar. They were crewmen from *The Drunken Molly*. The very same crewmen who had caught me in a lasso as I fled with my sister from the glen to the meadow, the very same crewmen who had stolen me away from my home. I looked up at the huge vessel on the scaffold. There was no need to guess the name of the airship that was hidden under that tarpaulin.

A figure appeared in the doorway of Mr Reeves' shack. At first it was only a silhouette, shadowed by the glare of the rising morning sun. Then it stepped onto the porch, and she was there before me, like a vision from my worst nightmares. Black braids dancing in the breeze, nerves twitching on her face. More than Rusty Reeves Mrs Zachariah was the one person I had truly hoped never to meet again.

7. Mrs Zachariah

Mrs Zachariah held her hand up to her brow, shading her fidgeting eyes from the sun's steadily increasing glare. She seemed to sway a little as she peered across the compound and tried to figure out who it was that was standing next to Rusty Reeves. "Gul?" she cried out after a moment. "Gulliver Quat? Is that you? It can't be. You can't possibly be here."

She lurched forward, knee length boots clomping on the wooden slats of the porch and almost fell headlong down the steps. Her black braids thrashed this way and that as she stumbled then managed to pull herself upright. "Gul!" she cried again, launching into a purposeful stride across the compound.

Moments later she broke into a sprint, running so fast into Quat's waiting arms that she nearly knocked him over. I saw the dragon bone leg shoot out and wedge itself into the gravel as he steadied himself. Mrs Zachariah hugged him tightly and nestled her cheek into the bushy bristles of his grey beard. "Gul," she sighed. "It's so good to see you." Her voice sounded somewhat different to the way I remembered it, a little more refined and softer in tone, perhaps the way it used to be back in Tennanbrau City.

"Have you brought news?" I heard her ask.

Over Quat's shoulder her eye seemed to catch mine. I saw a flicker of what I suspected might have been recognition and slunk cautiously back behind

Lullabeth's considerable bulk, leaning slightly to left so I could still watch what was going on from one side of her big shoulder.

Mrs Zachariah pulled away from Quat and cupped his beard in her hands. "Have you brought news of my bonnie captain?" she asked, looking up at him. "Have you brought new of Nathaniel?"

"Nathaniel?" said Quat. "You know all there is to know about him, Isabella. From what I hear you last saw him right here at Forgsnur's Footprint."

Mrs Zachariah released her hands and stepped away from Quat. Her whole body seemed to stiffen. The nerves on her cheeks began to twitch once more. She looked around the compound and it seemed to me that in that instant she didn't have the slightest clue where she was. Then she whipped her braids violently back over her shoulders and jutted her chin forward. "The impostor, you mean?" Her voice once more assumed the harshness I'd grown accustomed to aboard *The Drunken Molly*. "It was an impostor who came here in the company of a band of Ghibelline, laying false claim to my husband's name."

Quat stepped awkwardly forward and attempted to embrace her once more. She pushed him away. "If that impostor has sent you here with some sort of deluded notion that you might be able to engineer a reconciliation, then you've has a wasted journey, Gulliver. There can be no reconciliation with someone who is not who he claims to be."

She placed her hands on her hips and turned her head slowly, taking in everyone who was

290

congregated in the compound of the reclamation yard. "My husband is dead, hear me? The great dragon hunter, Nathaniel Zachariah, is dead. Dead to the world and dead to me. So plead all you like Captain Quat. Your pleas will fall on deaf ears."

"I have not come here to plead on anyone's behalf," said Quat. "I have come with a proposition that I wish to put to you of my own volition."

Mrs Zachariah narrowed her eyes. "What sort of proposition?"

Quat replied with a series of questions of his own. "What is the cause of all our woes, Isabella? What was it that took my leg and destroyed my ship? What was it that took Nathaniel's good looks and befuddled his thoughts so much that you now think of him as naught but an impostor? What was it that damned near smashed *The Drunken Molly* out of the sky?"

Mrs Zachariah's eyes jittered left and right. She chewed her lip. Little flurries of snow danced about her in the wind that animated her black braids. "The Sow." She spoke the words as a whisper. "The White Sow."

"Exactly," said Quat. He placed a hand on her shoulder. This time she didn't attempt to push him away. "We're cursed, you and I," he told her. "Cursed by our association with that monstrous she devil. Bad things befall us. Ask my men what happened when we attempted a simple hunt for dragon breath. One of my crew was near roasted alive."

I wanted to call out that it was Quat's headstrong decision to fly straight into a thunderstorm that was to blame for his woes and not some perceived superstitious curse. But the desire not to draw any unnecessary attention to myself made me hold my tongue.

Mrs Zachariah began wringing her hands in apparent consternation. "Cursed?" she wailed. "Is that what it is, Quat? Is it a curse that took my bonny baby away from me? I held him for a moment in my arms and he died."

"I know, Isabella," said Quat. "I was there."

"You were there, Gul," agreed Mrs Zachariah. "You were like a father to me. But it was Nathaniel who should have been there. Instead, he was off hunting the Sow."

"Aye," said Quat. "She had him as bewitched as we are cursed, Isabella. Still does. But together we can end it."

"I fully intend to end it," said Mrs Zachariah, bowing her head. "Nathaniel is dead. My husband is dead. I am manufacturing bombs to wage war on the Ghibelline. They're as much to blame."

"Avenge him by all means," said Quat. "But don't waste time on the Ghibelline. Work with me to bring down the White Sow. End the curse once and for all."

Mrs Zachariah looked up. "She's strong, Gul. Strong and ferocious, you know that more than any man alive."

"I have a plan, Isabella," said Quat. I saw the dragon bone leg shift a little in the gravel as he changed positions. "Can we sit and talk? It gets tiring after a while for a one-legged man to stand around like this."

Mrs Zachariah called over to the men seated at the long breakfast table. "Clear those things away. Make space."

Hurriedly the men began stacking the dishes and gathering up their cutlery.

Quat swung around. "Fetch me the Low County lad. He needs to be part of this conversation." Before I had a chance to do anything Lullabeth had grabbed my shirt collar and was hauling me across the compound to the table.

***

Quat and Mrs Zachariah took their seats side by side on the long bench. Lullabeth forced me to sit down at the opposite side of the table. Despite the sun being full in the sky now the air was growing even chillier, and the snowflakes were thickening by the minute.

"You know this boy?" asked Quat, nodding over at me.

Mrs Zachariah looked at him and then at me. "Fetcher?" she said. "What are you doing here?"

"Ask him," I spat back, finger accusingly jabbing at Quat.

"You're so young," said Mrs Zachariah. "Whatever was I thinking of hiring someone as young as this as a fetcher?"

"You didn't hire me," I told her. "You kidnapped me. And so did he!"

"Kidnapped?" The nerves on Mrs Zachariah's face began twitching. She turned again to Quat, eyes searching his bearded face as if hoping for some clue that what I was saying might be untrue.

293

"Never mind that nonsense," said Quat, dismissing what I had just said with a wave of his hand. "We have far more important matters to discuss." He reached inside his jacket and produced Slug's the battered copy of the picture paper. "Cast you eyes over this, Isabella."

He flicked through the pages until he found the illustration of me clinging to the back of the White Sow. "This is the lad's tale," he said, greasy finger pressing down on the page. "After he fell from *The Drunken Molly* he rode the Sow straight into her lair."

"I didn't fall," I corrected. "I was deliberately hung down on a rope as dragon bait."

Mrs Zachariah's face snapped up at me, blacks braids swishing though the air. "Bait? Who would do such a terrible thing to a boy so young?"

I just grunted in frustration. There was no point in reminding her. She only ever seemed to hear half of what anyone told her and managed to swipe away anything that seemed too inconvenient from her memory.

"The lad knows the location of the Sow's lair, Isabella," continued Quat. "He knows where we can find her."

"I don't," I protested. "I can't remember."

Quat ignored me. "We can bring her down, Isabella. You and I together. We can end the curse once and for all."

"May I?" asked Mrs Zachariah, the tone of her voice altering slightly once more as she nodded at the picture paper.

Quat slid it to her. For a moment she gazed down at the picture of the Sow gliding through the canyon with me on its back. Snowflakes fell and melted onto the page. Then she flicked backwards through the pages till she came to JJ's depiction of herself up on the gantry of *The Drunken Molly*, eyes wild and furious, serpentine braids writhing about her like a nest of vipers.

"Is this truly how I look, Gulliver?" she asked. "Is this what I've become?"

Quat wrapped his big arm around her shoulder. "It is not what you have become that matters," he whispered into her ear. "Not what the Sow has made of you. It's what you will be when we are rid of her once and for all."

Mrs Zachariah wriggled free from him. "What will I be?"

"What you once were," replied Quat. "When we are free from her curse, we will all be what we once were, you and me and Nathaniel, even the lad here. When this is all over, he'll go back to his family in the Low Counties."

"But I won't be the same," I said, remembering a discussion I'd had with Fenisnoor back in the Beehive. "*Whether we like it or not things never entirely go back to the way they were – and neither do we.*"

"Remember how it used to be, Isabella?" said Quat, scowling across the table at me. "The fine clothes you once wore? The perfumes and the jewellery? The parties and functions you were invited to as the wife of Tennanbrau's most celebrated dragon hunter? All of that could be yours

295

once more. We can regain what we lost. If we work together."

"Captain Zachariah is looking for you," I blurted. "He's coming to the tundra to search for you. He's to negotiate your surrender."

Mrs Zachariah's hand shot out and grabbed my wrist. Her fingernails bit into my flesh. "The impostor is seeking me out?" she spat. "The confederate of the Ghibelline is coming here? The airship thief wants to negotiate *my* surrender?"

"He's been sent here by Emperor Julian himself," I said, struggling to free my wrist. "There's an ISC Patrol with him as well."

Mrs Zachariah released her grip and shoved my hand away.

"Some chance they'll have of getting me to surrender," she said. "I've assembled an army. Every man here is loyal to my cause. I already have an ISC patrol held hostage. And I have bombs."

"That's why you're in such trouble," I said.

Quat scowled at me once more. "Ignore the boy, Isabella," he said. "Once we have taken the Sow your past misdemeanours will be forgotten. So long as none of the patrol members have been harmed."

"Not a hair on their heads," said Mrs Zachariah. "I have them locked inside the hold of *The Drunken Molly*. They are well fed. Their crafts are on the gondola deck, hidden beneath the tarpaulin."

"Good," said Quat. "Now see what you think of my plan."

He reached for a bowl containing three hunks of bread that had been left to one side of the table. He placed one piece of bread on the table. "Imagine this is the entrance to the Sow's lair," he said, placing the other two pieces of bread at either side of the first.

"*The Drunken Molly* will lay anchor to the left of the entrance," he continued. "*Beauty's Daughter* will be anchored to the right. We will lower bait into the entrance. When the Sow is enticed out, we will drop some of the bombs you have manufactured down on her. The explosion will disorient her. Our rope gunners will fire their lassos. We will have crossbow marksmen stationed on the decks of both airships. They will release their bolts to weaken her further…"

Mrs Zachariah looked down at the picture paper. "It seems that the Sow's lair is deep within the nesting grounds of the dragons," she said. "They would be incensed by our presence, protective of their young and their un-hatched eggs. We'd be under constant attack, Gul."

"That's where your army comes in, Isabella," said Quat. "There will be an armada of scavenger ships at our flank. They will take down the dragons and raid the nests. They will be allowed to keep the spoils and we will take the White Sow. It will be a glorious and historic day for all."

"You still don't understand that I really can't remember where the Sow's lair is," I pointed out.

"We'll take you to the mouth of each and every canyon in the mountains if we have to," insisted Quat. "Sooner or later, you'll recognise the place."

"I won't," I said. "I was terrified, clinging onto the Sow's back. It all happened so fast."

Quat scratched at his beard. "I may have a solution," he said after a while. "For a moment back there when I ordered the hunt of the Hammerclaws I had a flashback to the dreadful day when the Sow took my leg and destroyed my airship. I could see everything as clear as day. It was as if I was right there."

He turned to Mrs Zachariah. "I reckon the same would happen to the lad if we were to take him up above the clouds and hang him down on a rope from the bait hatch. I reckon if we did that it would all come back to him, damned quickly."

My hand trembled as it reached up to touch the scar that had healed on my chest. Wide eyed with fear I looked from Quat to Mrs Zachariah. I realised that they were both as mad as each other. That made me even more scared.

8. Angus

I was confined to one of the huts and warned not to move from there until someone came to collect me. The door was locked. I was left with a mug of water and some dragon meat jerky. I drank the water but could not bring myself to eat the jerky. I sat on a wobbly stool and watched through the dirty window as some of the crossbow marksmen from the scavenger ships took target practice, firing their bolts into a chalk outline of a dragon drawn onto an old section of airship hull resting against the perimeter fence.

Elsewhere a rope cannon had been set up beneath one of the scaffolds. Lassos were being launched at a sort of windmill contraption that I supposed was meant to mimic the up and own motion of dragon wings. I could also hear gunfire coming from deeper down in crater where I assumed they'd set up some sort of rifle range. Mrs Zachariah really had assembled an army. I scanned the grey skies, hoping to see the metal clad gondola of *The Hargmir* descend through the fat snow clouds. I couldn't believe that they hadn't realised that the first place they should look for her would be Forgsnur's Footprint. It seemed so obvious now.

I studied the bulky shape hidden beneath the tarpaulin. I now knew this to be *The Drunken Molly*. I found myself wondering about the ISC patrol members being held prisoner there. Part of me wished I'd been locked in the hold with them. At least then I wouldn't have felt so hopeless and lonely. If they were anything like Sergeant Caulder, they would surely by now be considering an escape plan.

I kept scolding myself for how much I seemed to have messed things up this time. No one who cared about me knew where I was. And I was soon to be dangled from a rope from an airship to try and force me to remember something I really didn't want to remember. And if I did remember, if it all came back to me, it could spell the end for the magnificent White Sow. I was supposed to be helping the cause of Friends of the Dragon and here I was doing the exact opposite.

Two or three hours must have passed before I heard the key turning in the lock. I immediately recognised the figure that stood in the doorway shaking snow from his shoulders. His hair, as red as mine, was a lot longer now and he'd started to grow the beginnings of a little beard on his chin. Despite this there was no mistaking, Angus Stonedyke.

I got up from the stool and Angus grinned at me.

"So, it's true, little brother. You came back."

"You're no brother of mine," I said.

Angus carried on grinning. "No need to be like that. We're both Low County boys."

"That still doesn't make you my brother," I told him.

"I'm doing you a favour here, Euan," he said. "I've been out with Smudger checking the traps we set for hares yesterday. You remember Smudger?"

I nodded. "The cook on *The Drunken Molly*."

"We got four big 'uns," continued Angus. "There'll be huge pot of hare stew for supper. Not as good as the rabbit stew our Ma's used to make in the Low Counties. No mushrooms, that's for sure. But there's onion and tatters that one of the scavenger ships brought in from Tennanbrau."

"What's this got to do with doing me a favour?" I asked.

"I was getting to that," said Angus. "That's why I wasn't here when you arrived, what with being out checking the traps and that. But when I got back and found out that they'd locked you in here I went straight to Mrs Zachariah and pleaded with her to release you into my custody."

"Your custody?"

"I'm to be your personal guard, mate. I'm not to let you out of my sight. But at least you won't be under lock and key any longer."

I sat back down on the stool. "Maybe I like it in here," I said.

The grin fell from Angus' face. He folded his arms over his chest. "The least you could say is thank you."

"Why would I thank you when you tried to kill me the last time I saw you?" I said.

"Did not," said Angus.

"You fired a cross bolt at me," I said, standing up again and pointing my finger at him.

"I was aiming at the balloon on that scavenger ship," he said.

"Well, you nearly hit me."

"Not intentionally. I was dizzy from that crabwort stuff your Ghibelline friends fired into the compound. I couldn't see straight."

"You're still not my brother," I told him.

He shrugged his shoulders. "But I am your guard. Now move it, Euan. I'm not hanging around in here all day."

I was tempted to sit back down on the stool and refuse to move. Then I remembered something that I felt sure would worry him far more than me being stubborn and pig headed.

"Have you seen your friend?" I asked.

His brow creased.

"My Friend?"

"Slug Martin," I said. It was my turn to grin at him. "He's here with your other friends, Fidget and Lullabeth."

The colour drained from Angus' face. "Here? How?"

"They came with Captain Quat," I replied. "Aboard *Beauty's Daughter*. And they're simply dying to see you."

***

It didn't take long for us to bump into Slug. Angus said he wanted to get in some lasso practice and literally pushed and shoved me across the compound to where the rope cannon had been set up. I suspected that he wanted to keep out of the way. He seemed nervous and kept glancing back over his shoulder.

Slug was sitting with his back to one of the scaffold legs, head bowed and hair flopping limply down as the snow swirled around him. Angus

302

clearly didn't recognise him and would have walked straight past had Lullabeth not stepped out and blocked his path.

"Well, well, well, look who we have here," she said, cracking her knuckles loudly.

Fidget appeared at her side, scratching the dry skin on his neck. "We were kind of hoping we'd run into you," he said, cocking his head and smirking at Angus.

From where I was standing, I could see Angus' hands shaking as he clenched his fists. "I don't want any trouble," he said.

"You should have thought of that before you dobbed us in to the law," said Fidget.

Lullabeth looked down at Slug. "Hey Slug," she said. "Look who we ran in to." When Slug didn't move Lullabeth gave him a nudge with the toe of her boot. "You listening Slug? I said look who we ran in to."

Slug raised his head slowly. He looked at Angus and exhaled a long, despondent breath. Slowly, back still pressing against the scaffold leg, he pushed himself upright. I saw Angus' fists tighten. "Hey," said Slug, somewhat lethargically.

"Hey?" cried Lullabeth, turning bright red. "Hey? Is that all you've got to say? After all your boasting about what you would do if you ever ran into Angus Stonedyke again?"

Slug swayed a little and his limp hair swayed with him.

Angus turned to me and whispered. "What happened to him?"

"Run in with a Hammerclaw," I whispered back. "Almost roasted him alive."

Angus held out his hand. "Let's just let bygones be bygones?" he suggested.

Lullabeth slapped his hand away. "What are you doing?" she yelled at Slug. "Get him! Get him back for what he did!"

Slug just slouched some more and slid back down the scaffold leg till he was seated again. His head slumped between his shoulders. Lullabeth cracked her knuckles. "If Slug won't finish this, then it's up to me," she grunted. "Grab him Fidget."

Fidget tried to grab Angus' arm. In the scuffle that ensued Angus stepped back and almost knocked me off my feet. He pushed Fidget hard against the chest and he went flying into Lullabeth, knocking the wind out of her.

"I'm doing a job for both Mrs Zachariah and Captain Quat," Angus warned them both. "I'm guarding Euan Redcap. If anything happens to me while I'm on their business, you'll answer to both of them. And that won't be pleasant, believe me."

Fidget looked up at Lullabeth.

Lullabeth shrugged her broad shoulders. "This isn't over, Angus," she warned. "It's not over by a long shot."

"You better watch your back," added Fidget, scratching vigorously at his neck.

Angus barged past them.

I stood there for a moment looking down at Slug. The kernel of an idea was forming in my head. An idea that might just help me escape the compound and the horrible fate that Quat and Mrs Zachariah had planned for me.

"Get a move on, Euan," Angus called back. "I want to get my practice in before supper."

9. Escape

"You enjoy that?" asked Angus.

We were back inside the little hut having just had two helpings each of Smudger's hare broth. I nodded my head grudgingly. After the stomach-churning experience of Bosworth's dreadful culinary offerings the hare broth had been the most delicious meal I'd tasted since leaving Tennanbrau.

The sun was setting in the sky now and the snow had eased off. Angus lit a couple of candles and placed them on the table in the centre of the room. There was a set of bunk beds in far corner. I was to sleep in the top bunk and Angus was going to take away the ladder, so that if I attempted to jump down in the night, he would wake up straight away.

"Trapping hares is no different to dragon hunting, you know," said Angus, wiping away the grease that had got caught in his half-hearted beard. "I bet your Pa sets snares for rabbits like every other hill farmer in the Low Counties."

"It's not the same," I said, watching him over the flicker of the candles.

"It is," he insisted. "It's exactly the same. It's almost the same as sheep farming. Your Pa sells the wool from the sheep the same way as a dragon hunter sells Dragon Breath. Every year your Pa sells off some of his flock for mutton and lamb. Some of them he even slaughters himself."

"It's not the same," I insisted. "Hares and rabbits and sheep are not being hunted to extinction."

Angus shook his head. "It's still the same thing, Euan. You sided with the wrong people. Friends of the Dragon just don't understand how important Dragon Breath is to Tennanbrau and the townships."

"I know all about that," I said. "You were the first to tell me."

"Well then you know it would be a disaster if we stopped taking Dragon Breath."

"There are other types of gas," I said. "Natural gases. Professor Mayhew has designed an airship whose balloon is inflated by one of those gases. I'm sure he could show everyone how the factories and all the other stuff that runs off Dragon Breath could use that gas."

"Mayhew?" spat Angus. "The leader of Friends of the Dragon? What would he know?"

"You haven't seen *The Hargmir*," I said. "It's a magnificent airship."

Angus shrugged his shoulders. "He designed an airship. Big deal."

I folded my arms and shot him a smug grin. "You have no idea who he is, do you?"

"He's an idiot," said Angus, grinning right back at me.

"Would an idiot have invented the rope cannon?" I challenged him. I began to pace up and down, the rickety floorboards creaking under my feet. "Would an idiot have invented the Dragon Breath Extractor?"

"What are you going on about, Euan?"

"Professor Mayhew," I said. "He was the one who invented the equipment you dragon hunters rely on so much. He realised his mistake and now he uses all the money he made to help finance the activities of Friends of the Dragon."

"Then he is definitely an idiot," said Angus, grinning again. "You shouldn't associate with idiots, Euan. Or, for that matter, turncoats like Captain Zachariah."

"Captain Zachariah used to be your hero," I said. "The way you used to talk about him back on *The Drunken Molly*."

"That was before I saw what he had become. Mrs Zachariah is right. Captain Zachariah is dead. He's no longer the type of person anyone in their right mind would look up to."

I could feel the anger boiling up inside of me and I knew had to change the subject. For the plan that had been forming in my head all day to work it had to be Angus who became angry, not me.

"What did you do to Slug and the other two to make them want to get revenge on you?" I asked.

"That's none of your business," said Angus, the colour draining from his face once more.

"You said we were like brothers," I shot back at him. "Brothers tell each other stuff."

Angus sat down at the table. His face became a blurred shadow behind the glow from the candles. "It was just after I arrived in Tennanbrau from the Low Counties," he said.

I sat down on the stool by the window.

"I was lost and hungry. I didn't have anywhere to go. The place seemed so big compared to the Low Counties. All those huge palaces and towering tenement towers."

I remembered my own first sight of Tennanbrau as Captain Zachariah navigated *The Hawk's Cry* between the high walls of those very towers.

"I'd run away from home because it was my dream to join the crew of a dragon hunting vessel. But now that I was there, I had no idea how to go about making that dream a reality. Somehow, I found my way to the Airship Terminus. Everyone I met there told me the same thing. No airship captain would take me on unless I could pay a retainer."

"A retainer?"

"It's a sum of money that is held in good faith against the risk posed to a captain by taking a chance on an inexperienced crew member," explained Angus. "If you get through your first voyage without any major mishap then you get the retainer back, along with your first wage."

"How much did you have to pay?" I asked.

"I didn't have any money," replied Angus. "Not penny to my name. It looked as if my dreams were never going to come true. Then I met Slug and his gang. And they took pity on me. They shared some of the scraps of dragon jerky they'd pilfered from Scavenger's Market and let me sleep in the old warehouse they were squatting in near the Terminus. And then they told me about their plan."

I pulled the stool up to the table. I was genuinely interested in what Angus was saying.

Understanding exactly what had happened between him and Slug was crucial to my own plan.

"Every year in Tennanbrau City the dragon hunters hold a grand ball," Angus continued. "They raise money for charity to help the widows and orphans of members of airship crews lost in the skies or killed while hunting dragons. Slug and the other two planned to steal the money at that year's ball. They had imitation guns they'd carved from bits of wood."

"And they asked you to join them?"

Angus nodded. "I'm ashamed now. But at the time it seemed the solution to my problems. It was the only way I could think of getting enough money to pay a retainer. I didn't consider the risks. We were going to wear wool sacks with eyeholes cut into them over our heads."

"What happened?"

"In the end my conscience got the better of me. At the last minute I went to the constabulary and told them everything. Slug and Lullabeth and Fidget were arrested and sent to the Pym Street Home for Wayward Boys and Girls. Slug got the longest because he was the ringleader."

I understood now. I had almost ended up in Pym Street myself. Even from my fleeting experience I could tell that the place wasn't somewhere you would wish on your worst enemy. And if you felt it was someone else's fault that you ended up there you sure wouldn't be too happy with that person.

"I was punished too," said Angus. "But my punishment turned out to be a blessing. I was sentenced to provide my services as ship's fetcher on *The Drunken Molly* under the captainship of Nathaniel Zachariah."

"You were a fetcher?"

"That's where most people start out, Euan. You've got a lot of experience now. I bet you could progress to become an excellent Rope Cannon Gunner."

"No, I couldn't," I said. "That's the last thing I'd want to be."

"Don't lie to yourself, Euan," he teased. "In your heart you know as well as I do that you really want to be a dragon hunter."

Again, I felt the anger rising inside me. "No I don't!"

Angus laughed. "The more you protest, the more I know it's true."

"He's tricking you," I blurted, realising the conversation was heading the wrong way again. "Slug Martin is tricking you."

Angus rose to his feet. "What?"

I shouldn't have said that. It would soon be dark. I was supposed to have done this first thing in the morning when I would have a whole day of daylight ahead of me.

"What are you talking about, Euan?"

I had no choice now. I'd have to see it through. I'd have to say what I had been planning to say. "Slug is faking it," I said.

I was never any good at telling lies, but I hoped that in the flicker of the candlelight Angus wouldn't be able to see the guilty look that was bound to be showing on my face. I smacked my lips and pushed on with the deception. "He's pretending to be all down and demoralised. He's hoping to lull you into a false sense of security. Then when you least expect it, he's going to get Lullabeth and Fidget to grab you and bring you to him. I heard them plotting this as soon as we found out Mrs Zachariah was here at Forgsnur's Footprint."

"Who does he think he is?" said Angus. "He needs to realise that I'm not the scared little kid he first met back in Tennanbrau. I'm a Rope Cannon Gunner and he's nothing but a petty crook."

He pushed the table to one side and headed for the door. "Follow me, Euan," he barked.

"Where are we going?" I asked.

"To have it out with him once and for all," came the terse reply.

This was what I had hoped for. But it was too soon. "You should wait till morning," I called after him. "Wouldn't it be better to confront him in the morning, after a good night's sleep?"

"No time like the present," said Angus. "Now get a move on, Euan. And keep where I can see you." With that he barged out of the door.

**

Angus shoved and cajoled me across the compound yard. I kept trying to convince him that it would be better to wait until the morning, but it appeared that I had done far too good job at getting him riled up. We passed the long table where the next sitting of scavengers and dragon hunters were tucking into bowls of Smudger's delicious hare stew. Some of them glanced up to see what the commotion was, then went right back to eating.

We found Slug near the fire. Lullabeth and Fidget were huddled up before it, empty stew bowls on their laps, but Slug was some distance away, head bowed and turned slightly, as if he was afraid to look at the flames of the fire.

"All right, Slug," barked Angus, marching up to loom over him and hauling me along by the sleeve as he went. "Let's have this out once and for all."

Slug looked up at him but didn't move. However, when I glanced over my shoulder, I saw Lullabeth lumber to her feet, followed swiftly by Fidget. "Come on," goaded Angus. "You think you can push me round the way you did when we first met? I'm a different person now and I'm not afraid of you."

"If you don't do something, I will," said Lullabeth, cracking her knuckles. I watched as Fidget slunk around to the other side. The two of them were surrounding him, ready to grab him at the slightest sign from Slug. Although this wasn't going exactly the way I had planned I knew I had to be ready to make my move as soon as the opportunity presented itself.

I looked over to Rusty Reeves' painted hut. Mrs Zachariah and Captain Quat were on the porch with Quat's coxswain. Under the glow of a couple of storm lamps they were pouring over what I assumed was map of the Far Tundra. I wondered if it would hold their attention long enough for me to be able to slip past them.

When I turned back Slug had risen to his feet. His head was still bowed. He spoke through the

313

limp curtain of his hair. "Did you know that I was almost burned alive by a dragon?" he asked.

"I'm not falling for that," said Angus. "I know all about your little plan."

"What plan?" asked Fidget, casting a suspicious glance in my direction.

Angus either didn't hear him or chose to ignore him. Nevertheless, he tightened his grip on my sleeve. "I'm not falling for it, Slug," he said. "So just stop the play acting."

"You want me to grab him, Slug?" asked Lullabeth.

"That's right," said Angus. "Get your friends to help you. You're nothing but a coward without them."

"Who are you calling a coward?" yelled Lullabeth and pushed Angus so hard that he stumbled backward and lost his grip on my sleeve. "You stay where I can see you, Euan," he said, finding his balance again. When he didn't make any attempt to grab my sleeve again, I took a surreptitious little backward step.

"I'm not scared of you either," said Angus. "You're nothing but a bully and petty criminal."

Lullabeth balled her fists.

"Do you know what it's like when you almost get burned to death by a dragon?" muttered Slug, addressing no one in particular.

"You're nothing but a snitch," said Fidget, jabbing a finger into Angus' chest. "Isn't that right Slug? He's nothing but a filthy snitch."

A crowd of scavengers and dragon hunters was beginning to gather, forming a circle around the five

314

of us, jostling to get better view. "If you're going to fight, just get on with it," yelled one of them. "Stop pussy footing around. Give us a bit of entertainment before we turn in for the night."

Some of the men cheered at that.

Angus pushed Fidget. "Don't you dare jab your finger at me."

Lullabeth gave Angus another shove. "Don't push him."

"Almost got roasted where I stood," said Slug.

I slipped back into the crowd.

Angus pushed back at Lullabeth.

Fidget tried to kick the legs from under him. The fact that he almost fell over was enough to help him dodge the punch that Lullabeth attempted to swing. I slipped right to the back to the back of the crowd. I could no longer see what was happening, but I could hear more exchanges of insults and threats. I looked over to the porch of the hut. Mrs Zachariah and Captain Quat were still studying the map and had not yet noticed the affray that was developing in the yard.

I turned and sprinted in the direction of the compound gate. As I ran past the long table, I saw that one of the rope cannon gunners had left his helmet lying there. I grabbed it and pulled it over my head to hide my red hair. As the shouts from the crowd grew louder, I took another glance back at the porch. The coxswain was looking over there now. I was running out of time. It wouldn't be long before he alerted the other two. Not long before someone put a stop to the fight. And not long after that they would find that I was gone.

315

I hesitated a moment, looking back at *The Drunken Molly*, hidden beneath the tarpaulin, considering whether it might be worth changing my plan. Maybe I could somehow sneak under the tarp and hide there until I figured out a way to help the ISC patrol escape. I soon dismissed the idea when it became clear the trio scavenger guards stationed there were not making any effort to move in the direction of the fight.

I sprinted for the compound entrance.

There was another scavenger on guard there, armed with a crossbow. On my approach he turned and aimed it at me. "You're needed straight away," I gasped. "A big fight has broken out and they need all hands to calm things down." He turned his head slightly, listening to the shouts that were echoing out from then compound.

"I'm not to leave my post," he said.

"I'm to relieve you," I told him. "I'm too small to be any good in helping to calm things down back there. But I can take over your post while you go and help."

He still didn't look convinced. I wondered if, despite the rope gunner's helmet, he realised who I was. "Orders of Mrs Zachariah herself," I added quickly.

He lowered his crossbow and rested it on his shoulder. "You keep your eyes peeled, sonny," he told me. "We don't want none of them Ghibelline creeping up on us in the dark with that crabwort stuff."

With that he began to sprint toward the compound.

Not even looking back at him. I ran through the dragon bone arch of the entrance. There was a discarded blanket that he had been using to keep himself warm lying crumpled on the ground. I grabbed it and draped it over my shoulders.

Although it was fully dark now, I could still make out the shadowy outline of the Serrated Mountains far to the North. I had once crossed the tundra from the mountains to Forgsnur's Footprint. My intention was to repeat the journey in reverse. All I had to do was keep running in a straight line.

The ground was hard and frozen beneath my feet. Flurries of snow were dancing once more in the air around me. The farther I ran from the reclamation yard the darker the tundra became. Maybe it was a good thing that I was making my escape by night after all. The tundra was so flat and barren that it would have been easy in daylight for anyone with a telescope to pick out my fleeing form. In the darkness I was going to be almost invisible.

I glanced back to try and see if anyone had yet returned to the entrance. It was then that I saw the trail of footsteps that I had left behind me in the blanket of snow that had fallen earlier in the day. They would lead anyone who wanted to follow right to me.

I began running in crazy circles, leaving what I hoped would be a confusion of prints that would be impossible to follow. Then I shrugged the blanket from my shoulders and dragged it behind me so it would wipe out my trail as I ran headlong for the far away mountains.

10. The Hunter's Moon

The snow flurries thickened so rapidly it took me by complete surprise. Soon it was coming down so thick that the moon in the sky above became no more than a dull glow. I could no longer see the Serrated Mountains ahead of me. When I looked back there was no sign of the reclamation yard.

The snow had started lying so deeply that the trail left behind by my footprints was filled up and covered within moments. There was no longer any need for me to drag the blanket behind me. Shivering I tied two ends of the blanket around my neck so I could use it as a cloak, much the same way as I had when I was first held captive on *The Drunken Molly*.

I pushed the rope cannon gunner's helmet firmly down, buckled the straps and ploughed on, head to the blizzard. I no longer had any idea if I was moving in the direction of the mountains. I just had to take it on faith that I was still walking in a straight line.

At one point the driving wind changed direction and whipped up behind me. Voices were dragged along with it. They were calling out my name. "Euan! Euan Recap! Where are you?" They knew I was gone and already there was a search party out looking for me. I tried to pick up my pace, but the snow was getting deeper and making it more difficult to run.

I heard the drone of an engine in sky somewhere to my back. They'd sent out a scavenger ship to try and find me. I should have guessed they would do that. Why did I never think things through before I acted?

The ground began to vibrate as the scavenger ship drew nearer. I glanced back and saw the lights from storm lamps arcing through the dense fall of snowflakes. She was flying as low to the ground as possible. I dived belly first into the snow and spread the blanket about me so that the falling snowflakes would lie on it. This way I hoped they would not see me.

The vibrations beneath me became so pronounced and the sound of the engine so intense that I felt sure the airship was right above me. I tensed, waiting for a lasso noose to tighten around my leg and haul me into the air. I held my breath and bit my lip. I could feel the downdraft from the turbines and clutched tightly to the edges of the blanket, in case it blew away.

Then the vibrations lessened. The noise of the engines receded. When I dared to turn around, and peek out from the blanket I saw that the scavenger ship had passed over me. It was heading in the direction I had been moving in. I rose to my feet and ran instead to my left. *West*, I told myself. *I'm running west. Once the scavenger ship is out of sight I'll turn again and run north for the mountains.*

***

Euan messes things up again, that was the new thought that kept echoing through my head. I hoped I was once again heading north but I could not be sure. The snow was still falling. It was lying so deep

319

on the tundra that all I could do was drag one foot after the other. The wind was piling it into huge drift, adding to my disorientation.

I wished I'd followed my second plan and somehow snuck under the tarpaulin onto the deck of *The Drunken Molly's* gondola. At least then I'd have had the chance to make contact with the ISC patrol. At least then I would have been warm.

It was pitch dark, not a trace of the moon amongst the thick snow clouds that had swallowed up the vast sky, not so much as a hint of the jagged outline of mountains ahead of me. I could hear nothing now but the ominous howling of the wind that often unbalanced me with its powerful snow filled gusts.

My teeth were chattering. Falling to the ground might have saved me from being detected by the scavenger ship but it had made my clothes damp. The cold bit into me, causing the scar on my chest to throb. The blanket hung sodden around my shoulder. The strap of the helmet was chafing my chin. My fingers felt too numb to loosen the buckle.

A story kept running through my head, the story of *Hargmir, Ghost of all Dragons*. Fenisnoor had told it to me when she explained where Professor Mayhew had taken the name for his ship from. According to the Ghibelline legend *Hargmir* was supposed to be made up from the souls of all dead dragons. She was said to prowl the tundra, waiting to take revenge on anyone who had wronged her kin.

I had been fetcher on one dragon hunting vessel and a galley hand on another. I had witnessed two dragon hunts and the cruel taking of dragon breath. The more I thought about it the more I convinced myself that I was just the type of person that *Hargmir* would be out to get. I started imagining monstrous shadows stalking me in darkness. I found myself jumping and drawing huge gasps of breath whenever it seemed I had caught something out of the corner of my eye.

If Hargmir devours me, I thought. *No one will ever know what happened.*

I started scolded myself again. *Stupid Euan. Messing things up as usual.*

I was so wrapped up in my thoughts that I didn't see what was looming up ahead of me till I almost walked straight into it. I gasped in shock again and took a step back. This was not my imagination playing a trick on me. It was something solid and huge and hideously twisted, part covered in snow, jagged pieces of it jutting skyward like mutilated dragon wings.

Could this be what the ghost of all dragons would look like?

I felt frozen to the spot. The wind blew the snow around me. My shivering intensified as my heart began to thump in my chest. The object ahead of me did not move. Was she sleeping? Or was she coldly observing me through hidden eyes, ready to pounce at the slightest provocation.

"Hargmir?" I said. "I'm a friend. A Friend of the Dragons. I may have been a fetcher on *The Drunken Molly* and a galley hand on *Beauty's Daughter*. But that was not by choice. I was kidnapped. Twice!"

Not a sound or the hint of any movement came from the object. It occurred to me that the sensible thing to do was to turn and run. But when did I ever do the sensible thing? Instead, I found myself taking a cautious step forward. Then another. Then another.

I was right up against the thing now. So close that it would have taken one snap of Hargmir's ghostly jaws, and I'd be gone. But I could see that it was not what I was imagining. Rather it was a chaotic pile of mangled metal and shattered timbers. Holding my breath, I wiped the snow away from the section nearest me.

There was a brass plaque attached to a long piece of wood, dented and blacken by the weather. I narrowed my eyes and saw that there were letters stamped into the brass. Although they had been badly tainted, they were still legible. I brushed away more of the snow and tilted my head to read what they said.

The Hunter's Moon.

I let out a gasp of surprise.

I'd stumbled upon the famous wreck of the airship that had crashed. I'd seen this looking over railings from the gondola of *The Drunken Molly* as she traversed the tundra looking for the White Sow. Angus had claimed that savage grey skinned Ghibelline had eaten her crew alive. But later Captain Zachariah had told me that it had been wolves.

Something else came back to me as I stood there before the wreck. Something Pa had once told me. "Euan," he'd said. "If you ever have to go into

322

the high hills to look for a lost sheep make sure you mark out places of possible shelter, crags or gullies, old trees with hollowed out roots and such like. That way, if the weather takes a turn for the worse, you'll have somewhere to wait it out."

That what this was. The wreck of *The Hunter's Moon* was shelter. Somewhere I could wait out the blizzard till the sun came up and I could once more see in which direction the Serrated Mountains lay. I stepped in amongst the wreckage, looking for something that I might crawl under.

The first section I found was a jagged piece of deck, resting against another section at an exaggerated angle. No sooner had I crawled under it than I discovered that it had a huge hole through which the wind was relentlessly gushing.

Next, I stumbled upon what might have been two walls of the captain's cabin, unevenly upturned so that they lay like a lopsided wooden tent on the ground. But when I crawled in there it creaked and groaned so loudly that I was afraid that the wind and the weight of the snow might bring it crashing down on top of me.

I thought that I might have to try and build myself a bivouac of some sort from bits of the wreckage. But then I came across a section of the gondola's hull that was still intact. I pushed at the rounded side with both hands to test how sturdy it was. It didn't budge an inch. I guessed that it had become partially embedded in soil that had subsequently frozen around it.

The only gap I could find was so close to the ground that I had to dig away the snow with my hands and then lie flat to wriggle under. But the hollow inside was big enough for me to stand up in. There was only a faint hint of wind blowing under the gap I had entered through. I quickly scooped through some snow and packed the gap. The wind ceased.

It was too dark to see anything but as I felt my way around, I came upon a crossbeam three or four feet above the ground. Somewhat awkwardly I climbed up, knowing that I would be warmer up there that on the hard floor of the tundra. Something was tangled around the beam. From patting and touching it I surmised that it was an old dragon net. An old dragon net that was miraculously dry.

I unravelled it from the beam. Once I had freed it I untied the blanket from around my neck and hung it over the beam to dry. Then I took off my shoes and socks and placed them at the far end of the beam. Then I removed my shirt and my trousers and hung them beside the blanket.

I wrapped the netting around me, once, twice, three times. I began to feel a little warmer. My teeth stopped chattering. I rubbed my hands rapidly together till there was enough circulation in my fingers to manage the buckle on the straps of the helmet. When I removed it, I could feel the rawness of their imprint on my jaw.

I placed the helmet beside my socks and shoes and pushed myself along the beam with my bare feet till my back was resting against the camber of the hull. The muscles in my legs were pulsing and tensing from all the running I had done. My breathing began to slow a little. I could feel my nerve ends tingling as my body heat slowly increased. My head slumped forward. I rested my chin on the scar on my chest. My eyelids began to droop. I felt myself drifting into sleep.

Then from outside there came a low growl. My eyes snapped back open. My head jerked upright. A second growl was followed by the sound of frantic scraping against the side of the hull. My heart started thumping once more.

Hargmir had found me!

11. The Pack of Wolves

I felt paralysed by fear. I had never encountered a ghost before. Let alone a ghost apparently made up of the ghosts of many dragons, all of whom were out to wreak revenge on me. From outside I heard another fierce growl followed by more urgent scratching against the outside the section of hull.

I wondered how long it would be before *Hargmir* drew breath and blasted the hull with a flaming ball of fire. I imagined the wooden structure burning all around me. An image of Slug writhing on the deck of *Beauty's Daughter,* swathed in blue flame, flashed into my head. Any minute now the same thing was about to happen to me.

I heard yet another growl and more scratching. Something came over me. A morbid sense of curiosity. It terrified me even to think of what Hargmir might look like, but at the same time I had this uncontrollable urge to see her, to know for certain how she appeared in all her dreadful splendour.

Without even thinking I found myself feeling all around the part of the hull I had been leaning on for gaps in the timber or knotholes that I might be able to press my eye against. I found instead a small area where the damp weather had rotted the wood and turned it fibrous and spongy. I pressed against it. With minimal effort my thumb popped through to the other side.

Leaned in and placed my eye against the hole I'd made. The icy air drew tears and made me blink. When my vision stopped blurring, I saw that the snow had ceased falling. The moon was casting an eerie glow over the blanket of white and the shadowy sections of the rest of the wreck. In amongst these I could see traces of my own footprints and in amongst my footprint a series of smaller paw prints.

For a moment I was a little confused by what I was seeing. Then I heard another growl. I angled my head so that I could look through the rotted hole to the direction from which it came. I had not expected for one moment what I saw there in the snow. Not *Hargmir, ghost of all dragons* - but a wolf. A huge, evil looking wolf, with sleek grey fur and a vicious looking muzzle, drool slavering from its jaws as it drew back its black lips and growled over its razor-sharp teeth.

This must be a descendant of the pack that had devoured the crew of The Hunter's Moon, I thought. The airship had come down in the part of the tundra that was wolf territory. It was not a ghost that I had to be worried about. But it was something just as deadly and just as dangerous.

As I watched the big wolf sniffed the air, no doubt catching my scent. Then he fell onto his muscular haunches and threw back his head. A dreadful, blood-curdling howl echoed out to the tundra. And away in the snowy darkness a chorus of equally chilling howls came echoing back in response. He was calling his clan to supper, and I was on the menu.

I held my breath when I saw a second wolf appear, and then another, and then a third. Two more joined moments later. Then finally a huge wolf, grey fur streaked in midnight black, came padding in amongst the wreckage. From the way he held himself and from the way the others seemed cowed by his presence it was clear that he was the pack leader.

The first wolf stood before him and growled; head slightly turned to the section of hull where I was hiding. The big wolf sniffed the air and then let out series of barks that sounded like instructions. Immediately the pack began excitedly yipping and yapping, dancing around in the snow and snapping at each other's legs.

The big wolf let out an angry howl.

He was like an airship captain giving orders to his crew.

The pack fell still and silent. They gathered before their leader. I saw his head tilt up and pulled my own head back, convinced that he had seen my eye pressed against the hole I'd made with my thumb. I drew a deep breath into my lungs and held it there. After a moment I heard scratching at the base of the hull. When I looked again, I saw three of the wolves digging at the snow with their front paws. It wouldn't be long till they crawled under.

Panic gripped me. What could I do? If I tried to slip back out, I would have no chance at all of escaping before they ran me down. The beam that I was on was raised above the ground, but I was convinced they could easily reach it, especially their leader. I looked up, trying to see if there was a way to climb higher. It didn't seem possible.

I thought perhaps I could unravel the net and try to tangle one of them in it. That way it might slow them down once they'd found their way in. But eventually they'd get to me. The closest thing I had to weapon of any sorts was the Rope Gunner's Helmet. I scrambled along the beam and grabbed it.

Pa's advice came back to me, just as it had when I was dangled on a rope as dragon bait from *The Drunken Molly*. "If you're ever charged by a ram smack it hard on the snout." I had followed that advice when the White Sow came swooping down to devour me. I could use the helmet to do the same with the wolves.

But there was seven of them and if they all got into the upturned hull it would be impossible to hold them all off. The sound of the scratching outside intensified. I was sure that I could see little chinks of moonlight seeping in from under the hull. Any minute now I was going to be torn to shreds by the pack of hungry wolves. I started to cry as one by one I said my goodbyes to each member of my family.

"Goodbye Pa. I'm sorry I never grew up to help you when some of your sheep got lost in the high hills."

"Goodbye Ma. I'm sorry I didn't help more with chores around the cottage."

"Goodbye Isla. I'm sorry I always messed things up on your birthday."

The wolves must have heard me because they started barking and snarling. I looked down and saw a black snout poking through the gap at the bottom of the hull. This was it. I gripped tightly to the rim of the helmet. I repeated the promise I made when I had been dangled from *The Drunken Molly* as bait on a rope. *If I'm destined to die like this, I'll at least put up some kind of fight.*

Then I heard another sound. The sound of one of the wolves yelping as if in pain. The digging came to halt. The snout withdrew rapidly from the bottom of the hull. Another yelp, followed by a drawn-out whine. I rushed back along the beam and pressed my eye back to the hole. The wolves were facing out to the snow-covered tundra, circling around as if in a state of confusion. One of them jumped and skidded a little way across the snow, as if it had been hit by something that had come at it from out of the darkness. It let out a squeal.

The big leader crouched low on his front legs, fur raised on his back, snarling viciously. It looked to me as if he was ready to launch himself into an attack. Behind him the rest of the pack seemed to be preparing to follow his lead. Then something hit the leader smack between his eyes. He howled in agony and furrowed his head deep into the snow, trying to relieve the pain.

Now shouts came out of the darkness. I heard many voices at once. The wolves were thrown into complete confusion. Their leader rose to his feet, pawing at his injured muzzle. Now three more of the pack let out strained yelps as flying objects came at them in quick succession.

The leader let out a last defiant snarl, then fled into the night, his pack dashing at his heels, tails swishing. I heaved a sigh of relief. I had been saved. Then my mood quickly deflated when it became clear that the most obvious explanation was that the dragon hunters and scavengers had found me.

All that effort, tricking Angus to make my escape, struggling through the blizzard, worrying about being stalked by the ghostly Hargmir, almost being eaten alive by wolves, it had all been for nothing. I was about to be captured again. Soon I'd be dangled from a rope in the skies above some high canyon.

Wearily I wiped the tears from my eyes and began to dress myself in my cold, damp clothing. My escape plan might have failed miserably but I had no intention of adding insult to injury by the letting them see me wrapped in old net with only my underwear to cover me up.

As soon as my clothes went on, I could feel all the warmth drain away from me. I began to shiver once more. I bit down on my lip in the hope that this would stop my teeth from chattering. Cautiously I pressed my eye to the hole once more. I wanted to see if Angus or anyone else I recognised was with the search party that had found me.

I hoped they had some warm blankets with them. I no longer cared if there was a scavenger ship nearby ready to transport me back to the compound at Forgsnur's Footprint. All I wanted at that moment was to be seated somewhere in front of a warm, crackling fire.

A figure appeared. The mossy green hair and the grey skin told me straight away this was neither dragon hunter nor scavenger. This was a Ghibelline tribesman. I felt hope once more rise in my heart. He lumbered in amongst the wreckage and then crouched down to examine one of my footprints, still visible amongst the chaotic mess the panicking wolves had made.

After a moment he raised his bulging bicep and gave a signal with his beefy hand. Three more Ghibelline appeared, each carrying a slingshot dangling down from their right hand. So that was what had been fired at the wolves. Stones from Ghibelline sling shots. I squinted my eye, positive that I recognised at least one of them.

After a moment three more joined the group. The tall one in the middle was immediately familiar from his distinctive gait. I had first seen him creeping up on Captain Zachariah in his chamber beneath the Serrated Mountains. I waited till I could see his face to be sure. My heart skipped a beat. There was no mistaking those craggy features, fierce but somehow friendly at one and same time.

"Illagnor?" I cried.

The Ghibelline chieftain's beady black eyes fell upon the broken section of the hull of *The Hunter's Moon*. He placed his big hands onto his hips. "Show yourself, stranger," he demanded. "Considering that you know my name and my kinfolk just saved from being eaten by wolves the least you could do is show yourself."

Needing no further encouragement, I swung down from the beam and scrambled back under the narrow space beneath the hull.

12. A Wounded Dragon

I awoke feeling so cosy and warm that I thought for a moment that I must have still been dreaming. I heard a hissing noise and when I turned my head, I saw little yellow sparks rising from the glowing remnant embers of what had been a huge campfire. Pushing myself up on my elbows I found that I was lying on a thick, furry pelt, with another similar pelt covering me.

To the side of the camp the snow-covered bits of the wreck of *The Hunter's Moon* jogged my memory and brought me into full wakefulness. I remembered the look of surprise on Illagnor's weather-beaten face when I'd emerged from under the hull. "Euan Redcap?" he'd cried. "What are you doing here?"

I started to try and tell him, blurting out everything in an incoherent ramble. But he'd held up his hand. "You're freezing," he'd said. "You look exhausted. We need to get you warm. We can talk in the morning once you've had a good night's sleep. Whatever you have to say can surely wait till then."

With a warm fur wrapped around me I had watched the Ghibelline tribesmen as they hastily assembled a fire from the dry wood that they had dragged with them across the tundra on their sleds. As soon as I slipped into the bedding they'd made up for to the side of the dancing flames of the fire my eyes had fallen shut immediately. My sleep was as deep as any I had experienced on the soft bed back in Professor Mayhew's apartment in Tennanbrau City.

I sat up fully now and saw Illagnor and his companions crouched on their upturned sleds at the other side of the embers. A cooking pot was by their feet, and they were tucking into something that had been shared out into wooden bowls. One of them saw me and nudged Illagnor.

"Euan, you're awake," he called over. "Come and join us for breakfast and you can tell me just how it is you come to be out here on the tundra alone."

What they were eating was some kind of gooey green porridge with stringy bits of fibre running through it. But it warmed the inside of my belly and tasted much better than it looked.

"I should have been back home in the Low Counties by now," I started, gulping down another spoonful. "But I stowed away on Professor Mayhew's airship."

I told Illagnor and his kinfolk everything that happened from being hauled up from the deck of *The Hargmir* to stumbling upon the wreck of *The Hunter's Moon*. It was like a repeat of the time I'd told the tale of my first kidnap, back in Captain Zachariah's chamber beneath the Serrated Mountains.

When I had finished Illagnor fixed me with his beady black eyes. "I don't know how your friends are going to react when they find out what you've done."

"My friends?"

334

"Nathaniel Zachariah and the others," said Illagnor. "They are camped in the foothills with their airship at anchor."

"The foothills?" I asked. "Why would they go to the foothills when Mrs Zachariah is at Forgsnur's Footprint?"

"It would seem they were given some false information concerning her whereabouts. They were of the belief that she had somehow managed to establish a base in the heart of Ghibelline territory."

"I need to get to them. It's worse now that she's made an alliance with Gulliver Quat."

"We will be returning to the foothills later this evening," said Illagnor. "But we have a small task to perform, and you will need to come with us."

"What kind of task?" I asked, placing my empty bowl by the fireside.

"One of our patrols has reported encountering a dragon with an injured wing," came the reply. "We are taking big risk being out here during the daylight. For weeks now Mrs Zachariah has been sending out scavenger ships to harass and intimate my people. But we are determined to tend to the Hammerclaw."

I remembered the Hammerclaw sow rising from the deck of *Beauty's Daughter*, noose still pulled tightly around her wing. I rose to my feet. "Illagnor, I think I know what's wrong. It's a rope. A lasso from a rope cannon. It's still attached to her wing."

***

I rode in Illagnor's sled while he trudged through the snow, hauling me behind him. My

335

clothes and my blanket cloak had been hung up to dry around the fire and, with the rope gunner's helmet on my head and a fur pelt around my legs; I was feeling warm and comfortable. When we'd left camp at the wreck of *The Hunter's Moon*, I'd tried to insist to Illagnor that I could easily walk and be a proper member of his band of Ghibelline. But he'd shaken his big, craggy head and ruffled my red hair with his calloused hand. "You're not used to conditions out here on the tundra, Euan. Distances can be deceptive. I need you to conserve your energy for the journey back to the foothills. We'll be doing that after sunset, and it will be too risky to haul you on a sled in the darkness."

The sky above was clear and blue now, not a trace of snow clouds, a crisp edge of frost in the air making conditions firm underfoot and conducive to the glide needed by the blades of the Ghibelline sleds. We were making good progress. I wondered if the real reason Illagnor wanted me to stay in the sled was because I might slow them down on foot.

Away in the distance I could see the scout that Illagnor had sent ahead stop and look up, turning left, and then left, and then left again, until he had turned full circle. I knew that he was scanning the skies for signs of any approaching scavenger ships.

Illagnor had warned that if a scavenger ship was to be sighted, I was to immediately dive under the sled while he and his kin led them away. "We don't want you getting captured again," he told me. "Mrs Zachariah's aim is to prevent us from wandering the tundra. It's her revenge against us for stealing the balloon from her airship. But the

336

scavengers she sends out don't have much patience. They'll chase us for a while, before they get bored and set course once more for Forgsnur's Footprint. As soon as they're out of sight we'll come back for you."

I watched the scout checking the skies and bit down on my lip as I looked up myself. I really hoped that a scavenger ship wouldn't head in our direction. I was terrified that if I did as Illagnor asked the wolves might come back. With only a sled to protect me I'd be even worse off than I had been the night before. But I also knew for certain that if Illagnor and his kin started to run I would never keep up with them, even if my fear tempted me to disobey him.

I worried about this for almost two hours, constantly glancing upward as the sun rose higher in the sky, listening for the thrum of a scavenger ship engine carried on the wind. I was so distracted that I didn't notice that Illagnor had come to a halt till the sled glided alongside him on its own momentum.

Up ahead the scout was crouched low on a small hillock of snow. He was pointing ahead of him and beckoning with his other hand for the others to approach quietly. "Climb down," whispered Illagnor. "And follow me. Walk slowly and make as little noise as you can."

I did as he asked. By the time we reached the hillock the scout was lying flat on his belly. We joined him, Illagnor and myself to his left, the others to his right. I saw immediately what he was looking at. Only a few feet away from us lay the wounded Hammerclaw.

She was a pitiful sight. She kept trying and failing, trying and failing to flap her wings and gain enough purchase to rise skyward. The lasso had become badly twisted, rendering the wing useless. The snow around her was churned up into muddy quagmire from her struggles. She looked exhausted, head slung low on her muscular neck, ridged tail hanging limply behind her.

All morning while riding on Illagnor's sled my throat had been aching. Now I could feel a sneeze building up inside me. I must have caught a chill from the drenching I'd endured during the blizzard. I tried to hold back the sneeze. My eyes began to water from the effort. Then I could not hold it back any longer. It exploded from me with such a force it sent a puff of powdered snow billowing before me.

"Atishoo!"

The Hammerhead snapped to attention. She turned in our direction. As soon as she saw us there came the tell-tale click-click-click of the little organs in her throat. She spread her jaws wide, but all that came out with her mighty roar was a dense miasma of grey smoke that quickly dissipated.

"The gas has not replenished sufficiently in her lungs," said Illagnor.

The Hammerclaw bowed her head as if she was ashamed. She tried to flap her wings again, pushing off with her hind legs. The good wing beat down against the snow. The damaged wing could barely move. She veered off at an angle and almost fell face first into the mire of snow and mud.

"Prepare the crabwort," said Illagnor.

338

Each of the Ghibelline held out a clump of crabwort root for Illagnor to light, the click-click-click of his flint stones eerily mimicking the sound the organs in a dragon's throat. I sneezed again as some of the smoke blew back into my face, immediately washing a wave of dizziness over me when I breathed in.

Illagnor's big hand guided me downwind of the smoke. The crabwort root was loaded into the cradles of the Ghibelline slingshots. They rose to their feet and began swinging their smoking missiles around their green tufted heads. The Hammerclaw let out a warning roar when she saw them, hacking up more grey smoke, interlaced with flickering silvery sparks.

Unperturbed, the Ghibelline released the smouldering crabwort roots. They went hurling through the air and landed all around the dragon, churning great gushes of smoke from where they sat in the muddy furrows of snow.

The Hammerclaw snorted and tried to bat one of the roots away with her front leg. All she succeeded in doing was making it smoke all the more. The smoke swirled around her like a mist. Most of it was rapidly sucked away by the wind. But a lot of it was inhaled through her flared nostrils. She tried to rise into the sky once more. Still the lasso around her wing thwarted her efforts.

I could see that she was weakening, succumbing to the sedative properties of the crabwort smoke, legs increasingly unsteady. But at the same she was fighting back, shaking her hoary head and stretching her long neck to gasp for fresh air.

Illagnor lit a second batch of crabwort root, which was duly launched from the slingshots. This second wave of smoke was too much for the poor Hammerclaw. With a strained bellow she fell to her knees, the swish of her tail slowing, slowing, slowing, slowing, till it fell completely still. She eased herself down onto her belly, her jaw resting on the muddy slush of the snow, her eyelids drooping shut.

Illagnor bade everyone to stay put till the crabwort smoke had dissipated. When he was sure it was safe, he sent his scout down to check that the Hammerclaw was fully asleep. The scout approached her with caution. Even in a drowsy state he could be sent flying with a mere flip of her tail. He circled around her, drawing ever closer with each circuit. Soon he was right up next to her, kneeling down in the mud, and stroking her head. He beckoned to us to join him.

The Ghibelline set to work straight away, unravelling the rope from her wing, and untying the noose of the lasso. They treated the rope burns and abrasions with the herbal healing balm they'd brought with them on their sleds. Then they examined every part of her for cuts and scratches, either suffered when she'd been hauled onto the gondola deck of *Beauty's Daughter* or self afflicted during her struggles to take flight.

I followed them, touching her scales, tracing my finger along the crevices on the muscular flesh of her legs, stroking her long tail, standing before

340

her, and feeling the warm air that gushed from her nostrils. She was both awesome and beautiful and I knew there and then that I truly was a friend of the dragon and that every moment I had from that day onward would be devoted to saving them from extinction.

"Illagnor!" The sudden cry jolted me from my thoughts.

When I looked the scout was pointing westward in the sky. Illagnor rose to his feet, his big hand gleaming with a film of healing balm. I stood beside him and looked to where the scout was pointing. No less than three scavenger ships were moving across the cloudless sky, their balloons clearly visible, smoke trails fanning out behind them from their turbines.

"What do we do?" I asked.

Illagnor held a finger to his mouth.

We all stood watching in silence as the Hammerclaw slept on.

"They're not coming this way," said the scout after a while. "It looks as if they're heading to the foothills."

"They've discovered the encampment," said Illagnor. "They've been sent to spy and report back to Mrs Zachariah."

"They think that's where I was headed," I said.

"It is where you were headed," said Illagnor. "Although you had no idea that the captain and the others had set up camp there."

"What we do?" I asked.

"What we intended to do all along," replied Illagnor. "We cross the tundra to the foothills at

341

sunset. Only we will need to make haste. I suspect that tomorrow Mrs Zachariah and Gulliver Quat will be setting out in great force to try and recapture you."

13. Fever

Thankfully there was no snow that night. As the sun set the Hammerclaw was roused from her sleep. We watched from the little hillock as she shuffled groggily around, shaking her big head to rid herself of her drowsiness. Every now and then she would fan out her wings, as if testing their strength.

The fits of sneezing that I'd been experiencing all afternoon had given way to a severe runny nose. I kept wiping it on my sleeve to avoid sniffing and attracting the dragon's attention. I could feel a dull tickle at the back of my throat and worried that I was about to start coughing.

Finally, when the sun was nothing but a tiny red disc on the horizon the Hammerclaw mustered the courage to beat her wings. They rose high in unison and swished back down, sending up puffs of snow. Realising that she was no longer restricted she broke into a trot, wings beating up and down and, with a final push from her hind legs, ascended skyward.

As she circled above us, she let out a triumphal screech. When she wheeled round and headed off for the Serrated Mountains we rose to our feet and stood watching in silence. Darkness fell quickly and with it a thick and frosty mist began to rise from the snow-covered tundra floor.

"We need to make haste," urged Illagnor.

The cough that had been bursting to escape from the back of my throat finally let loose. My shoulder jerked forward as I hacked and hacked. I could feel a terrible headache coming on. Beneath my cloak and the lasso gunner's helmet I was starting to sweat as the beginnings of a fever took hold.

"You're getting worse, aren't you?" said Illagnor.

"I'll be fine," I lied, sniffing loudly.

Around us the freezing mist was growing thicker. The cold air irritated my throat and lungs and made me cough even more. "Won't we get lost in this?" I managed to ask between bouts of hacking.

"The Ghibelline have traversed the Far Tundra for thousands of years," Illagnor assured me. "We could find our way to the foothills with our eyes closed." He handed me a coil of rope. "Tie this around your waist. Leave a good length hanging down at your back." He tied another coil around his own waist and showed me how it should it look. "We walk in single file," he said. "Each one holds the rope of the one in front. That way no one gets separated, and no one gets lost."

Sniffing and coughing I tried the rope around me as shown.

"Bargner will walk ahead of you," said Illagnor, pointing to the Ghibelline who had been acting as our scout. "Hold tightly to his rope and walk in his footprints. I will be behind you. If you stumble I will catch you. But I warn you we will be moving at a fair pace."

***

344

The fog that developed out of the mist was far thicker than anything I'd ever seen rolling down from the high hills back home. Bargner was walking only a few paces in front of me, but I could not see him. I just had to hold on to the rope and hope for the best. Equally the only indication I had that Illagnor was behind was the taut pull of the rope tied around my waist and the rhythmic crunching of his big feet against the frosty crust that had formed on snow.

I felt terrible. I seemed to be alternating between bouts of sneezing and bouts of coughing. One minute I'd be shivering uncontrollably, the next sweating profusely. My head was throbbing. Pain constantly jabbed at the back of my throat. The muscles in my legs felt stiff. It became increasingly difficult to put one foot in front of the other.

I've no idea how long I managed to trudge through the mist in that terrible fevered condition, perhaps no more than an hour. Was it more than that? Was it less than that? All I know for sure is that as my cough grew steadily worse my chest grew tighter with each new bout of hacking.

Then a horrible, sickening dizziness came swirling over me. The snowy ground beneath my feet seemed to sway as if I was standing on an airship's gondola. I lurched forward, struggling to keep up with Bargner's dogged pace. Suddenly I was falling. Before I hit the ground Illagnor dashed forward and grabbed me. I felt myself swung high into the air and perched firmly onto his broad shoulders. We were not moving. It seemed I had brought the whole Ghibelline procession to a halt.

"Pass me down Bargner's rope," said Illagnor.

"You can't carry me," I protested, my voice coming out as a raw croak. "I'll walk."

"You're ill, Euan," he said. "You've done well to make it this far. I've had heavier loads on my shoulders before now."

Coughing again I passed down the rope.

"Head out," barked Illagnor.

We began to move forward.

"Rest now, Euan," said Illagnor.

Legs hanging limply down over his shoulders I held onto his bony head. Soon my own head slumped down. I nestled my cheek against the mossy tuft of his hair. The cold fog swirled all around. When I breathed in it made me cough. Slowly my eyes fell shut.

***

The first thing I noticed was a strong, keenly aromatic scent that was somehow slackening the tightness in my chest and helping me to breathe more easily. My head was resting on a soft pillow and there was a blanket pulled up around my shoulders.

Somewhere nearby I could hear the low murmur of voices. I didn't open my eyes straight away. I thought that I might be dreaming. I drifted back to sleep for a little while. Then I became conscious of the smell again. I swallowed and found that my throat didn't hurt half as much as it had, and my headache seemed to have eased a little.

I forced my gummy eyelids apart and looked up. I seemed to be inside a tent of sorts, canvas flapping in the wind. I coughed. It was just a single cough. It didn't set off a bout of hacking. I blinked the sleep out of my eyes. It was then that I caught a glimpse of someone inside the tent with me. For one terrible moment I thought that I had been captured and taken back to Forgsnur's Footprint. I pushed myself cautiously up onto my elbows. My mood lifted when I saw who was hovering at the foot of the makeshift bed that had been made up for me.

"Fenisnoor!" I cried, finding myself filling up with genuine elation.

"How do you feel?" she asked, a smile breaking on her craggy face.

"Fine," I replied. "Well better than I did at least."

I wrinkled my nose. "What's that smell?" I asked.

"Mashed crabwort leaves," came the reply. "I rubbed it into your chest. Crabwort root has a sedative effect, but the leaves are good for fevers and respiratory conditions. You were in a bad way when Illagnor and others arrived."

I was about to ask where Illagnor and Bargner and the rest were when the flap on the tent was jerked roughly to one side and someone else entered. I recognised the ponytail and the leather waistcoat straight away.

"Hari." I sat up a little straighter.

Hari placed her hands on her hips and scowled at me in a manner that immediately put me in mind of my sister Isla. "Don't you Hari me, Euan Redcap," she snapped. "You are in serious trouble!"

14. Back Amongst Friends

Once I was dressed, I did as Hari had told me to do and emerged through the flaps of the tent. The air on my face was chilly but nowhere near as cold and icy as it had been on the tundra. The sun glinted sharply in my eyes and made me blink.

When I'd finished squinting, I saw that both Hari and Fenisnoor were standing before me. Beside them stood Captain Zachariah, Professor Mayhew, and Sergeant Caulder. Behind them all mingled and milling together were various Friends of the Dragon, Coxswain Grisling and some of the crew of *The Hargmir*. Hovering nearby were the other members of Sergeant Caulder's *ISC* patrol. Some way further back Illagnor was in deep discussion with a huge band of Ghibelline. It looked like his whole of his tribe, men women and children, were there.

"Hello," I said, my throat still a little raw.

They all looked at me. I knew from their faces that Illagnor had relayed to them everything that had happened to me since I left Mr Highbrae and took the road to Pennington Vale. Suddenly they all seemed to want to scold me at once.

"What on earth possessed you?" demanded Captain Zachariah.

"How could you be so reckless?" said Professor Mayhew.

"I warned you once before about the consequences of running away," said Sergeant Caulder.

"You were lucky that Illagnor found you," said Fenisnoor.

"Think about how worried your parents will be," said Hari, flipping her ponytail petulantly back over her shoulder.

I felt like the old Euan again. The one who always ended up getting told off for messing things up. Had it been a few months earlier I think I might have burst into tears right there and then. But it quickly came to me that I wasn't the old Euan any longer. I had changed. Everything that I had been through had changed me. I straightened my shoulders and looked them all in the eye one by one. "I'm sorry," I said, giving a little hint of an apologetic shrug. "But I honestly don't regret what I've done."

Again, I was faced with a stony wall of silence.

Then JJ stepped forward. "Well, if you think this means I'm going to draw another picture paper about your new exploits you've got another thing coming," he said. "I've got more than enough on my plate as it is."

The silence held a moment or so longer. Then Hari snorted as if she had been holding in a laugh that was desperate to escape. Professor Mayhew turned, and when he saw that Hari was gripped by a fit of the giggles he started laughing too. Captain Zachariah threw his head back and chortled throatily. Fenisnoor let out a huge, booming guffaw. Sergeant Coulter's face creased with mirth. Soon everyone was laughing and, without even realising it, I found that I was laughing too.

Hari came and punched me playfully on the shoulder. "Let's get some breakfast, stowaway," she said. "But don't go thinking you're forgiven."

***

The camp was set on a gentle slope of hardy grass, sheltered by irregular grey rocks to one side and a thicket of shrubs to the other. I counted two-dozen canvas tents like the one I had woken up in. A little further up the slope the anchor of *The Hargmir* was embedded deep into the soil with four or five tether ropes tied to the rocks. Above them the huge hull of airship hung on her balloon twenty or so feet up the air, swaying as the ropes creaked and strained.

Upturned crates had been set out around a campfire. Hari sat me down on one of them.

Breakfast consisted of scrambled eggs and the type of hard biscuits that were part of the staple supplies always carried on airships. This was washed down with mugs of a hot and sweet herbal drink that I suspected was based on a Ghibelline recipe. I found that the taste of it all was somewhat overpowered by the strong smell of the crabwort leaf mash that Fenisnoor had rubbed into my chest.

Sergeant Caulder sat next to me. "Did you see the ISC patrol back at the reclamation yard?" she asked me. "Are they safe?"

I swallowed down some egg and nodded. "I didn't see them exactly. They're being kept in the hold of *The Drunken Molly*. The whole airship is under a huge tarpaulin. But I heard Mrs Zachariah say that they were being well looked after."

Sergeant Caulder sighed. "I would rather that you'd had sight of them."

"I did think about trying to help them escape," I said. "But it wasn't possible. They were too heavily guarded."

"You did the right thing," she assured me. "It wouldn't have been right to put yourself at risk."

With that she rose and went off to discuss the matter with the rest of her patrol.

Now it was Captain Zachariah who came and sat next to me. He put his arm around me. A lopsided smile appeared on his molten face. "It's good to see you, Euan," he said.

I nodded my head. "It's good to see you too."

"How is she?" he asked. "How is my Isabella?"

I wasn't sure what to say. I didn't want to offend or upset him. I cleared my throat. "I think she's getting worse," I said. "I think Captain Quat is *making* her worse."

"Aye, Euan," he said. "Old Gulliver Quat has a habit of bringing out the worst in people. I know that from all the years I was his second in command."

"He wants to kill the White Sow," I told him. "He thinks she's some sort of curse."

"I suppose in a way she is," said the captain. "But a curse that is self-imposed. One that is born out of greed and ambition."

"I think it's the desire for revenge that's the curse on Mrs Zachariah," I said. "She blames the White Sow for what happened to you and what happened to your son."

Captain Zachariah bowed his head. "I know, Euan. And I would give anything in the world to change things."

Without warning our conversation was interrupted by Professor Mayhew rattling a spoon against a tin plate. "Let's call this meeting to order," he said.

I might have guessed there would be a meeting. Friends of the Dragon always convened meetings when there were important matters to discuss and important decisions to be made. All eyes, including mine, fell on the professor.

"We know that at some point this morning Mrs Zachariah and Gulliver Quat will be heading this way," he said, running his hand over his grey whiskers. "We have to decide what to do when they get here."

"We could just pack up camp and fly *The Hargmir* higher into the mountains," suggested someone.

"That would just end up as a game of cat and mouse," said Hari. "We should stand our ground. We can't let them bully us."

"Why don't we just hide Euan?" suggested someone else. "They've no proof whatsoever that he's here with us."

"Gul Quat is too wily to fall for that," said Captain Zachariah. "He'd call our bluff. He'd ask us to join him in searching for Euan on the tundra. It would be highly suspicious if we refused."

"The solution is very simple," said Sergeant Caulder. "With the assistance of my patrol I will

352

place both Quat and Mrs Zachariah under arrest for kidnap and other misdemeanours."

"That didn't work out well for the last patrol who tried," said Hari. "It's likely that we're going to be massively outnumbered."

"I've sent messengers to the other tribes of the Ghibelline," said Illagnor. "They'll heed my call and come to our aid.

"That should at least even things up," said Fenisnoor.

"Still," said Hari, "I don't see them just willingly surrendering themselves into custody. They've gone too far already."

"Couldn't we just stick to the original plan?" asked JJ. "Nathaniel speaks to Mrs Zachariah and persuades her to surrender. If that happens it would surely put Quat at huge disadvantage."

"I always thought that if I was able to get her on her own, I might be able to talk her round," said Captain Zachariah. "But if she's with the others she'll be belligerent and confrontational. She'll insist that I'm an impostor and refuse to speak to me, especially if Gul Quat is egging her on."

"What are we supposed to do then?" asked one of the young activists from Friends of the Dragon. I thought she looked to be around the same age as Hari. "Fight them? I didn't sign up for this expedition to fight people."

"Yes, you did," said the clean-shaven youth who was seated on the crate next to her. "When you signed up as a Friend of the Dragon you signed up to protect dragons against people who would do them harm. Look at all the times we've been harassed and jeered at when we were handing out leaflets in Scavenger's Market."

"This is not the same thing," said the girl.

"It is," insisted the boy.

I felt that I had to say something. "This is all my fault," I interrupted. "I messed things up for everybody. If they come for me, I'll just go with them."

"You most certainly will not," said Sergeant Caulder. "When Illagnor brought you to the camp last night he effectively placed you under the protection of the Imperial Sky Patrol."

"Besides," said Hari. "If you went with them then we really would have to fight. We couldn't just stand by and let them carry out their plan to kill the White Sow."

A call rang out and echoed against the hillside. "Airships ho!"

The call came from above us. Everyone looked up. A crewmember was waving down at us from the gondola of *The Hargmir*. "Armada approaching across the tundra."

"How many?" Captain Zachariah called back.

The crewman raised a telescope to his eye. After a moment he called back down. "Two dragon hunting vessels and at least a dozen scavenger ships."

"It looks as if the time for debating is over," said Professor Mayhew. "We are just going to have to stand our ground and see what develops."

354

15. The Stand Off

In silence we watched the armada of airships approaching across a sky that seemed to be growing increasingly dark and foreboding. Captain Zachariah dispatched orders to coxswain Grisling to raise anchor and take *The Hargmir* up into the cover of the billowing grey cloudbank. He himself remained on the ground.

Before *The Hargmir* ascended Sergeant Caulder had her patrol members climb the rope ladder up to the gondola where they were to stand ready to launch their craft from the deck. She too stayed behind on the ground. Despite the odds she remained stubbornly insistent that she was going to attempt to execute an arrest.

We moved down from the campsite to the edge of the tundra. As the wind whipped around me, I tightened the strap on the rope gunner's helmet and pulled my blanket cloak around my shoulders. Hari stood next to me shivering slightly but chin nevertheless jutting forward in defiance. Illagnor kept watching for the arrival of the Ghibelline tribes. He had sent his messengers in all directions, some to the east and west of the tundra, some up into the Serrated Mountains, some down in the labyrinth of caves beneath. Yet there was no guarantee whatsoever that any of them would reach us on time.

As the armada drew ever closer, I saw far away in the distance the outline of a flock of dragons diving in and out of a huge pillar of swollen black cloud. They were too far away for me to be able to make out what breed they were. But it comforted me to know that for once the focus of the dragon hunters and the scavengers would not be on them.

***

It took almost an hour for the armada to arrive at the foothills. As it ploughed steadily towards us, I could feel my heart beating faster and faster. Not knowing what was going to happen next was making me anxious. But I wasn't afraid. I was with friends. They were like my second family. I knew they wouldn't let anything bad happen to me.

The airship engines fell silent. They hovered in the air above the tundra, scavenger ships fanned out behind *The Drunken Molly* and *Beauty's Daughter* in a vast array of coloured dragon wing balloons. *The Drunken Molly* herself sported a patchwork balloon of many shades and hues. I guessed that it had been made from scraps that Rusty Reeves had stored in one of his huts in the reclamation yard.

Beauty's Daughter was the first to begin a slow descent, followed moments later by *The Drunken Molly* and then several of the scavenger ships. They stopped twenty or so foot from the ground. Wicker basket cradles were eased over the sides of the gondolas and lowered to the ground.

Mrs Zachariah emerged from one of them, along with some members of her crew. Angus Stonedyke was amongst them. A second cradle from *The Drunken Molly* bore the three captured ISC patrol members, hands bound behind their backs. Gull Quat and some of his men were in the first cradle that came down from *Beauty's*

356

Daughter. Slug, Fidget and Lullabeth were in the third. From the cradles lowered from the scavenger ship emerged a scruffy looking militia, armed with rifles and crossbows and cudgels.

We all huddled closer together and stood facing them. I could feel the tension in the air. Hari reached out and took my hand. I wasn't sure if she was trying to comfort me or comfort or herself. I saw Illagnor and Fenisnoor scanning the foothills and the tundra. The Ghibelline tribes were still nowhere to be seen.

Gull Quat came hobbling towards us, Mrs Zachariah striding at his side, hem of her long coat snapping at her boots, members of her crew pushing the ISC hostages ahead of them, armed scavenger at the rear. Hari squeezed my hand tighter. "Don't worry," she said. "They won't bully us into giving you up."

I felt a little twinge of guilt when I saw that Angus was sporting a black eye and a split lip. But it seemed that he had put up a considerable fight. Slug Martin had a big bruise on his cheek. He was walking with a bit of a limp. It seemed though, from the way Lullabeth kept casting daggered glances at Angus that the fight I had engineered hadn't resolved anything between them.

Quat stopped several feet from us. Mrs Zachariah stood at his side, braids dancing at her shoulders in the wind. Their men fell in behind them. Captain Zachariah stepped forward, pulling up his hood, as if suddenly ashamed once more by his appearance.

Quat leaned predictably on his dragon bone leg. "Seems we have us a bit of a standoff here, Nathaniel."

Captain Zachariah ignored him and spoke instead to his wife. "It doesn't need to be like this, Isabella."

The nerves on Mrs Zachariah's face began to twitch. She scowled at him. Her lip curled in distain. "Impostor," she breathed.

Now Sergeant Caulder stepped up beside Captain Zachariah. "Isabella Zachariah," she announced. "I have a warrant for your arrest. Charge one – the abduction and unlawful detention of ISC patrol members, Laurence Higgs, Alicia Barnis and Thomas Rundell. Charge two – engaging in acts of harassment likely to be of detriment to various treaties signed between the Emperor Julian and the tribes of the Ghibelline. Charge three – the previous abduction and unlawful detention of Master Euan Redcap of the Low Counties."

Mrs Zachariah looked confused. "Euan Redcap? My fetcher? Who abducted him?"

"You're not in any position to carry out an arrest," interrupted Quat. He held up his hand. Behind him the scavengers raised their rifles and crossbows.

Sergeant Caulder was not intimidated. She stepped closer to Quat. He towered over her. She had to crane her neck to look up at him. "You, sir, are under arrest yourself."

"Show me your warrant," challenged Quat.

"You know as well as I do, that I need no warrant," said Sergeant Caulder. "I have sufficient grounds to arrest you for the abduction and unlawful detention of Master Redcap on a second occasion."

"You're outnumbered and outgunned," said Quat. "How exactly do you plan to execute an arrest?"

"I am assuming that neither yourself, nor Mrs Zachariah wish to be considered outlaws with no prospect of ever returning to Tennanbrau City," said Sergeant Caulder, her voice never faltering.

"You should listen, Isabella," said Captain Zachariah.

"Why would I listen to someone who is clearly in league with an imposter?" she spat back at him.

"Will you surrender peaceably?" asked Sergeant Caulder.

Quat threw his head back and laughed. "When we return to Tennanbrau it will be to a hero's welcome," he roared. "We will be celebrated as the ones who finally brought down the accursed White Sow. If any charges are laid against us, we will be acquitted on the basis of guilty, with mitigating circumstances. Because everything we are accused of doing has been for a glorious purpose. In any case when the wings of the White Sow are hung in pride of place over the throne of Emperor Julian, he will no doubt offer us an unconditional amnesty."

A wild cheer went up from the dragon hunters and the scavengers.

"Are you resisting arrest?" asked Sergeant Caulder.

Quat shook his head and sneered. "I am saying your attempt to arrest me has no prospect of success. Instead, I wish to offer you a deal." He gave a wave of his hand. The three ISC patrol members were bundled roughly to the front of the crowd. They didn't look as if they'd been mistreated in any way. They looked more humiliated than anything. I suppose they thought that the fact they'd allowed themselves to be captured brought shame to the Sky Corps.

"I propose an exchange," said Quat. "These three for Euan Redcap."

"Absolutely not, Gul," said Captain Zachariah.

Quat leaned forward again and rested his weight on his dragon bone leg. "It's a good deal, Nathaniel. Three adults for a single Low County boy. Does the maths. I think you know who is getting the best side of the bargain,"

"That boy is under the protective custody of the ISC," said Sergeant Caulder.

"He is also under my legal guardianship," said Professor Mayhew. "Until such time as he is returned to his parents."

A huge smile spread beneath Quat's beard. "Thaddeus Mayhew," he said, in a somewhat mocking tone. "The inventor of the rope cannon and the dragon breathe extractor. I've always wanted to meet you face to face. Without your inventions the dragon hunting trade would never have taken off."

"Then allow me to show my latest invention," said the professor.

He turned and signalled up the hill to one of the men who had been left behind at the encampment. The man lifted a flaming torch from the campfire and waved it back and forth. Responding to this *The*

360

Hargmir descended slowly down from the cover of the clouds.

"This is my airship," said the professor, as Quat, Mrs Zachariah and the others craned their necks. "You will notice the unique design of her balloon. This is because it is filled with an alternative gas, one that occurs naturally beneath the ground. In the future there will no need at all for anyone to hunt dragons for their breath."

"But we are dragon hunters and scavengers, Mr Mayhew," said Quat. "Are you expecting us to give up our livelihoods? Should we condemn ourselves to poverty just because you have a misguided conscience?"

I could hear angry murmurs rippling through the crowd.

"There will be work," the professor tried to assure him. "There will be opportunities for entrepreneurs. The gas must be extracted from beneath the ground. There will need to be excavation projects and boreholes and pipelines."

Quat looked appalled. "You want us to be miners and labourers? Proud dragon hunters and brave scavengers?"

The dragon hunters began to jeer. The scavengers shook their weapons in the air.

"We've wasted enough time with this nonsense," said Quat. "Take the deal I've offered you, or we shall take the boy by force."

The scavengers aimed their weapons at us once more.

Hari squeezed my hand.

Angus moved to the side of Mrs Zachariah.

"Come on, Euan," he said over his split lip. "Just come with us. No one needs to get hurt."

Just then a shout went up from the gondola of *The Drunken Molly*.

"Look to the east."

Depending on which side of the standoff they were situated everyone looked either to their left or their right. Approaching fast in tight formation came a grey mass of figures. It was one of the Ghibelline tribes. There had to be more than a hundred of them.

"This changes things," Fenisnoor called to Quat. "Do the maths."

"There will be more of my people coming down from the mountains," added Illagnor.

Quat didn't seem at all fazed. A smug grin formed beneath his beard. He gave another signal with his hand. Within moments on of the scavenger ships broke off from the main grouping and headed across the sky in the direction of the approaching Ghibelline.

The Ghibelline kept coming. They were moving fast, running at a steady trot rather than walking. I could see that they were armed with spears and shields. When the scavenger ship was directly above them round objects began to be hurled over the deck railings. Everyone gasped as these objects exploded as soon as they hit the surface of the tundra, immediately felling those who were at the head of the advance. The smoke from these explosions was thick and grey. As it washed back over the Ghibelline warriors. They slumped and lurched and fell. Row by row they succumbed, till not a single one was left standing.

"We thought we'd give you a taste of your own medicine," chuckled Quat. "We mixed up a potent little cocktail of crabwort root, dragon breath and gunpowder."

No sooner had the words left Quat's lips than we were cruelly subjected to mocking laughter from the dragon hunters and scavengers on the ground. There came shouts of derision from the crew of *Beauty's Daughter* and *The Drunken Molly* above our heads. Even Mrs Zachariah was a managing a smug little smile.

They were all so focused on gloating that none of them noticed Sergeant Caulder sending a signal of her own up to *The Hargmir*. But I did. I watched as three ISC patrol craft, with their oblong balloons and bicycle-like frames, rose from the gondola, one in the lead, the other two to either side.

The ISC patrol members peddled their craft and steered the handlebars so that they were right in amongst the armada before anyone else even realised what was happening. The lead vehicle was deftly manoeuvred till it was level with the balloon on the nearest of the scavenger ships. The patrolman stopped peddling. His vehicle hovered in position. He reached back and withdrew his crossbow from the sheath strapped to the back of his leather jerkin. Before the coxswain of the scavenger ship could react. He had fired a bolt straight into the balloon.

The high-pitched whistle as the dragon breath escaped from the hole that the bolt had torn into the dragon wing membrane of the balloon could be heard from down on the ground. Dragon hunters and scavengers scattered in the face of the airship's rapid descent. It hit the ground with a terrible crash that shattered the hull timbers of the gondola. Crewmen dived clear of the wreck as its jet-black balloon collapsed flaccidly down onto it.

"Surrender now," said Sergeant Caulder. "Or I will have my men bring down both of the dragon hunting vessels."

Quat looked furious. Mrs Zachariah's head was jutting left and right as if she didn't really know what was going on. Many of the scavengers were searching the ground for weapons dropped during the panic to escape the falling ship. It seemed once more that I was the only one looking at the sky. I saw one of the rope cannons on *The Drunken Molly* swivelling around. The cannon barrel was raised and pointed at one of the ISC vehicles. A gunner was taking aim.

"Look out!" I cried.

But I was already too late. A rope lasso was speeding through the sky. It fell around the shoulders of the patrolman. As the noose tightened, he was hauled from his seat. He fell and jerked to a violent halt as the rope reached its full length and noose pulled even more tightly around him. With no one to steer it his vehicle spun wildly away, narrowly missing a head on collision with another scavenger ship.

Quat sneered at Sergeant Caulder. "You were saying?"

It was at that moment that one of the captured ISC patrol members decided to make a break for it.

364

It was Alicia Barnis, the only woman in the patrol. She barged into the dragon hunter who had a grip on her shoulder and sent him flying. Then sprinted towards us. As she ran the other two ISC members began scuffling with their captors.

Alicia had almost made it to where we stood when there came an audible click and the sound of something slicing through the air. Alicia fell and rolled awkwardly, hands still lashed behind her back, blood gushing from the entry wound of the crossbow bolt that protruded from her thigh. With no regard whatsoever for her own safety Sergeant Caulder ran to her aid.

The two other patrol members stopped struggling.

"Surrender the boy now," demanded Quat. "Before there is more bloodshed."

Hari pulled at my hand and guided me behind her. "They'll have to go through me before I let them take you," she promised.

The scavengers had regrouped. They began singing the Dragon Hunters Sky Shanty, as if it was some sort of war cry. The dragon hunters themselves joined in on the refrain.

Now I was born in Tennanbrau
Haul away above the clouds
And grew as tall as I am now
Haul away above the clouds

"Enough!" The raw voice of Captain Zachariah echoed above the din. "Take me instead of the boy."

The song trailed off into silence. "You?" asked Quat.

"The boy is not the only one who knows where the White Sow has her lair," said the captain. "Was I not dragged there, lashed to her side on a lasso rope? Was it not in her very lair that I was scalded beyond recognition by her fiery breath? Take me, Quat. I'll go willingly if it stops this madness."

Mrs Zachariah's eyes began to jitter. "Yes, yes, yes," she cried. "Take the imposter. When it is over. When the damned Sow is dead, and the curse is lifted, I'll have my bonny captain back."

"You can't," pleaded Hari. "It's just playing into their hands."

The captain pulled back his hood and nodded his molten head to where Sergeant Caulder was desperately trying to staunch the flow of blood from the wound on Patrolwoman Barnis' leg. "I don't want to see anyone else getting hurt," he said and took a step forward.

"Don't," I cried. "It should be me!"

Hari gripped my hand tighter, seemingly determined not to let me go.

Then, a sudden shadow filled the sky above us. I caught a glimpse of white scales and black talons. The gust from the downbeat of a powerful set of wings almost knocked both Hari and myself from our feet.

16. The White Sow

"The White Sow!" cried Illagnor. "We helped to heal her when she was wounded, and she has come to our aid in our hour of need."

Huge wings spread wide the Sow went gliding over the unconscious bodies of the Ghibelline tribe. Screeching she beat her wings and rose skyward then turned into a dive. Swooping low beneath the gondolas of *The Drunken Molly* and *Beauty's Daughter* she came in with her legs pressed close to her creamy white belly, so close to the ground that Quat, Mrs Zachariah and the others had to dive to the ground to avoid being hit.

One scavenger wasn't fast enough. The sow grabbed him in her black claws as she rose. He screamed as she dropped him, and he plunged to the ground. As she rose her white-scaled back hit the hull of *The Drunken Molly*. The repairs that had been made to the hole torn there during her previous encounter with the Sow gave way immediately, splintered hunks of reclaimed wood falling earthward.

I saw the lassos from three rope cannons fired from the deck of *Beauty's Daughter*. One of the nooses managed to tighten around the Sow's right leg. She pulled back against it and when the airship tilted precariously one of the rope gunners went tumbling over the railings. The Sow roared and a powerful jet of flame shot from her mouth. The tarred timbers on the side of the gondola took light.

The rope that bound her quickly burned through and snapped.

The Sow beat down on her wings. The balloons of both airships rocked from the turbulent gush sent out by them. The Sow raked the balloon of one of the scavenger ships with her claws, shredding the dragon wing membrane to ribbons. Her tail swung round and smashed straight through the gondola of a second scavenger ship. She rose skyward.

There was chaos in her wake. Both *The Drunken Molly* and *Beauty's Daughter* were yawing back and forth. There was a gaping hole exposing the hold of *The Drunken Molly*. Crewmen on the deck of *Beauty's Daughter* were leaning over the side, trying to beat out the fire with dragon nets. Scavenger ships were desperately attempting evasive manoeuvres to avoid the downward plummet of the two stricken vessels, narrowly avoiding colliding with each other in the process.

I watched in amazement as the two remaining ISC patrol members deftly steered their vehicles through the pandemonium. They were going to the rescue of their fellow patrol member, who was still dangling from the lasso rope that had dragged him from his own vehicle. One of the patrol members went past him to the left and sliced straight through the rope with a knife. The second came in lower and caught him by the collar of his jerkin as he fell. With what seemed to me amazing strength and balance he swung his colleague around so that he could sit behind him. Mission accomplished they peddled swiftly to *The Hargmir*.

Away in the distance the White Sow was wheeling around again in the grey sky, preparing for another attack. On the tundra the dragon hunters and scavengers who had been slowly rising back to their feet crouched fearfully low again. I saw Quat wrap his big arm protectively around Mrs Zachariah's shoulder.

Taking advantage of the situation Illagnor and Fenisnoor ran forward and wrestled the two remaining ISC hostages free and rushed them back to our ranks. Some the Friends of the Dragon, including JJ, dashed to where Sergeant Caulder was still tending to Alicia Barnis and helped her carry the wounded patrolwoman to safety.

The Sow was almost upon the armada once more.

"Everyone down!" cried Captain Zachariah. "She's coming in fast and low."

Hunkering down we watched as the Sow drew closer. "She's so beautiful," said Hari, crouching beside me. "How could anyone ever wish her harm?"

When she was almost upon the armada the Sow sent an intense ball of fire hurtling before her. The speckled balloon of one of the scavenger ships erupted into yellow flame. Within seconds the dragon breath inside the balloon exploded in a deafening blast. The shower of sparks that rained down in its aftermath set light to the gondola of the ship nearest to her.

As the first scavenger ship fell to the ground and the second was swallowed in flames the Sow came gliding through the smoke and debris, her wings and her tail sending the remaining scavenger ships into dizzying tilts and spins. She leaned slightly so that one mighty wing faced the ground and the other faced the sky and came roaring through the space between *The Drunken Molly* and *Beauty's Daughter*. I saw lassos being launched from the rope cannon emplacements on both ships. But she was far too fast to catch.

She came over our heads only a foot or so above us. All of us turned to watch as she rose again into the sky above the foothills, only narrowly missing *The Hargmir*. Her wings were beating rapidly. She climbed high, heading for the Serrated Mountains themselves.

Captain Zachariah stood up. He waved with both hands up to the crew on *The Hargmir*. "She's going to come back in once more," he yelled. "Take evasive measures. Move the ship to safety."

I heard the engines and turbines start as *The Hargmir* turned and drifted west, slowly at first, then picking up pace. Out on the tundra dazed scavengers were lurching from the wreckage of the two fallen ships. Above them a third was fully ablaze. Any minute now the balloon would catch light. Bits of splintered timber were still falling from the shattered hull of *The Drunken Molly*. The fire on the side of *Beauty's Daughter* had been extinguished, but black smoke was still swirling all around her.

I could hear everyone shouting in panic. Amongst the shouts I picked out Slug Martin's panicking voice. "See what dragons can do? See

370

what dragons can do? They can burn you. They can burn you alive."

Then Fidget's voice, "c'mon, mate. It's over. She's gone."

And Slug again, "she's not gone. She'll be back. She'll roast us alive!"

Then Lullabeth, "shut up, Slug. You're an embarrassment."

I saw Quat struggle upright and wedge his dragon bone leg to the ground to gain balance. He began calling up similar orders to those of Captain Zachariah. "Move while you have the chance, damn you. Don't just wait till she smashes you to smithereens."

The turbines on both *The Drunken Molly* and *Beauty's Daughter* began to rotate and churn. Then over the sound of their engines came another sound. It sent a cold shiver down my spine. It was the dreadful sound of crazy, maniacal laughter. When I looked for its source, I saw Mrs Zachariah dancing an insanely wild jig, legs kicking high, arms flailing about. The braids of her hair were cracking like whips. She looked as if she had finally lost her grip on reality and had no clue whatsoever where she was.

I turned to see if Captain Zachariah had noticed. But he was facing the foothills.

"Here she comes," he yelled.

I looked to where he was pointing and saw just the faintest outline of the Sow descending through the heavy clouds. It was when I turned back again to look at the tundra that my eyes fell on Angus Stonedyke. Unlike the others, who were scattering in all directions, he was rushing about with his head low, seeming to be looking for something on the ground. He picked something up. It took me a moment to realise that it was crossbow. I saw him check that it was loaded with a bolt. Then he raised it to his shoulder, spread his legs wide to steady himself, and placed his eye to the sight.

His straggly red hair hung around him. He chewed his lip to focus his concentration. I knew exactly what he intended to do. Based on past experience, I wasn't at all sure how good an aim he was with a crossbow, but I knew that he was certainly accurate with a lasso from a rope cannon. He had stationed himself right in the path of the Sow's approach. I looked over my shoulder. She was coming in fast.

I had to do something.

Hari yelled in surprise as I leapt to my feet and charged towards Angus. I could see him tracing the sky with the crossbow in the exact same manner as he would have done had he been in the cockpit behind a rope cannon. I could see the tension in his legs and the fixed determination that had settled on his freckled face.

He was going to take his best shot.

I ran at him.

It was only much later that I recalled hearing the click as the bolt was released from the crossbow. I dived for his legs and his knees buckled under the impact. He hit the ground heavily, momentarily winded. Seizing my advantage I yanked the crossbow from his hands and hurled it as far away from us as I could.

Angus rolled over and rose onto his knees, gasping to regain his breath. Turning his head slightly he looked up to the sky. Then he lurched to his feet. I backed away, fearing he would launch a wild punch at me, but his eyes were firmly fixed on the sky.

"I did it!" he yelled. "I can't believe I actually did it!"

I looked up. The Sow was twisting in agonised spasm in the sky directly above us, front legs pawing at the tiny bolt that protruded from her pale neck, patch of red blood growing wider and darker on her white scales.

Angus slapped me hard on the back. "I told you, Euan. All those months ago back on the *Molly,* when you were bunking up inside the chicken coop, I told you it would be me that brought down the Sow. I told you I'd be the one."

It seemed that for a moment everything fell eerily silent. Everyone had his or her head upturned. Captain Zachariah, Hari, Professor Mayhew, Illagnor, Fenisnoor, Sergeant Caulder, Mrs Zachariah, Gul Quat, Slug and Fidget and Lullabeth, Friends of the Dragon, ISC members, Ghibelline, dragon hunters and scavengers. All watching as the beautiful White Sow quaked and trembled in her final death throes.

The Sow beat down on her wings. I held my breath. For a moment I managed to convince myself that it wasn't half as bad as it looked. That she would rise, wheeling in the air, setting course for her lair deep in the canyons of the Serrated Mountains. That Illagnor would dispatch some of

373

the Ghibelline. They would sedate her with crabwort root and apply healing balms to treat the dreadful, penetrating wound.

But she didn't rise. Her wings faltered and she fell several feet, blood from the wound streaking back over her creamy belly. *Beauty's Daughter* came edging close to her, rope cannon gunners adjusting their positions to take aim. The Sow roared but failed to produce fire in her breath. She lashed at the airship with her tail. It thumped loudly against the hull, but all of the power was gone from her. All it did was set the gondola rocking.

Lassos were fired from the cannon, three in quick succession. Not one of them hit its mark because the Sow fell once more. This time it appeared that she could not even muster the strength to spread her wings into a glide. They folded in at her side. She went into spin, tumbling four or five times before she hit the ground, howling in agony as snow billowed all around her from the impact.

Hari screamed.

As the Sow flailed and writhed on the hard tundra floor Illagnor and Fenisnoor ran to her aid. At the same I saw several scavengers running in the same direction, withdrawing bone saws and gutting knives from sheaths and scabbards. Hari saw them too. With JJ and several of the Friends of the Dragon behind her she too began running towards the Sow.

Quat was hobbling around on his dragon bone leg, waving his arms frantically up at *Beauty's Daughter*. "A breath extractor!" he yelled. "Send down a breath extractor and some vessels. We'll take what we can before she breathes her last."

Angus was chasing after the scavengers. "It was me who brought her down. I get first choice of the spoils."

Mrs Zachariah and the captain stood facing each other. "Soon she'll be dead, imposter," she said, ticks twitching on her face. "And when the spell is broken my bonny, bonny captain will come home to me."

Illagnor and Fenisnoor were both crouched low, trying their best to get close enough to the Sow so they could pull out the crossbow bolt, dodging this way and that to avoid the strained lashing of her tail. Hari and the others formed a semi-circle in front of them, blocking the advance of the scavengers.

"You'll have to kill us before we'll let you past!" screamed Hari.

"With pleasure, girlie," said one of the scavengers, brandishing a boning knife.

"I was the one who brought her down," said Angus. "Don't any of you forget that."

"Stand aside," said Quat, hobbling forth with the apparatus of a dragon breath extractor that had been lowered down from his airship. Behind him came several crewmen lugging clay dragon breath vessels, uncorked and ready.

Now Professor Mayhew, Sergeant Caulder and the escaped ISC patrolmen joined the Friends of the Dragon. More dragon hunters, including Lullabeth and Fidget fell in behind Quat, some of them armed with scavenger crossbows and pistols they'd retrieved from the ground.

Up above *The Drunken Molly* and *Beauty's Daughter* aligned themselves to face *The Hargmir* now stationed directly above the dying Sow. Two ICS patrol craft rose from the deck and crossed the sky to confront the regrouping scavenger ships.

"Looks like we have another standoff," said Quat.

I looked around. The only other people not engaged in this second confrontation were Alicia Barnis, lying on the ground and pressing a rag against her wound to staunch the flow of blood, Slug Martin, rocking back and forth as he hugged himself and repeated over and over. "She'll burn them all to death. You'll see. She'll burn them all to death."

Finally, there was Mrs Zachariah, ticks still twitching as she watched the captain with unrestrained anticipation. "It's not going to happen," I heard Captain Zachariah tell her. "I am what I've become, and you are as you are. And nothing can ever change us back."

His words were interrupted by the sound of Illagnor's voice, roaring in fury. "No!"

I looked and saw the Sow's eyes fall firmly shut, her head slump to the ground, her tail fall still.

"No!" yelled Illagnor again.

"She's dead!" screamed Fenisnoor. "The White Sow is dead!"

The Friends of the Dragon turned to see. Some of them fell to their knees and began crying. I felt a lump come to my throat. The Sow's wings twitched.

376

I thought they might beat down and miraculously she would rise again. But it simply wasn't to be. The wings fell limp around her. She was dead. The White Sow was truly dead. Tears spluttered so violently out of me that my chest hurt. Over my sobbing I heard Mrs Zachariah asking. "Why are you still here, imposter? Why is the spell not lifted?"

My grief turned quickly to anger when I saw the reaction of the scavengers and dragon hunters. They were cheering wildly with Angus Stonedyke lifted high on their shoulders, the hero he always wanted to be. "Stand aside," demanded Quat. "It's over now. Nothing any of you can do. But there may still be a residue of breath left in her lungs. We'll cut her open and take what we can."

The scavengers moved forward making threatening gestures with their knives and saws. Sobbing, but still defiant, Hari and the others shuffled closer together and tried to create a barrier between themselves and the Sow. Half of the dragon hunters raised the crossbows they'd picked up. The other half aimed their guns. Sergeant Caulder and her ISC patrolmen picked up stones and tested their weight.

"It doesn't have to be like this," Professor Mayhew attempted to reason.

Quat raised his hand. "On my word, lads."

I held my breath.

Then three things happened in rapid succession that changed everything. First the dark clouds opened and sent down a torrential deluge of hail and sleet so powerful that everyone automatically crouched low into a duck. It rattled against my rope cannon gunner's helmet and stung my cheeks.

Next, gliding in through the lashing sheets of icy rain, came dragons. Hundreds of them, of every breed and size; Horned Ridgebacks, Treacleshells, Common Greens, Speckled Shortwings, Crimson Jaws, Lesser Wind Gliders. They filled the stormy sky, circling in a huge and ever-growing procession, one by one swooping down to glide over the body of the White Sow, as if to pay their last respects.

Some of the dragon hunters raised crossbows and pistols to the sky, attempting to take aim through the relentless downpour. Shielding my eyes, I caught a glimpse of *The Drunken Molly* and *Beauty's Daughter* ploughing into the midst of the circling dragons, rope cannons swivelling to offensive manoeuvres as scavenger ships moved in below to await the spoils.

There would surely have been a blood bath had the third thing not happened.

From the foothills there came a mighty, thunderous roar, so loud it shook the ground beneath my feet. When I looked through the mist of the rain, I could see that the hillsides filled with hundreds and hundreds of grey figures. Illagnor's messengers had brought the Ghibelline tribes from the mountains and the caves.

"Go!" they roared, thumping their spears against their shields. "Leave this place!"

The scavengers began to back away in awe and fear. Quat signalled the dragon hunters to lower their weapons. "We're going to back down?" cried

378

Angus. "But I downed the Sow. I get first share of the spoils."

Now, out on the tundra, just beyond where the Sow lay, the Ghibelline who had been rendered unconscious by the crabwort root began to wake up. They staggered to their feet. "Go!" they roared, in unison with their comrades assembled on the foothills. And Illagnor and Fenisnoor joined their voices too. "Go!"

Now the Ghibelline on the hillside and the Ghibelline on the tundra roared as one.

"Go! Leave this place!"

After the briefest moment of hesitation, the scavengers turned and fled. The dragon hunters followed suit. Angus hung back a little before he too broke into a sprint. Quat hobbled away as fast as he could. *Beauty's Daughter* descended once more. A lasso was lowered down. Balancing on his dragon bone leg he managed to get his good foot into the noose and was hauled skyward.

"This isn't over," he railed, shaking a fist at us. "We'll be back for our spoils. You hear? We'll be back for our spoils."

I looked to where Captain Zachariah and Mrs Zachariah still stood facing each other through the hail. His hood was pulled down and sopping wet around his shoulders. Her braids were limp and sodden. "It's over, Isabella," he said to her. "I'm here. I've always been here. I'm the same man inside that I always was. And I've always loved you."

Mrs Zachariah took a tiny, hesitant step forward. I honestly thought she was about to embrace him. Instead, she hissed through her teeth. "Imposter!" Then she turned on her heels, stumbled headlong into the deluge, and was gone.

17. Home at Last

The Hargmir passed slowly over the glen where I had once gone with Isla to pick mushrooms for her birthday stew. Leaning over the railings I could see the outline of the little gurgling brook where I used build dams with stones and catch minnow with my sock. The drone of the airship's turbines changed tone as she dropped to a slow descent. Now we were passing over the meadow where a lasso thrown down from the deck of *The Drunken Molly* had hauled me by my leg up into the sky above. Ahead I could see my father's sheep dotted along the hillside that ran up from the back of my cottage. A thin trail of grey smoke was rising from the stubby chimney, dragged across the sky by the breeze.

I felt a hand on my shoulder. "Excited?" asked Captain Zachariah.

"Nervous," I replied, feeling the knot in my stomach pull a little tighter.

"That's understandable," said Fenisnoor.

"I'm going to miss you, stowaway," said Hari. When I turned to face her, she pinched me playfully on the cheek with her finger and thumb.

We had spent the winter months at the camp in the foothills of the Serrated Mountains. After the hasty departure of the dragon hunters and scavengers we had waited till the sleet eased and the sky emptied of dragons then set about wrapping the body of the White Sow in large nets. These were hauled up on ropes lowered down from *The Hargmir*.

Slowly and solemnly the airship rose to the mountains and passed through the canyon that led to the Sow's lair. We were going to leave her there to rest in peace and dignity where there was no risk of her being defiled and butchered by dragon hunters or scavengers. It was during the intricate and laborious task of lowering her into the cave mouth and dragging her deep into the gloomy depths that the Ghibelline stumbled upon the nest she had made for three large, speckled eggs. Suddenly from being downcast and demoralised by her cruel passing we were all lifted by a new sense of elation.

The eggs were tended and cared for throughout the long, snow driven winter, till they finally hatched with the first thaw of spring. Two of the hatchlings were male, the crimson colouring of the boar that must have been their father dominant amongst the odd layered scales of pinkish white.

The third was female. She was albino. Her scales and her wings as pure and white as that of her mother. She was the White Sow reborn. By the time *The Hargmir* departed the Far Tundra she was gliding and soaring back and forth through the canyon, growing in size and stature with each day, easily outpacing her two brothers.

Friends of the Dragon had devised a cunning ruse to try and protect her from the attentions of dragon hunters and scavengers. It would play upon the superstitious nature of airship crews. They engineered a rumour that the ghost of the White Sow had returned to haunt the skies above the tundra and that the crew of any dragon hunting vessels or scavenger ship who encountered her would be both cursed and doomed.

Of dragon hunters and scavengers, we had seen little over the winter months. Occasionally when thunderstorms gathered in the south and flocks of dragons danced amongst the thunder and lightning, we would see the outline of either *The Drunken Molly* or *Beauty's Daughter* or some other vessel in from Tennanbrau steering in amongst them to steal their breath, scavenger ships trailing low behind them.

Some of the more vocal members of Friends of the Dragon wanted Captain Zachariah to use *The Hargmir* to disrupt these hunts by getting between them and the dragons and blocking the trajectories of the lassos. Professor Mayhew overruled this, pointing out that his ship only had a sufficient supply of natural gas left for the return voyage to Tennanbrau.

But once *The Hargmir* had returned to Tennanbrau there were plans to bring matters to a head. Sergeant Caulder was going to recommend that an Imperial Airship with an Air Corp battalion be dispatched to the Far Tundra to arrest detain Gul Quat and Mrs Zachariah, who were both now considered to be outlaws and fugitives from justice. She was also going to apply for an arrest warrant for Rusty Reeves for aiding and abetting known criminals and for allowing his compound to be used for illicit purposes.

Friends of the Dragon had plans too.

Through their study and observation of the dragon population they had amassed a wealth of statistics and data with which to lobby and petition those of influence within the Imperial Palace. Professor Mayhew was going to press for an audience with Emperor Julian himself, in order to explain in more detail the benefits of his alternative gas in maintaining airship travel.

But their boldest plan involved the paintings that JJ had made; wonderful paintings that depicted dragons dancing in amongst thunderclouds and soaring through blue skies, or gliding through tall canyons, paintings of dragon sows tending nests of eggs or dragon boars teaching hatchlings to fly.

There was to be a grand public exhibition of these paintings. Despite the importance of dragon breath to the economy the population of Tennanbrau knew very little about dragons. Their knowledge was limited to tales of the supposed bravery of dragon hunters and the various by-products of the dragon trade they haggled over in Scavengers' Market.

The exhibition was designed to open their eyes to the beauty of these creatures and the tragedy that would occur should they be hunted to extinction. It would build on the message delivered through the pages of 'The Tale of Euan Redcap' and further prick the conscience of Tennanbrau's citizenry. Pride of place would be JJ's heart wrenching masterpiece 'The Death of the White Sow', a painting I had yet to see anyone look at without shedding a tear.

Part of me wished that I could be there on the opening night of the exhibition to see the reactions for myself. But I knew that was not to be. I was going home and this time I was determined that I would see it through to the moment I was at last reunited with my family.

Besides *The Hargmir* had new fetcher. One that I had trained myself. Slug Martin didn't flee with the others back across the tundra. We had found him trembling amongst the wreckage of the fallen scavenger ships. It had taken some time to get him over his trauma. But he was a different person now, a reformed character, a conscientious fetcher, and a committed Friend of the Dragon.

The Hargmir manoeuvred to a slow, shuddering halt above my cottage. The anchor was lowered down and dragged a moment before it caught in the peaty soil. Two rope ladders were rolled over the sides of the gondola.

"Ready?" asked Hari.

I looked down and saw my parents and my sister coming out of the kitchen door. Following them came Alicia Barnis, who had been sent ahead to alert them to our arrival. She still had a slight limp from the crossbow bolt that had penetrated her leg.

Professor Mayhew followed Hari down the first of the ladders. Sergeant Caulder and Fenisnoor took the second. "We're next," said Captain Zachariah. He pulled up his hood. "There's no need," I said. He shrugged his shoulders. "Force of habit. I always feel the need to hide my face till people get to know me better. I said nothing. I looked around, wondering how long it might be before I stood on the deck of an airship gondola again, wondering if I'd ever in my entire life see a live dragon again.

I watched the captain disappear over the side. Some of the crew came and shook my hand. Grisling apologised to me again. Slug hugged me. Then I saw JJ with his paints and easel. "Are you not joining us?" I asked. "A bit later," he replied. "I want to watch from up here, so I can paint the scene when you finally make it back home." I nodded, then, with a sigh, I climbed over the railings onto the first rungs of the ladder and began making my descent to the ground.

Pa's dogs seemed highly suspicious of me. When I jumped from the last ladder rung to the ground, they ran to either side of him, growling protectively, as if I was a stranger. "You've grown," said Pa. "You look a bit broader too."

I nodded, feeling unexpectedly awkward.

I cleared my throat. "That would be from all the carrying stuff I've done as ship's fetcher."

"He's a credit to you," said Captain Zachariah and squeezed my shoulder with his hand. Now Pa nodded. He too seemed somewhat awkward. He stroked the head of one of his dogs. I noticed how Ma kept staring over my shoulder, her eyes wide, her mouth dropped open. When I looked round, I realised that it was Fenisnoor she was looking at. Living all the way down in the Low Counties she'd never been in the presence of a Ghibelline tribeswoman before.

"This is Fenisnoor," I said. "She's a good friend of mine. I have plenty of friends amongst the Ghibelline."

A little smile broke out on Ma's face. Fenisnoor smiled back, craggy grey features creasing as her lips turned upward. Ma had something rolled up in her hand. She kept twisting it tighter and tighter. It was a copy of JJ's picture paper, *The Tale of Euan Redcap*. It was no doubt the one I'd given to Mr Highbrae to deliver with my letter home.

I nodded at it. "Wait till you hear everything that happened after that, Ma."

She seemed to blink away a tear. "Don't you dare tell me anymore, Euan Redcap," she warned. "At least not yet. I've had enough nightmares as it is."

Isla stepped forward. Her red hair was cut shorter than she used to have it and there seemed to be fewer freckles on her nose than I remembered. "Trust you to pick today of all days to come home," she said.

"Today?" I asked. "What's today?"

"It's my birthday, Euan. You've been gone a whole year."

I felt suddenly guilty. "Oh no!" I cried. "Have I messed things up for you again?"

"You haven't messed anything up," she replied. "Having you back home is the best birthday present ever." She ran to me and wrapped her arms so tightly around me that I could hardly breathe. "I missed you so much, baby brother," she gushed.

When she finally released me Pa shooed away his dogs and held out his hand. When I shook it, I was surprised to find that my own grip was almost equal in strength to his. Over his shoulder I saw Ma dabbing away her tears with the sleeve of her blouse.

Somewhat embarrassed she turned and bustled away toward the kitchen door. "I made a huge pot of rabbit stew," she called, not looking back. "There's more than enough for everyone."

The End